QUARANTINE I

"How's Will?" someone shouts. "And Tom."

Tom. His name was Tom. The boy who bled on my jacket.

Devin doesn't say anything, just puts his hand to his eyes to block the light. Someone else calls out, "What did you see past the gate, Dev?" This rouses him. He moves his hands and speaks in a voice that needs to be lubricated. There's blood on his teeth, and someone gasps.

"Soldiers. Wearing those suits. Full mask and everything. A tank."

Everyone gets really quiet. A couple of people discreetly back away from him.

"They're dead." His voice cracks.

BOOKS IN THE WELL'S END SERIES

The Well's End
The Dark Water

SETH FISHMAN

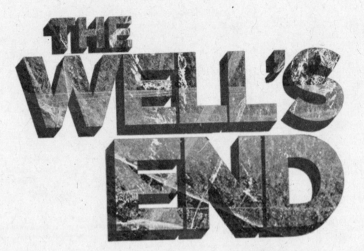

THE WELL'S END

speak

An Imprint of Penguin Group (USA)

SPEAK
Published by the Penguin Group
Penguin Group (USA) LLC
375 Hudson Street
New York, New York 10014

USA * Canada * UK * Ireland * Australia
New Zealand * India * South Africa * China

penguin.com
A Penguin Random House Company

First published in the United States of America by G. P. Putnam's Sons,
an imprint of Penguin Group (USA) LLC, 2014
Published by Speak, an imprint of Penguin Group (USA) LLC, 2015

THE LIBRARY OF CONGRESS HAS CATALOGED THE G. P. PUTNAM'S SONS EDITION AS FOLLOWS:
Fishman, Seth.
The well's end / Seth Fishman.
pages cm
Summary: "16-year-old Mia Kish and her friends search for answers when a mysterious illness
brings their Colorado community to its knees"—Provided by publisher.
ISBN 978-0-399-15990-9 (hc)
[1. Virus diseases—Fiction. 2. Survival—Fiction. 3. Adventure and adventurers—Fiction.
4. Boarding schools—Fiction. 5. Schools—Fiction. 6. Fathers and daughters—Fiction.
7. Single-parent families—Fiction. 8. Colorado—Fiction. 9. Science fiction.] I. Title.
PZ7.F5357Wel 2014
[Fic]—dc23
2013022716

Speak ISBN 978-0-14-751436-3

Printed in the United States of America

Design by Annie Ericsson

1 3 5 7 9 10 8 6 4 2

To Marget, my superhero, my tiny dancer

1

WHAT'S THE FIRST THING YOU REMEMBER?

I've heard the Question before. Who hasn't? But when someone asks me, the Question has a different meaning. It's not often
that the whole world knows who you are, has known you forever, has given you a nickname. Baby Mia. They still call me that.
Strangers still call me that. Baby Mia, who fell down the well. Like
a nursery rhyme. When someone asks about my first memory,
what they really want to know is *do you remember the well?*

Do I remember the well? I was four years old in 1999, when I
became famous. I broke my arm, two ribs and my nose—it's still a
little crooked. People tell me that they honked their horns when I
was pulled free, that they hung the picture of me bundled and ban-
daged on their fridge for years. Baby Mia, who fell down the well.

But truthfully, there is no memory. Only darkness. Considering how deep I was, maybe darkness *is* the memory. Blackness,
water up to my knees, lucky it was August and it didn't rain, a
peanut butter and jelly sandwich lowered in a Pink Power Rangers
lunchbox. My memories are the stories everyone tells, the stories about where they were, what they were doing, about the time
Baby Mia fell down a well.

Reporters come and go. When my mom died (blizzard, pine

tree), at least a dozen inquiries came through. As if what I most wanted to do after my mother's funeral was talk about my stint underground. The funny thing is, underground was all I could think about. My mother was going to be cold down there, dark, with no one to save her and with no one watching and holding vigils and honking horns and crying.

I'm sure that's what reporters wanted to hear from me.

But I admit that something about this reporter feels different. For one, he *looks* different. No wrinkled, collared shirt underneath a wrinkled beige sweater. No notebook and no smell of fast food. He's clean-shaven, his cheeks looking almost crisp, like a banker. But he's not in a suit. Instead, he's wearing a tight fleece, hiking boots and dirty jeans, as if he's just returned from a stroll in the woods. His brown hair recedes hesitantly back up his forehead, leaving a small tuft up front. He smiles gently enough, and he has a notepad and paper, but he hasn't pulled out a recorder of any sort. I'm not sure I remember ever doing an interview where there wasn't a recorder. Staring at him, I find myself uneasy and keep wiggling in my chair. He seems distracted, uninterested in me and the story, which, I'm embarrassed to say, is making me jealous. We've been sitting here on a cloud-covered Thursday, in the conference room of the main faculty offices at my boarding school, Westbrook, for about ten minutes now, quietly bouncing our legs. We're waiting on my father.

The reporter—his name's Blake Sutton—glances at his watch and sighs, then pulls himself to his feet and goes to examine the class photos strung evenly along the walls.

"Your father is in one of these photos, isn't he?"

These are his first words since *nice to meet you.* At least we're done with the staring contest. "That's right," I say, pointing down a few frames from where he's standing. "Class of '78."

Mr. Sutton shuffles over, bends and squints at the photo. He shakes his head a little and looks back at me, then to the image. "Quite the similarities." It's true: we both have the same high cheekbones and small foreheads, same wavy brown hair, same camera-shy smile.

"I guess," I say, bored already. Why do I agree to do these interviews anymore? Maybe it's time to stop. As if reading my mind he turns back to me and claps his hands together once and then pushes his right fist toward me—*the mike's on you*—and asks me what the local attractions of Fenton, Colorado, are.

I don't roll my eyes, but it's close. "What? Are you talking about Gracie?"

"Gracie?" he asks, returning to his seat.

"The tallest sycamore in the world." She's five miles up the road and a few hundred yards into the tree line, and it takes five kids holding hands to ring around her trunk.

Mr. Sutton smiles, and his teeth are überwhite and straight and thick. "I didn't know that."

"You didn't? It's true. Did you know that Fenton has the only Roman aqueduct in North America? It's handmade of over a million bricks."

He leans back now, impressed, letting me run the show. "What else you got?"

"I've got annual migrations of locusts, and we're the home of the national-chicken-thigh-eating competition." Suddenly I'm relaxed, in my element, having answered this line of questioning dozens of times, the familiarity of this back-and-forth a comfort. He's not taking any notes, but whatever—at least he hasn't asked me the Question yet.

The door opens behind me, and since I'm staring at Mr. Sutton's face, I get a good look at the moment he sees my father walk into the room. He grins, his lips parting slightly, and I see his tongue peeking out ever so slightly like a giddy dog. And then he seems to realize what kind of face he's making, because he straightens up and stands, extending his hand. Dad hasn't come into the room yet. He's still in the doorway.

For some reason, I don't move. I feel off-kilter, like I'm missing something very important. After a short while, Mr. Sutton lowers his hand, unshaken, and backs into his seat.

"Please, Mr. Kish, join us." He nods toward the empty chair next to me. "I was waiting for you to begin. Mia's been telling me all about Fenton."

The boards bend under my dad's feet, and he moves to kiss my head. "Hi, hon," he whispers, and takes a seat. He's clenching his jaw over and again, the bone protruding from his cheek like a twitch as he stares intently at Mr. Sutton.

"Dad?" I ask, sensing something wrong.

"Mr. *Sutton*," Dad says, not acknowledging me, "when I agreed to this meeting I didn't know it would be with *you*. I have to get back to work soon, so why are we here?"

Mr. Sutton nods his head knowingly, but ignores Dad's question. "Yes, yes. Late nights at the Cave nowadays?"

My father grips the chair tight enough for the wood to creak.

4

There is no Take Your Kid to Work Day with my dad. In fact, I've never met another employee of Fenton Electronics. I think about the tunnel he drives into every morning on his way to work. The one that's behind steel doors. I've only ever seen the entrance of the Cave—a nickname since before my time—because all us kids do it in the summer: take our bikes to the door, dare each other to pedal up and knock. Not many people actually work up the guts to do so, but I have. Not with anyone else, though. It was in the snowstorm; it took me a couple hours to walk there. It was after Mom died, and Dad wasn't picking up his phone. I beat on that door for fifteen minutes until it opened, and there he was, warm as can be, totally clueless. But that's all I've seen. Behind him was a long driveway and then another steel door. Like an air lock; I bet the two doors are never open at once.

Dad doesn't talk about work; I've just come to accept it. Everyone has. He goes into the mountain and then comes home. He makes me lunches and watches my swim meets. He only admits that his work is classified, that he programs code for the government; my dad says the mountain helps keep their electronics cold. But he also says that the code he programs is boring, basic stuff. I believe him. Why shouldn't I?

"Why are you here?" my dad asks again, this time through gritted teeth. And suddenly I realize, just as my dad already knew, that Blake Sutton is not here to see me.

Mr. Sutton raises his hands, palms up, in a shrug. "You *know* why I'm here . . ." He pauses, taking in my father, then looks at me and smiles again. "To interview your beautiful daughter, of course. What a story! Falling into that well must have been incredibly

5

terrifying." His voice has taken on a familiar tone, one I've heard dozens of times, almost baby-talk. It's the buildup to the Question. And here it comes: "I have to ask, Mia. What is the first thing you remember?"

I have it all in my head. I've said it enough that sometimes, for no reason at all, I find myself rehearsing the speech. In bed, walking to class, in the pool. But before I even have a chance to open my mouth, Dad blurts out, "Mr. Sutton, I think you should go."

The reporter shakes his head sadly and points at my dad. "Testy, isn't he?" he says to me, like it's a joke and I'm on his side. I've never seen Dad like this, and I feel helpless and uncomfortable, itchy and unable to scratch. "The thing is, Mia, your father's right. I shouldn't be here. I should be in the Cave right now, granted a 'tour'"—he actually uses air quotes—"of Fenton Electronics, as I have requested so many times before. I'm sorry to use you this way. Your story really *is* quite incredible."

"I don't get it," I say—I can't help myself. "Dad, what does he mean?"

"I mean," Mr. Sutton says, answering for him, "that Fenton Electronics has some pretty big secrets, and it is my job *as a reporter* to make sure the doors of the Cave are as wide open and forthcoming to the public as they ought to be." He gesticulates with his hands held apart in front of his face, as if he were describing a huge fish he'd caught. Then he stands and gathers his bag and the heavy jacket that he's laid on another chair and heads for the door, but stops and turns back to us. "Did you know, Mia, that I've been trying to get into the facility for years now? That I've been stonewalled the entire time? No interviews, no responses. But there's a

6

time limit to how long they can keep this up. And *that's* the reason I'm here. To let your father know that if he doesn't grant me access by this weekend, I'll have to make it happen by other means." He opens the door and steps through, staring intensely at Dad. There's a vein that has snaked its way onto his forehead, slithering up under his receding hairline. I swear his lips glisten, as if they were soaked in spit. "Maybe, Mr. Kish, I'll bring young Mia with me to show her what her daddy really does."

Dad's out of his chair in a flash, but Mr. Sutton closes the door in his face. He moves to the doorknob, but I call out, "Dad!" and he freezes. He stands there for a moment, his hands clenching and unclenching, his body heaving. Unlike the reporter, Dad's in slacks and a tie, his undershirt peeking through the thin white cotton of his button-down. There's a thick line of sweat running down his back, even though it's winter and the room is chilly.

"What's going on? What's he talking about?"

One thing my father has always been is quick to smile, and quick to forget—or hide—his anger. He turns to me and does just that: his forehead smooths, and his bushy eyebrows lose their furrow. He seems old, suddenly, as if his hair went from salt-and-pepper to gray instantly and the bags under his eyes became permanent and not just about his recent spate of late nights. Dad's always seemed young for his age, looking late thirties when he's really in his fifties, but at the moment, he projects *old* and a sort of helplessness I don't like being witness to.

"Oh, Mia," he says, his voice tired and even a little bit sad. "He's just some crackpot conspiracy theorist. He's been trying to get in for years, writing letters, leaving threats in our mailbox, calling the sheriff. Of course we have secrets, but you know that. We handle government contracts, which necessitate a certain level of secrecy."

"But what makes your company so special?" I ask. "I mean, why here?"

Dad mulls this over. He *has* been coming home late and devoting more time to the job. I know because he's never home when I call. He gets obsessive, and it's tough because I live here at Westbrook, on campus, and I can't be home to make him dinner and take care of him. When I don't have a swim meet, I visit him on weekends, and I often find the house a mess, delivery boxes everywhere and laundry needing to get done. But now something's worse. I have the feeling that, even though he's staring right at me and talking directly to me, his mind is back in his lab. He's fidgeting, ready to leave. I've never seen it this bad. The reporter must have really spooked him.

"Dad?" I ask again, vying for his attention. I imagine the pages I've seen lying on the kitchen table. The notes. The blueprints. Does he actually keep state secrets out for me to see? No idea what they're for, of course, but I'd be an idiot if I couldn't take a shot in the dark: "Is it about those computer chips you're designing?"

He jolts, shocked. I definitely have his attention now.

"What are you talking about?"

"What?" I say, a little embarrassed at being so forward. "You leave your paperwork around the house. Who do you think cleans it up?"

"Well," he finally says, not without some reluctance, "custom programming for microscopic analysis is one thing."

I get a thrill hearing this; my dad programs top-secret computer chips? But for what, microscopes?

"But that's not what this guy's talking about," he says, going on. "I don't like that he's here speaking to you as a way to get to me." Dad comes close, takes me by the shoulders and looks me in the eyes. Whenever he does this, he looks first at my left eye, then my right, back and forth and back and forth, and it's superdistracting. "Mia, listen . . . if he calls you and tries to set another interview up, don't let him. Stall him and let me know, okay?"

"Relax, Dad. I wouldn't anyways; he's really strange. And I won't even be around. I've got my race in Durango this weekend. Remember?" I don't bother mentioning my birthday on Sunday. It will just give him something else to forget about.

He pauses, then smiles. "Right, right. Okay, great. Just trust me on this one, okay?"

I nod, feeling a tremor of fear flutter in my stomach. Why *would* this reporter stalk me to get to my dad? I think of his muddy shoes and imagine him staking out the Cave, watching my father come and go. "Are you sure you shouldn't call the cops on him or something?"

Dad raises his eyebrows and smiles weakly. "I wish. No, he's harmless, just annoying." I don't believe him, of course. I've seen him try to make me feel better before. "Listen, hon, I have to get moving. You'll call me if you see him?"

"Sure . . ." I follow him into the hallway, and he kisses me on the head again, something I normally hate in public but now, even with a few faculty members coming and going, it is exactly what I need.

I head the opposite direction, toward central campus and my dorm. On the way, I pass the dean's office, with its great mahogany doors spread wide, and I see him. Mr. Sutton. He hasn't noticed me at all, and for a moment I'm stuck in the doorway, watching this strange man who freaks my dad out so. The thing is, he's just standing there, shaking Mrs. Applebaum's hand. I stop and put my back to the wall, listen for a moment. Mrs. Applebaum, the dean's secretary—most students love her—is asking about his piece. If he got everything he needed. If he had ever been to Fenton before, or Westbrook. Mr. Sutton says, Yes, absolutely, then asks about last week's snowfall.

I shake my head, entirely confused by the encounter, and push my way out the glass doors of the building and into the quad. The weather is sharp, the wind biting; the sidewalk is sure to be covered in ice. It's dark, and I think I can see my dad's car pulling out of the main gates, heading for the Cave.

I breathe the cold air and move quickly along the path from lamp to lamp, trying to stay in their light. I don't do well in the dark. But this time, with my dad acting all weird, it's worse than usual. I'm sucked back in, like I'm in the well, feeling the darkness around me, all through the campus and blanketing half the world. Just like my first memory. I think of my friends hanging out in the dorm, entirely unaware of this discomfort in my skin. I think of my dad in his car, the air only just now turning warm, his hands clutched tight around the steering wheel as he drives onward, through town and down the snowy roads, catching up to whoever else works at Fenton Electronics as they go one by one through the air lock and deep into the mountain.

2

THE WATER IS COLD, BUT YOU DON'T FEEL IT FOR MORE than an instant. It's supposed to be cold. Anything warmer than seventy-five degrees, and you're in a sauna, muscles floppy and useless. I'm under for almost the entire first length of the pool, then it's all breathing and eyes, rotating my breaths to see the competition in the adjacent lanes. Look left, look right. My body knows what to do, my breath comes in even bursts, my muscles begin to slowly burn, and I watch the girls fall behind, unable to leech off my wake. Even with my drag suit, designed to slow me down and work me harder, by the time I come out of my turn at the end of the pool, they're a full body-length back. By the time I touch the finish, I'm all alone.

No one congratulates me, not even Coach Hart, who sees me as his gift horse and picks on me more than the others because, heck, they aren't going to make it to nationals. He's turned swimming into a solo sport, despite the fact that I also anchor the relay. During meets, he runs up and down the edge of the pool shouting "WOOP WOOP," telling me where he is, giving me signals like *kick harder, double tempo, you're falling behind.* To push me, he had me swimming with the boys, which immediately pissed off the girls. Thirty of us spending six hours a day together on different sides of the pool, and no girl who would talk to me. And while I didn't realize that this would happen, I didn't really care at first. The boys were fun, crazy and cute together. I guess I never thought about how they'd react to being beaten by a girl. For about a month, I went side by side with the best in the state, winning a couple races too, watching the boys watch me, feeling sexy for the first time in my Lycra Aquablade suit. I thought they were my friends, and maybe they were. Maybe the boys didn't mean any harm, but I'm alone now, back to beating the crap out of the girls. All because of the time when I was tapering at practice the day before a big race, doing laps just to stay loose, and I saw one of the talented boys, Eric, swimming underneath me, crosswise, faceup, and I smiled at first because I wanted to, because I was into Eric. He's taller than me, looks good with his swim cap on or off. His blue eyes are so bright you can see them through his goggles. But then I heard laughing above my head, and Eric rolled over and his Speedo was down and he was mooning me, which was funny enough, but then there was another boy, Steve, passing by Eric and his wiener was out, flopping like a third leg, and when I came up gasping for air, they were all exposed, swimming around me like dirty dolphins, laughing to tears.

I might have been able to get them all expelled, but probably not. Their parents own the world (Eric's from Manhattan, his father a vice president at Goldman Sachs, his uncle a congressman), while my dad works in a cave. Coach Hart saw it all and did nothing. Well, not nothing. He put me back with the girls, who no longer wanted me. So I swim faster now, just to get away from them.

At one point in my life, I swam to win. But the summer before last, I watched the London Olympics, saw Phelps after twelve years and that many medals; I thought, *what's the point?* I'll swim my way into a good college and then give it up. Or at least give all this *team* sport mumbo jumbo up.

I rest my arms on the pool's edge, my nose sucking in the chlorine, and watch Jo make her dive from the platform. She twists perfectly, her tall body a ball of muscle and slick edges, and then dissolves into the pool. I smile. At least I have one friend in the pool *area*. I've known Jo forever; she's one of six townies at Westbrook Academy, though we weren't always this close. Her father teaches AP Calculus, which is why most people think Westbrook let her in, but watching her dive, I know that's not entirely true. She, like everyone at Westbrook, has a legit talent. The standard entry formula is obscene wealth and power coupled with talent, but if your father teaches at the school and you get invited to the junior nationals for platform diving, that usually works just fine too.

"Mia!" shouts Coach Hart. "Get your ass back in gear."

I look around, startled, and I see all the other girls already on the starting blocks watching me, their eyes encased in plastic, their expressions dull and robotic. They hate me. I might hate them too.

I climb out of the water and shake my limbs, loosening my muscles, stretching my neck. Back to the block, where this time Hart tells us we're going to hold our breaths and swim under for fifty meters, then freestyle back, then under for fifty, then back. Ten times. They're called "over-unders"—surprise, surprise. And I'm the best at them too. No wonder my teammates don't like me.

. . .

Jo's dressed first and leans against a locker next to mine, humming a country song I sorta recognize, looking effortlessly perfect as usual. It's eight thirty at night, our second practice of the day and last before the meet. Normally, we'd be up at five thirty going at it again, but Coach gives us one off to rest the muscles. How thoughtful of him. I'm in my flip-flops, trying to avoid getting plantar warts, and am scrambling to change. Everyone else is gone, Coach made me do a few more laps, and Jo is kind enough to wait almost every day. For the morning sessions, that means we're usually late to first period. Now, she's off in her own world, her lips puckering a touch, as if she's about to actually sing, when suddenly she bolts upright and grabs my arm.

"Shit, I meant to tell you."

"What?" I ask, slipping my shirt over my head.

"Odessa's throwing a party tonight."

I groan. Of course she'd throw a party on a Thursday. Odessa's one of the other townies, and she lives next door to Jo and me. We all live there, in what the students like to call "Scholarship Row," though I have seen Odessa's house, and I know for a fact she doesn't need a scholarship to attend Westbrook. The thing about Odessa is that she's done all she can to connect to the others, to prove that she isn't some new-blood rich girl from a backward town that doesn't understand the ins and outs of social convention. Usually that means she's nowhere near our hallway. Unless she throws a party. And a party the night before we travel to a swim meet means no sleep will be had.

Jo's not concerned. "Oh, come on, Mia. It'll be fun."

14

"What?" I ask, incredulous. "You're actually trying to convince me to go?"

She shrugs, her eyes on her phone. "It's not like you'd sleep through the noise anyway."

"And it's not like you have to be rested to jump off a board." I sort of expect to get a rise out of her at that—despite her perfectly choreographed boredom routine, she's fiercely competitive—but nothing. Her thumbs are moving fast, and she doesn't look up. When I first became truly close with Jo, it was a late night just like this. I heard her splashing into the water over and over again as I swam laps. When I finally pulled my goggles from my eyes, I saw her climbing the concrete stairs. She was running, hurrying to do another dive, pumping her legs until she made it up the platform. I remember watching her compose herself and balance on her toes, bounce, fall, do it again. I'd seen her around and knew who she was, but never did I expect her to be so dedicated and hardworking. By the next year, we were roomies. She told me, later, that she thought I was cool because I could beat the boys. I thought she was cool 'cause she could get them. Which has me thinking.

"Todd'll be there?" I ask, tying a shoe and looking up from my crouch.

She flashes a grin. Jo's a real friend, so it's rare that I can get genuinely annoyed with her, even if she's trying to drag me to a party to be a wingman when she knows I need the sleep.

"Maybe we can get Rob to come," I venture, my way of relenting.

"Already texted him," she replies, and as if on cue, my phone buzzes. I take a look, and it's Rob, responding to Jo and adding me in.

Long day?

Jo and I share a smile. Rob, another townie and friend who lives across the hall, has a way with understatement. He's probably at his computer, his desk lamp the only light on, plugging away at some code or other—his hobby. Sometimes I wonder if he's in Lulz Security or Anonymous.

Absolut, Jo texts back, which, of course, pops up on my phone too.

I thought Mia's idea of unwinding was Seinfeld *reruns.*

Apparently, I type, *2nite it means following Jo to Odessaville.*

O fun, he replies. *I'll remember to shower. C U soon.*

We pause near the big gym doors, each taking an involuntary breath against the cold. I'm not looking forward to tonight, but the alternative is lying on my bed with a pillow over my head getting more and more annoyed at Odessa's high-pitched laugh. Maybe Rob'll cheer me up. He always does.

Westbrook Academy is, as elite private boarding schools go, a relatively new creature. Created in the '60s by a new breed of wealth, the creators mimicked Groton or Milton or Dalton and bettered. Westbrook's buildings are state of the art, but look like Gothic castles, like a mini Oxford or Cambridge without the cold drafts. Each student has the option of a single, and rooms are equipped with bathroom, living room and kitchen. The professors were poached from the best universities in the country, the coaches from the big state schools, the students from the czars worldwide.

Entitlement is a way of life at Westbrook. But, I have to say, there's nothing easy about the curriculum. Sure, kids smoke pot every night, their doors open, waving the student RA in to take a

hit. But my classmates have goals or come from families that demand goals of them. No one would be caught dead with less than
a 2250 on the SATs. Without a 4.0. Without an acceptance letter to
higher learning, traditionally known as the four-year vacation from
Westbrook. Good grades are greatly rewarded, pep rallies are for
academics as well as sports, and you actually win a snowmobile if
you're the valedictorian.

Sometime in the early 1990s, kids around the country began to
hear of Westbrook. And, to Westbrook's credit, most didn't get in.
The sprawling dorms, built for the future growth, stood half full or
even empty for years. My father was one of the first townies admitted to the school. His picture hangs, as that weird reporter noticed,
in the school's administrative building. And I was one of the first
to be given alumni treatment. Now the cup is brimming, a cascade
of royalty. If you thought you were special as a kid, rich or brilliant
or perfect in all ways, here you're nothing special at all. It's like that
drag suit I wear when swimming. Westbrook feels tough, makes
it hard on you while you're at it and then, when you're out, everything comes more easily than you could ever hope. Dad decided to
stay in town, to work at a place with a scary nickname, but I want
to use Westbrook for more. I want to stop being a Fenton claim to
fame and start being something else: unrecognizable and not at all
a baby anymore.

The room Jo and I share is crammed right next to Odessa's. The
thin walls do nothing to muffle the sound of laughter and hip-hop.
We've both just showered at the gym, so we go straight into prep,
which for me means jeans and a T-shirt and sitting on my bed

watching Jo try on a few sets, and then bend forever over her vanity.

"You want me to pluck your eyebrows for you?"

She kicks her leg vaguely in my direction, as if to shoo me away, her face remarkably still in the process of applying eyeliner. Jo likes to do color, and she moves quickly on to an eye shadow called Midnight Plum. I think I'd look like a clown with that stuff on, but I can't help admiring the way it shimmers against her pale face.

"I still don't get how your hair looks that good after all the chlorine," I say, recognizing that I sound a smidge worshippy and glad she doesn't take advantage of it.

"You're way too down on yourself," she replies, glancing at me in the mirror. She's probably eyeing my wide shoulders. "You just don't take any pride in your swimmer's bod."

I stare at my arms and see a ribbon of muscle. "I doubt being beaten by a girl is a big turn-on for a guy."

"I don't want to hear that talk tonight, okay? We're going to Stanford, the best school in the country for swimming, where we'll meet the best boys in the country for swimming, and you'll find a tall and limber boy you actually respect because he can beat you in the freestyle, and you'll get married and have dolphins for kids. Until then, relax and have some fun."

Aside from the dolphins, I'd say Jo knows exactly how to talk to me.

There's a knock, I shout for him to come in, and Rob enters with a bottle of Absolut Citron and two shot glasses. His hair's wet, combed into an ironic part, so slick it looks like it's glued to his head. The style matches perfectly with his mail-order Warby

Parker glasses. His T-shirt is tight and red, with black Korean characters arranged in thin columns. I'd think that lame, except Rob's mother is Korean and he speaks it fluently. He can be cool in two languages.

"Where's yours?" I ask. He plops Indian-style on the floor, back to Jo's bed, and pulls out a flask from the inside pocket of his All-Saints coat, a black semiwrinkled thing that drapes well over his bright shirt.

"All scotch all the time," he replies, and taps his calculator watch to emphasize the point. He pulls out a bottle of Zyrtec and pops a couple pills, which he claims stops him from going red in the cheeks when he's drunk. His words, not mine.

"Ugh, you sound like them," I say.

"No," he spits emphatically. "*They* sound like *me*."

There's a loud crash next door and then a muffled cheer. Someone screams and runs past our door, his voice a lesson in the Doppler effect.

"Sounds like we need to get moving," I venture, partly so we can get back already. It's not that I don't like parties; it's just that I have this amazing ability to get beer spilled on me. Jo seems to agree, because she pops her lips, adjusts her breasts and then cranes her neck *just so* in a seductive pose, her lips pursed, the lip stain glaring against her pale skin.

"All right, all right," Rob says from the floor, where he's been watching the whole thing. "I'll make out with you, Jo—get over here."

He smiles big and wide and raises his flask. We take a few shots, which I hate but readily admit get the job done more efficiently than beer in a plastic cup. There's a moment, as we all sit together, where Rob slows his sarcasm and Jo actually snorts when she giggles, and I *feel* myself start to enjoy myself and look forward to the night. It happens out of nowhere, magic. Most of the time, I'm trying to find my way out of a situation, but tonight I'm going in, arms open. I wish I could figure out how to harness that magic and use it whenever. But I'll take it for tonight if the universe is offering.

I consider it a good sign for Jo when Todd Silver opens the door; he's clearly pleased to see her. His eyes catch ahold of me, and his brows go up, but he's not going to complain. I'm an enigma, made fun of, but not a pariah. Baby Mia jokes aside, there's only so much flak you can give the hot girl's friend before the hot girl stops liking you. Jo buffers me with her sheer looks.

Todd's wearing plaid shorts and a sports coat. He's got an abnormally deep voice, which goes beyond sexy to just odd. But he is, undeniably, a hottie. Jo's always had more friends than Rob and me, and at things like this, I often find myself hovering on the edge of a conversation. Do parties work for Jo just because she's so ridiculously perfect? I always joke that I don't know how she gets such amazing diving scores with those breasts. Sometimes I feel like I'm holding her back from some other side of herself. Another life she could be leading. But she never seems to mind or care. I think that's what makes her such a good friend. I wonder what makes me one for her.

Todd ushers us in, keeping a keen eye on Jo. "I wasn't expecting to see you tonight, before the meet and all," he says, but she's being uncharacteristically awkward around him and is smiling too much. She must be pretty drunk already. I've never felt the need to try to save Jo from a boy situation, but there's a first time for everything.

"Todd," I say, and he looks at me with reluctance. The music thrums across the room, and with one glance, I take in much of the crew team. "I hear Odessa's trying to do body shots with every boy at Westbrook. True?"

He laughs and winks. "Just had one myself. You're next," he says to Jo, pinching her arm. She giggles like an idiot.

"I'll try a shot," Rob offers helpfully. Todd's a tall one, six foot four, and he peers down from his chiseled face at little Rob, wondering who interrupted him. Rob just takes it, radiating indifference, his lips turned the barest centimeter upward. I grab Rob's arm and pull him away.

"Impressive," Rob says when we get past a few floating groups of our classmates into a spot where we can actually stand and talk. "We made it through the door before she abandoned us."

"She's not abandoning us, Rob. She *likes* him."

"Jo likes everyone," Rob replies. He's not so wrong; taking in the large living room, I can already find three former boyfriends. To think of the things I know about them just from the noises that came from the other side of our room as I went to sleep. There's Vance, with three balls. Trevor, who screams like a girl. Phillip, who gets kinky in Spanish.

"My *fellow* townies!" The line is filled with such self-effacing irony that I can only imagine it coming from Odessa. Rob doesn't even bother sticking around. He mutters something about getting us beers, and I'm left to face the scourge of our hallway. She's sitting on a couch with Rory—smarmy punk Brit—smoking a cigarette. She takes our arrival in quick stride.

Odessa grew up down the street from me. We used to be friends, maybe even best friends. When we found out that we both got into Westbrook, we snuck out after curfew to Baskin-Robbins to celebrate. When we found out our class schedules, we called each other immediately. A couple years ago, during the first days of school, we sat together at lunch. And then, in a shifting slide, her veneer began to change. She's not an awful person. She doesn't put me down or forswear our old friendship. But she plays it a bit like a joke. Like a relic from another age. The thing is, at Westbrook, status really *does* matter. When you're dealing with families who go back generations, whose surnames sit on university gates and products in the supermarket and presidential campaigns, families that send their kids to Westbrook from their own kingdoms of politics . . . let's just say that Westbrook is a petri dish of the national social scene. I can't believe how seriously some of them take it all; I know a few who literally won't speak to me because I'm a townie. Odessa has spent the past two years climbing her way slowly into the richie social stratum. It helps that she's legitimately rich on her own, if newly minted. From the looks of his hand placement, Rory certainly doesn't seem to mind.

"I heard you had another newspaper interview," he tosses in, his accent making this sound more serious and, therefore, more jackassy. "Another go at extending your fifteen minutes of fame?"

I feel my stomach sink. "You know I don't like to be interviewed, right?" I think back to the reporter and what he said about Dad. He was creepy, sure, but my dad didn't really earn any stars on behavior either. I wonder what Dad's doing right now at the Cave and just how classified whatever he's doing is.

"Oh, come off it," Odessa drawls, knocking Rory's hand away

from her pasty thigh. She's eternally cute and childlike, and no matter how much makeup she applies or tweezing of her red eyebrows she does, her face will only ever remind people of Pippi Longstocking. "Ever since you and I were kids, you were always so smug about those interviews." Suddenly her face lights up and she jumps from the couch and gives me a hug, her arms not going entirely around my body because of the cigarette. Typical move by her, the insult and hug. Brilliant, actually. I'm forced to awkwardly pat her back. She smells like men's Armani cologne—a new trend for the girls on campus—and nicotine. "Oh, it's been so long. I've missed you, Baby."

"You too, Odessa—"

"Can I get you a beer, Des?" This from Jimmy, near the fridge, Odessa's on-again, off-again boyfriend. I have no idea what their current status is, but I do know that it's never Jimmy who ends the relationship. Jimmy's the final townie at Westbrook, the lone Latino here too, which should be a double whammy against him from the richies and their sheltered ways. But Jimmy is just too big an alpha male (and comes from too much real estate) to be ignored by the gaggle of wealth at the school, despite his race and Fenton upbringing. Jimmy plays every sport and plays well, but he has this look about him that has people underestimating him left and right. Innocently dumb with short, buzzed hair and a wispy mustache, like a surfer bum in the wrong state.

"Definitely need a beer," Odessa replies, not really looking at him, which leads me to think they are in off mode. Poor Jimmy. He glances my way, offering me a beer too.

"Um, sure. I love PBR." I shrug my shoulders and grimace for the barest of instants. *Did I just say I love PBR?*

Jimmy pulls a blue-and-red can out of the fridge and tosses it to Odessa, but she totally misses it; the can slaps to the floor and makes an ominous fizzing noise. She inspects it for a moment before handing it off to me, a ticking time bomb. Jimmy laughs and pulls another, opening it himself and delivering it to her. Odessa takes a chug and surveys her party, leaning her weight backward onto Jimmy's chest while she begins a nice little rant to Rory about Mr. McPherson, an English teacher I like. I see Jimmy rest his chin on her head, and I think, not for the first time, that that boy has it bad.

I go into the kitchen and pop the can slowly over the sink, but right when I think I'm in the clear, it spits a mist on my face. Awesome. At least no one saw that. I cut my losses and leave the can in the sink.

"Here." A boy I have never seen before holds out a paper towel to me. He looks vaguely northeastern. I've seen the style plenty around campus: pale skin and dark hair, lips that fade into the skin and eyebrows that flare out at a point. This one has a small birthmark under his left eye. I take the towel and lean against the counter next to him, wiping my face. He must be someone's older brother come visiting.

"Thanks," I say, and then we stand there, side by side, taking in the scene. I curse myself for not having anything to say, but all I can think of is that I have nothing to say. He's not really paying any attention to me anyway. I could narrate for him, tell him that over there's my best friend, Jo, and the guy who is nibbling at her neck is Todd, whom I'm going to have to see a lot more of soon, if not tonight. There's Rob, who's watching Rory fiddle with the music and put on Vampire Weekend, a band Rob absolutely hates but I secretly like and feel bad about admitting, so I don't. He makes eye contact with me, finishes off a beer and raises his hands in the air, mouthing *DONE!* And sure enough, he makes his way to the door and out into the hallway. Probably back to his room and his gaming. I wish he spent more time in the real world. I think I said that to him once and pissed him off.

I glance over at the stranger but can only see his profile. His palms are behind him on the counter, as if at any moment he's going to pull himself up and sit, and I can see the veins stand in his forearm and disappear up beyond his black polo. He's wearing a Livestrong bracelet; he must've got it before Lance Armstrong copped to doping. Weird he still has it on, though. Everyone I know threw theirs away.

I wish I had another beer, so that I could at least have something to do.

He glances over at me, then at the beer in the sink behind me and grins. "You okay?"

I nod and magically find something worthy of saying. "Are you visiting?"

He looks around the room, then shakes his head. "Nope. New student. Transferred in this morning."

Midsemester transfer? His parents must be able to pull some pretty weighty strings. "Yeah? You liking it?"

He makes a face. "I don't know," he says seriously. "It's weird—I have the exact same friends back home. Like, I know what to expect here, you know?"

"Totally," I find myself agreeing, without really understanding what I'm agreeing to.

"But I *should* be worried. If I were the new kid back home, I'd be treated horribly. No one would give two shits about me. *I* certainly wouldn't." He takes a sip of his beer. "I'm waiting for that to start here."

He's got Westbrook figured out, that's for sure. "I guess day one is a free pass," I say, trying to be playful.

His eyes catch mine, really taking me in for the first time. He has to flick his thick hair back off his forehead to do so. A small scar whitens along his jaw. "Yeah," he says, "could be worse."

I can't tell if I'm flattered or not, but I'll admit the attention is pleasant.

"Hey," he says suddenly, straightening up, "you're that Baby Mia girl, aren't you?"

I shrug, all pleasantness fading straight away. "I guess so."

He sees my reaction and winces apologetically. "Ugh, I bet you hear that a lot. Sorry. It's just one of the few things that came up when I Googled Fenton before I came here. There are tons of pictures of you online. Must be annoying."

It *is* annoying. What teenager likes her yearbook photos splashed on the internet? Why did I wear a bow freshman year?

"If it makes you feel any better," he goes on, eyeing me, "I think the story is legitimately impressive." I open my mouth to respond, but then he spots Tiffany Van Stavern across the room and tosses a *one sec* her way. She's wearing a short green tube dress. When she leans forward, I swear I can see her underwear. At least he seems embarrassed when he says, "She invited me. I'll see you around?"

I look down at our feet—he's in Sambas—and he doesn't wait for me to reply. Of course Tiffany had already spotted and managed to get the new kid to the party; her nose job must have given her special powers. I wish I could go interrupt Jo, but she's too far gone, smiling shyly downward and playing with a beaded necklace I made for her last year. Her favorite flirt game with Todd is to punch him in the gut. But the hand she has on his stomach now is playfully rubbing up and down, and I'm almost embarrassed to witness the scene, like I'm a Peeping Tom because I can't find someone else to talk to. I'm stuck by the sink, watching the party go by.

The fridge opens next to me, and there's Rory, pulling out a couple beers and leading me back to the couch he's been perched on. There are others here, people I know, and they're playing quarters or dancing lazily or shouting out the window. There's the new kid, leaning in to speak with Tiffany. Rory's pretty close, his gaze on my cleavage. Disgust rises to my lips. He pokes a hole in the can's side with a key and hands me the beer.

"Chug it," he commands.

I'm tired of all this and make to leave, but he tips the can and spills beer on me. I'm so annoyed, so angry at this spiky-haired douche that I actually give him what he wants. I know he's just goading me. That he wants to get the boring townie to do something "crazy," but I can't stand the sneer on his face and the plaque between his teeth. I pull the beer from his hand, pop the top and shotgun it down. Because, fuck you, Rory—I can be just like anyone else when I want to.

The beer tastes like burnt ginger ale and smells worse. Rory watches with openmouthed fascination, which only infuriates me more. I finish the first beer and pull his can to my mouth too. Odessa sees me chugging and literally runs across the room chanting "Ba-by, Ba-by," which everyone quickly takes up, and I can't help but feel a rush of adrenaline as I finish the beer and throw the can onto the floor. The crowd cheers, and Rory tries to kiss me on my cheek, his breath hot and rancid, and I have to press hard to push him away. He tosses his shoulders and smirks like, *whatever—you missed your chance.* For one disturbing second, I imagine my life as Rory's girlfriend, cheering him on at rowing competitions and wearing his button-down shirts. Todd could stay at Jo's and I at Rory's, and we'd double-date everywhere, and that wouldn't be so bad.

Rory makes a beeline to Tiffany and taps her on the shoulder and kisses her on the lips when she turns around. Rory's a dick. Tiffany rolls her eyes and turns back to the new kid, who's clearly confused by the whole thing. He tucks his hands into his jeans and flicks his hair away again as he did before. I kinda like that gesture. Rory puts his big calloused hand on the new kid's chest and gives him a gentle push. Maybe he's wasted, or maybe he's just so totally not expecting this, but the new kid loses his balance and falls backward, knocking over and shattering a lamp that I know for a fact is from the '70s and is worth a couple thousand dollars. I almost scream in worry, but close my mouth before I make a fool out of myself. The music doesn't stop, and the crowd barely notices. But I see Odessa bolt into his face and push her finger into his forehead. The newbie's got some patience, because he just grits his teeth and pulls himself up and then slips from the room.

My head swims, and I fall back down to the couch; it's so much more comfortable here. The lighting in the room is perfect—a hazy warmth—and the music bounces in my feet.

My phone lights up.

Miss Kish, can I trouble you for a follow-up meeting?

Who's this?

Blake Sutton.

I'm confused. He has my cell number, sure. He called me to arrange the meeting. But why is he texting me? Why so late at night? The phone flashes again.

U still partying?

Not Sutton this time, but Rob, and I almost gasp in relief.

Rob!!!! Where r you?

In bed. All OK?

Come over! Things r weird.

Ha, course they r. But I'm saving it up for ur big day Sunday.

Bday for me! Bday weekend starting now! Come over!

Ha. K crazy. I'm going to bed. Have fun.

Boo, party pooper.

OK, Mia. Goodnight. Turning phone off.

Sleepnight!

I type, pretty proud of the expression I just made up. Jo's gone, and Odessa's door's closed, which might mean nothing at all or might mean I can actually go home now. There are eight or so kids in the room, but no one's talking to me. My phone flashes again.

Would love to connect. Let me know . . .

I try to ignore the message, the memory of my father's seething anger at this strange reporter, and sink deeper into the couch, listening to the music and the voices merge into one.

3

THE MORNING ISN'T TOO WEIRD. EXCEPT FOR THE
hangover.

I've never drunk like that before. Sure, I've had a couple beers,
a shot of something from time to time, but I've never spent a full
night drinking. Most of the richies have—they take tailgating very
seriously, prepping for college, so they say. But not me, and when
the sun hit my eyes this morning, I thought someone was poking
a needle into my skull.

The rest of the night was a blur. I guess Jo kept pace, alcohol-
wise, because later on, we found ourselves holding hands in the
bathroom while we puked. For the first time since I remember,
though, I didn't need the bathroom light on to sleep. Seems like
being blackout drunk is a good way to cope with my little night-
time phobia and unwanted texts from strange men. I'm sure the
school psychologist would be pleased.

No amount of brushing cleans my teeth, and the smell of alco-
hol on my skin makes me gag, but we're walking in a loose clump
with other students toward the quad, the open space between all
the academic buildings.

"You have to drink more water." Jo's holding out her Nalgene.
She's wearing sunglasses today, and her face is so sweaty she has to
push them back up her nose time and again. "And eat some bread."

"Ugh, if I put something else in my stomach I'll vomit on Mr. Geller's floor."

"Thank God we didn't have practice today."

Even the thought of doing over-unders makes my thighs hurt. I can't honestly imagine being in good enough shape for the race tomorrow. At least I usually don't have to be at my best to win.

"And don't worry," Jo adds. "I know you don't want a party for your birthday. We couldn't top Odessa if we tried."

I roll my eyes, but am pleased she has brought it up. "I don't need anything, Jo."

She smirks, which is less effective than normal because of her sunglasses. "I know you, Mia Kish. Don't pretend your birthday doesn't mean anything. It's okay to like having one."

"Especially big seventeen," I respond in a singsong way.

"Almost old enough to vote."

"Not really anywhere near old enough to drink." I wince, feeling my headache against my skull.

We get to the doors and file in behind the other students, putting on our game faces. Jo squeezes my arm and turns to her first class. I watch her for a second as she spots Todd by his locker and approaches him, her books held to her chest like a girl from the '50s. He steals her sunglasses and puts them on himself, and she gets an excuse to touch him while trying to retrieve the frames. I shake my head; I couldn't imagine trying to be cute today.

First period, European History, is buzzing when I arrive. As if no one else in the entire school had anything to drink last night.

There are ten people in the class, and we all sit around a big table, no desks or anything. That's the way it is here, a low

31

teacher-to-student ratio, a close learning environment. I put my stuff down next to Rob and take a seat. He's lost on his iPhone and barely looks up. The phone is sealed in an enormous OtterBox, one of those cases that are huge and designed to withstand water and dropping from, like, a hundred feet—one of many things people hassle him about. He's sporting headphones, and the music is loud enough for me to know he's listening to Pavement. Rob's an indie-music freak, half hipster, half goth, and is generally half a year ahead of the rest of Westbrook when it comes to the cool bands. Whenever someone starts listening to a band that he's been preaching for months, he rolls his eyes and takes them off his playlist. But only for a week or so; he loves the music too much to let it be sullied by a petty hatred of his classmates.

I get a text. *What up, Mia?* It's from Rob, who doesn't look up from the phone.

I laugh and text him back, adding Jo into the thread. *Wish u were there longer.*

Yes! Where U go? Jo comes back.

Rob pops off his earphones and glances up at me, his long hair covering tired eyes. "You okay?" he asks. "You look awful." Compared to us, Rob didn't drink very much. He probably had a nightcap with his tiny flask and went to bed.

"Screw you," I say, and vaguely mean it. Rob left me there last night, and now I feel like an idiot, hungover, remembering it all. It would have been nice to have had him there when Sutton texted. "You were supposed to be my wingman."

"You said you didn't need one!"

"That was Jo, Rob. You shouldn't have left me there."

Rob's a good friend, but if he's one thing, it's defensive, and calling him on anything is like inviting yourself to speak to a brick wall. He sighs dramatically, returning his attention to his monstrosity of a phone.

Then someone shouts my way. "Yo, Baby, I hear you made out with Rory last night. Truth?" This from Geoffrey, from Seattle, six foot three, lacrosse captain, Princeton bound. I know that might sound appealing, but his father, a lumber magnate, kills trees for a living, and Geoffrey looks like a billy goat.

I close my eyes for a second to replay the night, terrified that I might have forgotten something. He went for my cheek, yes, but I would rather puke my guts up than kiss him. I look across the room at Rory, who's making out with an invisible me, his tongue going deep down my invisible throat.

I can imagine Rory spreading lies about me to his boys this morning, them hungry for stories of his night's conquests. I'd spit at him if my mouth wasn't so full of cotton.

Mr. Geller comes in then, so I can't say anything, I just cross my arms and sink into my seat, hating this morning more and more. Geller's the enthusiastic type, fairly young and always in a sports coat. He often tosses his curly hair excitedly as he lectures about the Habsburgs and the Bourbons (both families with descendants in attendance at the school). He goes to his chair but remains standing, puts down his book, begins to flip pages and without looking up, asks, "Who has something to ask me about the reading?" He always starts class like this, and we never answer. Even if we're all legitimately smart, no one is going to fall for such a sucker question. Ask him something about the reading and then spend

33

ten minutes answering his follow-ups. Today, though, I can barely hear him. My blood is pulsing so hard in anger that I can feel my ears go deaf.

"He's lying, you know." Rob's still keeping his head down, but he's spoken up, and Geller tilts his head in confusion.

"What's that, Rob?"

"I said 'he's lying.' But I guess what I meant was 'Rory's pathetic if he has to lie about something like that.'"

"You mean he's gay!" shouts Freddy Prince—his real name.

Geller, still confused and sensing that he's losing our attention, shouts, "I don't accept that kind of derogatory language in my classroom, Freddy."

At the same time, though, Rory jumps up from his seat. He's not as tall as his roommate, Todd, but he's a heavyweight on the rowing squad, which means he's an angry built little guy. He's not looking at me at all—I might as well not exist. Rob's not only made fun of him in public, but he's gotten other richies to laugh at him. He takes a step toward Rob, his normally pale face flushed crimson, and points an angry finger.

"Why don't we ask Baby Mia?" he says, his voice a growl. "Or have you been wishing all along she was sucking *your* dick?"

This isn't particularly funny to the rest of the class. And considering that Rory is threatening a student in front of a teacher, he's already going to be in a ton of shit. But maybe it's the hangover or maybe it's the way he's talking to Rob or maybe it's the way Rory will push or take whatever he wants, but suddenly I'm up, the textbook full of glossy maps and mini print covering ten thousand years of history in my hand, weighing five, ten, twenty pounds, and before I can think, I smash Rory in the face, his smile disappearing into a picture of Elizabeth I. Rory topples over backward and hits the floor hard, rolls over and spits bright blood from his mouth onto the white linoleum. There's no noise except for the thumping of my own heart. And Mr. Geller has me by the arm. He drags me outside and throws me toward Dean Griffin's office.

"What were you thinking, Mia!?" he says, his voice sounding honestly confused. "You're lucky I pulled you out of there. He'll punch a girl." Mr. Geller runs both hands through his hair to get ahold of the situation, sucks in a breath and then looks back at me, his face set. "Get to the dean's, and if I find out you didn't make it, I'll have you expelled." He pauses, moves toward the door. "I mean it, Mia."

He slams the door shut. I can hear Rory moaning, and my hands shake. There's blood on my Converses. I walk, dazed, toward the dean's office, down a long hallway filled with tall and shiny trophies, some of them mine.

I can't take my eyes off the blood, and I keep thinking of last night with a puddle of shame in my stomach. Does everyone think I hooked up with Rory? Has he already managed to convince everyone that I'm just another conquest for him? I wonder what he said. *Baby Mia's not a baby anymore! Did you see her chug that beer? She chugged more than that!* My hand feels heavy, the weight of the book still there, the sound of his nose breaking. I'm at the entrance to the dean's office, an enormous old-growth oak, split and cut and fashioned into two doors, supposedly donated by a school alum from the keep of his castle in France. They are big and heavy, hard to open, and standing there, I think that if I knock, I'm going to have to go home forever. I let a stupid asshole get to me.

My father will be so disappointed. Mom would have been too.

I raise my hand and knock, but the wood's so thick I barely make a sound. I try again, harder, and at the same moment, an alarm goes off. Not the fire alarm. This one sounds different. Is farther away but somehow louder. There's an up and down to it—*eeeeerrrrrrrrrrrrrr-RRRRRRRRRRRRRR-rrrrreeeeeee-RRRRRRRRRRRR-rrr*—and I'm frozen, listening to the school's sirens, my hand still in a fist. My hangover headache goes into overdrive, and I can barely move. The sirens mean forest fire. Or tornado. Or nuclear attack. Or baby down a well. Anything that demands *pay attention, something's wrong*. But there's something different now. I've heard them before, and usually they echo off each other around town. These are solo, tinnier, only from the school. Why would the school's alarm go off on its own?

There's a squeak of feedback as the school's announcement system goes live, and then there's the dean's voice, but I can also hear it though the doors, where the speaker system is.

Students and faculty, please make your way immediately to Dylan Auditorium for a mandatory general assembly. This is NOT a drill, but note that we will not be sending students back to their dormitories as would normally be the case with our alarm system. Repeat, ALL students and faculty to Dylan Auditorium immediately.

There's a rustle of the speakers turning off, and almost immediately, the great oak doors pull wide to reveal Dean Griffin, a short man—he's smaller than I am—his face long and lined, and when he frowns, his wrinkles smush together and terrify everyone. He's been using that frown for decades, and was even a teacher here when my dad attended. He's the only member of staff I know who

36

isn't scared of the rich kids. He's someone I actually fear and respect in equal measure. And he's staring me in the face.

"Miss Kish," he says, his voice steady, but his eyes roving about, "you, having been raised in Fenton, know what that noise means more than most of the students here. I expect you to report to Dylan immediately. Tell everyone you see."

"What's going on?" I ask.

"You will be informed in due course. Now, to the auditorium!"

And he's gone, the great doors ajar, and I see his secretary, Mrs. Applebaum, lying on the giant green visitor's couch, her hand dangling to the ground. Dr. Seymore, the on-staff physician, is on his knees bending over her, a mask covering his mouth. There's a breeze pushing Applebaum's tacky silk shirt around in small ripples, but otherwise she's not moving, and from here, she looks pale, gaunt, her hair grayer and tossed about. I can't move. I saw her just yesterday, shaking that reporter's hand. I take a step closer.

The siren is so oddly captivating. I look out the window, past the snowy fields of the quad and beyond the lake toward the outskirts of Fenton, where I can see Route 467 winding down the mountains. The road is busy, and for a second, I think nothing of it. But then I realize that there are trucks, many of them, and they're camouflaged.

"The army?" I say aloud.

Dr. Seymore looks up and waves me away. "You're not supposed to be here."

I startle, and beyond the doctor, I can make out Mrs. Applebaum's face more clearly now, her lips ringed in blood, her face somehow as wrinkled as the dean's.

"Is she going to be okay?"

"You need to leave, now. Do you hear me?" he yells. "Go!"

I shuffle back out the door and into a hallway now filled with students, all heading to Dylan. No one is worried; there's an atmosphere of abandon—we've been released from classes early and can screw around. No one seems to get that something is going on. I feel like I'm holding a terrible secret, but I'm not 100 percent sure what it is . . . There are some high fives, a girl named Robin pulls Seth Winter's saggy pants down, and he chases her clear out the doors where I'm sure, if I caught up, I could see him piling snow down her hoodie.

I follow them blindly, in a daze.

Before I hit the outer doors, though, I walk by Mr. Geller's room and see that the class is already emptied. I see a trail of blood on the floor, and the other students do too, giving the stream a wide berth. I walk right through it and out into the quad, listening to the up and down of the siren. It's like a hypnotist's call to arms. The sun's bright, despite the cold, and I squint away the searing pain in my head from last night and the incessant siren buzz in my ear.

You can't see the highway from this vantage, so there's no panic or even realization of the soldiers, of what I've seen. There's music playing from a portable speaker someone's lame enough to lug around, and a few groups huddle around cigarettes. Someone even whipped a Frisbee out of nowhere. I can't see Jo or Rob. There are teachers slowly herding us toward Dylan, capturing the milling mass and pushing us through the doors. The snowy quad makes the task easier, because most of us stick to the plowed walkways and don't want to trudge through the deep snow.

All alone in a crowd, I look down at my shoes and the blood there. The wind is cold on my skin, and I shiver and pull out my phone. It rings a few times before he answers.

"Hi, honey, what's up?"

"Dad, the school sirens went off."

His voice gets real serious real quick. "What is it? Tell me everything. Did you see the reporter again?"

"What?" I say, pulling back the phone to look at it. What did the reporter have to do with sirens? "No, I didn't see him, but he texted me last night to try to meet up again."

"You didn't, did you?" Dad's voice is aghast.

"Dad! Of course not. Who cares? The sirens are going off!"

He's quiet, but I can hear him fiddling with something in the background for a second. "I just linked to the emergency grid, and there's no alarm in town. Are you sure it's the sirens and not an ambulance?"

I roll my eyes and raise the phone into the air for a few seconds and then bring it back. "Can you hear them now?"

"Yeah, but do you see anything wrong? A fire or something?"

"No," I reply, biting at a cuticle. "But I see army vans coming down the highway toward the school, and we're supposed to go to an assembly because this 'is not a drill,' and Mrs. Applebaum's sick, so I don't—"

"What did you say?" His voice is urgent.

"Mrs. Applebaum's sick . . . I don't know with what."

"Did you touch her?"

"Dad, no! She's in the dean's office lying on the couch. The doctor's with her. Dad, what's going on?"

"Mia," he says, his voice very clear, intent in a way I have never heard before, "I want you to leave the school. Right now. Come to the Cave—no, wait. This might sound weird, but go through the woods and get to Wilkins's. Tell him I sent you and that you need to get into the Cave."

"What are you talking about? How would Wilkins know how to get into the Cave?" My hangover is gone, dwarfed by the alarms ringing throughout my body. The one person who is supposed to take care of me is telling me to run. "Why can't you just come and pick me up?" I know my voice is cracking, sounding like a whine, but I don't care.

"Oh, Mia, Mia. I'm so sorry. This must be really confusing. You're right. Listen, you just have to trust me. You have to get off campus and make your way to Wilkins's at the aqueduct, okay? Please listen to me. Will you go?"

"What about Jo? And Rob?"

There's a pause. "They'll be fine, Mia. I'm going to tell you something that may scare you, but you're strong and I think you can take it, okay?"

I don't answer, and hold my breath. The students are almost all into the auditorium now, leaving only me and a few stragglers. Mr. Banner, Jo's father, is making his way toward me to walk me in.

Dad continues. "Mia, all of this has to do with me. If you leave now, *right now,* then nothing at all will happen to your friends, to anyone, and everything will be okay."

It's hard to take in what he's saying. But just then the phone beeps and loses the connection. I look down at it and have no more bars left, nothing: *Searching.*

"Mia," Mr. Banner says. He puts one arm on my back and leads my numb body toward the door. "Hurry up, now. We have to get in there."

"But I need to leave," I say quietly. I believe my father, but I don't believe this is happening.

Mr. Banner pulls up short and looks at me straight on. "Mia, Jo's already inside. So is Rob. I'll be in there too." He's talking to me like I'm a baby. "I know the sirens are scary; I bet somewhere deep down you remember them from the well, don't you?" That is the farthest from what's on my mind right now, so out of left field that I can only stare at him dumbly. Mr. Banner is an attractive man, tall with prematurely gray but sexy curls and frameless glasses. Jo's been given a lot of hell from the girls about him. Crushes abound in calculus land. But here he looks sallow and thirsty, confused away from his equations.

"Okay, just go on in, and everything will be fine. As soon as we figure out what's going on, we'll get you two girls packed for the swim meet and out of here. I promise."

I think about what my dad said, and how Rob and Jo are inside. Everyone's inside. I can't just take off like this. Mr. Banner would follow, I don't have any snow gear on, and most of all, I want to know what's happening. I'll wait, I'll talk to the others and then I'll go.

"You coming?" Mr. Banner asks, nodding toward the door.

In retrospect, I probably shouldn't have.

4

DYLAN IS ONE OF THE OLDEST BUILDINGS ON CAMPUS, originally built as the school's performance venue and, with the help and ingenuity of one of Westbrook's leading architectural alumni, is now an impressive hybrid building, half old marble, half exposed glass, an enormous room big enough to attract real music acts from across the country. Though, of course, Fenton-ites are rarely able to secure tickets at face value to see Radiohead or Bruce Springsteen when they come; recently graduated alums return in droves and snatch up the preferred tickets. Only alums and current students get tickets at the first-come, first-served price. I've made a killing selling my seats.

When I get inside, it looks like the students are rioting. Or as close as they can come. Turns out it wasn't just my phone that lost service, but apparently every phone on campus. And for a prep-school crowd at a mandatory school function, that's tantamount to chaos. Paper balls are being thrown everywhere, but mostly there's just shouting. A sort of voiceless swell of complaints and anger from those who are very good at complaining and being angry.

I see Jo and Rob parked near the front, and they wave me into an open seat. Rob's probably more upset about the lack of signal than the others here, but aside from twirling his enormous case in his hands, he doesn't seem to show it.

"What do you think's going on?" he asks me once I'm settled.

Jo beats me to it. "Dad says there's a bad gas leak and that soldiers are coming to evacuate us." She must be feeling better, because her sunglasses are off and her eyes are shockingly wide open.

"Then why are we all sitting together here?" replies Rob, his usual dubious self making a good point. Today his shirt says WE MISS YOU TEBOW. His hair drifts down his face along the edges, like sideburns, and he pulls at a tuft now, something I've come to recognize as distraction and worry. I don't say a thing to my friends about Dad's warning, but only because I don't see any use. Why add speculation to the fire? We're here for a reason, and the professors will tell us what to do.

A paper ball flies past my face, and I search the seats behind me. Everyone is where they should be, sitting with their friends along fault lines that sometimes are too difficult to make out. In the far back are the seniors of high pedigree, and everywhere else is territory worth fighting over. But I'm not interested in just *any* face. I just want to make sure I know where Rory is, so I can plan my escape route after this. And sure enough, there he sits, about eight rows back and on my left, glaring at me from behind a balled-up bloody T-shirt. He's already starting to sport two black eyes, an improvement, if you ask me. Next to him is Jimmy, who leans over and tries to poke his nose. I'm too far away to hear what they say, but Rory isn't pleased and slugs him in the arm, which, for a guy as built as Jimmy, means nothing.

Someone's hand not too far over from Jimmy catches my eye;

Odessa's waving at me and then points slowly over to Rory and mouths, *Nice job!* I can't believe she even cares. I hate that she plays all the sides. And now she's gone, already back to her friends, laughing loud enough to be heard over the entire student body. I can make out Todd, arms over the chair next to him, way up top. He tosses me a nod and indicates that I should get Jo, but I don't have the energy to play messenger girl.

I settle back into my chair and glance at Jo, who I realize could probably sit somewhere else. But I'm not ever scared of that type of thing. Since freshman year, she has proved fiercely loyal, and we three basically subsist as our own little clique. Not nerds, geeks, losers. Not even townies. I just think we're good friends. I remember what Dad said, about how he wanted me to leave now without her. Or Rob. She sees me looking and gives me a quick pucker of her red lips, but the tension under her skin is visible. We're all freaking out.

Not so far away from us on the row, I find myself staring at a newly familiar face. The boy from last night, sitting by himself. He's keeping his eyes down, rolling a pencil between his fingers, when he glances up and catches me staring. His eyes are brown, a comforting color, but near the pupils they shift to a bright and vivid yellow. I realize I didn't get a good chance to stare last night. There's something magical to these moments when a new kid doesn't know the cliques and is willing to speak to or hang out with anyone for the first few days. I kinda feel sorry for him; coming into Westbrook junior year and trying to find a way through all the un-spoken rules must be a nightmare. And considering how he fared last night, he's probably worried about putting himself out there again. That or he's sitting near us because of Jo. I always have to keep her in mind when it comes to vagrant boys. She notices him too, grabs my arms and squeezes hard, and suddenly I'm wishing I didn't look like a burned-out marshmallow.

"Who's that one?" she whispers to me.

"I met him last night. Didn't you see him?"

She smiles knowingly at my tone of voice, and I roll my eyes. How quickly do the worries of the world disappear when there's a new boy involved?

"What's his name?"

I shrug. "I don't know . . ."

Rob leans over me and whispers to the new kid. "Hey, newbie, what's your name?"

I try to sink into my chair to distance myself from Rob, but the new kid glances at me anyway, a hint of a frown on his face, causing the scar on his chin to flare white again.

"Brayden," he says, giving a small wave that jiggles the yellow band on his wrist. "I'm Brayden."

"Cool," Rob says, and then leans back in his seat, not offering his name or ours. He tugs his sideburn again and leaves it to us. Typical Rob.

Just then, a door near the front of the stage opens, and out come the professors. All of them. The procession is odd, like we're in some sort of dictatorial regime, because they seem to march to preappointed spots around the room. Mr. Banner is there; he takes a place at the end of our aisle and shoots Jo a smile and a wink.

Dean Griffin steps onto the stage and in front of the podium, a single piece of wood with the school's emblem, a mountain lion, carved into its face. We at Westbrook are fond of carving things from single pieces of wood.

The dean taps the microphone, sending feedback through the speakers, and my head reacts like a tuning fork just went off in my ear. I squeeze my eyes shut, and when they open, the place is still. It's the gravity in his voice that gets my attention.

"Students of Westbrook, for the moment, we are not fully apprised as to why we were asked to sound the siren."

Jo's forehead wrinkles and she looks at her father, who shrugs, clearly thinking his natural gas story had been true. There's a release of breath in the room; now that there's nothing to be reported, everyone can stop caring. As if to emphasize the point, Eric, the guy who mooned me in the pool, raises his arms and goes, "Wooo hooo!" and everyone laughs, but the dean shouts so loud spittle flies from his mouth and past the podium, almost to me.

"SILENCE!"

The place settles, curious more than scared. But there's a growing tension here—it's palpable—and a good chunk of the student body feels it.

"Silence, I say," he continues. "You don't seem to understand the severity of the situation. I wonder about the merits of full disclosure, but I'll not have your parents assuming we did anything but. We have been, for reasons currently unknown to me and the faculty, ordered by the military to shut down campus activity and classes. I have no news from Fenton, and am not entirely sure whether they are under the same restrictions we are, but I have been informed by several faculty members that our phones and internets are down." There are some snickers at his obvious lack of modern web understanding, and the dean pauses long enough for them to settle. I imagine him thinking, *Maybe it's just as well. Let them think there's nothing wrong; this might be easier.* He steels himself for what must be the really bad news. "This means that, for the time being, no one is to leave the school grounds and we are to place ourselves in voluntary lockdown." There's a huge swelling uproar from the crowd. Today is Friday, and half the class probably has trips planned to Vail or Aspen and their families' winter condos. You'd think by the level of indignation that we've been told to eat mud or something. No one gives a crap about what's really going on, but told they can't go skiing, suddenly they think the teachers are fascists. A few kids ball up paper and toss it toward the stage. One hits Rob on the head. He flicks his hair out of his eyes and settles lower into his seat.

"So they *are* always like this."

I see that Brayden has moved to the seat next to me during the chaos. He's leaning in, a small grin on his face, conspiratorial. It's funny how much you can see when you're close to someone. I can't help but notice the beauty mark under his left eyelid, like a counter to the scar on his jawline. Or the fact that his lips are moist, not dry like most boys' during the winter. Or that his hair is long enough to reveal the beginnings of a cowlick. The small bits that make him a whole. Maybe I should be hungover more often, if this is how observant I am. Ugh, what if he's the same way? What if he can smell my barf breath?

"Who, the teachers?" I ask him, confused. I can feel Jo tense next to me, straining to hear what we're saying. Rob's less subtle and swings his head down to listen.

"The students. Don't you remember our chat last night?"

I remember him getting kicked out of Odessa's party. Things going sour for him just like he predicted. "They only get this way when you take away the gifts Mommy and Daddy bought." Of course, this kid doesn't live here, so he's from somewhere else—he's probably rich himself, and I'm putting my size-six shoe all up in my mouth.

"I call mine Mum and Dada."

I can't help it and let out a burst of laughter, which, I must say, is worth the jackknife to my headache.

"Miss Kish!" The dean's shout finally bursts through the noise of protesting students. "From them, yes, I get it. But from *you*? What if your father is in danger? What if *you* were in danger and your father had no way of knowing? And yet you *laugh*! All of you laugh!"

The place goes silent, everyone staring at me, and the wave of fear and embarrassment hits me at the same time. I can't breathe, and I double over in shame, which makes my head and stomach hurt and matters much worse. He's just making an example of me to the other students, but he's right. The siren went off here, but Dad seemed to know what was going on. And here I am, ignoring both my father and the dean, laughing in their faces. I try to stand, and Mr. Banner comes over and helps me. I can see him scowling at the dean. He takes me out a side door into the cold and scoops up some snow and gives it to me to suck on, an odd gesture that somehow is exactly what I need and probably wouldn't have been done by any other teacher. Jo's there, and so is Rob, but not Brayden. Won't ever be speaking to him again.

"Don't worry about the dean, Mia," Mr. Banner says. He's got one hand on my shoulder, and he crouches in front of me, forcing me to look him in the eye. "Nothing's going on at the Cave. Nothing's going to be a problem here, either, okay? Griffin is just a testy old—"

"But why is the army here, then?" My voice doesn't feel like my own. It's weak and sad and soft, and it dribbles from my mouth like spit. I don't know why I'm all worked up, but the sirens are still going, and I can't help but think of Mrs. Applebaum and the way she looked. Dean Griffin said *lockdown*, but what does that *mean*?

I can hear the dean's voice through the brick wall. Now he's telling us that class is canceled but will resume on Sunday to make up for it. We'll have Saturday off, but are not allowed to leave campus for any reason. The crowd is none too pleased. There's some shouting, then loud applause from the student body, and a couple seconds later, the door bursts open and a senior, Devin Harris, strides purposefully out. A large group of his friends are close behind, cheering him on. A few of the teachers from the room try to impede their progress, but there are just too many kids. Devin gets to his Mercedes SLS and hops in, and so do a couple of his friends, who immediately roll down their windows and lean halfway out, cheering and raising their hands and sticking out their tongues. One even does a mock Taylor Swift "heart" gesture, and the crowd cheers.

Devin spins his tires and peels out, fishtailing on purpose in the snow, drawing an even larger cheer from the crowd. The whole student body must be outside now. The dean is near the door, watching with disdain. I turn around, looking for Brayden, but can't spot him. And then I feel ashamed to have shifted my thoughts so quickly from my father to him. I grab Jo's arm, and we watch the boys together. Rob leans in, sticks his head between the two of ours and rests his chin on my shoulder. I guess it's that easy. Just get in a car and drive away. I don't have one, of course, but Rob has an old 4Runner, and I'm sure we could take that. Dad said to go through the woods, but it would be so much faster by car.

"They're idiots, you know?" Rob says, his voice so close it echoes in my head.

"Yeah," I respond automatically, though maybe they aren't. For the moment, I don't feel the need to participate in Rob's perpetual negativity.

Devin has reached the end of the parking lot and zooms down the long entrance to the school, a small tree-lined road that runs three-quarters of a mile before it hits the campus's surrounding brick wall. Beyond the entrance is a roundabout that leads to the nearest county road, but you can't see it, as there is a row of pine trees in front of the towering wall, so that from this far away, the border of the school looks like a forest. The only drivable way in and out of the school is through the front gate, a wrought-iron fence, intricately shaped and perpetually open. We all watch Devin and crew streak for freedom as if we were in a movie theater at the closing credits, except when Devin hits the roundabout beyond our view, something must've gone wrong. At first we can hear him honking, long impatient hand-on-horn honks. Then there's a series of loud pops that echo harshly around the mountains, and the whole school, all assembled in front of me, ducks involuntarily.

We hear Devin's tires screech again—he's taken the roundabout in a full circle and is suddenly bursting back toward campus and into view, going way faster than before. The hood is riddled with bullet holes, but not the windshield, and some absurd part of me says, *at least they weren't trying to* hit *the students.* The car bounces and swerves and then, in one twist, he can't control the wheels and no amount of winter-driving experience can save him. The car plunges into one of the enormous oaks lining the road, about fifty yards out, and one of his friends, a stupid kid named Will, a nationally ranked welterweight wrestler, shoots through the front window and lands in a clump in a snowdrift.

The students erupt. Dozens begin running toward the car, but just as many mill about, screaming. Another clump scatters in all directions, heading to the dorms or into the auditorium. Jo's dad shouts, "Holy crap, stop!" and tries to physically prevent some of the kids from moving toward the wreck. I take off for the car, though, because I have to know what's stopped them and why. Without a glance, I know Jo's right next to me. I'm running hard, feeling the slick of half-salted ice on the concrete beneath my feet, and I hear Rob calling for us to slow down. He was never much of a runner.

I feel my body burst with adrenaline, my fear pushing me even faster, my mouth filling with a weird need to spit. There's a surreal moment as I run, as I get closer to the car, where I feel my body slip into itself the way it does when I swim. When my legs move at a rhythm and my breathing is even and I know I'm performing as well as I can. At those times in the pool, I go on autopilot and get lost. My mind wanders now, doing a quick lap of the crazy of the past two days. First the reporter, then Rory, then the lockdown and now this. How can they shoot at a *kid*? Suddenly Dad's tone of voice on the phone makes sense; something's going on here that's very, very real. I try not to think about how the school's exit is blocked, how I missed my chance. I should have listened to him. I should have believed. I should have left. I can't help wondering if we're fucked. The worst part of it is, if Dad's right, if everyone *would* have been okay if I had just left, then all of this is my fault.

A few kids are already sprinting back to the school through the snow, to get the campus doctor in residence—of course Westbrook has a state-of-the-art medical facility, but only I know that Dr. Seymore is in the dean's office—and a few others are calling 911, only to remember that their cell phones are useless. Other teachers are running around too, herding students, hustling our way. They look as lost and confused as we are.

The car is smoking, though I can't tell if it's from the tree smashed into its hull or the bullet holes. Lots of them, strafed across the front. Will is moving—at least he was lucky enough to land in the soft snowdrift—but Devin isn't, and neither is the other kid, someone I don't know, though I've seen him around. You see everyone around.

A lot of kids are crying, and a couple are starting to pull Devin and the unnamed one out of the car, but I shout, "No, don't move them. Not yet!" I get closer and push someone out of the way. Devin had his seat belt on, thank God, and he's breathing. There's a huge gash on his forehead from a piece of glass, but the now-deflated airbag seems to have saved him. There's a bruise and a series of cuts on his neck from where the seat belt dug in. I take his pulse, and he seems okay, so I look in the back. The other kid, the one I don't know, he's bent awkwardly on the seat, too high, his head way back and resting in a hole in the rear window, a crater that left a web of cracks through the remainder of the glass. There's blood dripping down, pooling on the back windshield wiper. I pull off my jacket and put it to the wound on his head.

Jo and Rob are off to the side, looking at me with a mix of *whoa* and *what the heck are you doing?* But my father taught me basic first aid, and rule number one is to apply pressure, so I have no problem sitting here until the doctor comes. It's not like I'm performing surgery myself. Speaking of, I look up, and there he is, Dr. Seymore, hurrying in his white coat, camouflaged against the snow. To my right there's a crowd around Will, but through them I can see Brayden on his knees, cradling Will's head, keeping it straight. He looks at me, then down at Will and back to me, and smiles, like he's saying, *check out this little coincidence, that we both* happened *to find two injured bodies in need of head holding.*

Then Dr. Seymore is at the car, looking in at Devin and quickly realizing, like I did, that there's nothing to be done for him at the moment and he's probably just unconscious. He turns his attention to me and the boy I'm holding on to, nodding in quick assessment.

"Good," he says. He turns and shouts at a few of the bigger boys, including Jimmy. "You guys, get over here and help me move him." Dr. Seymore takes my place, and I step back, letting them work.

At this moment, there's a loud screech and everything freezes. At the end of the driveway, the gates of Westbrook are being dragged closed. What's worse is that the men doing it, soldiers, carry guns and are covered head to toe in white hazmat suits. No one makes a move toward the gate to stop them. They snap the gate shut and walk away, like ghosts.

I find myself standing apart from it all, blood on my shirt and all over my jacket, which I hold in a ball in front of me. I lift the jacket to my nose on impulse and take a whiff, and it really does smell like iron. The blood coagulates on my knuckles before my eyes. This kid's blood. Mr. Banner takes my arm, and he and Jo walk me to the dorm. I search for Rob and see him alone in the field, waving his huge cell phone in the air, searching for service. Mr. Banner looks weird, like he's aged from all the stress of the past two minutes. I swear his hair is grayer, and longer, and when we get to the door, he coughs like my grandfather used to, the kind of coughs where we cringed and flinched and tried to ignore the rattling in his throat.

Mr. Banner gags and then dry heaves into the snow. I try to be concerned for Jo's father but have to battle my own stomach, which never likes the sound of another person's upchuck.

"Ugh, I'm sorry, Mia. How gross. And after you were so amazing back there, I can't even stand the sight of blood. Listen, go take a shower, get some rest. We'll handle this." He looks at his daughter. "Take care of her, okay? Take care of yourself." He gives her a big hug. And while they embrace, I can hear him whisper, "Don't leave your room."

His voice sends shivers down my body, and when I pull away and head toward the dorm, everything goes slow and bright. My body still aches from last night, a migraine on the verge, but adrenaline is dashing through me so hard I'm considering turning off and heading toward the pool. Maybe laps would help and I can

54

focus on them to take my mind off whatever this is. I'm afraid. Somehow my dad had an inkling about what's going on. Maybe he has access to military broadcasts. But he's locked behind double steel doors, and it sounds like he's not going to come and get me. And I'm here, when I should be gone. I swallow hard, take a breath. That could have been me. If I'd gotten in the car and tried to drive out of here, that could have been me. My fingers tingle, the cold starting to seep in. Dad had said everyone would be safe if I left. And I could have left out the gates and on foot through the woods. But how could that have changed anything? Devin would still have hopped in his car. They'd still have tried to get away.

Rob's joined us, his teeth chattering in the cold. He's a little baby, I realize. We all are. I take Jo's hand and then Rob's, and they both squeeze mine, but it's hard to feel comfort when there are students running and crying and screaming in confusion all around us. We get to the dorm entrance, and Rob turns and takes a picture of the wreckage on his phone. I give him a look.

"One day," he replies, frowning defensively, "someone will want these pictures."

He's probably right. I think of the hazmat suits and the gates slamming shut and the sirens. I think of the parents cut off from their kids. Someone will want to know what's going on. Someone will have to find out.

THE RUMORS OOZE THEIR WAY THROUGH THE WALLS
and into every student's ears:

There are soldiers around the school, and they'll kill anyone
who leaves campus.

We are being held hostage for ransom, for our parents' money.

A nuclear reactor melted down in a secret facility, and we're all
going to die of radiation poisoning.

No one knows there's anything wrong—no one in town, not
our parents. We are alone.

Some rumors are probably entirely false; some undoubtedly
true. Either way, we're all on our last nerves. The dorms feel like
prison, and it's not hard to imagine every person you know sitting
on their bed, staring at the cracks in the wall.

The faculty is fairly conspicuous in their absence. The RAs are
patrolling the floors, making sure everyone stays in their dorms,
but they're just overwhelmed seniors. We haven't seen a teacher
in hours, and there hasn't been an announcement on the PA system for longer than that. The last one was a frantic plea by the
dean imploring us to stay indoors. I wonder if Mrs. Applebaum is
okay, if the dean was so frantic because he was concerned about
his stalwart secretary.

Amber, the ever-initiative-taking class president, apparently snuck up onto the roof of the dorm and reported to everyone that there's a ring of soldiers surrounding the school, and yes, they are in hazmat suits. She said she couldn't make out any roadblocks near the town, but it was hard to be sure. Westbrook is its own estate by design, hidden from Fenton and the rest of the world. Dad said the sirens didn't go off in town. Maybe the rumors are true.

Jo, Rob and I sit together, saying very little. There's a good view out the window, and we take turns staring across the field. It's dark, the school strafed in the light of hundreds of lampposts, and I'm in the perch now, watching for glimpses of the soldiers through the gate and along the walls. I've never felt this helpless before. Sometimes I even find myself tearing up, but mainly because I don't know what to do. It's like trying to thread a needle or solve a Rubik's Cube or some other doable but frustratingly difficult thing where I must clench my fists and hold my anxiety in. I wonder if Dad's arguing with the soldiers, trying to get through, trying to get me out. I draw trees in the fog on the window. I keep forgetting that my phone has no service and picking it up to check for messages. Jo's taking it all much better than I am. Todd's in another dorm, but he promised to sneak over whenever he could, and she seems content to wait. She flicks on old-school Madonna, which Rob grunts at—I know he secretly has a thing for her. I wish I could be as composed, but instead I'm crawling through my own skin. Other students are gathering in their rooms, huddled together, whispering about how their parents are best friends with the governor, a general, the president, and how they'll be airlifted soon. I remember the urgency in Dad's voice. We can't wait for help; we have to leave now.

I've just started to create a mental map of any and all possible escape routes when I see a figure stumbling from the infirmary. Since we're all sequestered in the dorms, no students should be coming from that direction. The figure trudges off the path and through the snow, struggling all the while, until finally he comes close enough to make out and I see that it's Devin. I feel a surge of joy, glad he's alive, glad there's something going on, and I shout, "Devin!" I turn to Jo and Rob. "Guys, come see this! He's okay!"

Devin gets closer, and apparently we're the only ones who've seen him so far. "He doesn't look okay," Rob mutters. And for once, he's not being sarcastic. There are a few bandages on Devin's face and neck, but they are bled through, and he's limping really badly. Behind him in the white of the snow, there's a blood trail. It's too dark to make out anything more, but he looks wrong, bigger in some way, like . . . swollen or something. Why'd they let him out like this?

Someone else has seen him now, and the front door to the dorm opens. A few kids hurry to put their arms around him and help him into the building. I hop from the window and head to the door.

"Where are you going?" Rob asks.

"Did you see him? Something's not right. I'm going to find out what's going on."

"But you don't know Devin."

"So?" I spit, exasperated and tired of Rob's indifference. I'm angry now, at Rob but also at myself. Maybe I could have done something, somehow. Maybe that's what Dad meant. "Who cares if I don't know him? I'm here, and he got shot at, and we're obviously in danger, so I'm going to figure out what the hell happened. I didn't ask you to come along, so don't give me any of your shit, Rob."

Without waiting for an answer, I open the door and head into the hallway. A few others have done the same, and when I look back, Jo and Rob are following at a discreet distance, appearing chastised. I'm huffing air but manage to be secretly pleased; this anger feels new and good to me. A channel for my helplessness. I hurry down a couple floors to the lounge near the entrance where some of the students have been hanging out near the fireplace and watching movies and playing pool and foosball. Devin's been placed on a couch in a seat of honor, and he's slouched, in clear pain, clutching his ribs.

"Are you okay?" This from Mindy, an RA. I know Mindy—she's in my calc class and likes to complain about her 3.9 GPA. She's also smitten with Devin, talks about him all the time, which is mainly how I know of him. "They let you go already? You don't look so good."

I peer in and frown. Devin doesn't look swollen, as I had initially thought. He looks . . . older. Like a bruised version of himself ten years from now. His jawline is full, stretching out from under the bandage. His torso and arms seem elongated; even his hair appears longer.

Jo's managed to catch up, and she whispers, "What's wrong with him?" I shake my head.

"How's Will?" someone shouts. "And Tom."

Tom. His name was Tom. The boy who bled on my jacket.

Devin doesn't say anything, just puts his hand to his eyes to block the light. Someone else calls out, "What did you see past the gate, Dev?" This rouses him. He moves his hands and speaks in a voice that needs to be lubricated. There's blood on his teeth, and someone gasps.

"Soldiers. Wearing those suits. Full mask and everything. A tank."

Everyone gets really quiet. A couple of people discreetly back away from him.

"They're dead." His voice cracks.

Mindy takes his hand. "Who, Devin? Will? Tom? Are you sure?"

He's shaking his head. "No. I mean . . . Yes, Tom and Will died, a long time ago. From the crash. At least, I think so." A few people have slumped to the floor. Zadie King is crying, holding a friend close. She was Tom's girlfriend. Others start to sob, bodies shuddering all around me. And I'm embarrassed that I'm not. But my mind is whirling; I can feel it trying to put this all together. I glance across the room, and there's a large mirror where I can see all the students in a semicircle facing Devin. I see Rob grimacing behind me, Jo using her finger to pull a tear from her eye. I see myself, my forehead creased, my eyes dark and empty, and I hate it, this feeling. That I'm stuck here and helpless. Zadie draws in a deep breath and controls herself, but Devin isn't done. He's still shaking his head, and I wonder how much that movement hurts him.

"I don't mean Tom and Will. I mean the others."

"Who, Devin?" Mindy is using the voice she uses to coax information from students about drug stashes and unwanted sexual encounters. Devin looks so tired, so gaunt, and as he sits there, breathing hard, I notice the tear in his shirt, the blood behind his right ear, the stubble on his knobby chin. He's a wreck, and he sounds it. Which makes everything he says actually feel all the worse.

60

"Everyone." He rattles, swallowing hard. Then he coughs, a long cough, wet and mucousy, right into his hand. It reminds me of Mr. Banner's cough, which sends alarms surging through my body. "Doctor Seymore. The nurses. Maybe Dean Griffin. They were sick . . ."

My stomach drops, and I immediately seek out Jo. My best friend looks like she's got a steel rod implanted into her spine, she's so stiff and unmoving. The room is dead silent, no one sniffs, coughs or even breathes. Mindy keeps stroking Devin's hand, like nothing has happened, but even the girl in the corner stops sobbing. I think they all think he's delusional, but something about the way he spoke has me inexplicably convinced he's telling the truth. I sidle closer to Jo, grab her hand in mine.

"Now, Devin," Mindy admonishes him, "what do you mean, that the others are all sick?"

"I . . . I don't know. Maybe the teachers too."

I raise my hand to Jo's shoulders, give a squeeze, but it feels like a hollow gesture of comfort. Maybe because I'm terrified myself. We're both stuck, rooted in fear, mesmerized by Devin's story. I can't help thinking, *If my dad knew this was coming, why didn't he try to protect us? If he knew this was coming, what else has he been keeping secret?*

Devin shudders and continues. "Some weren't sick. Like, Dr. Seymore, Mr. Geller, Mr. Brent, Mrs. Applebaum. They weren't sick—they were dead."

Now there are gasps, and my stomach takes a bigger lurch. I saw her, Mrs. Applebaum. Right before the sirens. I saw Mr. Geller, right before the sirens. I saw Dr. Seymore, not hours ago. Now they're dead. And I find myself hoping that it's just them . . . Just six people dead. The room feels smaller, tiny, with all these people in it. The ceiling lights seem to glare, and everyone can't stop talking over one another.

"We have to help them," Jo mutters to herself. I look at her, and know she's right. But she's not going to say it again, not louder. I was the only one who heard her. So without thinking, I take a deep breath and repeat what she said for the whole room to hear, ignoring the quiver in my voice.

I swear someone coughs, "Baby!" Real appropriate, dickweed. But everyone's paying attention, so I go on, feeling my nerves steady. I look in the mirror at Rob's and Jo's reflections, and they're watching me, listening, urging me on, I can tell.

"We have to help them," I repeat, pushing each word out of my throat. "No one knows what's going on, and people are getting hurt. We need to control the situation. Which means we need to confirm Devin's story." A few murmurs of agreement. Devin raises his head to protest but coughs instead, spitting up some blood on his shirt. Someone screams. Everyone except Mindy has backed away now. She wipes his mouth with her sleeve.

"Devin," I say to him directly, "you're sure about what you saw?" He nods, so weak it's all he can do.

"If someone's hurt," I go on, to everyone else, "we have to help them. We have a responsibility." I pause, take everyone in with my stare, these blank, terrified faces. "Any volunteers to come with me to check on the dean and the infirmary?"

Rob's hand is up, like we're in a competition. Jo's is too, and that makes sense; she wants to find her dad. No one else has moved a muscle. There must be sixty kids crowded into the lounge now—word leaked that Devin is here—and they all stare at us, the townies, doing the dirty work.

"This is your school too, you know," I shout loud enough to feel my throat scratch. I'm suddenly so angry at everyone that I want to punch something.

"What if it's Ebola?" Freddy Prince says, just loud enough to make out.

People move even farther from Devin. Mindy stops petting him and stares at her hands, wipes them on her pants.

"It's not Ebola," I reply, shaking my head, thinking of the odd symptoms Devin is displaying. "I don't know what it is. None of us do. And we won't unless we go find out. To do that, we need more volunteers."

Devin, out of nowhere, stands up and tries to walk but then collapses onto the floor and sort of lolls his head around, letting out a long sigh like a tire deflating. Half a dozen girls scream, and I'm kind of surprised I don't myself, if only because of the shock. Someone steps out of the crowd near the stairwell and hurries forward, and I'm taken aback at seeing Brayden. He's clearly worried, his lips pinched tight, and he pulls up the sleeves of his waffle shirt. I can't help but notice the fine thread of muscle, an athlete's body—I guess I know why he's at Westbrook. Probably plays football, a quarterback poached from another school or something. He doesn't look my way, instead he kneels next to Devin and checks his bandages and his forehead, and carefully peers into his eyes. I know it's a stupid thought, but I remember when Brayden said how awful things would be for him here, and I bet he wasn't imagining this.

"I need some ice," he says to no one in particular. "Does anyone here have any codeine?"

A dozen hands shoot up. Brayden shakes his head.

"I've got Adderall!" someone shouts helpfully.

"One of you get the codeine." He looks expectantly at Mindy, but she just shakes her head and sniffs, like there's no way she'd leave Devin's side. Brayden keeps searching, his eyes landing on those that have already volunteered. "You—Rob, right? Go get the ice and also a cloth and a bowl of water. Someone get Devin here to a room and lay him down, and Rob, I want you to put the cloth over his head and the ice against his ribs here," he says, pointing to where Devin's holding his side. "Then I want you to give him codeine, two pills, and let him sleep. Someone watch over him, okay?" This boy, this mysterious boy, stands up with a groan like an old man, then claps his hands together, his face bright and angular and so full of determination that I'd think he's been training for this. "I'll go check out the school with you."

Everyone's suitably impressed, murmuring and moving to do what he said, but there are no more volunteers. Rob gives Jo a squeeze and then looks at me and, through his glasses, I see his dark eyes flick significantly at Jo. And why wouldn't he be worried for her? We haven't heard from Mr. Banner for hours, and now Devin's telling horror stories. *She's fine,* I mouth, not convinced myself. And with one look back at the useless mass, we open the glass doors and move out across the shifting snow.

6

THE HALLWAYS HAVE NEVER SEEMED SO EMPTY. THE lights are on, and they fill the place with a buzzing glare so bright that our footsteps have shadows. Some of the classrooms are lit as well, but all are empty. We check each anyway.

When someone tells you everyone's dead, it makes peeking your head into a room a terrifying thing. I find myself tiptoeing and have to mentally force myself to stop and put my heels on the linoleum. We scuffle our way past trophy cases and the Wall of Giving, a list of donor names on gold plaques—fourteen-karat gold plaques. I bend, involuntarily, to check out an old one: SEBASTIAN AVERY, FOR HIS WONDERFUL DISCOVERY AND THE CURIOSITY THAT GUIDED HIM. Dad used to talk about him, Avery, his favorite teacher from when he was a student here. A light goes out ahead, and I jump. "Sorry," says Jo, her finger on a switch. It's Mr. Geller's classroom. I see the bloodstain still on the floor. Brayden is squatting like a tracker, staring at it.

"That's mine," I say.

He looks up, flicking his hair out of the way. "Really?"

"Well, I made that come out of Rory Boddington's nose."

Brayden smiles. "I don't blame you," he says. "But I didn't think you had it in you."

I'm not really in the mood for jokes or lighthearted conversation, so I can't help it when my voice goes steely and I say, "Sometimes people just push you too hard, you know?"

"I *do* know," he responds, without a trace of jest or mockery. Beyond the cute birthmark beneath his eye, I feel like I can tell who he really is for the first time. I remember him being pushed at the party, him helping the injured boys and volunteering. Maybe, wherever he came from, he's a different boy, aloof and popular, but here, in this new and outsider place, maybe he's forced to be a little like me.

Brayden stands and looks into the empty room, his gaze careful, like he's looking for something specific. "Why are you so good at this?" I ask.

He turns to look at me, his deep brown eyes thoughtful. "I'm an Eagle Scout."

I give a rueful chuckle, expecting him to admit he's joking or something, but he's already focused elsewhere, apparently being honest. More a nerd each second. And then he hushes me. He actually hushes me. He steps toward Geller's desk.

"Check this out."

Jo rubs her pale arms, a nervous habit of hers, and is clearly eager to move on, but the tone of his voice has her curious. Brayden is bent over a cloth on the ground. A handkerchief. It's thick with red, a deep stain of blood.

"Oh, my gosh," Jo cries, her voice literally echoing out the door down the empty hallway. She clamps her hands over her mouth, eyes wide.

I take her by the arm, knowing she's transferring everything she sees here to her imagination about her father's whereabouts and condition. "This doesn't mean anything, Jo," I say, but what I'm really thinking of is Mrs. Applebaum's mouth, the blood dripping, and Devin coughing, hacking blood onto his chest.

Brayden kicks the handkerchief, then makes eye contact with Jo and holds it, his voice calm and reassuring. "Don't worry about this. It's from Rory, not Mr. Geller. You can tell by how it leaked onto the handkerchief in that weird pattern. It's a drip; if it were a cough, it would look more splattered."

Jo pulls her hands across her forehead, grabbing her blond locks and pulling them behind her shoulders. She sucks air deep into her lungs and nods, even manages a smile that seems to bring some warmth back into her pale cheeks. "Got him good, didn't you, Mia?"

I laugh, each breath dissipating the pent-up nerves I have and steadying my hand. Brayden smiles, kindly—unnervingly adult of him—and says, "Let's get going. I didn't move here to spend all day in school."

As we follow him out the door, I glance down at the blood on the handkerchief. I give it a kick, imagining Rory at that moment, and the handkerchief flips over. A splatter pattern. Jackson Pollock on a dark day. I peek to see if Jo's looking but she's not, which I'm grateful for, and hurry after them.

"So hold on, why Westbrook?" Jo asks Brayden out in the hallway, where we are starting to creep less and speak more normally. They walk side by side, and I notice that they're almost the same height. She tall, he average. His Sambas squeak along the floor, and he reaches behind himself to scratch his back. It's hard to imagine the chaos Devin spoke of.

Brayden glances over at her, shrugs. "My parents moved here. They found this enormous estate for sale and thought it would be a good retirement place. They love the country. I don't know—I wish they'd waited for me to graduate high school, but they didn't want to lose the property."

Jo frowns, thinking. "Wait, you moved into Furbish Manor?"

"Yeah, their name is still up on the entrance to the drive."

"Whoa, the Furbishes," she goes on. "You must be rolling."

The Furbishes were pillars of the community, early gold rush miners who hit it big, then bought the general store, took on real estate, cattle, and eventually built half the gas stations in the surrounding hundred miles. But about three years ago, their private jet crashed on the way to a family vacation, killing them all, every last Furbish. It was a huge local tragedy. I knew two of the kids; they went to the same elementary school as me. Their house, their estate, was hundreds of acres of prime forest, pasture and river. I knew that someone had snatched up the gas stations, but I didn't know anyone had bought the manor. Whoever did had to be worth millions.

"You think that we must be rich because we moved into a ghost house in the middle of nowhere?" he replies, his voice becoming heated. His ears go flush.

"No," Jo says, "I just . . . I was surprised, that's all."

"Me too," I join in, backing her up. "It's a crazy place. My dad and I used to hike behind the estate and in their fields. I thought it would be turned into a museum or something."

We walk almost to the end of the hallway. He doesn't answer for a while and then finally admits, "Yeah, it *is* a crazy place. We moved out here last week, and I basically spent every day roaming the house and the woods for hours on end. I've never had a backyard before."

I try to picture him out in the woods behind the manor, backpack on, roving across trails and exploring the land. In the snow it must have been hard going. Lonely. I wonder what he thought of while he was out there.

"Do you like it here?" I ask.

He stares at me, his scar flashing white. "That's a weird question. This is all really messed up."

I shake my head, trying to ignore the hallway. "No, I mean in Fenton and at Furbish."

He's quiet. "Furbish isn't exactly the place I'd go for fun."

We turn the corner, the infirmary in sight, and everything changes. I had just started to relax, to disbelieve, when we see the feet. We freeze, all three of us, rooted there staring at the blue socks and the khaki pants and the brown leather shoes pointed toward the ceiling, halfway out the infirmary door. I can't breathe, and I try to swallow this all away. Brayden crouches and steps forward like a fighter might, in a stance. I take Jo's hand, and we might as well be at a haunted house, clutching each other close, following Brayden slowly, waiting to scream.

Brayden stops suddenly and stands up, stunned. He's not even looking at the body, whoever it is. He's looking into the infirmary, his face turning pale. I move my eyes down to this man, this old man I don't recognize, whose face is marked with spots and lined with sagging skin. He's pissed his pants, and is nose is peeling, and his chapped lips are stained with blood. His legs are splayed

69

haphazardly, twisted over each other. I take a breath and follow Brayden's gaze into the infirmary, then feel like I've been hit by a truck. The old man, his hair somehow plastered into a perfect part, is lying in the doorway because there's no more room.

Every chair, bed, desk, inch of floor is covered with bodies sprawled in various positions. No one moves. No monitors beep. Just bodies upon bodies. And the weird thing is that even in my horror, I realize something: I don't recognize anyone. They're all old people. Really old and withered people. As if a home of geriatrics were bused in to die. That's the last thought that flits through my head before Jo gags and vomits all over those brown leather shoes and then falls to her knees to try to clean it up with her scarf.

Brayden and I both move at the same time to help her up, and she gives in pretty easily. Apologizing, her eyes tearing. I can smell her puke, and it's making me nauseated. Who are these people? Where are the teachers? I don't understand. My hands begin to shake, and I tuck them into my armpits to keep them still. I have never seen a body before. Now I've seen thirty, forty. Now I've seen a graveyard.

"Hello?" a voice calls from up ahead, around the corner, down another hall. "Is someone there?" The voice is weak, frail. I'm reminded of that old commercial: *I've fallen, and I can't get up.*

Jo and I look at each other, startled by the voice. We hurry on toward the sound.

"Hey, wait a sec," Brayden shouts. But we ignore him, round the corner and there, on the ground, halfway down the hall and almost to the infirmary door, is a man, sprawled, looking at us, his face so wrinkled I can barely see his eyes. I don't recognize him, but after seeing the infirmary, I guess I shouldn't be surprised.

The thing is, when you see something like that, a broken human being, you don't keep running. I even put my hand to my mouth—I can't help it—and suddenly Brayden bumps into us. We're all sent falling, and it's Jo who lies face-to-face with the old man.

"Help?" he whispers.

This close, I think my first inclination was wrong; maybe I *have* seen this man before somewhere. I'm embarrassed to think that I ignored this guy for my first two years and now he's calling out for me. Maybe he was a janitor or something.

"Oh, God," Jo says, her voice shaking.

"It's okay," I say to her and to the old man. I take his hand, with its thin skin and heavy veins. "We'll get you help. Everything's going to be okay."

"Mia," Jo says, her voice weak. She has a hand on my ankle and is squeezing hard. "He's wearing my dad's tie. I bought that for him for Christmas. *That's my dad's tie!*"

I squint, take a closer look. It does seem similar to what Mr. Banner was wearing this morning, but I don't really remember.

"JoJo?"

I freeze; so does Jo. The old man used her nickname—there's only one person I've heard call her that.

"What did you call me?" she says, almost accusingly. The old man bends forward, his eyes rheumy and blank.

"Is that you, JoJo?"

She crawls forward, touches his face with a shaky hand. "Dad?" Her voice is so soft I can barely hear.

"No way," I say, backing up. "Jo, no way."

She turns to me, ignoring Brayden, her eyes melting in tears. She breathes deeply, sucking back snot. "Can you help me? I can't do this. Please, check his wallet or something."

The old man is twitching, like he's having little convulsions. I don't know if I can do what she's asking. But Jo would do anything for me. She always has. I feel Brayden's hand on my back, gently encouraging me forward. So I grit my teeth and move, my eyes almost closed, and pull the leather wallet from his back pocket. Inside, there's a Colorado driver's license registered to Brett Banner. I feel ill and try to hold myself together for Jo. Biting my lip, I show her the license.

"What's going on?" Brayden asks finally, as if thinking now were the appropriate time for clarity. We don't answer him, just stare at this old husk of Jo's dad. His bloody mouth and wheezing chest.

"This is impossible," I whisper to her, to myself. "Someone must be screwing with us."

"JoJo, I think I hurt myself. I can't. I can't move. I can't really. Breathe."

"Dad," she says, steadying her voice, "this isn't funny."

But she reaches out a tentative hand to his head, which is now empty of hair but for a small tuft around his ears, white as the snow outside. His head is covered in spots, and he's drooling into a small puddle. I wonder how long he's been here. This impostor, this old Brett Banner. This man who seems to have aged a lifetime in a day. I can't help but think of my own dad lying on the ground somewhere, calling my name. The hallway is quiet. He tried to get to the infirmary, just like all the others.

"Dad?" Jo asks. "Dad, tell me what happened."

"JoJo. What's going on? I can't see. I can't . . . Where's your mother? Wait—don't touch me. You might get it."

Mr. Banner closes his eyes and lays down his head. I'd say Jo's more scared than sad, and so am I. He seems to stop breathing, and I don't know whether I'm supposed to mourn or start CPR. But he's right—we might be exposed to whatever this is. Far too exposed already. I don't think we should be near him; it's too dangerous. I hate thinking like this, but I wrap my arms tighter around my friend to keep her from touching him again.

Brayden seems to get this, but still he moves to check for a pulse. His eyes flick up to Jo, then back down to the body.

"Jo, I don't know what to say." He's doing better than I would. I'm surprised I can still stand. "He's gone."

I feel her body begin to heave and choke on her own tears. I hold her close, my eyes glazed. Whatever happened to Mr. Banner must have happened to the other teachers. I think of the infirmary and the bodies piled within. All faculty members grown inexplicably old. I think of Devin, looking like an older version of himself. Holy crap, my body is itching to move, screaming at me to run the fuck away from here as fast as I can. I imagine the feel of his papery skin. I look at Mr. Banner; is it too late for us?

"Mia?" Jo whispers. "What's happening?"

I stroke her hair. "I don't know. That might not be him. It can't be." I feel stupid saying this—everything makes sense, even if it doesn't. Whatever's going on is making people age and die. Fast and furious. And Jo's dad is now dead. And my dad seemed to know something was coming. He tried to warn me. I feel her body shuddering against mine and try to ignore the fact that Dad didn't try to warn anybody else.

"It might be." We both turn toward Brayden, Jo snorting cry-snot, trying to control herself. He's been back down, digging through the old man's pockets, and has found his keys and cell phone. He hands them both over to Jo and steps back.

"What're you doing?" I ask, disgusted both by his rooting around in a dead man's pocket and by his touching an infected body.

"She has to know for sure. She has to *believe.* Otherwise she'll never let him go." He pauses, looks at me, and for the first time, I see that he's scared too. He just knows how to hide it better. But I can see it in his eyes; they're large, his thick brows higher, his forehead creased. He's just a better actor than me.

Jo's staring at the keys to her house. She flips open the phone, and it's clearly her dad's. I see something, but she flips it back down again.

"What's that? A message?"

She sniffs. "So what?"

But I swore I saw something, a name I'm incredibly familiar with. "Open the phone. Look at it. Whose message is that?"

Jo does, and we both look. There's a message icon—two, actually. They're from my dad, clearly downloaded before the service outage. He *did* try to warn someone.

Jo's eyes catch mine, and for a second, we just stare at each other. Yesterday we woke up and fought over who would shower first. Now this, this insanity. Jo retrieves the voice mail and presses

74

the speaker phone, and after a delay, we hear my dad's voice, saved on the phone's message service.

Brett, it's Greg Kish. I know this might sound weird, but I'm worried that something bad's about to happen. I'm not sure what, but I wanted to call you to warn you. Mia is there alone. I can't help her. I need someone, an adult, to keep an eye on her, and I hope that for the next few days, you can do that for me. If you see anything suspicious, call me, okay?

The phone goes silent, and we all look over at the body lying facedown. Brayden's eyes shift from body to phone to me, puzzlement written all over his face.

"How did he call after the phones went down?" he asks.

I shake my head, looking at the time stamp on the phone. "He didn't. He called yesterday." *Yesterday, right after I met with the reporter.*

"Why did he call then?" Jo asks.

I consider telling them more, but instead find myself shrugging in confusion. Dad called Mr. Banner after we met with that fake reporter. He *did* know something was going on. I should have listened to him and run when I could. Jo pushes for the next message, which was left about fifteen minutes after the first, and I stare so hard at the phone that I think I see him, my dad, driving in the car from campus to the Cave, phone to his ear, speaking softly but earnestly, pleading with Mr. Banner to save our lives.

Brett, it's me again. I know that last message was strange, and I'm sorry. Please, please, don't say anything to Mia to alarm her. Just . . . listen. If something happens—anything you think that might be strange—take Jo and Mia and go straight to the aqueduct. The caretaker, Wilkins, he'll get you into the back door of the Cave. If you can't find him, if he's gone into town or something, try my phone number.

The message ends, and I blink away tears, both at his voice and in relief to know that he wasn't such a monster. That at least he tried to warn someone else. Dad told Mr. Banner about the aqueduct, about Wilkins. Suddenly I'm hit with a wash of frustration, of anger. It didn't matter; Mr. Banner is still dead, and my father still knew something was coming. He *knew*. If he had acted on it, instead of just sending these cryptic messages, everyone might be alive now. Or at least Mr. Banner would be. Where is my dad, anyway? Why wasn't he here before this all began, pulling me away?

"Listen, I know things are insane right now," Brayden says, taking the phone from Jo, as if that will make things better. "But clearly there's some sort of outbreak going on. Something moving quickly and killing everyone. We're quarantined for a reason, and we shouldn't be *here*. We could get sick. Your father, Jo—even yours, Mia, judging by the call . . . they wouldn't want you to stay here. We have to go tell the others. We have to put Devin in an isolated room. Try to keep healthy."

I let Jo stare for another moment, then say, "He's right." And he *is* right. He's so collected and calm, even while being scared. I wish I had his poise and felt confident helping my best friend through this. I want to close Mr. Banner's eyes. I bet the eyelids are soft.

I swallow my own grief and walk Jo back the way we've come. She moves slowly, being led, and finally I lean her against the wall, where her head bangs back hard and she sucks in her breath.

In the silence there is nothing, only the sound of my heart beating, reverberating in my head so fast I think I'm deaf. But I'm not deaf, because I can hear the front doors open, crashing against the walls with a bang. For the briefest of moments, hope swells in my chest. My father's come to save us! I look around the corner, toward the doors, and see three figures. I see soldiers and guns. Brayden takes a step forward, but I grab his arm and pull him and Jo back around the corner.

"Oh, shit," I say.

"What?" Brayden asks, confused. "Even if the soldiers are quarantining us, they still want to help."

"Like they did when they shot at Devin?" Jo whispers, her bitterness fresh and raw, especially standing ten feet from her dead father.

"He was probably being an idiot, not stopping, trying to break the quarantine," Brayden replies, somewhat callously.

I hear them, but can't really understand. How can I explain it to them, what I saw? There were two soldiers with guns dressed in hazmat suits coming into the school. Between them, walking without a hazmat, was a third figure. Blake Sutton.

7

"WE HAVE TO GO."

Jo knows me well enough to hear that there's something different in my voice. "What is it, Mia?"

I stare at her, trying to push out the smallest whisper I can
imagine. "I *know* that guy. I met him yesterday. He interviewed me
and Dad, but afterward Dad warned me to stay away from him."
I'm feeling guilt bloom in my stomach; we don't have much time,
so I blurt out, "Right after the sirens, dad told me to leave campus.
Just like he told your dad, Jo. He *knew* something bad was going
to happen, and I think this guy's the key."

Brayden, who's crouching at our feet and peering around the
corner, whispers up at us, "He's here in the quarantine with a killer
virus and no hazmat suit. He's more than just the key."

"We have to get off campus." I stare hard at them, willing them
to agree, but it doesn't take much. Jo nods immediately, her face
grim, and though Brayden is new, is in an unfamiliar place, doesn't
know me or anyone, I can see that he trusts what I have to say. He
mulls my words over in his head, checking angles, and I see the
moment he agrees, his face almost upticking. I don't know why,
but I want to smile. I have to fight the urge. But he's making me

feel strong, purposeful. The opposite of the loneliness I feel in the swimming lanes.

"Okay, good," I continue. "We have to get Rob."

I expect him to pause again, but he doesn't. He's all in.

"Through the pool!" Jo says, and she's right. It's a way out that will take us far from where Blake Sutton is. I put my finger to my lips and shoo her forward. We go single file, crouched, moving quickly, trying to keep our sneakers flat against the tile to avoid squeaks.

Soon we're at the small glassed corridor that connects to the gym, then to the pool, a sort of indoor/outdoor walkway, the most dangerous part of our trip, as it's where we are most likely to be seen. We peer through the window, fogging up the glass with our breath, but can't see anyone. What we can make out are spotlights, moving across the school, along the walls.

"That makes getting caught easier," Brayden jokes. I nudge him quiet, and we move on, staying low, into the gym, where the smell of sweat and wood immediately hits me. The pool is connected through the locker rooms, and we're about to go through the girls' locker room when I get an idea. "You guys go through the boys' and see if the equipment room is open. Get some ski-team gear, something warm. Anything we might need for being out in the cold at night."

"Where are you going?" Jo asks, her pale face almost blue in the dark.

"We shouldn't split up," Brayden adds. His brown eyes are intent, trying to figure out my plan, but I need to be alone in the girls' locker room, so I shake my head.

"Just trust me," I say, and then add, "Grab some hand warmers too, while you're there." Jo looks confused, probably just still in general shock at seeing her dad transformed and dead, but complies, and the two are off to the other side of the gym, their bodies flinching at each occasional squeak along the hardwood floors.

Good thing I often get dressed alone, so I'm used to it being so quiet. It's weird, though, like my locker combination should be different. But no, 18–31–17 still works. *Click.* I wince, pull open the squeaking door, and then wince again. Naked is not how I'd like to be found by anyone who might come inside. I strip out of my layers—though, after considering the logistics, I leave my underwear on. Against the cold air, my mind screams, *hurry up hurry up hurry up*. Of course I have a swimsuit in my room, but not one like this, and I pull on my full-body suit, two legs, up to my waist. Jo and Brayden are probably digging through the equipment room, finding weapons. I feel like I can almost hear them, whispering.

But suddenly I *do* hear a sound, like plastic on plastic and the gush of heavy breathing. I immediately cover my exposed breasts and try to turn my head, but a muffled voice shouts out, "Stop moving."

My throat's so tight I can barely breathe, and my body's so cold it's starting to shake. Perfect timing to be as helpless as I've ever felt. Halfway naked, I don't think I can move my hands to defend myself even if I wanted to.

"What are you doing here?" the voice asks. There's a click, and suddenly I'm bathed in light, even more self-conscious.

These men, they're soldiers. Brayden's right: they're supposed to *help* us. I take a deep breath and say, "I'm a student here. I was just getting some things I need for my dorm. I . . . what's happening?"

I peek over my shoulder and see him, this large white suit with a gun trained on me. A flashlight is affixed to the barrel, blinding me from any details.

"Did you see anything?" the soldier asks.

"What do you mean?"

"Did you see anyone sick?" he replies, his voice echoing around the locker room.

It's an odd thing, wallowing in this type of fear. I feel as if my senses sharpen. I notice my dry teeth, the tightness of my skin, the pulse of my heart in my fingertips. I'm all alone. "I saw the teachers, yes, but . . ." I try again. "Just let me put some clothes on."

"Don't move!" he commands again, moving closer. "You have to come with me."

"But what is this?" I ask, all my questions bursting forth. "Why is everyone dying? Who are you?"

He doesn't answer, but grabs my arm and pulls me toward the door. His plastic glove bites hard into my skin, and I try to fight down the panic that's growing in me. I don't know if he's helping or hurting. I don't know what to believe.

There's a squeak and then the loud thud of a body and helmet hitting the tile. I turn, see Brayden twirling a baseball bat in his hands, calm as can be. His eyes are so intense they appear to smolder. I'm agog watching him, feeling my body heat up instantly, life returning to my limbs in a jet of boy crush and hero worship.

Brayden kicks at the soldier's foot, then, satisfied, he looks up at me and blushes. "You okay?" he asks, his voice soft and caring.

"You just hit a soldier? What were you thinking?"

He frowns, his lips thin and his forehead wrinkled. "I was thinking he was trying to take you somewhere you didn't want to go while you were naked."

I turn, deathly embarrassed at my bare chest, and pull the suit into place, trying hard to ignore that he just saw me topless. Fully clothed, I stand up and take the still body in. We're in trouble now.

"I didn't know you'd actually be changing in here, otherwise I'd have n-n-never . . ." He stutters, thinking about what he's saying. "I would never—"

"See me naked?" I offer helpfully.

"No. I mean, not that. I mean, maybe . . . but I'd never—"

"Barge in and knock a soldier unconscious?"

He nods his head thankfully, but I can see him checking me out. It's a weird thing, to be cognizant of his eyes roving my body, making me feel for the first time in a long time like I don't need to hurry out of the pool and to my towel. I find it odd to recognize the difference between Brayden's look and, say, Rob's innocuous gaze. If Brayden hadn't walked in on me naked by accident, would he have ever bothered to do so on purpose?

I look down at the soldier and realize how different his body is from the dead we just saw, how animate and sensible. Limbs angled the right way, the suit rising slowly with each breath.

"He's fine," Brayden reassures me. "He'll wake up crying, but he deserves it."

"Yeah, and he'll be happy to come with all his buddies and their guns to find us in the dorms." I'm scaring myself, growing more terrified by this quarantine by the second, but am somehow equally

82

exhilarated. Maybe it's being in the locker room, but my body is as bouncy and eager as at a swim meet. Brayden laid someone out for me, and it's hard not to stare. I wonder if he has a soccer bod like Jo says Todd has—all six-pack and legs. I take a second, gather myself, trying to think of his face as merely two eyes and a mouth. We have more pressing matters in the world.

"Thank you," I squeak.

He comes close, picks up my jacket from the ground and slips it over my shoulders. "Not sure why you were in here changing, Mia, but you need to stay warm, okay?"

I nod mutely, the warmth of his breath on me. Is it weird that I'm surprised at how minty it smells? He reaches up slowly with both hands and places them tenderly on the back of my neck, his palms just under my jaw. I close my eyes and lean forward, but instead of his lips brushing mine, they land softly upon my forehead and linger, pressing against me gently. I'm pleased by how good it feels, and as he pulls away, he hovers his lips near my forehead and kisses my eyebrow the same way. I don't know what to do with my hands, so I put them against his coat, but even with the thick padding of his jacket, I can feel his body. He moves his hands to my hips, and they rest there like miniature fires, burning through my suit.

He leans back, leaving me swaying, absolutely dazed. I can hear Jo coming, whispering, "Guys? Where are you?" but I don't move. I can't. I can only stare into his eyes.

"Mia," he says, almost inaudible.

"Yeah?" I reply, a breath.

"I like you."

I giggle, I can't help it. "You do?"

He nods seriously, then traces the ridge of the crook in my nose. "I even like this."

He looks proud, excited, happy. Jo rounds the corner and sees us, standing over a body, our faces smiling, not fifteen minutes after finding her father dead. I feel an immediate, awful guilt wash over me and hurry to get on the rest of my clothes.

"What happened?" Jo asks, her arms full of supplies. She looks steady, purposeful, her face more flushed and her thin brows bent over her eyes. I'm not sure, at this very moment, that she can realistically process what she walked in on.

"We have to go," I say, searching the floor for my clothes.

Jo bends to hand me my goggles, which had fallen from my locker. She's slow about it, sidestepping Brayden, who is making a show of checking the soldier again. I look at her, her grief-stricken face. She smiles. Not a big one, not an *I'm happy* one. But she glances at Brayden and smiles for me. And that makes her the best friend in the world.

We have to sneak back across campus. There aren't many soldiers, and we know our way around the school, but they're there, standing near our dorm, guarding the entrance. This is what a quarantine is all about, right? No one in, no one out. I wonder why they waited so long to get on campus in the first place. But now we've no choice. If we're caught, we might be held long enough for the soldier we knocked out to wake up and then we'd be in serious trouble.

Our room is on the third floor, so no climbing in the window, but there are two side entrances and one basement entrance, and there appear to be only three soldiers assigned to guard the entire area, making rounds, wandering the grounds near the doors. We wait until they turn the corner and then we take off; I have my magnetic key-swipe in hand. The snow gives way under our feet, slowing us down, and for a moment, I'm terrified we'll be caught, but we make it to the doorway. I swipe the card, and there's a loud *beep* before the green light flashes, then the *click* of the bolt retracting. *Hurry,* I think, and we pull the heavy door toward us. A soldier appears at the building's edge and starts speed-walking our way. We slam the door shut, hearing his body bang against the door right after.

"We told you!" he shouts, his voice muffled through suit and door. "Stay inside!" Then he kicks the door. I let out a sigh of relief. He must have thought we were trying to get out, not in.

We all share a dazed look.

"And now we have to sneak back out there?" Jo asks.

I shrug. "It's the only way."

"Okay," Brayden says, hefting the baseball bat he felled the soldier with. "I'll get to my room and meet you at yours in ten minutes. Ready to go by then?"

"Definitely," I reply, trying to sound confident. His gaze lingers. His body doesn't want to move, and I see it fighting to stay. It's the cutest thing ever, watching him want me. But finally he turns down a hallway and disappears, and we jump up the stairs to ours.

I'm not surprised to find Rob in our room, standing by the window, biting his nails. He whirls around at our entrance, his usually indifferent face etched with concern. He's in a blue sweatshirt with the hood pulled up, spikes of his black hair peeking out in disarray.

"Where were you?" he asks, angry and jealous and concerned all at once. He takes a look at Jo and his face softens, knowing intuitively what we found. He's always been a sensitive one. "Oh, man. Shoot." He goes right for her and gives her a hard hug that her arms don't return for a second—and then they do, desperately, and suddenly she's crying. I can't help it; I join them, and for a moment, what might be the only moment in a long while, we mourn her father.

"How'd you know?" she asks, sniffling, pulling back to look at Rob.

"I could see it on your face," he replies in a whisper.

I'd like to go on hugging my friends for longer, but we don't have time. "Rob," I say, taking charge, pulling them both back to me, "we have to leave campus . . . now."

He nods to the bed where a backpack is already waiting. Again, Mr. Astute.

"But we can't leave," Jo says, her eyes out the window. She's hugging herself and rocking gently on her feet. "It has to be a virus, right? What if we've got it now, by being there? We weren't wearing suits." She turns back to us. "What if we spread it by leaving?"

"We're not going to see anyone," I say, shaking my head.

"You don't know that," she replies. "And what if we infect your dad?"

I shove down the image of him folded in wrinkles and coughing up blood. "We won't, Jo. He'll know what to do. He *told* us to come."

She rubs her face with her hand, her purple sparkling nail polish at odds with how we're all feeling. "Whatever, Mia. He's your dad. You decide if you want to infect him."

I'm stung by her words, but try to let them go, considering what she's just gone through. Rob's pretending not to watch the exchange. He's putting on his deep brown North Face jacket and fiddling with the zipper. When we don't say anything for a while, he glances at me.

"I've been on the roof with some of the others," he says. "It's true, they've got us fully wrapped in soldiers."

I frown and go to the window, peer out toward the gates and see an armored vehicle parked there, spotlights set high, shining across the walls. "Where are they the thinnest?" I ask, though I already have a strong hunch about this. It's integral to the plan.

He bites the inside of his cheek. "At the lake."

And why wouldn't they be? Jo and I share a look. The lake makes up a section of the eastern border of the school. It's more of a frozen pond, really, but big enough to hold crew practice in and to ice-skate on for fun.

"How many?"

"Five," he replies instantly. Rob's never wrong about numbers. "One patrolling the school side, four in the woods beyond. Looks like they'd rather steer clear of us."

"We all have skates?" I ask, worrying more about Brayden than anyone else. It's practically mandatory for every kid in this area of Colorado to have skates. They nod anyway. Rob says he'll be right back and runs to get his.

In that moment, our first alone, I check in on Jo. "Are you okay?" I ask lamely. But what else can I do? I'm distracted by the need to get moving, by my own nagging guilt at us being here still, by the new kid who's packing downstairs. I realize that I'm not the only one with a single parent here. I'm worried about getting to Dad while Jo gets to realize that her mother, Nancy, is at home, oblivious to her husband's death.

But she doesn't have any idea of what's going on in my head. She only sees me asking, sees the concern in my face. She smiles sadly and says something I would never have imagined: "Let's just get out of here first, then do all the 'are you okay?' stuff." I kiss her hand and then we turn, energized, to pack our things and grab our skates.

There's a knock on the door, which means it can't be Rob. I smile and rush to open it, but it's not Brayden either. Instead, Odessa and Jimmy are there, both with bags, Odessa with a Tumi roller. They hurry inside.

"What are you two doing?" I ask, freaking out, imagining our escape blown.

"After all my late-night parties, you of all people," Odessa says, sitting on my bed, "know how thin these walls are." She smiles her innocent smile, but I can tell how worried she is. Her bright red hair is tucked haphazardly in a bun and she's chewing her lips, gnawing at them.

Jimmy looks even bigger than usual, his heavy down jacket like a comforter wrapped around his shoulders. He has a wool cap on his head and looks like an Inuit. The door opens, and there's Rob, who peers at them and then—it's almost funny—his shoulders sag as he accepts their arrival.

"Odessa," Jo says, zipping up her backpack, "we're going, you're not. I'm sorry. That's too many of us. You'll be fine here."

Jimmy shakes his head, his jacket rustling loudly. "No way. Not after Devin. Not after all the crazy that's gone down."

I feel my hands go moist. I look at Rob. "What happened to Devin?"

But Rob doesn't answer, his face suddenly haggard, and instead it's Jimmy again, his eyes out the window. "He's started to get weird. Something's happening to him. His voice went all deep, and he started losing hair on his head."

"It took ten minutes," Rob says, agreeing with Jimmy in a quiet voice. "I watched it happen."

"Is he dead?" I ask, fearing the worst.

Rob shakes his head. "No, he just looks like a guy who's prematurely balding. It's weird, like he's suddenly thirty-five years old." That's odd, I think. He's not dead, just aging. He might have been bound to go bald as an adult. I guess since he was younger, he has more time to age?

"We're not staying here," Odessa says, looking as earnest as I've ever seen. She pulls on a tight red Gore-Tex jacket and a pair of earmuffs that look like headphones. Her freckles pucker in worry. "Mia . . . we just want to go home."

"Since when has that been the case?" Rob asks. He's never really liked Odessa.

"What?" she snaps back at him. "You aren't worried about your parents? I'm not allowed to care about my family?" He looks chastised and ducks his head. She's staring at me, entreating me to understand.

"What if you're infected?" Jo barks, angry, unmoved, bringing up the argument we just had, and I can tell she's unable to bear speaking of someone else's parents. "What if you give them the virus?"

"What do you mean, virus?" Jimmy asks, his face alarmed.

"What did you see in the school?" Odessa asks at the same time. "Is it true? Are they dead? It's a virus?" I realize that she looks different, and it takes me a moment to get that she's not wearing makeup. Wow, it's been years since I've seen that. More important, I understand that she's not messing around with us. She's serious, scared and looking for help. I don't want all of us to fight, and I don't want to have to explain everything we saw in the school, to keep bringing up Mr. Banner in front of Jo, so I search my closet and pull out an extra Arc'teryx backpack and throw it at Odessa.

"We don't know if it's a virus, but it looks that way. Drop the rollie, fill this up. Jimmy, go get your skates and Odessa's. And some water. Hurry."

Just then another knock. We freeze, but Rob peeks through the eyehole, gives a thumbs-up and opens the door. Brayden's there, the only one smart enough to dress all in black. His thick eyebrows shoot up at the numbers in our room, but I'm just as surprised that he's brought his own skates. Surprised and, almost irrationally, proud. Even Jimmy grunts, gives him a bump on the way out.

"Got everything?" I ask.

"Think so." He turns to Odessa. "Hi, I'm Brayden. Newly designated townie."

Odessa's smile is firm and confident, her usual self. "Welcome to the club. We're the only real people at Westbrook." She always says that sarcastically, but this time it feels genuine.

There's a hiss of static in the air, and we all flinch and glance up involuntarily at the announcement speakers. A deep voice begins to speak slowly, carefully, enunciating each word.

Students of Westbrook. Do not be alarmed, but please listen.

This is clearly not Dean Griffin. There's no way Griffin is still alive, as old as he was. *From now on, please stay in your rooms. Soon you will be visited by a soldier, so do not be alarmed; they are merely registering your presence and are going to hand out information on the new schedule that will be in place during this short quarantine. You are NOT to leave your rooms under any circumstances. I assure you that the incident at the gate this morning was completely unavoidable, and we are deeply sorry for your losses. There will be no further incidents of this nature as long as you follow these instructions. Please, children, let us help you.* He pauses to cough, but it sounds normal, not deep and hacking like Devin's viral one. *One final note: I'd like to ask Miss Mia Kish to come to the office, please. Mia Kish—to the office.*

My body locks up. Even though they're my friends, the stares of everyone in the room make me feel weak and naked. Like they could turn me in to the guards at any moment to help themselves. It's him, isn't it? Sutton, standing in the dean's office without a hazmat suit or a care in the world. He's ordering me to come to him. Dad warned me not to meet with him. He warned me about a few things. *Dad,* I think, *I won't ignore you this time.*

Jimmy bursts into the room, his bulky brown skin glistening with sweat, skates swinging from the laces he's clutching in his fists. He heard the announcement too, of course.

"We have to go, *now,*" I say.

Odessa finishes shoving her clothes into the bag. The others put on their winter jackets, their gloves, their hats. We are very quiet and very efficient. No one asks why I was called to the office. No one thinks I should go. I see Jimmy help Odessa tighten her straps, and she looks grateful as his huge hands grip her shoulders comfortingly. I guess they are on again.

"Mia," I hear, and I turn to see Brayden standing at the window. It's a small room, but he's carved out a very tiny nook of privacy, and I join him.

"What do you see?" I ask, craning my gaze out to the courtyard. It hasn't snowed in a few days, which is lucky. Though bad for covering tracks. I don't see anything special, just one soldier pacing leisurely along the path.

"You're going to be okay," he says, his voice urgent with belief.

"I know," I respond, almost automatically. He called me over here to make sure I was okay. I smile, a genuine one, and try again. "If you bring your bat, I will be."

He looks at it, leaning against the bed. Then he grabs my fingers lightly. His hands are sweaty; so are mine. "I will. And I'll protect you."

There's no noise, not at all, and suddenly I turn to everyone else. They're ready, no more rustling or packing, all just waiting to get moving. I set my face serious, and Brayden does too, though his dark eyes shine at me.

"Where to?" asks Jimmy, looking so intense under his cap that he reminds me of a bulldog.

I look at them all; they look back. Rob nodding to himself, already agreeing with me, his upper lip sheened in sweat. Jo knows the answer; she's heard my dad's message, and her face is grim and determined. Jimmy and Odessa next to each other, his enormous hand resting on her curly head as she leans against him. And Brayden's holding his bat. *We can do this,* I think, for the first time. And so we will.

"We're going to the aqueduct."

8

THE SNOW IS THICK ON THE EAVES, HANGING HEAVY and full. It clings to the windows, sits gently on the frozen lake. It spills from the mouths of the gargoyles that line the ledges of the great halls. Lights flash in the woods, on the hills, bright strobe lights that burst across the fields as they pass through the gaps in the trees. There are smaller lights too, flashlights held by guards, men that squeak as they walk in their white suits. The lights are on in the dean's office. They're waiting for me.

We have a plan, but we're already exposed and in danger. There are no excuses for all six of us, bundled as we are against the weather, to be casually breaking out of our dorms for an evening stroll.

Odessa and Jimmy are crouched against the wall at the back of our line. They're breathing fast, clouds of mist billowing from their mouths. Closer to me are Rob and Jo, the former with his mouth covered in a black scarf, his gothness quite useful for espionage. Jo's scared; she's pressed as close against the wall as possible, so that the ivy that hangs above us seems to reach for her. Brayden, directly behind me, grabs my hand to steady me. I start, fighting the simultaneous feeling of fear and pleasure—I grab some snow, squeeze it to slush to help me focus. There can be no distractions now.

The nearest guards are twenty feet away, staring at the quad. They're whispering, but are too far away for us to make out what's being said, and then they move on, following a well-trodden path, ignoring the vast expanse of open snow.

I motion with my hand, and we move, skirting the wall, scrunchy step after step, the drift shin high in places. Whenever someone comes near, we crouch like before, sometimes lying flat on the ground in the snow, letting it provide cover. I'm wearing thermals, ski bibs and three pairs of socks, and sweating so badly my eyes sting. As we move, I grab some snow and stuff it in my mouth to cool down. Rob sees me and does the same. Pretty soon, we're all sucking on snow.

The lake is on the other side of campus from our dorm, and is the only gap in the wall aside from the front gates. We're almost there, about fifty yards away on a small hill overlooking the school. From our vantage, I see clumps of soldiers patrolling in pairs. On the other side of the lake, we see the soldiers Rob mentioned, fanned out, right in our way. I can see the statue of Socrates too, a Westbrook make-out point; technically, it's off campus, but it has such a perfect view that it's not hard to understand why it was built there. I'm sure whichever alum donated the funds for the Greek philosopher would totally love its more general use. I'm nervous, because I had hoped we could just skate over the lake silently, easy and quick, but with the soldiers so clearly keeping watch on the other side, there's no way we can make it across without being seen. I guess we'll have to go with Plan B.

I glance back and spot a massive army truck parked near the school. The glass front doors of the school open, and out come two more soldiers carrying a limp form, clearly a body. Then another set of soldiers joins them. There's a hollowness in my gut, an anguish for all the dead. I check if Jo's okay, and she's not, her eyes are as wide as they get, and she's shivering. I catch Rob's gaze, his face slack and sad. He pats her arm. I wish I were able to help. But I can't, because Plan B calls for me to go solo.

I point at Jimmy, who's in the rear, and indicate down one side of the hill toward the lake. He frowns, confused as to why he's leading now, but starts off. I guess football players are good at taking orders. The others follow, staying low. I grab Brayden's shoulder, and he stops. I start pulling off my jacket and boots and bib and hand them to him along with my bag, which has the rest of my gear. He doesn't question me, which I can't help but love, only reaches for my skates. I shake my head and toss them into the snow.

"When you get down there, tell everyone to put on their skates. Then wait for me to distract the guards."

"What?" he asks, his voice in a panic, steam puffing from his mouth. He rubs the birthmark below his eye as if it's bothering him. "Where are you going?"

"A different way. It's safe. Trust me."

"I'm coming with you," his says, his voice firm. The funny thing is, his conviction makes me feel stronger, more capable. Like now that I have someone talking to me like this, there's no way I'm going to screw it up and get caught. The others are halfway down the hill. I push him in their direction.

"Trust me, Brayden."

He stares for a beat, angry even, a vein shivering on his forehead, but then nods reluctantly. Before he goes, though, he scrambles back up to me and pecks my lips, quick and cold but exhilarating and wonderful. "Be safe, Mia." Decision made, he's gone, hurrying off to the others, and I'm alone, trying to catch my breath.

Below me, I see another set of doors open, these near the dean's office, and four soldiers emerge, striding purposefully across campus. Straight to the dorms. I'm willing to bet my room is where they're going. My nerves, already frayed, splinter. But at least I know I can't wait. We have five minutes, tops, before they discover I'm gone. Ten minutes before they find our tracks. *Now or never*—I think this to myself like a mantra over and again to beat my fear, pushing out of my crouch and down the other side of the hill and to the far end of the lake, away from my friends.

I can trace the outlines of the others in the air as they huddle in the trees about fifty yards down, waiting for me, wondering what I'm doing. But I'm not sure I know, myself. What I do know is that they have to be far away from me, just in case I'm caught, just in case this doesn't work. Ahead of me is the lake, iced over, and beyond that are the hills and forest and bright strobe lights of the hazmatted soldiers. Socrates is pointing at me, telling me this is a stupid idea.

The lake is about a quarter-mile across, but it narrows significantly at one point, exactly where I'm headed. There, it's only about the length of our swimming pool to the other shore. The water flows stronger there, thinning the ice, making the area notoriously dangerous to skate on. Signs dot the edge: they are bright red, with a stick figure in water, drowning, his mouth a big O. It says DANGER, but honestly, that's an understatement.

I approach the edge and take off my scarf and socks and stand shivering. The water sloshes gently out from a broken hunk of ice. The water's dark, the snow along the edge of the lake turns to mush and then disappears into the deepest black liquid. I stare like I would at the pool, waiting to jump, but knowing I'll hate the first moment, that instant of near shock when the cold hits my body.

I grab a couple of icy rocks, and with a few careful plunks, I crack the ice more, a splash of liquid hitting my ankles, numbing my toes. There's a hole about three feet across now. The size of a well. I stare at the darkness, and there's nothing else. My father, my friends, the soldiers, the virus, all of it gone. Filtered out as my eyes zoom in.

"I can't," I whisper, but no one hears me. I think I stutter; it's hard to tell. I take deep breaths like I'm supposed to, hyperventilating purposefully, getting as much oxygen into my body as possible, as if that's an excuse for any delay. But I don't move. How can I? What the hell was I thinking with this plan?

There's a crunch in the snow. The others must have sent someone to help me. For a moment, I hope it's Brayden, and I know I'm pulling a sheepish smile onto my face. I glance over but instantly drop down into a crouch, impressed by my own reflex, because a soldier is walking up the bank this way. Beyond him, I see the outlines of my friends move, as if to duck deeper into the brush. I glance at the hole, where the ice appears to be glowing, pale and sickly.

The soldier's flashlight cuts a path to the trees inland. He won't expect to find me here; he's not even looking my way. But he's walking on the edge of the water, and my clothes are here in a small clump, along with the jagged hole. We're screwed. My fear of the murky water is gone, or rather, overwhelmed by the fear of being found out and letting everyone down, so without thinking too hard or looking behind me, I pick up my scarf and socks and slowly walk backward into the water, goose bumps so hard and strong they break my skin. I feel like a duck in the worst way possible. The water is so cold it burns, the thin band of its surface rising like lava up my legs, but the soldier is close, and I've no time—just years of experience getting into freezing water (if not *this* freezing). I clomp my teeth down on my tongue, feeling the fleshy muscle and squeezing until I can taste the copper of blood in my mouth. I shove what few clothes I have under the ice, goggles squeezing so hard over my eyes that my head aches. I fleetingly wonder what the soldier would make of me, a blue, shivering girl in a Speedo, goggles on, rising from the water. The Lady of the Lake. He'd probably freak out and run back to campus. Or shoot me. Both bad options.

I'm grateful for the pain, for the distraction from the panic that's going through me. Before swim meets, we always sat alone, listening to music, jiggling our legs. Day one, they told us, if you panic, you're done. Panic makes your blood flow quicker, makes the oxygen dissipate. I breathe out, as if I had air stored in my toes, and then in, inflating myself, my body, and with a masochistic dive, I'm under.

Swimming was a fear for a long time. Darkness still is. It has taken me years of obsessive combat with my own neuroses to get into a bathtub, then a kiddie pool, then the Olympic-size one at school. Now I can almost get into a pool without flinching. R.E.M.'s "Nightswimming"? Not my favorite song.

I'm immediately numb and swallowed in the black. So numb it's hard to move my arms and legs. It's not like I was loose, ready to go. I kick, pull, swim through the turgid water, the moonlight faint above my head as it squeaks through the opaque ice. I am the fastest girl my age in the United States. I have been known to swim this distance in 23.3 seconds. But I can't today. Because I can't see anything. My goggles don't work. I don't know where I'm going. There's no noise, no splashing beside me or cheers or screams. My muscles are sluggish, and I don't even hear my own wake, because I'm trapped under the ice. Stuck. No perfect 68 degrees Fahrenheit. Suddenly, I want up. I involuntarily jerk, and my head bumps the ice. The panic sets in, and I can feel my body simultaneously begin to shut down and scream for help, my muscles burning. For a moment, I stop swimming, let the panic overwhelm me and slam my fists into the ice. I imagine that it bends or cracks, but I'm not sure. I look around, unable to see even a foot ahead or behind, just a wall of swirly black, and suddenly I'm back in the well, freezing, floating, waiting to die.

There's a moment passing before me, an eternity when I see my hands flutter near my face. When I can't help but think in the small of my mind, a little voice, something my dad whispered:

> *Baby Mia, who fell down the well*
> *scratched her legs but then felt swell.*
> *Spent a couple days underground—*
> *we pulled her up, safe and sound.*

I didn't die in the well. I survived. I got out. I'm alone this time with no one to help, but I'm not a baby anymore. I can do something about it. I force the panic back down my throat. Because if I panic, I might as well be dead already. The water feels resistant against my skin, but not cold any longer, and I take that as a bad sign. In my ice-smacking mini freak-out, I didn't keep track of my direction. I have no reference point. I'm in an empty room filled with water, and there's only one way to the door. I'm shivering, but my lungs don't care; they are starting to clench, as if someone were squeezing them from the inside. Even with all my training, I'm running out of air.

I pick a direction and swim, fast now, as fast as my lethargic body will move. I keep my head against the ice, skimming. If I'm swimming upstream or downstream, I'm gone. The only hope is across the current, toward the near shore. If I accidentally turned around, back toward the campus, I could be caught and certainly won't be able to try this again. But then it gets brighter, the moonlight real and not an opaque haze, and I can almost see the moon's shape. The ice must be thinning. I feel a surge of heat, the adrenaline spiking, and I push on, my muscles screaming, and suddenly the lake's bottom jumps up to meet my arms and stomach and I'm there, thrashing through the ice, making tons of noise when I'm supposed to be quiet but can't possibly make myself be.

A bathing suit, even a full-body one, is not a wetsuit. It's not built for scuba, and I'm shivering immediately. Violent shivering. My fingers don't work. I want to curl up into a ball. There's a cloud in front of me, and I rip off my goggles to see that it's my breath.

"F-f-fire," I stutter stupidly to myself, breathing shaky. My mind is nearly as slow as my body. I know there's no fire, there are no clothes, I'm still in my bathing suit. The only good news is that I am on the correct side of the lake. But I'm nowhere in the clear yet. If I don't get some warmth, I'll freeze.

You'll have about six minutes before you freeze to death, our coach had said after one of the boys jokingly asked if we could practice in the lake. *If you run, if you keep moving, keep your blood pumping, you might make it to eight.*

"Eight minutes." The ground is rocky and hurts, but quickly turns to snow and my feet become lumps of ice. I run, using whatever momentum I had underwater. Up the hill, step by step, to the make-out spot where Socrates points beyond me to the school as if to damn us forever. I can see lights from up here, the town still twinkling. Maybe the virus hasn't spread yet. Maybe the quarantine actually saved the town. Maybe Dad knows what to do, maybe his secrets were to protect me. The hope is all I need to wake me up.

Socrates has long been known to have cracks, deep fissures that run from his base to his waist, gaping enough for students to shove discarded cigarette butts and silly love notes into his belly. The board of directors has approved a restoration, to take place in the summer when the snow is gone. And until then, there's a crude support system of two beams placed against Socrates's side, anchored in the snow. They've been sagging for weeks, a joke around campus: we are the richest school in America, and we can't afford a proper fix-me-up. I'm not sure the others would have agreed with this plan, and now I'm having second thoughts, but there's no way out.

I don't wait. I don't have time. My frozen feet bend the first board, cracking it hard. Two kicks, and it goes. The second bends but doesn't break. Instead it's my foot that feels like it snapped. I groan but keep kicking, slamming with my heel until the wood shatters.

Then I grab Socrates's big, stony arm, lock my grip and pull as hard as I can. My feet are stabs of pain, but that might be good, blood beginning to circulate. The statue groans, but doesn't break, and I give a desperate, involuntary scream, realizing that my eyes are full of tears at the pain and the cold. I keep pulling, jerking myself backward until there's a snap that's so loud it sounds like thunder, and I let go to scramble away. Socrates lists forward, powdery chalk spilling from the cracks, and then slowly twists off his support. The huge statue goes tumbling, very loudly, down the hill.

The noise is so loud, so *not quiet,* that I freeze, almost literally, but then think, *One minute left—go go go go go go go.*

The soldiers can't be far away. I hobble on, my legs burning, almost falling more than running. The snow covers rocks and branches, and I trip once, twice, my hands scraping against them.

The spotlight flashes, and suddenly there are loud voices coming my way. I duck, ignore my body shutting down and hold my heaving breath as four soldiers run by, their white suits blending in the snow, their rifles clinking. They don't say anything, but they're probably miked up—something Rob would be proud of me for thinking. They move down the hill, still in my sight, and they might stay there for a while, so I have to slip behind the tree. But I can't. My body doesn't want to move. My legs are cramping.

I twist my head toward the lake and see them, the others, skating quickly across the surface, using Socrates as a distraction to get to the far side. They are a breath of life, and I'm up, stumbling toward them, unable to scream even if I could, even if it wouldn't bring white-suited soldiers my way. But I wave my arms. They feel like logs attached to my body. I can feel myself shutting down. It won't be the virus that kills me; it will be the water and the cold and myself. My friends are fifty feet away, but if I fall into the snow, my body will be hard to see. I have to get to the shore. I feel a sharp pain in my foot, and the white of snow comes tumbling before me. I can't feel myself breathe. The white turns black, and the numbness fades away.

9

THERE'S HAIR IN MY FACE.

I take a halting breath, and it goes in my mouth, tasting of lavender. I spit it out. My hands and feet burn, and I can't tell if I'm able to wiggle them or not. I'm on my side, and there's something heavy holding me down. For a moment I panic and squiggle: I'm in the worst nightmare of my life. But when my eyes focus, I don't see the moon, and I'm not lying in the snow in my bathing suit. Instead I see thick wooden beams high overhead.

Someone is humming.

"You're awake," a voice whispers in my ear. Right in my ear. I jump, but since I'm unable to move, it's more like a jolt. Brayden? So close—I tense up, but inadvertently lean back into his body, feel his enveloping heat. Two arms clutch around me and squeeze me in, and I recognize the calculator watch and suddenly I'm juggling warmth and disappointment with the best happiness I've ever felt.

"Rob!"

"Don't move—you're okay. We're in the equestrian barn, huddling for warmth." He pauses. "It's my idea."

"What happened?" But I remember what happened. I swam into nothing and came out alive. I'm an idiot—what a stupid plan.

"I don't recommend finding your best friend in a Speedo

lying in the snow. You were blue, completely. Totally matched the bathing suit. We threw a blanket over you and rubbed you, but Brayden"—here his voice twists a touch in admiration—"he said we had to get you to a heated place fast."

That's right, the barn. I'm glad they thought of it. Off campus about a half-mile into the woods on a winding road. The equestrian team at Westbrook is aces, best around. The horses are kept in a state-of-the-art facility across the water, heated in the winter, cooled in the summer. A perfect place to take me. I lift my neck to look for Brayden but can't see much.

I'm spooning Jo, and she pushes against me and says, "Shhh, stop moving. We have to make sure you're warm enough." She moves her hair out of my face, and I can see the necklace I made for her. I pull gently on it.

"But we have to keep moving."

"We will, soon," she says. "Let's just make sure you're safe and feel better." She's not wrong. My feet burn, and my head aches.

Rob keeps going, his voice muffled in my ear, the heat of his breath a surprisingly nice thing to feel—I guess you almost freeze to death, and what used to be gross is now a godsend. "Jimmy picked you up and said you were a block of ice, and I swore we lost you. But when we got here, the heat was working, no one was around, and there was hot water, so we doused you in it and . . . It's been a couple hours. You don't remember that?"

"No," I say. I don't remember a thing. Did all five of them stand over me as they poured warm water over my body? Did they strip me naked to do that? I can feel myself dressed now, nothing wet, so they must have. The idea of the boys watching makes my defrosting extremities feel even worse.

"Well, you started shivering like crazy, but that's better than before, when nothing was going on, so we dried you off and put you in clothes—well, Jo and Odessa did, real quick—and then Jo and I huddled against you until you fell asleep. You snored pretty badly." His voice goes sheepish. "I'm glad you're okay."

I feel a tug at the tone of his voice. I knew Rob was a friend; he has always been. But he's not really one for emotions, and to hear it, to feel him pressing against me to raise my body temperature, it's a simple reminder that he's truly in my corner.

"I snore because I broke my nose falling down a well," I say, though I'm pretty sure he knew that. "Thanks, Rob. I mean it."

"Hey," Jo protests, "I'm glad you're okay too!"

I laugh. "Aww, Jo? Jells of Rob, are you? Can we please sit up? I feel like I'm trapped in a cocoon."

We all move at the same time and pull in different directions, making it impossible to free ourselves and causing us to laugh more, like we're kids in sleeping bags on my bedroom floor.

"Wrestling time?" Jimmy says, suddenly looming over us with a crooked smile. "Don't mind if I do." And he proceeds to flop down on us, his massive frame covering me completely, pushing air from my body—and a groan-giggle that leaves me helpless.

"Get offfff," moans Jo, and he does, holding out his hands to pull each of us to our feet. I'm first, and when I stand, my legs feel like they're asleep. Pain shoots up to my thighs, my legs buckle and I almost fall, but Jimmy holds me steady.

"You okay, Mia?" Jo asks, a mother hen. "Jimmy, let her go."

"No," I say, looking around for the first time. "We don't have time; we've been here too long already." I grit my teeth and force myself straight, and am rewarded with the gradual disappearance of pain. "Where's Brayden?"

"He's gone," Odessa says grimly, not bothering to move from her perch near the window. There's a noise, a clanking and shuffling that's unfamiliar, but it finally connects: horse hooves on the floors of the stalls. An odd background music.

"Where'd he go?"

"He's been gone for over an hour," Odessa says. The sky is still dark, but even under cover of night, we're lucky they haven't found us. Odessa sits right underneath one of the barn's lights, and I can see her sweaty cheeks, her freckles glaring. Her red hair is breaking into its frizzy parts. As if she heard my thoughts, she retwists it.

"Relax," Jimmy says, slapping Odessa playfully on the leg, the only part of her body he can reach. "Your boyfriend will get back soon enough." He's joking, of course; you can tell by the way his jaw tightens—I know that, we *all* know he likes Odessa. But the thought of her thinking of Brayden like that still makes my stomach churn.

Jo takes my hands and holds them up to her face. "Let me see." They are pale and dry. Unfamiliar. Jo doesn't say anything, though, and she pushes me back down to the ground, and then pulls off the pair of socks I'm wearing, which someone must have sacrificed for me. Stuffed inside the socks are a couple of the hand warmers I had asked them to get from the locker room. But despite the help, my feet tell a different story than my hands. The skin is red, bursting angry red that shifts toward a darker shade of purple at my toes.

"Wiggle," Jo commands, her brow lined with worry.

I do, and wince at the pain. She prods each toe to find which provokes what degree of wincing, and all of a sudden, I have something else to worry about. My pinkie toes on both feet and the middle toe on my left don't feel a thing when she prods. The big toe on my left is darker than the rest. When she bends it, it feels like someone's giving me an Indian sunburn on an actual sunburn. I bite my lip, and Jo's blue eyes flick up.

"We have to get to a doctor."

"What doctor?"

"I don't know why your dad wants us to go to the aqueduct when we could just get to Fenton and to a doctor and warn everyone what's going on. I mean, what if there's a huge viral outbreak?"

"Jo," Rob says, his thin frame seemingly smaller than usual, hiding behind his voice, "we have to trust Mia's dad. He knew something was going on—if it *is* a virus, either he'll help us or not. Either way, we can warn the town and the authorities about what's going on then."

"And see our parents," Odessa throws in.

Jo's face swerves into a grimace that she recovers from admirably. "Yes, and that too. But I say we can do all that way better in Fenton."

I shake my head. I want to recover that undeniable childhood feeling that Dad knows everything. If he tells me to go to the aqueduct, then to the Cave, that's where we should go. "Listen, I'm not just making this up. There's a reason why Dad is pointing us this way." I look at Jimmy, who's got a skeptical look on his enormous face. "Jimmy, Odessa, you decided to come with us, and I know you could leave at any time, but you should stay. We can't risk running into others and passing on whatever it is that's infecting the teachers. Dad knows what he's doing. Just help me get these wrapped again and let's get to the Cave. He'll tell us what to do."

I flash back to the sight of Sutton walking the hallway, and then the sound of his voice on the intercom. He doesn't just want to speak to me. He *needs* me for something. And all of that at the same moment of this infection? Dad told me to stay away, he told me to go to the aqueduct. And we will.

There's a knock on the door, a great metal sliding thing that has a chain on it but no lock. The chain is secured by a wooden board stuck through the links. Jimmy picks up the baseball bat and stands near the door, arm raised, ready to break open whoever comes through. Rob is off to the side, breathing hard, a rake in hand, waiting for Jimmy's word. Even Odessa takes part, climbing high into the loft where they store the extra hay and peeking through the window to get a better angle.

Like a sailor in a crow's nest she calls, "All clear. Only Brayden. He's got stuff with him."

"What stuff?" Jimmy shouts back.

"Open the door, Jimmy," I say, a bit louder than I intend. But no one seems to mind, because they're thinking the same thing. Jimmy pulls the wooden board out and lets the chain fall to the floor.

The door slides and Brayden hauls in two garbage bags, which he tosses at Jimmy's feet. "Put that down, J. You'll poke some-one's eye out." He sees me, and his face warms up, shooting crow's-feet along his eyes and a single dimple on his left cheek. So that's what he looks like happy. "You're awake? That's great. How're you feeling?"

"I'm okay."

Jo snorts, wipes the sweat off my forehead. "She's got frostbite, probably."

Brayden's face crumples in concern.

"Well, almost okay. Where were you?" Did that sound demand-ing? I'm happy he's back, but oddly sad he wasn't here to be with me when I woke up. Or hadn't wrapped his arms around me like Rob. *Where was he?*

Brayden looks amused. He doesn't bother to answer and instead opens a bag, glances over at me and Jo and then says, "Jo—you like PB and J?" Her eyes light up, but then she gives a little shake of her head. "I'm allergic to peanuts," she says.

He's not fazed a bit and follows with, "Tuna?" She nods eagerly, and there's a sandwich bag thrown through the air, which she rips into with a greed that makes my own stomach so jealous that I feel like I want to throw up. I have no idea when I last ate.

"Where'd you get all this?" Odessa asks, climbing down from the barn.

And I want to know too. Sandwiches? "Yeah, what did you do? Rob a picnic?"

He glances at me, doesn't ask what I want, and tosses me a roast beef. "No, I took it from an empty house."

There's a cold silence at this. At the implications. My hands freeze on the sandwich bag wrapper, and I think of the town in the worst possible scenario. Empty, filled with stiff bodies, premature grandpas and grandmas. Has the virus spread somehow?

Reading our minds he says, "No, no, I don't think so. The cars were gone, and we are sorta desperate. So I helped myself." He sees us staring. "What? You don't like your sandwiches?" He tosses more around.

"No," I heckle, hobbling over to him. He meets me halfway and clutches my elbow. "But I think it's pretty darn sweet that you broke into someone's house and then stood there and *made* us sandwiches. Like our little mom."

Brayden puts up his hands, not at all apologetic, then reaches back into the bag and starts tossing Lay's Potato Chips, Funyuns, Gatorades and apples all around. We snatch them up, eating some, packing the others away. Rob starts to gather our things, and I sit to stretch my legs. Jo sidles by and whispers, *"He brought us food—he's a keeper."* The sandwich was good, too, but I guess no one here would realize that the best sandwich I've ever had in my life came to me in a lunchbox when I was down the well. But that's just a haze. This is real. This is a pocket of warmth, a full stomach, and a group of determined friends. We made it out of the school, we're all together. If we got this far, we can make it to the Cave. If we make it to the Cave, everything, somehow, will work out. I know it. I'm not an idiot; I know that Brayden took this food from an empty house. That there are soldiers nearby. That people are dying. But before, it was all the beginning of the end. Now, watching Jimmy gnaw an apple and then toss the core over his shoulder, I feel vaguely in control. I rise to my feet slowly, the ache still real, and hobble over to the stalls. The first horse is a black mare, pure black, no white spot between the eyes or anything. She huffs at me, and I hear her tail swish in the stall. I hand her my apple. I need it, but she might not see anyone else for a while, not with the students stuck across the lake. I place my hand on her forehead, the hair so short here it feels almost like skin. She pushes against my palm, like a cat, and I rub lightly, tenderly.

"We all ready?" Rob asks. And we are. Even Odessa's already packed. We've been junked up on nerves and have barely slept, but we're still ready to move and should really take advantage of the darkness. Jimmy coughs, and even though it doesn't at all sound like Mr. Banner's cough, or Devin's cough, we all stop and stare. Even Jimmy freezes, like he's been caught stealing or something. His face is white and suddenly, for the first time, the big guy looks scared. He rubs his fingers lightly on his thin mustache and tries to smile. I'm surprised when Odessa steps forward and gives him a playful push.

"Don't scare us like that," she says quietly, only for him, but we all hear it.

He stares at her, still lost in fear, and she pushes again. I see his face melt, a smile form, and he takes a breath. I test my foot—it moves okay, if a tad numbly—and heft my bag onto my shoulders. The others do the same. We take each other in, realizing this is going to be the last warm place we'll have until we're safe, and I feel something good grow between us all. It's thick and tangible, and we bask in it together.

10

JIMMY IS OUR TOUR GUIDE NOW. HE COMES TO THIS area in the summer to mess around, smoke pot. Though by the way he tended the horses before we left—made sure they had enough feed for a long wait, rubbed a couple down—I wonder if he's secretly a member of the equestrian squad.

The aqueduct is about four miles away, which triples in length when you think about the snow. I don't like the idea of wandering around in the dark, but there's no real choice—we've been here a few hours already, and if we really are being searched for, we'll be found soon enough.

Jo glances down the hill toward the school and her dead father. I take her hand and whisper, "Onward, right?"

She nods, and I know she's feeling it, a gnawing if undeserved guilt. What would I do? I feel a swelling at the pit of my stomach, and I shove away the thought of the virus spreading in the school and my classmates getting weaker and older. After the cough, I've kept a good eye on Jimmy, but he seems fine. Still, the whole group is somber, game faced. All humor is gone, except for Brayden, who smiles warmly every time he catches me looking. It's safe to say he's smiling a lot. It's safe to say I'm glad when he does.

We walk single file, carefully, trying to minimize noise. The pace is excruciatingly slow, and my bad toes start to hurt pretty fast. I can feel one of them, my big toe on my left foot, squish against the front of my boot, like a blister giving way. I try not to think about it, but every step's a reminder. Jo glances at me with concern, but I wave her on. We push through the hills, deeper into the woods, pausing occasionally to listen for any soldiers, but there's nothing. Every once in a while, we get a glimpse of the town below through the woods. The lights still blaze from all the streetlights and from the occasional house. There's St. Anthony's Cathedral, its spire marking the center of town, Palmer Square, the two streets off Main that are rowed with tiny shops and the post office. I've never been here, in the woods, not like this. But I've been down *there* hundreds of times, have looked up this way and have never wondered how empty the forest might be.

It's impressive how unerringly Jimmy leads us in the dark. The baseball bat in my hand has long since turned into a walking stick, and I find, after an hour or so, a desire to swing at low-lying snow-covered branches. The air is cold entering my lungs, but feels good. And as the night deepens, I somehow grow warmer. My toes stop hurting, which, honestly, I think is a very bad sign. I wiggle them around experimentally, but I'm not sure they move in my shoe. Nothing for it but to keep going. My pace settles into the even beat of swimming laps in the pool. We all unconsciously step in time. Jo grabs and breaks as many low-lying sticks as she can find, snapping them with her gloved hands. We're all covered, our faces blocked by heavy caps, some pulled low. I can't tell what they're thinking.

I can't tell how they're feeling. Whether Jo's eyes are glazed, lost in memories of her father, or whether she's focused on her feet. Without faces, we're just parts of a whole, and if not for Brayden's occasional glances back at me, I'd think I was on an escalator or something. We're tired, our breaths heavy. And we shouldn't speak anyways. So we trudge. And I admit there's a comfort in it all.

Two hours in, we take a break. About halfway there. Two miles in two hours. Coach would be disgusted, hills, safety, snow be damned.

We're out of Gatorade, so we're eating the snow for water. "Not too much," cautions Rob. "It's not so good for you."

"Is that true?" Odessa asks, her mouth full. She spits some out, and Jo hisses, "Don't do that!"

"Don't do what?" Odessa replies. She digs into her jacket pocket, pulls out a cigarette and lights up.

"You could spread the virus," she says.

"What," Odessa says, incredulous, "a deer sniffs this tuft of snow and contracts it? And don't scare me like that. I don't have the virus. My hair isn't growing, and it's not turning gray." At this she takes off her blue cap and shakes her curls. Fair enough; they seem just as bouncy and out of control as usual.

"We should keep moving," Brayden says from his perch up ahead. He pats Jimmy on the shoulder, and like a dog doing his bidding, Jimmy stands, pulling up his scarf to cover his chapped lips. He hefts a big piece of wood to use as a staff and then begins pushing through the snow. It's about a foot and a half deep here and hard going, though, frankly, we are lucky it's even this thin. I didn't think, until now, about how tired Jimmy must be, being the snow breaker. We walk in the wreck of his footsteps.

I find myself at the end of the train, Odessa directly in front of me; she tosses her cigarette still lit into the snow. You can hear the *hiss*. She's wearing tighter, formfitting ski clothes, of course. Trying to be sexy even here.

"You know," she says over her shoulder in a hushed voice, "I miss my Berkins."

"Your what?"

"My stuffed bear. Dumb, I know. Berkins is his name. I have a stupid stuffed animal, and I wish I could just go get him."

I can't see her face, but I can tell by the hitch in her breath that she's tearing up.

"I hear you. And I guess that's the point of all this, isn't it?"

"What, my bear?"

"No," I say, trying to sound reassuring. "Getting back home, safe and sound."

She turns to me and stares for a moment, her eyes glistening, and I think I see the corner of her lips turn, almost a smile. But only for an instant. Then those eyes squint, suspicious and confused.

"What the—"

I turn and follow her gaze and freeze up, slinking into a ball on my knees. I motion for her to do the same, but she ignores me. Jo, who was ahead of her, has just rounded a slope, and I don't dare shout or make any noise.

About five yards away, there is a pair of feet. White feet, hazmatted, sticking out from behind a trunk. Odessa glances back at me, then she tiptoes forward as much as she can. Each toe landing is a huge crunch, louder than anything I've ever heard. I twist the bat tight in my hand. Odessa only has a kitchen knife, courtesy of Brayden's foraging.

I'm about to move forward to take the lead when she whispers, "Hello?"

I freeze again, search frantically for another soldier. Odessa is right up to the feet now, and she's bending over, seemingly at ease. I step closer, joining her, my breath sending white puffs into the air fast now.

Slumped against a tree, helmet tilted to the side, is a figure in a hazmat suit. I can't see into the suit at all, the glass is dark and glossy. It might as well be empty. It's holding a handgun in a dangled grip, and its square helmet is slumped at an odd angle. There's a triangular badge on the suit, and closer inspection reveals a cloud and a lightning bolt and the words DARKSTORM SECURITY. These soldiers aren't US Army at all! They're hired men, like Blackwater in Iraq. Sutton's army.

My lungs tighten, and I fight for breath. This is a man who might have shot at Devin. Who is probably out here searching for us.

"Odessa!" I hiss. "Let's go!"

She bends forward. "Hello?"

The body jerks up and grabs her by the jacket, pulling her in.

"Why aren't you sick?" it demands, its voice gravelly and weak. Odessa screams, shrill and high, sending snow toppling. I dash forward and grab her hand and tug. I kick the arm holding her, again and again, until it finally lets go.

Odessa turns to run, but there's a loud *crack* and she's spun, twisting in what would be a perfect dive off a board, and then she's down, blood spraying from her leg into the snow. The soldier doesn't stand up, doesn't even try, though I'm not sure he could. But he's pointing the gun lazily at her, then over to me, then back to her.

"WHY AREN'T YOU SICK?"

Odessa closes her eyes, and for the briefest moment, I wonder what she's thinking about. Her family home in Fenton? Her richie friends? Regret for being here? Or is she dying, the shock setting in, knocking her out? Her eyelashes flutter; she doesn't move.

There are fast crunching footsteps, but I don't dare look; I don't want to scare the soldier. And then Brayden leaps past me, snatching up the Louisville Slugger from my hand, and in the next motion, he smashes it into the hazmat suit's face. The gun discharges again, wildly, hitting nothing, but sending an echo around the woods. Odessa moans, and Jimmy rushes to her side. The visor is red now, covered in blood from the inside. Brayden raises his bat again anyway, and I open my mouth to scream to shout to tell him to stop smashing his face in please don't kill someone in front of me—

"Put the bat down!"

The voice is muffled, and I turn to see Rob and Jo with their hands up, now fully surrounded by five more of these guns for hire, all in the same hazmat suits, surrounding us with machine guns and bright flashlights.

For a moment, the only noise is the deep, adrenaline-fueled breathing of Brayden. He's holding the bat up, as if in a batter's box, and his eyes flick from one to the other. *Put the bat down, Brayden.*

I can see him size up the odds, his chest heaving, tallying in his mind. Somehow, he's actually considering taking them on. His foot moves gently toward the gun in the injured hazmat's hand.

"Put the bat down, Brayden," I say, shaking my head. I try not to look at the broken body at our feet. A part of me thinks Brayden can pull it off—disarming the entire group of soldiers. But I don't want him hurt. More than anything right now, I guess even more than getting to my dad, I don't want him hurt. Odessa starts coughing, and her lips are blue. Jimmy's got his hand pressing hard against her thigh, and there's blood dripping through his fingers. His eyes are wild, and his hair is sticking to his sweaty forehead. Brayden watches her for a moment, his jaw set so tight I can make out the bone through his skin. Odessa passes out. "Put the bat down, Brayden." Rob's lips are tight, but he's the one who said it, not me. His glasses are fogged from all the exertion, and he's resting his hands on the top of his head, breathing hard through the nose. He repeats what I said again, slowly. Brayden swallows and drops the bat deep into the snow.

It's only while riding on the back of a snowmobile, holding tight to the plastic body of the soldier who is driving, that I really think about Brayden's fingers going slack. About the bat falling. About how easily he crushed the face of the fallen soldier. I get it, he was protecting Odessa. And he was protecting me, but the intensity of his swing, like bringing an ax down on a piece of firewood, determined and deadly . . . I have never seen anything like it. I have never seen someone so ready to kill. And with his bare hands too.

The wind burns my face and makes my eyes tear. We're riding in a single-file line—like before, only this time in custody—at an easy pace, up and down the hills and through the woods. The snowmobiles came after we surrendered. Enough for each of us to have our own escort, and two more to make sure we wouldn't jump off the back and flee. Not sure we'd bother trying anyway.

Involuntarily, I squeeze the soldier in front of me tighter. It's like squeezing a sleeping bag.

After Brayden dropped the bat, a soldier came up and, using his foot, pried the mask off the man on the ground. He was alive, wheezing bloody bubbles past his lips. There was no mistaking his long gray hair and his wrinkled skin, despite the smashed face.

I felt a cold come over me, my brain working slowly, but terrified at the implications, and a quick look around the group revealed a similar response. Not only had the virus spread, but it was somehow infecting men *in hazmat suits.* Jo probably thought of her dad, because she vomited immediately, heaving into the snow, and the men shouted *"STAY PUT"* when Rob and I tried to move toward her.

One of the hired goons checked the dying man's dog tags and reported back, "It's Brenner, sir."

The commander, whatever his rank in the security company was, shook his plastic head. "Brenner was first response, right?"

"Yes, sir. He was on patrol at Westbrook when we got news of their escape. Squad three."

"He's pretty far out."

"Sir?"

The commander paused before heading toward his snowmobile. "He's pretty far out to be infected."

‧ ‧ ‧

My nylon jacket squeaks against the suit of the soldier on the snowmobile. "Hold on," he says, perhaps being kind, but through the muffle of the suit, I'll never know. We zig through the woods, faster than I thought possible, and at first I keep ducking my head at the branches. I try to see the others, but when I turn my head, I freak out and feel like I'm about to fall, so I just hug the disturbingly warm body in front of me and hold on.

Far away, a gunshot echoes in the hills. It sounds familiar, that gunshot. I picture all of us flinching on our perches on the back of the snowmobiles. Probably thinking the same thing. One of the soldiers must have finished the job Brayden started, a bullet to the head of the dying soldier. A mercy kill.

If the soldiers in special suits are dying, I don't want to even think about what's going on in my body right now. I wonder if the school is quiet, empty of life, full of hundreds of prematurely aged bodies.

I'm not sure how long we're on the snowmobiles. The twists and turns through the trees make me nauseated, so I keep my eyes closed. I end up pretty numb, almost falling asleep against the shoulder in front of me, my burning toes the only thing keeping me awake.

Without warning, we pull into a clearing that, despite it being dead of night, is bright as day. I put one of my hands up to block the glare. We're in a broad field, but to my right, I can make out a paved road running parallel to our path. On the other side of the road lies an equally large field. I peek over my driver's shoulder to stare at the wall that looms before us. There are spotlights, big baseball-style floodlights, both stationary and shifting, resting on tall towers that rise over the brick wall. Shadows are up there too, men with guns, I'm sure. They're probably peering at us right now, each one assigned a face to crosshair. Ready if we do anything crazy. Beyond the wall is a mansion, a huge house, and it takes me a second to put it all together, but the moment I do is the moment we get close enough to the gate to make out the words FURBISH MANOR engraved beautifully into the metal. I gasp and try to see Brayden, but he's too far up in the convoy to make out.

Did they take over the manor like they took the school? Are his parents being held hostage, trussed up in the basement? Or worse, sick and infected? If I was groggy on the ride here, I am pulsing now, my teeth tingling and every hair on edge. I find myself squeezing the soldier's body in front of me so hard that he yells at me. We slow to an idle, still in line, and I see a couple of guards inspect Jimmy's snowmobile up front. I try to stand in my seat to get a better look at Brayden, but he's just staring ahead. Jo turns, though, and mouths, *What is going on?* I shrug. The gate to Furbish is massive enough to accommodate any military vehicle. The guards wave Jimmy's guy on, and we inch forward, like in traffic. Brayden is up next, but this takes longer. The guard speaks into a walkie-talkie, conferring about something. Then he pulls off Brayden's cap, leaving his hair spiking and staticky. Brayden snatches for the cap, but the soldier bats him gently away. He points somewhere inside the manor, and the driver nods and veers off to the side. They recognized him for some reason. They *know* Brayden by sight. Did they report his arrival? Why would the guard have orders to do that? Why are they here at Furbish Manor at all? My stomach shifts uneasily as we pull forward in line, no one else receiving the same treatment.

Once inside the manor, I can tell that the guard towers are makeshift, easy-to-assemble metal scaffolding no better than glorified deer blinds. The courtyard in front of the mansion is filled with other impermanent setups. Tents and small prefab buildings line the place, and I can only assume those are the barracks. Darkstorm logos splash on fabric and tarp but on none of the vehicles. I see Humvees with big guns on top, and trucks; one tank is sitting just inside the outer wall. A whole row of snowmobiles. Something's weird, but it takes me a minute to figure it out: the soldiers walking around inside the walls aren't wearing hazmat suits.

"Where are you taking us?" I shout over the engine. Though I assume the mansion is the answer, sitting like this has me feeling alone, and I can't just diffuse my fear by making jokes with Rob. I squeeze my arms tight. "Come on. You don't have to tell me anything you're not supposed to. We aren't the bad guys. We're just kids. Where are we going?"

"Quarantine."

I laugh. "We already were quarantined."

He shakes his head. "Detox, observation, testing. Quarantine."

I don't like the word *testing*. I prefer *quarantine*.

The convoy pulls up to the mansion, as expected, and we're all ordered off our machines. But our escorts don't get off; they just back up and scoot away, and suddenly we're huddling together. Jimmy's pawing at his tiny mustache, making me nervous. Jo nudges me, and I look up and gasp, as shocked as I've ever been; I see Brayden on the marble front steps to the house. He's talking to Blake Sutton, who's standing there with his legs together, his arms crossed and a hand on his chin, nodding occasionally, listening intently. I can't make sense of this at all. My stomach turns over just watching the two of them speak. Brayden looks, somehow, small next to the older man, as if Sutton owns this place. And, considering the soldiers everywhere, maybe he does. Brayden points our way.

"What the crazy is going on?" Rob asks, taking in the scene.

"Brayden must know that guy," Jo says, her voice hurt.

"No," I say. But I can't tear my eyes off him, desperately trying to put two and two together. "No way. They've got Brayden's family. That's why they're here. He doesn't *know* Brayden."

Sutton puts an arm on Brayden's head and further tousles his hair. Then he makes eye contact with a soldier and nods toward us. He doesn't look at me, not at all, just turns and walks through the tall wooden doors of the house.

"Looks like they get along pretty well," Jimmy says. This is, I realize, the first time he's seen the man.

"I don't get it," I murmur. Sutton *knows* Brayden? And they're here, at his parents' house, using it as their base?

"Mia," Jo says, her face twisted in concern. She's got a lock of her hair and is brushing her lips with it back and forth while she muses aloud. "Who even is Brayden? He transferred to Westbrook, what, a minute ago? And he's superhelpful and knowledgeable, and now we end up at his house that happens to be controlled by this guy who's chasing us?"

The pieces of the puzzle clink into place, sending a bout of rage shooting across my skin. "No way," I say, but Jo just shrugs, weary and resigned. I feel the urge to pull off my jacket I'm fuming so much. Rob takes my wrist, but I shake him off.

Brayden comes down the steps toward us, a small smile on his face, looking as charming as ever.

"What are you doing?" I ask through gritted teeth.

"We're gonna be okay," he replies, genuine relief in his eyes. As if he doesn't care at all for what these men have done to us. "They're not going to hurt us."

"How do you know?" Jimmy asks, readjusting Odessa in his arms.

"Mr. Sutton said so. He's bringing us into the house."

I am blind. I am boiling. Even if Brayden isn't one of them, he's betraying me anyway. I move before I think and push Brayden into the snow.

"You asshole!"

He doesn't try to get up, he just sits there, arms raised in defense, shaking his head. "Mia, I swear I don't know why they're here."

"You're one of them, aren't you?"

"Of course he is!" Jimmy shouts, egging me on. He's angry too, his round face bright and shiny. He's holding Odessa up, but she's limp, her lips pale and her head lolling to the side, leg streaked red against her fitted suit. A new set of guards arrive, clearly there to handle us. They're watching, momentarily surprised by the infighting.

"Mia, please," Brayden begs, and his face is so pale the scar there brightens white. His yellow bracelet dangles like an inexplicable lie.

"You show up out of nowhere, you move into this place and then you're sent as a mole to spy on me. You fucking bastard!" I'm so angry I spit, spraying his face, but he doesn't retaliate. Instead he starts to tear up. For some reason, that makes it worse, and the instant before the guards recover, I kick Brayden in the face.

11

THEY LOCK US IN AN EXTRAORDINARILY LARGE ROOM, what might have been a ballroom if Fenton were known for balls. The floor is polished wood, and there are two enormous fireplaces and mahogany chairs with bird-patterned cushions lining the wall. There are windows, but we're four stories up. At least we overlook the entrance, so we can see what's going on outside. It's four in the morning, and the darkness hints of day. I'm so completely wired I couldn't sleep if I tried. Rob, the only one of us who even bothers to try to find cell reception, pulls out his OtterBox, but can't find a signal. My phone can't go more than a day without charging, so it's probably dead anyway. I stuff myself onto a window ledge, draw my knees up and look into the courtyard. I'm having a hard time calming down, partially because I'm not sure what's wrong with me. Two times in twenty-four hours I've smashed in a boy's nose. What am I doing? I'm barely the type to speak up at a dinner, much less retaliate.

A snowmobile starts up outside, catching my attention. I try to zoom in on the soldiers. I don't see Brayden. And they didn't bring him in with us. So I must be right. He *is* working with Sutton. Surely that justifies a kick to the face.

Odessa's on the floor, her head resting in Jimmy's lap, and I want to focus on feeling sorry for her, because I do, but my stomach is so knotted that I can't focus. I rest my head against the glass and close my eyes and try to think of the pool, of my even breaths and of the nothing in the water below me.

"Hey," Jo whispers near me. She runs her hand lightly on top of my head.

I sniff and shake my head. "I can't believe it. Why set us up like that?"

"I bet that's why he went out for food back at the barn," Rob offers, coming close. Jo shoots him a look that I see, and he makes a face. "What? It's true!"

"Guys?" Jimmy says; Odessa's red hair is pressed against his chest. He's looking tired. Bigger. His hair is longer, not much, but definitely noticeable. "Des needs help," he begs, like there's something we can do about it.

Rob moves toward him, but I grab his arm. Rob's taken off his winter coat, and his arm feels thin and reedy. He looks down at my hand, then at me, his small nose flaring. I shake my head slightly, and he's still confused, but then Jimmy coughs. A deep, retching cough. He looks at his hand, terrified, but there's no blood. Not yet, anyway.

"Yeah, you're right. Stay over there, okay? Don't come near me." Jimmy's face is serene, not a wrinkle of worry, and he speaks so calmly and with such bravery that my heart aches. I shove all the pain of the betrayal into my body, far away, and jump from my seat. Jimmy's dark skin pales, like I'm coming over to him or something, but I'm not. I feel bad skirting him and Odessa, but I have to, and soon I'm banging on the door.

It opens pretty quickly, a big white door designed to blend into the wall. A soldier, unsuited, with a brown buzz cut peeks in. His tan, pimply face makes him seem young enough to enroll at Westbrook.

"What?"

"He's sick"—I nod at Jimmy—"and she needs a doctor."

The soldier's eyes widen, and he slams the door in my face. But I can hear him on his walkie-talkie, speaking frantically. I skirt Jimmy and Odessa again and go back to the window. We all sit expectantly, but nothing happens. Jimmy coughs some more, but never with any blood—each time he shows us his palm, and it really does give me a sense of relief. Like each cough is a game of Russian roulette that he keeps winning. And for a while, we don't say anything. And then we don't say anything for even longer, now afraid to speak. Rob moves to another window and starts outlining the snowmobiles and trucks in the fog.

"Where are they?" Jimmy finally asks. *I don't know,* I think, but I only shake my head. He gently puts Odessa down, resting her head against the floor, and then moves to the door, which he starts to kick, shaking its frame, sending a deep *boom* around a room clearly designed for great acoustics.

"Let us out!" He screams and kicks, his big body moving almost rhythmically, like a logger against a tree. Again, scream and kick, the tendons on his neck get rigid and tight. The door makes a splintery sound and actually gives, but not in a serious way. Toying with him. He keeps going, breathing hard, his red-and-white ski jacket soon comes off, and his tan muscles flex underneath his tight gray

Under Armour. He looks like he could break open the walls with his bare hands, and even though we're just watching, dazed, it's slightly disappointing that this huge specimen of a guy, our best shot to protect us from harm, can't kick open this door.

I gaze around the room. Rob's chewing his nails, eyes purposefully elsewhere, Jo's face is set, staring at Odessa. They hear his kicks, of course. Both of their shoulders flinch with each one, but they're detached and gone. I wonder where? Rob, maybe, is thinking of his parents in Fenton. Jo is probably trying not to think at all.

"Jimmy," I say, but he can't hear me. My throat aches. "Jimmy!"

He glances over, a bloom of red on his round cheeks. He doesn't stop kicking.

"Stop that! It's not helping."

"Screw you, Baby. I'll do what I want."

I stand up, pissed now. "Baby? *I'm* the baby? You think kicking the door like that is going to get us out of here? Real matu—"

But then there's a *click*, and the door on the opposite side of the ballroom opens.

Jimmy stops, his foot resting on the door he's been kicking. He pulls back, looking smug. I'd laugh or hug Jimmy if I thought it was safe.

Three men walk into the room, their boots striking the floor in deep, matching thuds. Two are in hazmat suits, probably newly donned, both of which are adorned with the Darkstorm logo. One has a gun, an automatic of some type, and it's trained on us. The other has a medical kit, a doctor. And the third I've seen before. He's not in a suit. He's not very tall, but he's imposing, even with his vaguely receding hairline and his simple black fleece and jeans. I find it strange that I've only spoken to him twice, that I know nothing about who he really is.

The three stop about fifteen yards away. I can feel Jo tense beside me. She should be tense. My mouth's dry, a by-product of the helpless anger I feel enveloping me. Sutton's staring at me, a friendly smile on his face, and he gives me a little wave. As if he's passing me on the street, as if we were neighbors. "Who are you?" I ask, my voice ripe with venom. His smile vanishes.

Sutton's gaze lingers on Odessa and Jimmy. Closer now, I can see that his face is rigid and dark, and it's clear that the past two days have taken a toll. There are heavy bags under his eyes, as if he's been up for a week straight, yet those weary eyes don't seem like a weakness. They look like he doesn't have to sleep, like he's never had to sleep at all.

"I know you won't believe me," he says, his mouth twisting with regret, "but I'm sorry to be seeing you again this way."

"Funny enough," I reply, almost automatically, "I don't."

He stares at me for a moment, seemingly to gauge my anger. His dark eyes roam my face. I will not make this easy for him.

"Mia," he says, his voice sounding sincere, "you don't understand. I need to contact your dad; he's the only one who can help your friends. This is all one huge mistake."

"You shooting kids at Westbrook was a mistake?" Jo asks, and I'm happy to see she's here at my side, not lost in grief. I give her a grateful smile.

"You're right," he replies, walking toward Odessa. "We should have gotten there sooner and sealed the exit, but we only meant to deter those boys. They ignored our warnings." He bends and examines Odessa's wound, not touching, just peering. Then he waves over the medic, who hurries to kneel at her side. "The thing is," he continues, moving now to Jimmy, whose face goes dark at his approach, "I set up that interview between us for a simple reason: it was meant to be a way of saying to your dad, 'I can get to your daughter, so you have to let me into the Cave.' Nothing more should have come from it."

"So to threaten him?" I say.

"I was obviously wrong," he goes on, paying no attention to me. Instead he reaches out a hand toward Jimmy's face. "Oh, yes—the virus is advancing to the tipping point." Jimmy flinches, but Sutton's persistent. He opens Jimmy's eyelids, peers into them one at a time. Then checks his pulse.

"What's the tipping point?" Jimmy asks from his perch on the floor. I want to know too, but I'm not about to offer my interest.

"Tipping point is a term that references the moment when the virus stops aging the body to any beneficial effect," he replies, his voice straitlaced like a doctor's and full of the same type of jargon. He pats Jimmy on the knee and rises. "I'm not sure if his heritage carries any genetic anomalies that withstand the virus more, but I doubt it. But don't worry. This means he's barely contagious. Good news for you all."

"Dude, I'm third-generation American," Jimmy says.

I catch Rob's eyes, which can't help but have a touch of accusation. They sense a missing link to this story. *Why haven't I told him everything?* I can see the question blazing.

"What about you?" Jo asks. She's been tracking his movement

like a cat might a dangled treat. Except there's nothing fun about Sutton. "You aren't afraid of catching the virus?"

Sutton touches his forehead with the back of his hand, almost absentmindedly, as if routinely checking his body temperature. "I'm afraid, Miss Banner. I'd be foolish not to be."

I want to ask why he's standing here with no hazmat suit but Odessa grunts painfully on the floor, distracting all of us. The medic cuts off her pants, exposing the bulbous wound splattered against her pale thigh.

"During the meeting with your father, Mia," Sutton says, regaining his train of thought—he barely looks at Odessa—"he clearly wasn't getting the point." He shakes his head, smiles at me, his teeth showing this time, bright against his tired face. "Stubborn guy, your dad. Always has been. You too, of course. When I saw how he reacted to my visit to Westbrook, how he made it clear he wouldn't help me, I knew I couldn't rely on him to make this easy, and that I'd have to use my men to contain the outbreak."

"But how?" Rob blurts out. "You only interviewed Mia a day and half ago. How did you know there'd be an outbreak?"

My veins go icy. I remember walking down the hall after my interview and seeing him in the dean's office. He was there, talking to Mrs. Applebaum. Holding her hand.

"You gave it to her," I say, my voice wooden. I remember how the meeting ended so quickly, but then this stranger stuck around campus, was just spending time in the office. Why would he do this? What does my father have that this man so desperately wants?

Sutton's eyes go dark. "I *told* you I didn't want to do that. But your father forced me to." I shake my head in denial. "Yes, he did," he hisses in frustration at me. He sounds more like a whiny kid than an angry mastermind. "Mia, you have no idea what's going on here, so please stop pretending. Did you know I told your father about the outbreak? That I called him up at the Cave and said his Baby Mia would get infected if he didn't let me in?"

"What's he mean, Mia?" Jo asks, confused.

"I don't know," I admit. "He knows Dad somehow. But he's lying now to get me to help him."

"Help me do what?" Sutton laughs. "Don't you get it? Your father told me he had *taken* you from Westbrook. He lied to me, maybe to buy you time, maybe not. And then he left you there in the middle of a viral outbreak. To die."

My hands clench. Dad had told me to leave the school, yes. But I had called him, not the other way around. He never tried to warn me.

"But the announcement asking for her," Rob puts in. "You knew she was at Westbrook."

"Not for sure."

"You had your hostages anyways," I say, my voice dull. "If not me, you'd just take the entire school captive." Even my running away didn't help. The only person who could have prevented this was my dad.

Sutton nods in agreement. He rubs at his eyes; his fingernails are long and dirty. "You'd figure a school loaded with kids, even without his daughter, would force Greg Kish to buckle. But nope, not at all. The virus spread more powerfully than I thought, I admit—some of my men have been infected, despite precautions."

That's why they're this far away, I think. *It has nothing to do with Brayden? They just needed to outrun the virus they let loose?*

135

"And now that some of my men are infected, we have to work faster so that we can save them too." He sees the look of disbelief on my face. "What? You think I wanted this? To kill innocent people? To kill *my own men*?"

He lets out some air, a sigh, and his body seems to deflate. I hate thinking this, but the thing is, he seems truly regretful. Like he really didn't want to. Like he had this master plan that just kept getting messed up and out of control and now people are hurt. Because of him, because of my dad.

"After your father refused to play ball, I had to cut the signals to Westbrook and the Cave to make sure they couldn't communicate with the outside world. And now the irony is, I can't even call Kish up to negotiate if I tried."

"Then what do you need her for?" asks Rob.

Sutton glances my way. "The Cave has cameras, lots of them. I just need to borrow Miss Kish here and have her wave to Daddy. That should be enough."

My stomach aches. I'm supposed to be his little puppet.

The medic clears his throat.

"I have to take out the bullet. It's fragmented."

Sutton waves the medic on. Jimmy rushes over to hold Odessa's head, stroking her hair. It's surreal, watching a soldier in a baggy suit dig into a bloody wound right in front of you. Jo's not looking, she's gone white, and I'm grateful to see Rob take her aside. Odessa's eyes are glassy, and I realize she's still in shock, still entirely dazed and unaware of where she is. She moans. Fair enough. I would too if someone were probing the inside of my leg with a tweezer, pulling out bullet fragments. He drops them into a little sack and puts that in a pouch.

"Will she be okay?" Jimmy blurts out.

The medic doesn't answer, and I catch Jimmy's gaze, trying to show some encouragement. But I might have twinged seeing the antiseptic—what might be iodine—come out. Good for you or no, that stuff hurts more than anything. My dad swears by iodine, though. I get a cut, iodine. I get a pimple, iodine. A mole looks too big, iodine. I remember countless times I sat on the dresser in his bedroom while he put the dropper against a scab or wound. I'd kick my leg back hard against the wood, again and again, probably shouting more than I needed to. But it always ended up a good memory, because then he'd blow on the iodine to dry it, to make me feel better. And we'd eat ice cream afterward while watching TV.

I do admit, though, I've never had iodine thrown on a bullet wound. And I certainly know this guy isn't going to blow gently on the hole in her leg. When the liquid hits, Odessa jerks completely awake and screams so loudly that foam flicks from her mouth. Jo, still huddled against Rob, starts to cry. "Don't," she says, reflexively. Everyone in the room looks at her, but she didn't mean to speak. Her tears drip with mascara in a thin line down her cheeks.

"Please, please stop," Odessa shouts. And the medic does. The skin around the wound is copper-colored now, and the edges of the entry hole are jagged, puckered up, gawking at everyone in the room. Odessa's gulping ragged gasps of air, and Jimmy's trying to softly shush her. Sutton watches with detached interest as the medic pulls out a needle and thread and stitches the wound in nice zigs; it all looks way easier than I thought it would be, especially considering that he's wearing gloves. Odessa sucks hard and moans each time the needle goes through the skin, but she doesn't scream again, and I'm impressed. I've had stitches before and, honestly, I don't remember them hurting, but that was with some local anesthetic.

"See, everyone," I say to include Jo, who's calmed herself down, "she's going to be fine." Then comes a syringe. I assume it's finally a painkiller, but only after he sticks the needle into her vein do I realize the chamber is empty. He's drawing blood.

I frown. "What's this for?" Sutton puts his finger to his lips, telling me to be quiet.

"What's he doing?" Jo asks, and there's panic in her voice. She's standing very rigid.

The soldier fiddles with Odessa's pale arm, retracting blood—not at all the way it's done in the doctor's office with a small prick and a vial. "Hey!" I say, louder this time. I don't like this. Sutton keeps his regretful face on, but suddenly I feel like we're lab rats. The soldier on the snowmobile was right. We are being tested, processed. I imagine students taken directly from Westbrook and kept somewhere else in the camp. Rows of vials, red with blood, line a shelf in a trailer somewhere, and anonymous men spend all day peering at our secrets. If they can take our blood, what else can they do to us?

I think to ask Sutton why he never wears a hazmat suit, but Rob spits out, "That makes no sense. She needs help, not her blood taken."

Jimmy seems to agree. I hadn't even noticed, but he's put

Odessa's head back down, and he's staring hard at the medic, his forehead so wrinkled he looks like a sheep. Then, without warning, he grabs the medic's plastic arm. "You want me to take that thing and poke a little hole in your suit, huh?"

The medic doesn't fight. He doesn't have to. The other soldier in the room steps forward and levels his machine gun right at Jimmy.

"Please let my man go. He's only doing his job." This from Sutton, who's speaking quietly, no threat in his voice.

"What, to take blood tests?" I ask.

"Yes, actually. She had an exposed wound. There's a virus going around. Your friend here"—he points at Jimmy—"is clearly at the tipping point. Why wouldn't we test her? Why wouldn't we test all of you? You're the one who asked us in here to help. We need to make sure she doesn't carry infection. How is that unreasonable?"

I leave Rob and Jo and approach Sutton, stand close enough to smell the spearmint on his teeth.

"Don't you think that asking us permission might be the reasonable thing to do?"

Sutton's eyebrows clench in anger. "Let my man go," he hisses, and for the first time, he actually seems pissed off. There's even a fleck of frothing spit on his lips. Jimmy tightens his grip on the medic and flips Sutton off. The guard now has his gun touching the back of Jimmy's head.

You stupid, wonderful idiot.

"You think throwing a tantrum is going to work here? You think I want to hurt you?"

Jimmy takes his idiocy to another level, butting his head backward against the barrel several times. Sutton waves at the guard, who in one simple movement turns the gun on its end and bashes Jimmy in the head. He slumps to the floor, almost on top of Odessa, who is so dazed she doesn't even notice. I rush forward, so do Rob and Jo, and the medic and guard step back to give us space.

Jimmy's mouth is open, his tongue lolling gently about inside. There's already a hefty bump on his head, but at least his eyes are flickering. Jo puts her hand on his chest and leaves it there.

"We can't just sit here," I whisper, feeling desperate.

"What we have to do," Jo replies at full volume, her voice tired and uneven, "is let them take our blood so they will leave us alone." She looks up at Sutton. "You *will* leave us alone, right?"

He smiles and raises one hand. "Scout's honor. It's all very simple now. I'll communicate to Mr. Kish that we have his daughter, then he'll open the Cave and let us in."

"But what if he doesn't?" Rob asks. "I mean, an entire school of kids didn't get him to open up the gates. He even thought Mia was there. Why would it work now?"

"It will," I say, somehow confident. Dad thought I was gone from Westbrook. My absence doesn't make him not helping the school okay, but still . . . "I'll speak to him. We'll stop this now."

"Good," Sutton says, clapping his hands once. He tilts his head to the side and peers at Jimmy. "I'd say that your friend probably has, what, twenty, twenty-four hours to live. But that's the good news," he adds, nodding at the medic to go ahead. "If the Cave opens up, we'll find a way to save him."

"How?" Rob asks.

"Ask her dad," he replies, but I'm barely focusing on that. The word *friend* has me thinking of something, a painful punch in the gut.

"Where's Brayden?"

Sutton waves me off. "He's with his parents. Friends of the cause."

I was right, I think, feeling a sudden impulse to punch something. He led them to us. And now he's somewhere in the house, reunited with his parents, duty done. I'm livid, and I'm sure Sutton can tell, because he's peering at me intently. Probably watching the vein on my forehead bulge. I feel sick, betrayed, and can't keep his gaze.

"What about us?" Rob asks, pushing his glasses up his nose. He's still wearing his ski coat, and the hood bobs behind him, making him look puffy and childlike.

"What about you?" Sutton replies.

"What if we're carrying the virus?"

Sutton squints at us too, then heads toward the nearest door, the one Jimmy tried to kick down. "Don't worry," he says over his shoulder. "If Mia's daddy doesn't open the door in the next twenty-four hours, you'll all be dead anyway." And then he's gone, leaving us with two soldiers, one with a gun and the other with a needle. My skin goes tight at the meaning of his threat. The virus is spreading that fast? Or will he just get rid of us with his own guns once we're useless to him? As awful as he is, the look of real regret I saw on his face has me doubting he'd just kill us. He doesn't seem the type. As if I know what that *type* is.

"May I?" the medic asks, breaking me from my thoughts, his voice soft and muffled. I look to Jo and Rob for help, but they just stare. I take off my jacket and hold out my arm. "I'm sorry about this. I wish I had vials. The majority of our equipment is in a mobile lab at ground zero. And now we can't get to it."

"That's okay," I respond, unable but to be nice when someone apologizes. I wonder what Sutton's paying these men to have them risk their lives like this. But I guess that's the point of being a mercenary—loyalty for reward.

He draws my blood, and I feel it. He doesn't take much, he gives me a cotton ball and disinfects the tiny hole. But I feel it. I slump weakly to the ground and hold Jimmy's and Odessa's hands, no longer scared of the virus after what Sutton said about Jimmy's tipping point. Or maybe I'm not scared because of the inevitability of it all. Twenty-four hours, he said. The medic takes blood from the others, and Jo and Rob stay quiet; we all do. We're stuck here, watching Jimmy age, waiting for something to happen that we should never have been involved in. I feel overwhelmed, tired, and as the medic and soldier leave, I haven't ever felt as helpless. Not even in the well.

"We're going to be fine," Rob says, in a rare display of straightforward reassurance.

Jo leans in to him and whispers, "We'll never be fine again."

12

JIMMY WAKES UP AFTER AN HOUR, AND THE FIRST THING he does is check on Odessa, who's still passed out. We've put our jackets over both of them, and he pulls mine from his legs, then groans and gingerly touches the back of his head.

"The dude clocked me."

I'm sitting in the window, watching the soldiers come and go outside, and for the past hour, I've been wondering if I'd see Brayden. It's hard to remember that he didn't grow up here, that this isn't his house.

"How're you feeling?" Jo asks Jimmy. She's used the time to gather herself, and I've been catching glimmers of life in her face. I'm glad she's taking the lead. Jimmy looks different, like a thirty-year-old version of himself. His voice is deeper, body more developed. I'd say that the virus, whatever it is, has hurried him to his thirties, but kept him in the peak of fitness. It seems almost cruel: it makes you strong before it saps your life away.

"Groggy," he admits, "but otherwise, yeah, I'm fine, I think." He stands up and heads to the door. "Gotta piss, though."

I do too. So do the others. He knocks, and a guard, now fully suited, peeks his head in. Soon we are being escorted one at a time to a bathroom down a hallway lined with ancestral portraits, plush carpet, and Ming or Hong or some Asian dynasty's vases. I have to go slowly, hobbling, as my foot isn't feeling any better. Wow, we are a full squad of injured kids. When it's my turn, I don't see anyone except my very own soldier, and while I go, I stare longingly at the shower, wishing I could wash the smell of the frozen lake from my hair.

On my way back, I can see that the hall continues beyond the ballroom, but to the right, the wall gives way to a banister and a stairway. My legs itch at the absurd possibility of making a break for it. I even move in that direction, the thick red carpet under my feet giving way, and the guard seems to sense this, because he wraps his hand around my arm and steers me toward the door. I'm still peering at the steps when suddenly Brayden sticks his head around the corner. His face starts upon seeing me, and he ducks quickly back out of sight. I almost scream, but clamp down my throat. *What's he doing? Why's he hiding?* Something inside me says to keep him a secret. Brayden pops his head out again, and motions something to me. I think he wants me to distract the guards. I almost shake my head no—I want to flip him off—but something tells me he wouldn't be tricking guards unless he wanted to help. My body tenses, and I feel the soldier shift his weight behind me, his gun clicking against his hip. I shake my head. I can't just mess around here. Brayden looks behind him, then turns back to me looking desperate. He mouths, *Please.*

It's quite easy, really, what with the hobble I actually have now. I should have been in drama at Westbrook. I pretend to snag my foot on the carpet, and fall forward to my knees. I even give a little cry. The guard reaches for me, and the one resting outside the ballroom turns my way. I stay on my hands and knees, saying *"Shit, shit, shit, shit"* lightly and holding one leg up, wincing in pain. Brayden's biggest problem will be my bathroom escort, so I roll over and grab his leg and squeeze, a pretty horrible thing to do considering that he probably thinks I'm infecting him. Unless he doesn't know the virus can make it through the suits. Who knows what kind of lies Sutton is feeding his men.

I don't see anything, but hear the faintest *click*. I assume the guards do too, but they stay where they are, staring at me, one trying to pull his leg from my grasp. I let go and slowly get up.

"You okay?" one of them asks. Sometimes it's hard to remember that they're humans.

I'm not sure if I'm okay. I just helped Brayden sneak into the ballroom, and I'm terrified to have to confront him.

"Hey," the soldier repeats, "I can get the medic."

I shake my head and answer weakly, "No, I'm fine. I'm just tired." I keep my eyes down and open the door, and they let me enter without another word.

Brayden's feet are dangling above the ballroom floor. Jimmy's holding him up against the wall by the shirt, like in a comic book. I can see the veins, fat and thick like worms, on his arms. I knew Jimmy was strong, but this is ridiculous. Brayden looks afraid, and he's got both hands on Jimmy's arms, but he's not struggling.

"Let him down," I whisper. Jimmy glances at me, then reluctantly lets Brayden fall to the ground. Brayden's lip is swollen, and there's a smear of dried blood on his cheek.

Rob stands next to me, looking down on him. "What do *you* want?" he spits. Rob's natural vitriol comes in handy sometimes.

Brayden looks past our legs to see Odessa lying on the floor. Jo watches, her chin bunched into a frown. Brayden's pale, and my first thought is *virus!* but I shake that away quickly, especially with Jimmy so close. If Brayden had the virus, he'd be aging. No, he's just different, changed. When I first met him he had a swagger, a confidence. That's gone. Now he's a shell.

"Please, Mia. You have to believe me." His voice trembles, sending his thick lip wobbling. His bloodshot eyes wander the room, looking helplessly at each of us.

"What do I have to believe?" I ask, keeping my voice down, trying not to alert the guards. Everything we say now seems more significant, dangerous.

"I don't know that guy. My parents don't know that guy. My parents aren't even here! They must have been kicked out when the soldiers moved in. Or maybe they were gone this weekend and I didn't know."

"Bullshit," Rob says, his brow furrowed. "This coming from the guy who just strolls down the hallway and into our prison cell."

"Yeah," Jimmy adds. "If that's the case, why did they separate us? Where have you been?"

"And why would Sutton lie to us about you?" I ask.

Brayden tries to steady himself and stand up. No one helps him. There's a very real part of me that feels sorry for him, and I know that's just the me who wants to believe him. I glance back at Jo, see her look of disdain and take strength from it.

"They separated us because Mia kicked my ass," he says ruefully, his eyes to the floor. "Then they put me in my father's study and took my blood, but didn't tell me a thing." I glance at the crook of his elbow and sure enough, there's a splotch of stained skin from the iodine. They took away his Livestrong bracelet, good riddance. "Listen, I know this might seem hard to believe, but I'm telling the truth. We haven't lived here long, but when my parents bought the place, they bought the blueprints as well. When we moved in, there was a weird door open in the back of my closet. A secret passage. I told my parents, and we pulled out the blueprints and found five more. You don't build a house like this without some extras."

Jimmy snorts in disbelief.

Brayden appears distressed at the sound, desperate. "It's *true!* Wouldn't you have explored this place top to bottom if you moved here? That's what I did. And the study has a passage that leads right into the hallway. It took them long enough to leave me alone. Now there's almost no one inside the house, so I snuck up here."

"So you're saying that your parents aren't here, that you had nothing to do with any of this, and you just *happen* to know about a collection of secret passages in the house?" I play it back for him so he can hear how ridiculous it sounds.

"No." He shakes his head. "I don't happen to know anything. A secret door was left open when we moved in. If it hadn't been, I might have never known."

"So is there one in this room, then?" Rob asks, eyes scanning the walls.

"No," Brayden replies, and for the first time I see him relax a little. Rob's question was a crack in our wall, a potential foundation for belief. "But there's one in a bedroom at the corner of this floor, that leads to the kitchen, and from there to the back door."

I stare at him, trying to read his face. "Mia," he says, speaking

147

only to me. His voice is soft. I've heard it that soft before. The others stare, and suddenly I feel extremely self-conscious, heat rising to my face. The thing is, I *want* to believe him. I want everything he says to make sense. "Please. You have to trust me. I would never lie to you."

We leave him in the far corner of the ballroom and make a circle around Odessa. Jimmy takes her hand, but doesn't break my eye contact. Everyone's watching me, waiting for me to make the decision. "Whatever we think about Brayden, whatever we do with him, we *have* to get out of here. That crazy bastard said he's going to use us as ransom against something my dad has, right? But he also said that if we can get into the Cave, then we'll be okay. Dad must know what's going on, there must be some sort of answer in there. And we don't have much time." I try not to look at Jimmy, but I can't help myself. His face looks so different now it's shocking, a full beard coming in stubbly over his cheeks, but I can see that his eyes are the same—young, confused and afraid. He knows he's in trouble.

"So we trust him?" Jo asks. She'd cleaned up her face in the bathroom, and her skin looks healthier, her eyes brighter. She's more here, more present. Not like she's over her dad, but she's not fading away into grief, and for that I'm thankful.

It's Rob who answers, all logic. "Well, I want to distrust him, and I *do*, but I think his story checks out."

"What do you mean?" Jimmy asks.

"So, right, he wasn't in the room with us, doesn't know what that Sutton guy said. Right now, we're where Sutton wants us. Captured, locked away, waiting for Mr. Kish to give him ransom or something. What does Sutton gain by setting us free? If Brayden wants us to escape, then, logically, he's not on Sutton's side." He pauses, looks around the place. "And I've been thinking. If ground zero is Westbrook, and the virus is spreading, then it makes sense that the soldiers would want to set up their base farther away from the school. Furbish Manor is perfect."

"This place makes sense then, huh?" Jo picks up the thread. "There's nowhere semiclose to campus that has this kind of facility." It's true, I think, picturing the map of the area. Furbish is the logical choice, considering the scenario. Solitary, big, walled, not too far from but not too close to Westbrook.

"So if he's telling the truth," I say, not fully believing but recognizing the possibility, which makes me feel guilty for kicking him, "then he showed up to a new school, got caught in the middle of a virus outbreak and then dragged to his own new house, to find his parents gone and his friends hating his guts."

"And you kicked me in the face!"

We all turn around, not realizing he had snuck up on us. He pats down his dark hair sheepishly. He's smiling, a tentative lift of his bloody and swollen lips, and I do the same. He seems to sense we need something more. "Guys. I know this place. I can get us out of here." He looks me dead in the eye, his face so sincere my heart stops. "I promise."

There's a pause, and then Jimmy grunts and slugs his arm. Brayden winces, and we all laugh; we can't help it. For the first time in what feels like days, there's something to laugh at. I guess it is all a matter of scale.

"Okay, how do we do this?" asks Rob, who gets on his knees near the window and peers out front. "Lots of soldiers at the gate."

"One of you," Brayden says, "knock on the door and make a guard come inside. Be loud and annoying enough that the other guard is distracted too, and I'll go out door number two at the end of the hall and clock him at the same time that you jump soldier number one."

Near the window, Rob shakes his head, probably imagining all the parts where we might get shot.

"There's something going on out there," he says, cupping his hand to the glass. "They won't let the soldiers in for some reason."

Just then, for the second time in as many days, alarms sound. They are loud, persistent and painful—and then, gunshots. Many of them. They sound smaller than I thought they'd be, but they're coming from everywhere, reverberating in the hills, like we're surrounded by a million firecrackers. A bullet smashes through the glass of one of the windows, and we all dive to the floor.

"What the fuck?" Jimmy shouts. He's shielding Odessa's limp body with his, and I feel a surge of love for the guy. We all look at Brayden, as if he's at fault. "I didn't know there were alarms here," he says defensively.

We hear footsteps running down the hall, and then the door opens. The guard only sticks his head through the door to check on us. He has to have seen Brayden, though I can't tell his reaction because of the suit. The surprise is blown. This is our chance, good or bad.

"Now!" I scream, trying to get up, but my toes ache in protest. Jimmy beats me to it, hurling himself off Odessa and sprinting to the door. The soldier pushes the door wider, trying to bring his gun to bear, but Jimmy gets there first in a blur of speed and simply smashes the door closed, with the soldier in it. The man's hazmatted head bangs hard against the wall, and he slumps to the ground. Jimmy peers out into the hallway, then waves us over. We pull in the guard, and Brayden unsnaps his walkie-talkie.

"Where's the other one?" I ask, already sweating.

"Must have gone to see what's going on." There's still shooting, erratic, but now there's a lot of screaming in the courtyard, and I can hear engines begin to rev up.

"Everyone," I say, rushing for my coat, "put your gear on. Jimmy, can you handle Odessa yourself?" He nods grimly, his dark eyes clearing away what has to be a killer headache from the blow to his head, and lifts her up into a fireman's carry as easily as putting on a jacket. She groans, opens her eyes.

"What's going on?" she asks, groggy.

"Des, honey," Jimmy says, his voice apologetic, "I'm going to have to run pretty soon. It's going to hurt some, but I need you to be quiet, okay? We'll be safe soon, okay? Odessa?"

"Okay, Jimmy," she says slowly. "I hurt already."

Jo comes up behind Jimmy and pats her cheek. "I know you do, Odessa. We're going to take care of you." I stare at her, both pleased and worried—she's fearless, acting less lost to bereavement, being herself. Thank God Jimmy's not as contagious anymore, or we couldn't help them at all.

Brayden's at the door. "You guys ready?" I look around, and we are. Ragtag, breathing hard, but we're ready. I feel adrenaline, like I would at a meet, and can't help but remember that I'm actually supposed to be in Durango warming up for a race. I'd be sitting alone right now, probably in our hotel room, staring at the wall. Headphones on. Imagining my hands parting the water over my head.

"Follow me," Brayden says, breaking into my thoughts, and disappears into the hall.

We don't see anyone, but there's shouting downstairs and the *thud* of boots. We move, slouching, as quickly as we can to the end of the hallway and then take a left, past the bathroom and to the far door, which opens into a pretty huge bedroom, king-size bed and all. There are even old mahogany dressers and drapery around a set of bedposts. There's a portrait of a man in a wig that looks hundreds of years old, and the carpet here is thick and white and spotted with new muddy boot prints. Brayden doesn't even wait; he moves directly to the walk-in closet and pushes aside a bunch of empty hangers, then pulls at the bar they rest on. A door cracks, and he pulls again, huffing at the effort. The door gives, and there's an opening into the dark.

He glances back. "There are no lights. The stairs are spiral, and there's a banister. Just hold it and you'll be fine." And then he's swallowed by the darkness.

We follow one by one, Jimmy and Odessa first, then Jo, then me, then Rob. I'm glad I'm in the middle of my friends, because as soon as Rob shuts the door behind us, I'm absolutely terrified. My throat is tight, and I just picture us going down and down, moving by feel, deep into a well.

Jo and Rob grab my hands. "Almost there, Mia," Rob says.

And he's right. It's over in a flash of light that proves to be

Brayden opening the entrance to the kitchen below. He sticks his head out, then closes the door, and we're engulfed in blackness again. I almost fall down the stairs.

"Okay," Brayden whispers. "We're at the rear kitchen door. When I open this, there's no going back. Something's going on, so they're distracted; we have to move quickly. Follow me right out the door, and we're going to run straight to the shed. The sun's rising, so soon we'll be visible, but if we keep moving, we can make it. Once we get to the shed, I want everyone on the ground. We'll crawl to an exit in the wall, then we're a ten-second sprint from the woods. Everyone got that?"

At first I nod, but then I hear everyone else whisper yes, so I do too.

"Jimmy"—Brayden pauses—"you got her?"

"I'm good," he says, his voice so firm I think he's almost angry. As an older version of himself, he seems bigger and stronger and more capable.

"Great. There's a block of knives on the counter near the door. If you can, grab a knife. Let's go!"

Brayden opens the door and slips out before my eyes even adjust to the kitchen light. Jimmy and Odessa go and then Rob's pushing me gently in the back, and I get down the rest of the stairway and out the door behind Jo to an empty stainless-steel kitchen. I remember to grab a knife—it looks like the others grabbed a couple too—and I get a small paring knife that disappears inside my fist. And then we're outside and running, my vision bouncing, flashes of light going off from the guns of the men on the towers behind us.

We make it to the shed and get on our knees, panting hard,

even though we only ran about twenty yards. I notice now that it's snowing lightly, beautiful big flakes that are oddly set against the firefight nearby.

Brayden's beaming. "We made it!"

"Yippee," says Odessa with irony, grimacing in pain. She must have woken all the way up, because Jimmy has put her down with her back against the shed and she's right there with us.

"What's going on with them?" I ask.

"Soldiers," says Rob, cocking his head to listen to the shots.

"Duh," Jimmy replies.

"No," Rob says, "I mean the others. Infected ones. Dying soldiers. They are fighting each other."

"How do you know?" I ask.

He shakes his head. "Right before the alarm sounded, I saw a group of soldiers come to the front gates, and they wouldn't let them in. It just makes sense. Remember how they killed that one in the woods? Remember how angry he was? Imagine you start getting symptoms, and you try to come back to the base to get help—"

"And they don't let you in," Jo finishes for him.

"Right, and they have guns."

"Well," Brayden says, snapping us back to the task at hand, "there's no better time for that than now." As if to prove his point, the walkie-talkie he took screeches, and there's a voice, unmistakable.

Corporal Johanson? Corporal? Answer, Corporal.

We stare at the device in dread. It's Sutton. I look up at Brayden and mouth, *Hurry!*

We are quiet and determined, even Odessa. Her eyes are dark

slits as she stuffs her sweaty hair under her cap. Rob bounces on his feet, all energy, flipping a knife he took from the kitchen back and forth between his hands, and Jimmy's a bull, taking gulping breaths of air. This is it.

"Jimmy, you take the rear," Brayden says. There's something immensely satisfying about everyone working together. No arguing, no overt fear. We've done something like this before, snuck out of a prison. We can do it again.

Brayden's face is grim. The men firing the bullets on the far side of the house aren't here yet. But soon that will pass, and we all know it. "Okay. Follow me, then. And *stay down*."

He moves ahead and runs us straight at the tall wall that surrounds Furbish Manor. Exposed, I glance behind us, but it's darkish and I can only make out flashes here and there. We hit the wall and skirt it, following Brayden blindly. I try not to think how incredibly dangerous it is to be this trusting. I have no idea where we're going, and we just handed our fate to the boy we know the least. I hope he proves us right. I hope I can release the pit that's been growing in my stomach since we got to Furbish.

Suddenly, Brayden disappears. I have to control the urge to scream. But then Rob goes too, and then Jo, and someone grabs my hand and I'm pulled into a well-disguised nook in the wall, where there's a thick metal door. We all fit inside the nook, completely hidden from everything. Brayden pulls on the door's handle, but it doesn't budge. He casts apologetic eyes back at us. "This locks automatically, and you need a key to get in or out, but usually I leave it open an inch. I guess they closed it."

"What do we do now?" Jo asks. I'm not cold, despite the snow, and I feel sweat dripping down my back. *Maybe we can just hide here*, I find myself thinking irrationally.

"Rob," Brayden says, turning to face the door, "boost me up."

"Are you kidding?" he replies. Brayden raises his hands toward the top of the wall and stands there, one leg up, waiting. Rob lets out a breath, and Brayden puts his big snow boot down hard on Rob's thigh. "Just don't get shot," Rob whispers. Brayden leaps up, grabs hold of the ledge, and Rob and I help push him to the top. Then he's gone.

"We're screwed," Jimmy says, staring at the sky.

A key rattles, then the door gives and opens. Brayden's there, a big smile on his face. "I keep a key under a rock near the door, just in case it locks when I go out." Without thinking, I give him a squeeze. His face lights up, the single dimple back in his cheek, and he presses my gloved hand. "Okay, straight into the woods," he says, facing the outside where, now, the guns seem louder and closer. He's still holding my hand. And then we run.

The cold air is harsh against my face, stinging me as we go. I can't see very well, and my eyes tear up. There's a blinding light of a flare gun not so far away, and suddenly I can see everything. Trees bent with snow sag in our way. Rob's high-stepping through the snow, Jo almost beside him. We run about fifteen feet before Brayden pulls me down. The others follow suit, and our bodies fall into the soft snow. There's shouting coming from just around the wall, very close. At that moment, I can make out white shapes moving through the woods to our right, running from tree to tree, infected soldiers approaching Furbish Manor. One, the closest, not twenty feet away, crouches and swivels his gun from side to side.

I hold my breath. There's a *crack*, and bark flies from the tree near the soldier. He ducks and returns fire, his barrel flashing. Jo's scooting forward on her hands and knees. The sky is full of small bright suns, flares hissing in the night and, then the very real sound of bullets whizzing overhead, like a whistle and a fist of air. Not at all like the movies. They're so close they hurt my ears, and I know that just one of them could rip me in half.

I swallow and move ahead, one leg in front of the other. I realize I dropped the knife and I search for it. Behind me, I can see Odessa pause, motioning me to go ahead. Jimmy is with her, a hand on her back. I can't find the knife. Screw it.

The air moves near my head, a bullet flying too close, and I flinch downward. The odds of getting hit by something as small as a bullet have to be tiny, I think—I hope. Soldiers, ones not wearing hazmats, are streaming from the front gate of the manor in our direction, taking positions in a crouch, aiming at the woods ahead of us. They probably should be in suits themselves, but I doubt they had time to put them on. The guard towers are bursts of light and smoke, their big machine guns swiveling this way and that, spraying forward, sending snow flitting into the air all around us.

The infected soldiers move like ghosts through the trees. They seem to be going slowly, but they aren't acting stupid or brain-dead like zombies. I imagine the men feeling older, weaker, but still with their faculties, still knowing how to shoot and be afraid of whatever is eating them from the inside out. I can see them call to each other, wave to each other, shoot and run and shoot. Mobile spotlights come on, bright and strong; they strafe the field, find a target in the snow and stick, keeping their beams steady like a Broadway show.

I can't help but watch, fascinated, as these spotlit men are picked off one by one. One buckles, his body spun in a circle and into the snow, his gun flailing in the air. I gasp. Steam rises from the body as it moves, twitching in place. The spotlight roves, shifts its gaze for another target.

"Mia!" Odessa has caught up with me and is tugging at my boot. "Keep going."

Jimmy is behind her, motioning for me to move. I take a deep breath. But the image of that body jerking backward replays. There must have been twenty or so soldiers that I could see attacking. Which probably means near fifty in all. That's a lot of crazy, desperate men, clearly infected with whatever their suits were supposed to keep out. I wonder why they don't just shed them. But then I know I wouldn't, because maybe the suits are doing *something*, slowing down the disease, keeping them from dying too quickly. I imagine that both sides are terrified. And not even of the bullets. One side of getting sick, the other of not getting better.

We crawl forward another twenty yards, angling away from the action, slithering over open ground as quickly as possible and moving directly toward the tree line, which is another forty yards off. We've moved fast, and the fighting is to our right; the spotlights seem to agree, barely coming near our path. I wait for Odessa to catch up, and shout/whisper, "How you holding up?"

She grits her teeth, but manages a smile, her face pale. We push forward together, slipping through the dirty snow, my body practically soaking in sweat.

Toward the battle, a lone figure breaks off from the attacking soldiers and starts running our way. He's moving quickly, his black boots flashing through the snow, his gun raised. My veins go icy, fear bounding through my body. Has he seen us? As he gets closer, I can hear that he's shouting something, but I can't make out the words. I instinctively cover Odessa and push her head into the snow, just as there's a splash of gunfire. The man jerks in mid-step and flips backward and sideways onto the ground. He's maybe twenty feet away.

A light follows him and grazes our position. I look over at Jimmy, who's right next to me, holding Odessa's hand. He's breathing hard, then spits in the snow. Blood. I see him see it and pretend not to watch as he covers it up. An ache goes through me; how long does he have now? There's a *hiss* from up ahead, and I see the others watching safely from the tree line. Why are we here and not with them? The snow feels refreshing against my burning face, and I wonder how we're going to get Odessa to the tree line if we have to make a break for it. The men are coming closer, the battle spilling this way as more sick soldiers attempt to flank Furbish. I try to focus on the spotlight dancing along the snow, coming close. But then it pauses—it found the body, registers it as dead, and like the Eye of Sauron, moves on to more pressing matters.

"Okay, let's go!"

And we squiggle forward as fast as possible. I ignore the pain searing up my feet until we catch up to our friends, who pull us to the safety of a concealed snowdrift, as if they were pulling us over the ledge of a building or a mountaintop we had just summited.

We huff deep misting breaths and try not to watch the massacre. The attacking, sick soldiers don't stand a chance. There's less gunfire now, sure sign that the rebellion is ending.

"We don't have much time," Brayden says. "They'll take stock as soon as this is over, and they'll definitely scout the woods for us. Jimmy," he asks, looking the big man over, "I know the woods around here a bit, but I have no idea how to get to the aqueduct from here. Still doable? You know where we're going?"

Jimmy nods, reclaiming the task we gave him when we left the barn, which seems like an eternity ago.

"And can you carry Odessa?"

He nods again, his big forehead set in a single, determined line.

"Good." He pauses, looks around at the group. We're all heaving, but we made it. He smiles. "Believe me now?"

Rob does something I never thought he'd do. He picks up some snow and throws it playfully in Brayden's face. The sky is getting brighter, and I can feel our spirits rise with the sun. If we were back at Westbrook, if none of this had happened, Rob's move would lead to a snowball fight. As it is, we just grin dumbly at each other.

"Okay, let's do it," I say, and everyone moves. We go single file again, Jimmy and Odessa and Jo up front, Rob, then me, then Brayden. We walk for five or six minutes before what's been creeping into my mind seems like it's worth doing, and another two or three minutes before I get the nerve. I swallow and grab Brayden in midstep. He looks at me, his nose red either from my kick or the cold, but either way, it's adorable. His eyes drink up my face—I can feel him doing it, and it makes my mouth go dry, and my toe, the one I can't feel anymore, it almost tingles.

I pull his hood over his head and stick my face in there with him, surprised at my own boldness. For a moment, we're alone. There's nothing but the sounds of our breaths and the slick of the nylon of our winter gear shifting against our bodies.

"I believe you," I whisper and lean forward, putting my lips on his, giving a soft kiss. They're swollen and taste coppery, and he winces, so I pull back apologetically but he puts his hand on my back and brings me closer, and I begin to shiver I'm so hot. When we kiss, I can feel the scrape of our chapped lips, and it's been a while since we brushed, but none of that matters. I close my eyes and am lost in his warmth, and when I come up for air, he's staring at me, his thick brows high, pushing wrinkles into his forehead. His mouth is open, and I see his teeth, white and a little crooked.

"What?" I ask, nervous.

"You're beautiful."

No one's ever said that to me. Not even my dad. That's something people say to Jo. It's so simple, but it feels like the last thing in the world I expect to hear, and I close my eyes in delight. I want to hear more, but I just grin, stupidly, and lower my eyes and there, in the snow, I see the footprints of my friends and realize that we're falling behind.

"I'm sorry about hurting you," I say, my hand against his chest.

He's tender, even with gloves on, and touches my chin, pulling me to his gaze again. His face is severe for some reason, and his lips thin. Did I say something wrong?

"Mia . . . I'm sorry too." He pulls me in for a hug, and while I'm there, I stare into the empty woods behind us, confused about his apology but not wanting to complain. "You ready?" he asks in my ear, his breath warm.

"Yeah," I reply and slip out of his grasp. I can still feel the lingering touch of his lips on mine. I wish I knew what just happened.

Turns out the others aren't so far ahead, because they've stopped and are pretending not to watch us. We catch up, but now I'm almost ill from embarrassment. Rob mutters something. *Nice one*, maybe. A favorite of his. I'm not sure.

"Well," I say, "better keep moving." I catch Jo's eye, and she has her head tilted, her expression set in a small grin. I make a face, and she laughs lightly, and that laughter makes me happy. It's all I can do not to laugh myself.

"I just need to sleep," Odessa grumbles, oblivious to it all, fading back toward the haze. She's not just in pain from the bullet, it seems, and I wonder if the wound is infected. She takes a sluggish step, and her leg gives out. Jimmy grunts and lifts her up to his chest.

"Let's go," he says, his voice tight.

Jo tries to help Jimmy, but her feet sink into the snow quicker than she can move them. She sort of stumbles along behind, holding only some of Odessa's weight with her outstretched arms when she can. It would look funny in any other scenario.

The morning arrives, gray turning into cloudy white. Sometimes I hear the *crack* of a gun behind us, but basically the battle seems to be over. The silence of our march, though, begins to bear down on me, and the moment of happiness I just experienced fades. If the battle's over, then Sutton's coming for us. Without me, he has nothing, just a rampant virus. I wonder, as I trudge along, whether I'm selfish for escaping. If I could convince my father to open the Cave, maybe Sutton would stop the virus from spreading. And that just leaves me cold, thinking of the dead back at Westbrook, of the soldiers, of it spreading slowly out into the world. This could be the beginning of an epidemic, and I'm running blindly to the safety of my dad, who, I know now, is a liar. He might have been keeping secrets from me for years. It's not that I don't trust him; the problem is that for the first time, I wonder if everything's going to be okay. I glance up ahead at Jo, who's still trying to help Odessa and Jimmy. And I realize that even if we make it through this, those three won't be fine. The school won't return to normal. Mr. Banner won't come back to life. Odessa's been shot and Jimmy's aged. I take a deep step into the snow, and then another. We're heading to the aqueduct, but I'm not sure anymore if it matters. I know we're hurrying, I know we're trying to get safe, but it might be too late to bother.

13

THE AQUEDUCT TAKES ANOTHER HOUR OF SLOW, PAINFUL hiking to get to. Each step hurts like hell, but I don't want to say anything. Cold toes don't mean a thing compared to a bullet wound. Jimmy can't carry Odessa that long, so we try to take turns, but none of us can really bear her weight, so it's more to give him a second for a break. He lifts her on his broad shoulders, fireman-style, her body slumped down, her curly hair swinging, playing with gravity.

Every once in a while, Jimmy has to cough, and he bends at his waist, Odessa still on his back, spitting blood on the bank to avoid contaminating the stream. We all watch quietly, refusing to make eye contact. Time is running out.

Rob keeps forcing us to walk for a few hundred yards or so in the shallows of a stream where our waterproof boots won't soak through. "To throw off any trackers," he says. I don't remember any dogs at Furbish, but I wouldn't put it past them. They have snowmobiles, though, and even without dogs, they should be getting close.

"There," Jimmy blurts out, his voice desperately tired.

He's at the edge of a clearing in the woods, his bloodshot eyes up in the air. Following his gaze, I make out a sharp hill that becomes more pronounced, bursting from the earth, one that breaks into a cliff face, a splotchy wall of dark red earth, spattered with icicle drips. And jutting from the cliff face is the aqueduct, a long brick waterslide that's supported by hundreds of columns as it transports water from the very heart of a freshwater spring all the way to Fenton. I follow the path of the aqueduct, and from here, we can see the outline of Westbrook's chapel. It looks burnt out, ancient.

"Do you think they can hear the gunfight down there?"

"Probably not," Brayden says. "Gunfire doesn't travel far through mountains."

Fleetingly, I wonder why he knows this.

"How do we get in?" Jo asks. "I don't see a way up there."

She's talking about the station, which stands at the point where the aqueduct enters the cliff. It reminds me of a lighthouse, with its cylindrical shape and circular windows. It's high up on the cliff, seemingly perched on a small outcrop of clay, and out of a hole in the bottom of the station jut the beginnings of the aqueduct, almost like the mouth to its long and flowing tongue.

Jimmy knows this one, though his face goes a bit sheepish. "Used to smoke pot and wander this area. Sometimes we'd climb halfway up for the view. There are stairs up the back. We have to circle around."

Like any story with a lighthouse, there is a man who works the station. A loner, known by sight in town, especially to us townies. The inevitable legends have grown over the years. Something for the students to fear, I guess—even the jocks, who go stand at the edge of the woods and piss as far as they dare in his direction, no matter that it's miles away. His name is Wilkins, and he has a white beard, a vast flowing thing that covers his belly. I have no idea how old he is, but he's not young. He always wears a cap pulled deep over his eyes. I've never spoken to him, but I've seen him a lot. In fact, for a while, I was sort of obsessed with him. The thing is, my father told me that Wilkins was the man who pulled me from the well. He used to remind me about him as if he was recounting the tale of a mythical hero. Dad said Wilkins came running from the woods with a shovel on his shoulder and started digging. Didn't say a word. He moved earth like it was nothing. Like it was his own daughter down there.

I've seen him see me, but we've never spoken. He nods. I smile. That's it. I'm nervous now to actually be meeting this savior of mine for the first time. But in some weird way, I think it's a sign that Dad wanted us to come here. Wilkins will show us the way and protect me somehow, as I like to think he's always doing. Like he's doing with my father right now, protecting the hidden entrance to the Cave. Our guardian angel.

We all stare at the station, no one moving. "I'll go first," I say, because I want to. And before anyone says anything else, I step in that direction. Except that my foot makes a MUCH louder noise than I expected. I freeze, we all do, deer in headlights. I hear the sound again.

It wasn't me.

"HIDE!" I hiss, and we all dive wherever we can go. Behind trees, a rock. Rob just lays himself as flat in the snow as possible. Odessa grunts in pain but tries to keep it quiet, and for a moment, we all close our eyes and hope for the best. There's the noise again, a static rumble, and I glance up to see Brayden, not having moved at all. He's fiddling with the walkie-talkie.

"Brayden," I whisper, annoyed.

"What?" he replies, clueless. "I didn't know what it was either at first; it scared me to death. But then when you all jumped to hide—" He chuckles. "Jo, wow, I had no idea you had that skill!"

Jo's far away and somehow managed to bury herself deep into a snowdrift. She digs herself up and shakes off the snow. "I'm a diver." She shrugs. Now that our hearts are out of our throats, we all gather around Brayden, who's gone back to messing with the device. It doesn't seem to be working.

"Can I see that?" Rob asks. Brayden hands it to him. This isn't the type of thing you buy at Toys-R-Us. There's a small keypad and a dial and all sorts of stuff I don't get, but that's what Rob does: he gets things. Takes them apart, puts them back together. A mechanic and computer geek in one. He takes off his gloves, and his fingers blur, and suddenly there's noise, coherent noise, loud and human, and it makes us all feel exposed.

The tone of the orders on the walkie-talkie shifts from routine commands to urgent anger. The voice gets familiar, and we know it's Sutton. He sounds an odd mix of desperate and assured. I can't help thinking that all this is getting out of hand for him. He didn't expect the virus to jump to his hired soldiers and spread as it did. Surely these mercenaries won't stick around for much longer . . . unless he somehow promised them the antidote. What's more dangerous, a bad guy with a carefully executed plan, or a bad guy with no control over his plan at all?

. . . *their trail*

We had trouble getting the snowmobiles across the water, sir.

But the dogs have them?

Yes, sir. The water lost the scent, but we're close.

Don't lose them again.

I'm sorry, sir.

It doesn't matter if you're sorry. If you can't find them, we'll all be dead soon.

The radio goes static, Sutton's final order being adhered to. We aren't so cold anymore. And when we look at each other, there's no relief that they don't know where we are, that we have a small a head start. We all stare up at the aqueduct, this imposing gash in the rock, and try not to think of what will happen if it's a dead end. Brayden checks Odessa's wound, and it's clear that she needs help. She's grown feverish, and I can see angry streaks of red under her skin, splitting off like veins from her stitches. It smells. It's infected. Jimmy tries to be upbeat, *we'll be there soon*, but Odessa's grim. And so am I. Brayden wipes the wound with some snow and covers it again, and Jimmy lifts her up. It's harder for him to do, and I can't tell if that's because he's been hefting her for a while now, or if the virus is starting its descent, making him weaker, older. I watch them with a stark realization: if we don't get help, and very soon, they're both going to die.

I'm no longer tired. It's hard to think of sleep when your world is ending.

The spiral stairs are metal, each step ribbed with thin, jagged splits to help a climber find purchase. Even so, there's ice pooling along the edges, dripping from one step to another. The railing is slick and cold and impossible to hold on to. We only have three stories or so to go, but each step burns my toes, and I can't imagine the pain Odessa must be going through. Jimmy is pulling her up step by step, and they're taking their time down below.

I'm first on the stairs, Brayden second. Below me, Rob and Jo are whispering, and I'd like to lean backward to listen in, but I'm afraid I'd slip and break my neck. Spiral staircase equals nonconducive eavesdropping locale. No one next to you, only the clanging of boots.

I keep moving and lead them to the top of the stairwell, where something of a porch appears, about big enough for all of us. There's even a chair, metal and covered with a thin band of ice, and a small bucket filled with cigarette stubs. Wilkins's patio.

Brayden doesn't look at me; his hand is cupped against a frosty window. His breath adding a layer of fog he keeps swiping at. I join him at another pane.

"See anything?" I ask.

"Lots of things. Not anyone, though."

"You think the soldiers came this way already? Does he even know they're around?"

"Probably. But it doesn't look like anyone's here at all."

Rob and Jo crest the top.

I bang my glove against the wooden door, but it doesn't make so much noise. I pull the glove off, feeling the crisp air on my hand, and rap on the window. It shudders, wobbling the reflections of the others.

"Doesn't he live here?" Brayden asks, chewing on his lip. It's still swollen, and he can't seem to stop touching it.

"I guess we'll find out," I say, and I reach for the doorknob,

somehow entirely surprised that it clicks open. I had definitely envisioned Jimmy using his elbow to smash in a window.

Everyone steps back and looks into the gloom as the door
swings wide. We can hear Jimmy and Odessa making their way up
the stairs behind us. He's whispering encouragement to her. I
feel a welling of emotion, a sadness. I never knew Jimmy, or *this*
Jimmy. He's not too bad a guy; he clearly cares for Odessa. They
finally mount the stairs, her arm draped over his shoulder, him
bent way down to accommodate her height. I can't really imagine
her getting through this without him. Jimmy's eyes find mine, then
flick to the open door. He grins, and I notice now that his beard has
grown fuller, more adult and complete, like a logger's.

"We alone?"

"Not sure," I respond.

"Hello?" he shouts. Everyone flinches.

"Why'd you do that?" Jo says, her voice more concerned than
angry. I can tell by the fear etched into her skin. The etchings are
getting deeper.

Odessa weakly swats at Jimmy. "You idiot. Don't be so dumb
right now, okay?" I find it oddly comforting that she can still be
mean.

"I can't help it," he says playfully. "I got hit in the head, remember? Who goes first?" he asks. And I see Brayden prepare to go,
but I step in front, again thinking of what they don't know, of how
I should be the one to explain ourselves to Wilkins, wherever he
is. Jo grabs my hand and then does this thing we do when we pass
in the hallways of Westbrook: we interlock fingers and then immediately let go, our palms together, sliding apart. At school it was

170

always a familiar greeting, a reassuring hello, and here it's doubly effective.

Inside it's black. Pitch as night. I instinctively reach for my cell phone to use as a light, but remember that it's dead. We're going medieval. I stand at the entrance, blinking, waiting for my pupils to dilate, trying to steady my breath. I've worked hard to feel comfortable *not* being afraid of the dark. But I'll be the first to admit that the dark isn't exactly my friend. And when I can't see *anything*, when I'm in a stranger's place, when I'm being chased by soldiers . . . well, these just aren't optimum conditions for me. My therapist, who I finally "graduated" from seeing last year, she'd call these moments "aversion tests," and I'm pretty sure I fail them when I want to be on my knees hyperventilating. And I almost do; I even squat, my palms sweating, but then I think of everyone waiting, of how if I just keep moving, like in the lake, I'll get there.

So I take a step, then another, ignoring my aching toes and willing my pupils to dilate faster. And suddenly an outline of a table forms. Then of a chair. Then of a TV, an old boxy one. I'm not about to flip on a light switch as a beacon for pursuing soldiers, but this feels like a living room from a family home, not at all like a professional workstation, a thought that actually comforts me.

"Hello, Wilkins?" I call, my voice echoing metallically, melding with the running water nearby.

"I thought we weren't supposed to do that," says Rob, his voice close, and it's all I can do not to scream. I turn and punch him hard in the arm.

"Ouch! What's that for?"

"Don't creep up on me!"

The others can hear us, and they file inside, and we all now stand, feeling useless, unable to even read one another's expressions.

"That's his name, Wilkins?" Odessa asks, her voice strained with pain. "I've always wondered."

"You've seen him around town, right?" I ask. "He's the one who pulled me out of the well."

Everyone's quiet for a moment. *Baby Mia, who fell down the well.*

"We need to separate and find the entrance to the aqueduct's tunnel," I say.

"Does anyone know what it looks like?" asks Jo. I can't see her face, but she sounds tired.

No, of course we don't. And we stand there for another moment, shivering and blind.

"Come on, guys. They're probably getting close," Rob warns. He's back near the entrance, peeking out the window.

We all move forward, in different directions, but it's soon very clear that there's only one way to go. A hallway, a door right beyond what I now see is a kitchen. The hallway is darker than the outer area, and I run my fingers along both walls as I walk and feel door frames to my left and to my right like mini speed bumps. Who knows how many rooms there are? "Let's split up," I say. "Everyone check the doors."

Some of them are locked. A couple are filled with discarded equipment or empty, never-used cots. As if this place used to be a big deal, filled with dozens of workers. Why would that be? Was this where the builders of the aqueduct slept? What's worse is that we can't really see any of this, we have to feel it out. The darkness is absolute; there's no light getting in, and I'm starting to feel the black creep into me. I grab a hand—it's Jo's. We squeeze, and I fight down the panic.

"So do you know this Wilkins guy?" Jo asks as we dig along.

"Not really, no. I've just seen him around. I figure if he's good enough to pull me from the well, and if he's good enough to watch over Fenton's water supply, he's probably good enough to trust."

She's quiet for a moment. "I hope your dad is right."

That makes me freeze up. "What do you mean?"

"You know, that this is where we should be. That he has an answer." Her words are full of concern; she's voicing what I've been trying to keep down for a while now. Are we too far gone to be saved? Should we even be here? But for some reason, her words have me on the defensive, annoyed that she'd doubt him. I own the monopoly on criticism against Dad.

"I'm sure he will, Jo," I say, my voice not entirely kind.

"I miss my dad," she says quietly, and I feel like a jerk. I pull her close, our jackets squishing loudly in the dark. It's weird; as soon as I'm taking care of someone else, I lose my fear. We're in the middle of nowhere, in a mysterious station in the dark being chased by hired men. But at that moment, I can only think of her, and how her hair smells oily and how her body is so small and how her mother doesn't know that her father's dead.

"You find anything?" someone calls from farther down. Jo starts, then sniffs. I can hear her wiping her face.

"No," I reply, "nothing. This place is much bigger than I thought it would be."

"Guys! Come here!" I think it's Rob.

Jo and I leave the room we're in and keep our hands close,

touching occasionally to make sure the other is still there. I can see better now, but only well enough to know I'm catching up with the others, not to tell who they are. I quell my unease at the faceless shapes and move closer.

"What'd you find?" Jo asks.

"Another hallway and some lights." I peer around a corner, and sure enough, there's another long hallway. But at the end is a door, ajar, with a glowing red light the color of an exit sign emanating from its depths. Rob's standing in the hallway waiting for us.

"What about the rest of this hallway?" Jimmy asks, and I try to count shadows. We're all here. I wait for someone to answer, but they seem to be waiting for me. Weird. Don't they realize I'm the one who gets panic attacks in the dark? I guess that's what happens when you volunteer to go first.

Given the choice of direction, I'll volunteer myself toward the pretty lights. "Um, okay. Jimmy, you leave Odessa and finish off the hallway, it's not long—"

"No way," he says, and I can hear the shake of his head against the nylon of his coat. "I'll take her."

"Fine." No reason to argue with him. "Hurry up, then, and come back. Everyone else, this way."

Jimmy helps Odessa stand and they leave, and it's only after they're gone that I think sending someone else with them might have been nice. A hand takes mine, and of course I think it is Jo's, but only for a second. I can't believe how soft his hands are.

"Hi," Brayden whispers in my ear. I smile—he can't see it in the dark, but I smile. Jo's hand is nice, but his is better. I hold it tight. "You sure this will get us into the Cave?" His voice is worried, scared maybe, and I'd like to imagine the fear is on my behalf. Maybe that's a little selfish.

"Not sure at all. But I trust my dad now. At least, I'm going to believe his lies were for my benefit." I can hear my friends' footsteps, their echoes behind me, and the red light seems to emit a *hum*, a *buzz* that filters into my thoughts. Dad's always taken care of me.

The darkness behind me grows more absolute with every step we take toward the red light. As if I'm losing the space I'm leaving. I can make out the others—Rob, Jo, Brayden—all bundled tight with me like we're in a haunted house or something, except this isn't a ride, we didn't pay to be here, and I'm not sure there's a way out. I should stop thinking, or I'll lose my nerve.

I push my back against the wall and tiptoe forward, and the others follow. When I get to the door, I do a quick peek around the corner and back, but don't really process anything. How do spies do that? The quick look, instant understanding of a scenario. I want photographic memory, but I'll settle for good results. So I do it again, slowly, keeping my gaze on the empty room, trying to shove my fear back down my throat.

No one. Just a room. I turn the corner and step in and am not surprised to find that red light does *not* provide the same level of comfort as a normal bulb. The others enter, and we find ourselves in what is clearly the control room of the aqueduct. There's a massive chair in front of a series of screens, a cockpit of buttons and switches, a few flashing lights. All of the screens are blank, except for one. It shows the front entrance, and the door is open.

"Creepy," Jo says, stating the obvious.

"Did we close that?" I say, my heart pounding.

Jo shakes her head. "I don't think so."

"Are you sure?"

"It doesn't matter. Either they are here and we're screwed, or they aren't." She always has a fine perspective on things.

Rob, seeing electronics, takes control with a grace that he rarely displays. He settles himself down in front of the oversize console and starts fiddling with a keyboard, bringing a monitor to life. "Looks like the backup generator has kicked in, but only for the mandatory systems. Maybe the soldiers started to cut the power around Westbrook and that outage affected this station. The water's still running, but we aren't going to be cooking any food in the oven anytime soon."

"Can you tell where the Cave entrance is?" Brayden asks, his tone urgent. "The soldiers are coming."

Rob shakes his head. That probably was the first thing he tried to figure out. Then he seems to reconsider. "Well, sort of, but no. Just that there's a gate labeled E9 that's blinking and looks like it could be an open door, but not sure where it is. This stuff isn't too complicated. Your Wilkins dude maybe wasn't the most tech savvy, so they probably kept it simple for him. I think the computer is almost more of a record keeper than anything else. All he ever had to do, I bet, was pay attention for any alarms or internal fuck-ups and read the display."

"He didn't do a very good job this time, huh?" says Jo. I give her a look. "What?" she counters, unapologetic. "Where is he? Why aren't the lights working? Why isn't he taking care of things?"

"Maybe he's in Fenton and now *they* are quarantined."

"Maybe." But she's dubious.

After searching the room high and low, Brayden's bent over in the corner, pulling something from the wall with an audible *click*. "This room isn't a total loss, though." He turns and waggles a flashlight in the air. "Bet there's one in every room, if only it were bright enough to find them."

Jo takes the flashlight from him. "Let's go test out that theory," she says.

Rob appears reluctant to stand up, and I'm about to say something when a shriek pierces the corridor, bouncing around the metal from every direction. We all freeze in whatever pose we're in, and a perverted part of my brain thinks that we look really weird. I swear our gazes all meet. And then we run.

Brayden first, squinching his shoulders tight and doing a little hop through the door into the corridor, then Jo, who gamely switches on the flashlight and sends the beam down the hallway as far beyond Brayden's feet as possible, so he can see. I don't dive after them, but grab Rob, who might just stay sitting he seems so comfortable in front of his monitors. I've already learned the lesson here, though, no more separating. Rob's body is probably as worn as mine and running on empty. Even if he wanted to leave, he seems to need me to yank him along. At least with the flashlight, we aren't running into the dark.

We round the corner and see the outline of Jo and Brayden at the door, stock-still, staring into a room. Jo's holding the flashlight forward but sort of looking away, her hair almost white in the light. Brayden, on the other hand, is in a squat and peering intently.

"What?" I ask, but answer my own question when I catch up and take in the room.

Odessa's babbling and crying, tears and snot down her face.

"I stepped on his head, I stepped on his face!"

She means Wilkins. The guy who saved my life is lying at our feet. His arms are rigid, legs stiff, and his massive beard is thick and gray and almost covers his entire wrinkly face. Jo turns and stares at me, her face pale, her red-rimmed eyes roaming everywhere, as if she can't focus or doesn't want to. I pull her to my shoulder, and she whispers, "I don't want to see this." And I'm sad, because another person we were supposed to rely on is dead, another person like her father.

"What happened?" Brayden asks, one of the first stupid things I've heard him say. Wilkins has the virus. It's obvious. And what's more obvious is that the virus is spreading. And maybe it's farther than we thought, than even the soldiers knew. Maybe the worry should be if the town *isn't* quarantined. Who knows how far this thing has spread? Maybe the world is screwed. The thought makes me dizzy, and even though I'm holding Jo, I kinda want to sit down.

Jimmy's shaking his head like he can't believe it. I guess he's taking it from another angle, since he's infected himself. His breathing is becoming labored, and his face is showing more signs of aging: his jaw is rounding out, and wrinkles are forming at the edges of his eyes. I wonder how fast it goes from here. I look around at the others: no sign. Yet.

"I saw that the door was inched open, so I shoved at it, but it was stuck," Jimmy says, as if to actually give Brayden an answer. "Something big in here, I thought—something fell, like a chair or mattress or something. So I pushed until it opened, about a foot or so. And then I stepped through. Couldn't even see what it was." He sucks in a breath and looks at poor sobbing Odessa. "That's when she came in after me. And stepped right on the dude's face."

"On his face?" repeats Rob dumbly.

Jimmy nods. "Yeah, on his face. She fell over, and I thought it was her leg, maybe pain or something, and she starts screaming. But then I felt around, and I know a beard when I feel one. Ugh, I think he shat himself too."

He did; he must have. The smell is toxic, though I'm not sure I noticed it before. Must have had the same effect on the others, because as soon as Jimmy mentions poop, we all try to stop breathing.

I reach out a hand to Wilkins's face. There's enough light generated by the flashlight to see him if I wanted to, but I don't. I let my hand quest over the contours and, though my body calls for me to flinch, I don't because I want this—to know for sure if my guardian angel is really gone. I take in the cold, yielding surface that is his forehead, then cheek, then nose.

"Mia," Brayden says, soft in my ear, "you shouldn't touch him."

It's too late for that, I think, and don't answer. He doesn't pull me away; no one does. So I guess we all think the same thing. If we didn't have the virus before, we do by now.

"I'm sorry," I whisper, but the others clearly hear me, because of course they're watching weirdo Mia touch the dead guy. No one is gonna ask why I'm apologizing to him; they leave me to it, and we have an odd moment of silence between us.

Jo touches my shoulder. "We have to keep going."

I take a breath, and it catches. I had no idea I was crying. If Jo tells me we have to get going, Jo who has so much more to mourn about than me, I'd best suck it up. Still, there's something about this

179

man I never actually spoke to. He's lying faceup; no one to pull him out like he did me.

There's a noise, persistent and shivering. An engine, a snowmobile, a shout, a gun—we can't tell from this far inside the aqueduct, but it's faint and growing louder. We all clue in to the sound; the noise is sharp and dominates the room. We don't like what we hear.

Rob turns on the walkie-talkie, and we stare.

. . . tracks, sir.

Good. A pause, the voice Sutton's. *Sergeant, the one called Mia. The girl. Make sure we get her. I don't care about the others. Please hurry—there isn't much time.*

As long as there's time for us, sir.

Don't question me, Sergeant. This is the only way.

Sutton's voice is apologetic, as if unused to giving orders.

"What does he mean, 'I don't care about the others'?" Odessa asks. She's leaning on Jimmy, her eyes wild.

"Who cares?" Rob yells. "They're almost here!"

Everyone's up, and we're back in the hallway, scrambling against each other for space, looking for rooms. We don't even know where we are. Jo smashes into a door and bends, grabbing her shoulder and cursing. I reach for her, but she grits her teeth and pushes me on. The door at the end of this hallway leads to a T-junction, and after a fruitless search to the left, Jimmy calls, "I got something!" and then, "Brayden, Rob, get here now."

By the time I catch up, Jo's acting as a standing spotlight, illuminating the three boys as they twist a submarine-style door, turning a wheel that's apparently pretty tight. Odessa sits on the floor, panting, trying to conserve her energy, and I realize how—in light of everything, of the virus and us running and how close we *all* are to danger—she's in pretty bad shape. Infection, probably the virus from being so close to Jimmy all the time, pain, exhaustion. It's a wonder she's even awake. I catch her eye, and she makes a face.

That's everyone doing something but me. The thing is, as soon as I heard the radio . . . no, maybe before, maybe as soon as we found Wilkins, I knew what I had to do. And standing here twiddling my thumbs clinches it. I take a couple steps backward and look down the black hall behind me. A number of seconds pass, not so that they notice me, but to let my eyes adjust. The hallway takes shape, and with a small smile, I toss away any thoughts of me being crazy. Right?

There's a *thunk* and then a spinning sound. Metal slides through a metal groove, and the door opens. The boys shout, even Rob, a guttural yawp, and I feel it too. We're going to live. From this far down the hallway, I can still see inside, a half cave, half manmade structure. Another red light shines on the wall, illuminating a series of machines with hoses twisting from their frames into a small pool of water. The pool takes up half the floor and separates into two thin channels that flow through two fairly wide-meshed grates. The rest of the floor looks like concrete, like the edge of a swimming pool.

"What's all this?" Jimmy thinks aloud. His voice echoes in the small space.

"Must be where the water is tested for purity," Rob muses.

"So one hole goes to the Cave and the other to Fenton?" Brayden asks, his voice showing relief and even excitement.

Rob squats, puts a hand in, then shakes off the water. "Sort of,

181

one should go farther into the mountain, to the original source of the spring, the other to Fenton. The thing is," he says, pointing at one grate, "the one that goes to the water's source should head on a separate route to the Cave. Otherwise there'd be three grates here."

Jimmy might have asked more, but we don't have time, and Brayden, as if reading my mind, hops into the pool, where the water sloshes up to his waist. He blows through his lips, probably because of the freezing temperatures on his poor unmentionables, and then bends and dips his foot through one of the large holes in the grate. He squeezes to the other side, then turns back and motions for everyone to follow. And they do, even Odessa gets up and is handed through by Jimmy to Brayden. I stand transfixed, watching it all from just beyond the door, which I've inched toward slowly this whole time. Jimmy goes for it next, and he scrapes himself pretty hard against the rusted grate, his body almost too big now to make it. I think tetanus first and then, with horror, of how that blood has the virus and how the water flows toward the town.

"Jimmy," I shout, "wipe that bar, stanch the blood!"

He looks back at me, confused, then he gets it and he slams his hand against his arm. Rob sloshes forward and whips out his cap and wipes down the bar, then throws the cap onto the ground, away from the water. By then, Jimmy has his arms wrapped, having ripped some of his undershirt into a bandage, for all the good it'll do.

They're all there, standing in the puddle, waiting for me. I bite my cheek, step back toward the station.

"Where are you going?" Jo cries.

"They'll find us here," I shout, walking backward, feeling the darkness surround me. "They'll track us down. And they'll know we came this way. The grates here won't stop them. We need something bigger. We need to make it hard for them to get up here."

"What are you talking about?"

I set my jaw. "We need to burn this place down."

Maybe I had it all wrong. Maybe I like being alone in the dark. All my life, I've shivered at the thought of a moonless night, and now I'm leaving my friends and heading toward it. I can feel my heart keep time with my footsteps as I run down the hall toward Wilkins's room. Maybe I wasn't done saying good-bye. *No,* I berate myself. *I have to do this. They'll find us if I don't.*

The room still stinks, and this time, I gag, really gag; my head goes down between my legs, and I bend, trying not to vomit all over the place. It takes me a moment to get my mind straight, and I'm painfully aware of how close his face is to mine.

Brayden found his flashlight against the wall, so I fumble against the edges of the tiny space, my hands roaming high and low. Then I feel it, a small flashlight, clipped in place just like Brayden's. I unsnap and light up. I can see better, but the beam is low, and it's hard to make anything out.

"Mia!" I hear my name echoing down the hallway. I can't tell if it's coming from beyond the grate or closer. I hope no one has come to get me. I hope they're smart enough to go on.

I cast the flashlight around, looking everywhere but at Wilkins. Each time the light leaves a space, I can feel the darkness suck in. I hear noises, echoes and engines, louder than before. I can feel our time fading. Up on a shelf, I see some books and then—there, a cigar. I reach for it, but no lighter. I grab a book off the shelf, then stop. *Cigar, lighter. Where do you keep a lighter?* Suddenly I want to smack myself. I squat again, clenching my nostrils against the smell, and hold a trembling hand out to touch Wilkins's cold body. I feel his shirt and follow the fabric to his belt. He's so big, so sprawling. A bear. His crotch is stained with urine, his mouth flecked with vomit. My mouth gobs with saliva. I take a deep breath and reach into his pocket, ignoring the wet I can feel through the fabric. I realize that he must not have been dead long when we arrived. If we hadn't been caught up at Furbish, he might still be alive and coming to the Cave with us.

I find a lighter and pull it out. I kiss his frozen cheek and whisper into his ear, "Thank you."

I rip a few pages out of the book. *The Gunslinger.* Never heard of it. I light up and set a few on fire, toss them onto the bed and watch them curl on themselves and die. My heart stalls. The room is metal. Even if I did get the bed to burn, it would do nothing in here. I'm in a friggin' submarine.

My mind tumbles, and I'm out of the room, where I can hear the voices of my friends much better, but I can't for the life of me figure out who's speaking. Even male or female, their voices are too distorted, but I hear their words: "Miaaaaaaa, get back here!" "I'm going to get her." "No, we have to go." I know this makes sense. I know they *should* go, but hearing the words feels like I'm being abandoned. At least I don't know who said them and who would abandon me. "Fuck you, you're crazy, she might need help." "You heard the radio, Rob! THEY'RE HERE!"

I wouldn't say that I'm going to ignore their cries, but thinking about them doesn't make me happier. So I run fast through the maze of corridors to the front room, the kitchen. I twist the burners on, no flame, as high as they go. One, two, three, four burners, and then slam myself against the door and peek out the window. Already the air smells of gas. I see lights beyond the window, little dots flashing outside, casting about. There's no way I can fill up the entire station in this amount of time. Still, it's the front room that matters. The stairs. The access point. I just need to leave the station hanging from the cliff like an empty tree house.

I light the book again and get it going, really going, then put it on the chair, which is wooden and obligingly lights up by itself. I can smell the gas more strongly now, and I try to blow away the fumes. I can smell my time running out.

I hurry to the hallway door and slam it shut. There's a gap in the floor, and I don't want any gas sneaking out, so I pull off my winter jacket—the first thing I can think of—and shove it against the crack, stuffing it in.

"Mia?"

Normally I'm sure I'd scream, but I don't have time to be afraid. I do have time to drop my flashlight, though. Someone's come back to get me, but I can't see beyond the shadow standing down the hall. I start running and grab the arm of whoever is standing there.

"Hurry! We have to run!"

And we do, side by side, and it takes a second and a few long glances to make out Brayden's face. His lips are tight, intense, and I love that he doesn't ask questions and just runs. I love that he came for me. That he probably talked Rob out of coming and then came himself. I love that he puts his arm out, his hand against my back, and pushes me forward, as if he understands exactly what I've done and is trying to protect me.

We get to the pool and dive in, just like the movies. But there's no explosion. We're in only three feet of water, totally soaked, on our hands and knees, and I can't help it: I start laughing. And Brayden shakes his head and lets out one disbelieving chuckle. He grabs my neck, his fingers warmer than the water, and he pulls me to him, and I kiss him, once, because that's all the time we've got, but it's a good kiss. The kind of kiss that makes me want more, to forget the dead man twenty yards away, the ticking time bomb thirty yards beyond, and the mass of soldiers who might be, even now, climbing a set of steel circular stairs.

14

BRAYDEN AND I SLOSH THROUGH THE DARK TO CATCH up with the others, his light our only guide, and it actually illuminates very little. A pale beam that he streaks across the rough-cut stone and the shallow water. After spending a while in the dark, following a light beam, you almost forget you're actually there. This small tunnel, it's different from the hallway with its empty rooms and economical space. The water runs lower here, shin high, with thousands of tons of rock overhead. I wish it weren't so narrow in here, that we could walk next to each other. If it weren't for Brayden's flashlight, I'd already be sniveling in a ball. The rock is familiar, and it does its best to remind me of the well.

But no, that's not exactly how I want him to see me. So I buck up, and we keep going, almost jogging through the water, our boots splashing out and in and out and in, and I'm trying to ignore the fact that for the second time in two days, I'm about to get hypothermia. My right foot has stopped hurting, at least. I think, at this very moment, that I'd rather no pain than the reminder, the dull ache of a lost cause. I can't imagine what my toes look like. We keep on, breathing hard. I time my breaths, like I do when swimming, trying to pace myself. I wish Brayden would catch my timing, but he just goes ragged—deep and wet breaths that break my rhythm. We'll be there soon, wherever "there" is. We have no other options. Find the entrance or freeze to death. No better motivator out there.

A couple hundred yards in, I think I can see the others. I motion to Brayden and point. They've stopped and are huddled together, shivering like a bunch of refugees. Jimmy has his fists clenched, as if he's ready to box, squinting into the light.

"Stop walking. Stay right there!" he shouts.

"What's he doing?" Brayden whispers to me, his voice slipping along the rocks.

I know what he's doing. Our flashlight probably blinds them, and they think we might be the bad guys. "Jimmy," I say, my voice amused, "do you really have so little faith in me?"

"It's them!" he cries, laughing, and the whole group surges toward us.

Rob and Jo give me a big hug, then Jimmy makes it a bear hug, and even Odessa pats me, weakly. She's in pretty bad shape, her lips so blue they look ultraviolet whenever a light hits her face.

"We didn't have a flashlight," Rob explains, almost apologetically. Whoever was in front must have lived in a nightmare. They probably had their hands on the wall at all times, feeling the slickness of the stone like the gullet of a beast.

"Oh, my God, that's horrifying," I say.

Jo's hair is wet, water dripping down the sides of her face. She smiles. "I thought of you and wasn't scared at all."

I'm suddenly ten times warmer and want to grab her into another hug, but Jimmy interrupts: "What'd you do?"

I think about the soldiers, and how I didn't have any time to really follow through with my plan. There's been no explosion. Nothing. The soldiers must have opened the door in time to air out the place.

"Nothing," I say, feeling useless. Sutton's going to catch us, and we're leading them straight to my father. "I did nothing."

"Stop that, Mia." Jo's face is pale and shiny and deadly serious, and she's trying not to shiver in the cold. Her eyes are tender, but steely, bolstering me.

Jimmy tugs at my ponytail playfully. "Yeah, Baby, at least you tried something."

The ground moves. Dirt sifts from the ceiling, then a flash up the tunnel.

"GET DOWN!" Brayden and I shout at the same time, and I dive forward, trying to knock everyone into the water. Jo and Rob catch me and look at each other for a second, then slam backward, a shock wave pushing us over. There's no flame overhead, no burning heat or near death. Just a huge gust of air and then a grumble, deep down in the mountain. Under the water, it sounds like a gurgle, like the mountain is about to spit up.

Jimmy pulls me out, and I gasp for air. He turns and plucks another shape from the water, and I see that it's Rob, struggling to right himself.

"Where's Odessa?" I shout.

"I don't know!" both Jimmy and Rob scream.

I plunge my hands into the rising water, watching with dread as it reaches my chest. I hear the others screaming and gasping for air and then the noise of the water turns into a roar and I'm alone, unable to hear a thing. There's no space for breathing; there's no space at all. I open my eyes underwater but don't see a thing except silky green filtered through the beam of the floating flashlight a few yards ahead. I slam my head against the ceiling and almost go blind in pain and think, *That's it. I've killed us all.*

And the funny thing is, at that moment I almost take a deep breath of water and just say, *Whatever. I don't care—take me.* It would be so much easier not to be afraid of this anymore. Of drowning, of the soldiers, of the virus, of losing our parents, of the dark. I float, weightless, feeling the water tickling at my lips, trying to get me to open up.

The moment lasts forever, and some part of my mind screams for help, hopes that someone, Brayden, Jo, Rob, even Jimmy, will grab me and save me somehow. But they don't. They're probably all about to die too or gone already. And then the water crests, pushes on, and starts to recede. Just like that. Maybe five seconds later, I'm on my hands and knees, and the water barely passes my elbow, and if I am going to die, it's because I'm hacking out a lung.

When I finally get control, I look for everyone else. I flip my hair back and scootch forward to help pull Odessa out of the water, where her face is lying half submerged in what remains of the wave. She's barely moving, her eyes semi-open. I slap her face gently; her cheeks are cold, like frozen meat, and I'm about to begin mouth-to-mouth when she coughs and spits up water. I rub her back while she vomits out some more, then rolls weakly onto her ass and leans against the wall.

"Am I alive?" she asks, her voice gravelly.

"What was THAT?" Jimmy screams from somewhere behind

me, and it's clear that his ears are ringing and he's overcompensating with his voice.

"THAT," I say, "is what I did."

Everyone's soaking wet, sitting on their butts, in a state of shock. But it's a pleasant shock. We're grinning, happy to be alive. For the first time, we feel like we've struck back and aren't just running from threat after threat. I try not to think of the possibility of a dead soldier or two. Probably they didn't make it up the stairs in time to get cooked. Maybe the station was empty.

Brayden's flashlight, the only thing illuminating the tunnel, flickers. He's not holding it, that's why—it's floating in the water, and we all sort of watch it cough, sputter and die.

"Win some, lose some," he says.

"Awesome," says Jo, and even she sounds fine, hopeful. "Okay, someone take my arm. Take everyone's arms. Link up, and let's keep moving."

I help Odessa stand, and someone grabs my sleeve. Jo has found me. "Hey," I say, "can you take Odessa's other side? I need some help here." She does, stepping in front of her, and I can feel Odessa's weight lessen.

"Everyone ready?" Brayden asks from a few feet ahead.

"Lead on, master," Rob calls back, his voice wet with typical Rob irony. There's a sound of sloshing, so I begin moving too. We walk forward in an odd shuffle, the space really too small for our arms to be linked. I fight the urge to head backward and see the damage, to see if there are bodies strewn about on the hill, their white hazmat suits camouflaging the soldiers in their death as they lie against the snow. I imagine—maybe I overimagine—standing at the edge of the hole we're in right now, gaping out at the forest below and seeing that *everything* has been ripped from the mountainside. Down below, there'd be chaos, burning rubble and the surviving men running back and forth. Someone would see me, raise a gun.

"Hey, the tunnel's branching," Brayden warns. "Be careful, don't go wandering off.

My chain link takes a couple steps forward and bumps into Brayden and Jimmy.

"Which way?" Jimmy asks.

"To the left," responds Brayden.

"How do you know?"

"I know."

It's Rob who backs him up. "He's right. The spring that feeds the aqueduct has to flow downhill, with gravity. Feel the flow of water here. Downhill is that way." He points to the left.

"So this is where the water branches to feed the Cave," I respond, going through the logic in my head.

"Exactly," Brayden replies. "From here we go down and deep."

"To the Balrog," says Rob.

I'm glad my dad made me read Tolkien, but apparently no one else has, because they're very quiet. And in that moment of silence, you can hear the water sluicing apart at the junction, trickling down the mountain. We're in a waterslide, one of the ones that's black and dark and not fun at all.

"Nerd," Jimmy says. Jo lets out a giggle, and I can't help but do the same. I'm sure Rob is glaring at us, but I don't care. It's like we're latching on to any reason to be happy. And the sounds of a laugh in this empty place float, reminding us that we still have bodies to laugh with.

"Okay, okay, to the left then," I say finally.

The entrance is wider than the previous tunnels. We go two at a time. I'm still holding Odessa, whose head is on my shoulder and whose breath is getting softer. I want to warn someone, but she might hear and get upset. I guess this is a moment when I recognize a problem and have no solution. I can only keep going and hope for the best. But with each sloshing step, I imagine the dark bacteria floating in the water climbing to her thigh and her wound. If she wasn't infected before, surely she is now.

We push forward, no end in sight, and the group gets quiet again. We could have lost someone, for all I know. Just step after step after step. The water at my feet isn't cold, and I feel like I have heavy weights attached to my legs. When do I get my toes cut off? When everything is resolved and we're safe and sound, I still get to look forward to my toe removals? Odessa's getting heavy, and I want to pass her on, but I don't think I should break the silence. It's a reverent, desperate sort of palpable feeling. The air growing closer, each one of us becoming more alone.

And when someone does talk—I don't know who—the words cut through the air like the voice of the Wizard of Oz. Dramatic and unreal, visible in the air. Then the words filter through to the real part of my head and become normal and mundane and incredibly important.

"What's that?" the words say.

Up ahead, impossibly small, is a pinprick of red light.

"Go, go, go," I urge, my mind woken from its stupor. The grunting noise I make is the best way I can point out our need for speed with Odessa.

The red light gets bigger, then brighter, until suddenly the tunnel opens into a room, the water leveled in a shallow pool across the ground. The room isn't very large, but it is large enough for a door, which is steel and thick and looks like a bank vault. Above and to the left, one red lightbulb, encased in a metal frame, alive with current.

"We made it," Odessa breathes, and my heart does a little jump. She's alive enough to care about herself.

"Where does the water go?" Jo asks. "Like, why does it end here in a pool? Isn't it supposed to feed the Cave?"

Rob moves to the edge of the pool and feels around. "There's a grate here, a small one. It must filter through this." He grabs Jimmy's hand and hauls himself out, his calculator watch waterlogged and dead. The two of them, their hair pasted wetly to their faces, turn and grab at Odessa's hands. We help her up, and then we all flop onto shore ourselves, six wet fish, trying to ignore the cold that's been settling in our bones.

"So this is what it was like swimming under the lake, huh, Mia?" Jo asks, her teeth beginning to chatter.

I try not to shiver at the memory. "Honestly, no. Not at all."

I didn't mean that as a rebuke, but it came out that way, and everyone's faces say *party pooper*, including Brayden's. So I turn my attention to the door. They have no idea what that experience was like. We're all scared, we're all on edge. Give me a break.

The security keypad is encased in plastic. I feel an ache immediately, imagining this as a telephone with a direct line to my dad.

I come so close to dialing my home number that I have to clench my fingers into fists, which is just as well because I now can start pounding on the door.

No sound. In fact, no sound and lots of hurt. Pure steel, thick layers of it—it's like punching a smooth wall. After three or four hits, I fold at the waist and shake off the pain in my hand.

"Your dad told you how to get in, right?" Jo asks. She's looking around at the others, nodding her head as if surely I have a plan.

I can't meet her eye. "No. I mean, kind of. He told me to find Wilkins. He said to tell Wilkins that we needed to get in the back door." We all think of Wilkins now, both of his wrinkled and riddled body and of the fact that it might have been vaporized in the explosion or burned to a husk.

Rob watches me closely; they all do, but he's the one who breaks the silence. "Okay, well now what?"

"Now what, what?" I snap. "You're the Geek Squad. Hotwire the door or something!"

Rob's face doesn't flush, so he's not really angry at the Geek Squad comment, but he does raise his eyebrow, which is Rob speak for *You've got to be kidding me*. I've seen him give the eyebrow to dozens of students and a few teachers. Never to me. Leave it to Rob to make me feel like crap with the careful manipulation of a strip of hair over the eye.

But maybe because it's me, or maybe because he really is our best shot, Rob's face heroically battles the eyebrow into submission. He sighs, one long one, then moves me aside to take a look at the keypad.

"Can you make it work?" Brayden asks.

"I don't know, maybe. Probably not. It's not like this was designed to be broken into." He peeks around the casing, then pulls along the edges. There's an audible click, and the casing comes off, revealing a bundle of red wires underneath the flat keypad. We all watch, entranced.

Odessa's leaning against Jimmy, passed out, and Jimmy pulls her pale cheek upward and gives it a little slap. She doesn't wake. He checks for pulse, an act only he and I are privy to, and I wait desperately for him to look up, which he does, sighing in relief. I didn't think Odessa's infection would spread so quickly, and while I can't imagine her dying from a thigh wound, I know it's a real threat. Blood loss, shock, lack of rest, lack of medication, her body is breaking down. And what if she has the virus? If she doesn't get medical attention very soon, she'll lose her leg. She could die. We're close; we're right here. Just get that door open, and we'll be fine. I know it. Jimmy's hair is all awonk, his beard scraggly and dripping with water. He looks haggard and scared. Not for the first time, I wonder if Odessa knows how much Jimmy likes her. Maybe that's what I don't know or realize: Jimmy and Odessa might have a childhood together as townies that I have no idea about, a memory of them playing in the snow as kids, sledding down Felix Hill. A history that predates the chaos of prep school, where Odessa became a new person and Jimmy just went along for the ride. Because whatever Jimmy is, he's looking at her in a way that makes me jealous. Not about *him*, per se, but about the way his face is so concentrated and caring, as if he were holding a baby or a kitten, his forehead furrowed but his eyes bright, the small smile to make her feel better. Wow.

I peer at Odessa's face, then do a double take. The thin light makes it hard to see, but something's wrong, and I don't like the icy feeling that's grabbing hold of me. Odessa's changing, her cheekbones sharpening and her lines becoming more pronounced. She looks more regal, like paintings of Queen Elizabeth, even with her head lolling about.

"We have to hurry, Rob," I whisper.

"I'm doing the best I can."

"But Odessa's aging."

Rob glances over his shoulder, mutters to himself and grimly sets back to work. The others stare, and Jimmy starts shushing her, even though she's passed out and not making a sound. Maybe he's shushing me.

"Are we all infected?" Jo asks, pulling off her gloves and inspecting her hands for signs of aging. She comes right up to me and sticks her face in mine. "Can you see anything, Mia? Any wrinkles? Anything?"

I have to pull back to actually see her, but I look, pushing her head to the side to get a better view in the dim red light. "I can't see anything in here," I say. I rub my hand gently along her skin, and though it's cold, like marble, it's smooth too. Around the eyes, the lips, the forehead. I bring my fingers down to her neck, and don't feel anything abnormal. She's watching me; the others are too. I smile. "You're totally as young and as beautiful as you've ever been."

"Lucky," Jimmy says, and I can't tell if it's a joke or a way to tell me that I was being insensitive. Maybe both.

Suddenly, Rob starts jumping up and down, little shivers of excitement. His hands are covered in wires, like tiny worms in his palm. I see him pull one out, then another, and switch the two. "This might just work!"

The red light goes off.

"Damn it!" Jimmy says.

"I didn't think that would happen," whines Rob.

"Well, fix it!" I say.

"I can't see which wires I just switched."

"Great, that's just friggin' great." Jimmy's huffing. Even in the dark, I can feel his body trying to contain his anger.

"It's okay, Rob," Brayden says. "Jimmy, shut up. He's doing the best he can. He's doing *something*. Give him some time."

Everyone goes quiet again, the gentle flow of the water the only noise—too relaxing a sound for the scenario.

"Hey, Rob," Jimmy says quietly into the dark, "I'm sorry. It's not like Mia's dad gave her the code or anything."

"Say that again!" Jo bursts out.

"What? Calm down. Jeez."

"The code!" Jo repeats. Her excitement is palpable, even if unseen, and we all start rustling. She grabs my arm and shakes me.

"Mia," she spits, "what did your dad's message say?"

"Huh? I don't remember. Not exactly . . ." I remember the voice, the sound of his voice. I remember the dark hallway and the deep wrinkles in Mr. Banner's face. I can't believe she remembers anything other than her dad's death.

Brayden, clearly our memory keeper, pipes up. "It said *if you can't find him, if he's gone into town or something, try my phone number.*" He wouldn't be the first Westbrook student with a photographic memory, but I find myself swelling in pride and gratitude for him anyway.

"This guy's beginning to creep me out," Jimmy says, but his tone is lighthearted.

Jo grabs my arm excitedly.

"What, Jo?"

"You don't get it?" she says.

"Call my dad?"

"Yeah." She says this slowly, like she's enunciating to a child. *"Try my number."*

I smack myself in the head. Literally. It *is* a phone directly linked to Dad.

"What's his phone number?" Rob says, his voice eager.

I pull out my cell phone before I remember the battery's dead. I curse. "Um, I just have his name on Favorites. I don't usually dial the actual number."

I know it's Brayden who puts his hands on my shoulders. "You can do this, Mia. You've dialed it before, right?"

I close my eyes, a redundancy in the dark, but it helps me remember. "I don't think he's changed his office line. Like, ever."

"What's your home phone?" Rob asks.

"974-585-2379."

Rob presses a button, and the keypad illuminates green. Even such a small light seems to warm us up, pulling us closer together. He presses the last button, and the pad makes a harsh noise, all of the numbers blinking red, then they go out.

"We need his office number."

I close my eyes again. "Come on, Mia. You got it," Jo says, and I hear Brayden shush her. He lets go of my shoulders, backing away, and I'm alone in the dark with numbers swirling in my head. I imagine myself in the lane, back and forth, Coach shouting at me. I hit the wall and turn. I was a little girl, and someone asked me how old I was. Four. That's how old I was when I fell down the well. Four. My dad has me in his arms and he asks, *What's your name?* I'm Mia, and I'm four. *Remember, Mia, if anything happens to you, and you can't find me, what is my phone number?* 799 Sycamore Drive, Fenton, Colorado 81937. *I'm glad you know your address, Mia. That's great! But I mean my phone number. Can you tell me what Daddy's phone number is?*

"974-317-9947," I whisper.

"You get that?" Brayden asks, but Rob's already pressing away.

There's a *beep* and a green light, a happy color and happy sound. Within the gigantic door, there's the whirl of steel moving against steel and then a *pop*. The door opens just enough to throw a squeak of brightness into the room, but with our sensitive eyes, it seems like a spotlight.

No one moves for a second and then—chaos. I've never been so glad in my life; we're all jumping up and down, and I think I'm crying. Jimmy's lifted Odessa into his arms, and she jerks awake, in a daze but smiling already, and Jimmy leans over and kisses Jo on the cheek and then tosses his head straight up and hollers, his tendons pulling tight. Brayden squeezes me close, and I don't want to let go but then Rob and Jo are there, and we're all hugging like best friends should. We're all so wet still that drops of water splash everywhere, like a small rain shower of happy.

"I never thought you'd remember that number," Jo admits, laughing. Rob's face is so hot that his glasses have fogged completely, and I can only see his grinning mouth below them.

"Me neither," I reply, and we keep holding each other, just *that* much afraid of what we'll find on the other side of the door. We might have gotten in, but we have no idea what exactly we've gotten in *to*.

The door takes the combined strength of all three boys to push open, and when it swings ajar, we're immediately blasted with a gust of warm wet air, a gross but welcome relief to the near-fatal cold we were all feeling. Inside is an enormous cavern, twice the size of a football field, carved straight out of the rock. The walls are rough, and the place feels like the inside of a huge egg. Peppered across the room are small buildings, twenty or so of them, steamy glass structures that rise from the ground and emit an almost iridescent light.

"Greenhouses," Odessa breathes, her voice so soft not everyone hears her.

"What did you say?" Something weird is happening to her. She's sweating a lot, but seems to be feeling better. Her eyes are sharper, more aware of our surroundings. She's actually *looking* at things and not lolling near death. It's creepy that aging for a teenager means becoming a fully developed human.

She looks at me and reaches into her jacket. "Greenhouses. Growing rooms. I used to work in them at Westbrook, for my fungi." She pulls out her pack of cigarettes and watches mournfully as she drains water onto the floor. She squeezes the pack and throws it onto the ground.

"Oh, yeah," Jimmy exclaims, a bit too loudly. He's trying to be as upbeat as possible around her. His beard is still so weird on his face, he's hard to look at. "You went off to that science fair competition for your mushrooms and stuff."

"Fungi. And their decay-life capabilities."

"Yeah, whatever—that stuff."

Just like me, Odessa got into Westbrook for a reason. She manages to hide her botany passion pretty well, but I remember her when she won Colorado's state competition. I bet the "science fair" Jimmy mentioned was actually the Intel competition. I bet she did pretty well there too. And by pretty well, I mean a twenty-thousand-dollar scholarship to a university of her choice. That might be a conservative guess: twenty thousand is for tenth place.

"What do greenhouses have to do with electronics?" Brayden asks. I shoot him a dirty look, and he frowns. But he's right. Something's wrong. I knew Dad was keeping secrets, but now any guesses I might have had about what happens here have gone out the window.

Even though I went Rambo back in the station, we don't want to take any chances, so we close the door behind us. It's just as difficult to do from this side, but there's a gratifying *beep* when it seals, and I can hear the sealing mechanism again, like ten Westbrook lockers slamming shut simultaneously. The thought is so mundane that I almost giggle at its normalcy, and I like that feeling of happiness. As if, with the door closing behind me, I can finally be secure. We made it. If I had stumbled upon it accidentally, the room would have been out of a horror movie—plant-filled, steaming structures in the midst of an empty cavern. But for some reason, they don't bother me at all, and I only feel utter relief. This place, the Cave . . . it's real.

"Hey, guys," Brayden says. He's been peering at the door, checking it out—probably to make sure it's really sealed—but now he waves his hand upward.

There's a camera perched above the door, flashing a red light, taking us in. We scream *hi* and *hello* and *help*, and I even shout, "DAD!" but no one comes running. After a short while, screaming feels foolish.

"This is the back entrance, I guess," Brayden says.

"Yeah," I say. "The main doors don't look anything like this."

"Then," Rob says, "I guess we should go on."

"But wait," Jo shouts, her voice echoing along the walls. "We can't just hurry ahead, remember? We'll give them the virus."

I've known this all along, but maybe I was stuffing that away because I was just following his orders. Maybe I didn't think we'd get here at all.

"What should we do?" I ask, worry in my voice.

"We have to help Odessa," Jimmy pleads.

We look over at her—Odessa, who is staring at her hands, her cheeks more flush than I've seen since we left Westbrook. "I'm fine, Jimmy," she says, lifting her leg experimentally. Suddenly she coughs—a fit of coughing—and some blood spurts past her lips and onto her shirt. She picks up the fabric in her hands and grimaces. Jimmy wipes it with his gray wool cap and then shoves it in her jacket.

I turn back to Jo. "We don't have a choice. A bullet wound is bad enough, but the virus . . ."

Jo takes a deep breath and nods. Her face is so tired, her eyes sunken. All of us are exhausted. We're a bunch of teenage zombies. "Okay. Okay. But, really, let's keep our distance at first. We have to."

Winding our way through the many greenhouses, I can't help but be curious. The glass is steamed over, but I wipe and peer in. Inside there are rows of plants on one side—ones I don't recognize, but that doesn't mean much—and on the other are rows of vials and lab equipment.

"Mia," Jimmy asks as we walk on, "what does your father *really* do?"

I shake my head, trying to push down my embarrassment. "I don't know anymore. I thought he worked with microchips."

"Maybe they use plant life to somehow power their electric grid," Rob suggests helpfully. He swipes at the steam of a window as we pass, leaving finger trails. "I mean, that's a pretty big deal, right? Biofuel? That's worth all this stuff."

"Maybe," I say, doubt creeping in. "This doesn't look like anything I know about biofuel."

"What do you know about biofuel?" Odessa says, her voice stronger and deeper than before. She's hobbling more on her own now, but it's apparent that the virus has taken hold—her face is adult, just like Jimmy's. Two thirty-year-old seventeen-year-olds walking arm in arm.

Jimmy looks over at her quizzically. She pulls him to a greenhouse, and they stand next to each other, looking at their faint reflections. She touches her face. She doesn't look like Pippi Longstocking anymore. She hops experimentally on her legs.

"I don't think you should do that," Jo says. We've all stopped and are watching her in amazement. I can't believe it. Five minutes ago, she seemed like she was almost dead, and now she's shrugging off her wound. I don't like not understanding what's going on.

"I feel better, though."

"I bet it's the virus," Brayden says. "It's healing her."

"What do you mean, healing me?" Odessa touches her wound tentatively, but scowls in pain. She's definitely not healed up.

Brayden points at Jimmy. "Look at him. He's a perfect version of himself in the future. He's older. And, if everything goes like we've seen, he'll start degencrating soon. But for now, his body is aging quickly, so maybe it's healing quickly."

Odessa tries to take another step and hobbles painfully. "Not quickly enough."

"At least there's something good from this, right?" I say.

"I don't know," Rob replies. "Why heal you and *then* kill you?"

I'm surprised when it's Jo who speaks. She's staring at something in the distance, lost in thought, but still here with us. I can guess pretty clearly where her mind is and feel an ache of sorrow for my friend.

"It has nothing to do with healing," she says, her voice slow and quiet. "The virus isn't taking years from your life, it's making you go through those years faster. Don't you dare think it heals."

Jimmy and Odessa look at each other, facing their own mortality, but I can barely register that. I put my arms around Jo, but at first she resists. Her body stays stiff a good ten seconds or so before she hugs me back. I hear her sniff, feel her shake. I can feel the others watching, respectfulness mingled with impatience. I'm ashamed to say that I feel some of the same things. I want to make sure Jo's okay, but I want to get answers, see my father, find some way to help everyone here. I grab her shoulders and look her in the eyes.

"We have to keep going. Even in here, we don't have much time."

Jo swallows, looking guiltily at the others before walking on. Brayden brushes his hand lightly against mine.

He whispers in my ear, "You're really an amazing girl, you know that?"

My body goes flush, and I duck my head.

"It's true," he says, and he kisses me at the outer edge of my eye and starts walking after Jo. I feel a happiness in me, one that moves to eclipse the doom we're living in. And I don't want it to go.

We're weaving our way from one greenhouse to the next, Odessa walking more normally.

We have just cleared the last greenhouse when Odessa gasps. My gut leaps, assuming the worst, but instead she's just pushed up against the final greenhouse window, peeking in.

"This is incredible," she moans, her voice deeper now, more sultry.

Brayden and I hurry over and wipe off another spot. Things look about the same as the last place, plants lined up in a chaotic jumble of greenery.

Jimmy asks, "What am I looking for here?"

"This." Odessa is still in awe. "All of this. I haven't seen *any* of it before."

"She's right," Brayden says. "This is crazy."

"What's crazy?" Jimmy cries, growing exasperated.

No one gets the point. Except maybe Brayden, who seems to

know this stuff. "Guys," Odessa explains, "my first paper made it into *Science* when I was thirteen. I've already won the Intel competition." *Aww*, I think. My earlier guesstimates were wrong. Forget the twenty thousand—you win the big prize, you get one hundred thousand bucks and a full ride at any school. I might hate Odessa now, even though she has a bullet wound in her leg and is a petri dish for a virus. "I'm as good a botanist as any in the States," she goes on. "And I don't recognize *one* specimen of flora in that room."

We squint again. Everything just looks green to me. Tropical. Odessa sighs, clear that we don't get it, and so she goes to the front of the greenhouse and opens the door. A red light flashes, and she's in. She digs around in the bushes and then comes to the window we're all looking through, with her hands full of fruit we've never seen before. One is like a coconut in a U shape, a long coconut banana. In her palm are some berries that look like black-eyed peas, except they're blue and white. Little eyeballs of color.

And here's where I start thinking this place is wrong. I mean, really wrong. We already know something's not right, but I really can't believe the Cave houses some huge microchip-processing plant after seeing this cavern. Dad's been lying to me, like, forever. I stagger back and look at the large space. Greenhouse after greenhouse. Why would Sutton want to get into the Cave? Why would he be so insistent, be willing to let loose a virus that he clearly can't control? Why would Dad want me to come here if he knew Sutton was looking for me?

I grab Jo's arm and almost double over in pain at the feeling in my gut, the reality I've been repressing since I heard his message on Mr. Banner's phone. My dad knew all about this. And if he knew all about the virus, and if he's been lying to me for years, and if he really doesn't work for an electronics company . . . then the virus came from here. Westbrook might be ground zero, but this is where it was spawned.

"It was made here," I say, out loud, unable to help myself.

"What," asks Jo. "What was made here?"

"The virus. It came from here—I'm sure of it."

"But why?" Rob asks. "I mean, a couple greenhouses don't mean end-of-the-world virus."

Rob doesn't know, he doesn't get it. I stare Jo down and watch her run through the logic. I could be wrong, sure. I hope I am. But suddenly all the clues from my life seem to stand out. The subscriptions to *Science* and *Nature* and dozens of other journals. The time I found a hazmat glove in the car. Dad's obsession with biological-warfare movies. All small things, sure. Even added up, they aren't concrete. Yet, my father . . . my dad. What if he *has* been lying? Who is he? What does this even mean?

Jo puts her hand to her mouth, then shakes her head and her eyes go hard, pissed off at me for even thinking such things. "No way, Mia. No way."

"No way what?" says Odessa, returning from the greenhouse, her limp barely noticeable, and clutching the banana-coconut thingy as a prize.

"Mia just blamed this whole outbreak on her dad, who, awesomely, we're heading for right now."

"I thought that Sutton guy was the one who caused the breakout," Jimmy says.

"He did," I reply, worked up. "But he's trying to get back in here.

There are exotic plants, my dad's been lying, and this place is a front. There might be antidotes here, sure, but that probably means the virus is from here too."

"This all makes more sense now," Odessa says thoughtfully.

"What do you mean?"

"In one of the earlier greenhouses I didn't make a fuss, but all I saw were toxic plants. Belladonna, hemlock, wolfsbane, oleander. Death plants."

"Why didn't you say anything?" I ask.

"Why would I? I'd only looked at one greenhouse. There are what, two dozen around here?"

"Socrates was forced to drink hemlock, right?" Rob asks, and I stare daggers at him for throwing us more off topic.

"Most famous suicide in the world," Odessa replies.

"But I don't get it," Jimmy says, perplexed.

"You don't have to get it," I growl, angry and embarrassed. "Just ignore me. Ignore that Odessa is holding a plant from Jurassic Park and that some crazy lunatic is trying to break in here. *Here,* not the town of Fenton. Not even the school. Ignore how all of a sudden everyone is aging and dying, and my dad *knew about it already from inside the Cave.*" I swing my arms around me. "Ignore the greenhouses. They're actually hobbies for an electronics company. Everything's superokay!"

They're quiet, gazing at the other greenhouses in the room, their foggy windows, their steaming roofs.

"Mia?"

The voice is familiar, but staticky. I follow the sound up into the air and spot a speaker on the lip of the greenhouse.

"Dad?" The anger that was gushing forth from me, collecting in each tense breath, dissipates immediately at the sound of his voice. I'm not angry at my father. I don't want to be. I can feel the smile growing, and desperately shout now, "Dad, Dad! Can you hear me?"

"Mia! You made it! Jo, Rob. Oh, my gosh, you guys did it. Are you okay?"

"Dad, Odessa's hurt. What's going on? Where are you?"

"We're farther inside the Cave. Quickly, what took you so long? Where's Blake?"

He means Sutton, who sounds so normal with a first name. "I don't know, Dad. We saw him. He tried to capture us at Furbish Manor. But we got here and blew up the aqueduct so they couldn't follow us in."

There's a pause. "And Wilkins?"

I press my hand to my head and close my eyes. "He's dead."

Another pause, just the hiss of static, but I can imagine his lips pursing sadly. "You've done an amazing job, Mia. Everyone. We're on the far side of the mountain in the command console. This place is huge, honey. You're deep, near the thermals. About twenty minutes away."

This place *is* big. "Tell us where to go. We can hike to it." I look at the group, everyone is standing straighter, breathing slow, hardly believing this is all almost over. Odessa stretches her leg again, nodding reassuringly at me . . . and reminding me. "Wait, Dad. Dad!"

"I'm here, honey."

"Odessa's hurt. She needs help. She's been shot, and we need to take care of her. But, Dad"—I pause here, worried about asking this—"do you know about the virus?"

"She's been shot? He shot a kid?" His voice is as intense as the speaker can convey.

"She's doing better," I reply. "I think we can make it. But Dad, the virus."

"We know about the virus, Mia." I feel a touch of the betrayal slipping back into my gut. He *did* know. I glance around, but only Brayden will meet my gaze.

"Well, it's spreading to the soldiers. *Through* the hazmat suits. We don't know why. But we could be carrying the virus maybe. I don't want to expose—"

"It's okay, Mia. It's okay. We know all about it. We're fine. And we'll take care of Odessa and your other friend too. I can see they both need some help." I don't know where there's a camera feed. Funny; my only friends used to be Rob and Jo. But of course he remembers Odessa from when we were kids. I wonder if Dad's actually thinking, *Who are those others, that new kid?* "We're coming right away; it's pretty confusing—so many tunnels it's like a maze. Just walk straight through the tunnel until you reach a fork. Stay there, and we'll find you. Just head fifty yards to your left, and you'll hit a tunnel entrance. I'm sorry we aren't there already, we're a bit short-staffed at the moment, but we're coming right now. Okay?"

I want to know more. Who's he with? Who all works here? Have I met them before in Fenton?

"Mr. Kish," Jo says, her voice uneven.

"Jo, hi. Are you okay?"

"Can you reach Fenton?" She pauses. "Have you heard from my mom?"

Dad's voice gets gentle, and I know he must have put two and two together as to why Mr. Banner isn't with us. "They cut our phone lines, Jo. I'm sorry. But we do still have high-intensity cameras posted outside the Cave, and there are no soldiers in Fenton itself that we can see."

I watch Jo physically relax, her body bend halfway as she sucks in deep bouts of air and tries not to cry. I know I should rush to her, but this time I'm just watching from a distance, as she heaves in happiness and relief. Rob takes my role, and she steadies herself in his arms. "So she's okay?"

"I'm sure she's fine, Jo." There's a pause, the static thick through the speaker. "Will you be okay?"

"Yes," I say, assuming he was talking to me. "Hurry, though, Dad. We need you."

"I will, Mia."

"Dad?"

Nothing, not even static.

"Dad?"

"Yes, darling?"

"Do you know what's going on?"

Pause. "I do, Mia. And I'm not going to let anything happen to you."

Coming through the static, my dad's voice isn't very convincing.

15

THE TUNNEL IS RIGHT WHERE HE SAID IT WOULD BE. There's something incredibly anticlimactic about arriving at the Cave only to find out that we actually have to hike through more caves. At least these ones are spotlit by lamps mounted near the floor. The passage is wide enough to walk two abreast, and as we move, our shadows bend and arc across the tunnel.

We find the fork in five, maybe ten minutes, though it's more like a T-junction, a tunnel going directly to our right and left. Jimmy and Odessa slump to the ground, and pretty soon everyone follows suit but me. I'm too anxious for that. Rob's even nodding off, his head leaned back against the wall, his mouth open so wide I can see his fillings. I pace up and down, taking ten steps either way, then fifteen, then twenty.

Suddenly I'm out of sight of the others, listening for footsteps. Funny that I don't hear him when he tugs on my hand. I give a little internal shriek of pleasure, but when I spin, Brayden's face is serious. The floor lights splash upward against his features, magnifying his scowl, making his lips look dark and his cheeks gaunt. He gazes down at his feet uncomfortably and plays with the zipper of his coat.

"What's going on?" I ask softly, hoping the group can't hear us.

"Mia," he begins, flicking his dark eyes at mine. I smile encouragingly, though my mind is racing with puzzles. "Listen. I just want you to know that . . ." He looks at me dead-on now, taking a breath and a step closer. I find myself holding my breath too. "Well, no matter what happens to us—"

I'm not sure why I say it. Maybe because he seems so upset. But I blurt out, "Nothing's gonna to happen to us." He considers this. Then, as if making a decision, he suddenly becomes someone different. A transformation that feels both disturbing and amazing. He pushes me against the cave wall, and I hit my head lightly against the rock, but it doesn't hurt so much and I can barely feel that anyway. Alarm shifts to pleasure as he kisses me, his hand tucking inside my shirt and coasting up from my hip to my side; his thumb is light against my abs, and I suck in a breath at his touch, unable to help myself. I can't move, and all I can do is press forward against him and let his hand cup the curve of my breast.

No one has ever touched me this way. A small part of my mind has always felt ashamed at that, at how the other girls at Fenton have done everything and I haven't. Even Jo lost her virginity last year. No one's come close to Baby Mia, but I don't feel like a baby anymore. I feel a burn, instantly too hot for my skin and my clothes, and I fight the urge to rip them off. I let him kiss my neck, and I close my eyes. He pulls away and disappears.

Literally, he disappears. And when I open my eyes, a flashlight beam hits me like a spotlight. I toss my hands into the air and stifle a scream. It all comes tumbling back in a rush, and all I can think is that they caught up with us. Sutton broke the door, and it's all over.

"Mia?"

The voice is familiar, but not Sutton's chiding condescension. "Dad?"

The beam keeps me blind for another moment, but it wavers and drops and a big shadow moves quickly and envelops me. I try not to think about the fact that two seconds ago, someone else had me in his arms, which Dad clearly didn't see. I'm incredibly happy he's here, my dad, but I'm flustered and embarrassed and would rather be in Brayden's arms. I feel awful even thinking that. And then I'm tired, completely exhausted. He smells medicinal, like Old Spice and cough syrup, and his grip is strong enough that I can't really get my own arms around him. I'm held like a baby and finally stop resisting.

"Mia," he says again, pushing me back to arm's length. Through the gloss of sudden tears, I can make out a woman politely standing off to the side. She's watching the exchange with unconcealed agitation. But my father's face holds most of my gaze. I sniff loudly and try to stop crying.

"You're here," I say simply, and then with dawning horror I push him away as fast as possible. "Don't come too close. I might be contagious."

I see scruff on his face and heavy bags under his eyes. And his smile is as economical as always, especially considering the fact that I might have just killed him with my snotty nose.

"Mia, don't worry. We know about the virus, and we're not infected and won't be." He laughs, his mouth open enough to see the coffee stains on his teeth. "Please trust me. You can relax."

"Greg," the woman says from behind him, clearly a reminder to hurry. She's a short woman in a blue jumpsuit, a one-piece that zips from the ankle to the neck. Her hair's tied back, like mine, but I can see some streaks of gray in the black. Despite that, she's very pretty, her nose pert and her skin pale and smooth. Though at the moment, her lips are pursed thin enough to be severe. *What's her problem?*

Dad glances over his shoulder. "Oh, yes, no time for delayed hellos. Veronica's right, we have to get moving. This is all a race against time, you know." I grab his arm, my grip more forceful than I mean it to be, and he squints at my hand.

"I don't know, Dad," I say, trying to keep my voice steady. Trying not to sound betrayed. "I don't know anything, do I?"

His face melts. "Mia, I know I haven't been completely forthright. But you're here, you're safe, and if you trust me, I'd ask that you wait just a little while longer. Then I'll tell you everything." He looks from my left eye to my right. I hate it when he does that. "Okay? Can you do that?"

I nod, annoyed but unwilling to let that break the good news of our reunion. He appears to notice Brayden for the first time. Brayden, the one who was just cupping his daughter's breast. I shiver at the thought.

Dad seems about to say something, but Brayden beats him to the punch.

"Mr. Kish," he says, holding out his hand, "my name is Brayden Cole. I'm glad to meet you."

Dad's just barely taller than Brayden, and I can see him sizing the new kid up. He takes the proffered hand and pumps hard, which is funny, the seriousness of it all. It feels like Brayden's about to take me to the prom or something. Dad claps his hand on Brayden's shoulder and says, "I don't know your story, but if you helped my Mia get here, I'm grateful."

Veronica snorts, and I give her a look, hopefully one that she'll understand translates to *I don't know why you are here ruining this for me.*

"Where are the others?" she asks.

"This way." Brayden waves and leads us on, though we don't have to go far before we find them all resting on the ground. Jo and Rob leap up and, unable to focus their delight, they hug me and then my dad. Veronica goes straight to Jimmy and Odessa and checks their eyes, their pulses, and glances at Odessa's leg; the bandage is clearly visible through the tear in her pants. I probably should tell her about my foot, but I haven't felt it in a while. It's just a heavier weight than usual, like a wet sock is wrapped around my toes and I can't wiggle it off. I catch Brayden's eye and give him a mischievous smile, but he looks chastened—happy, sure, but he's not exactly sending me any signals. I could use ten minutes alone with Jo to complain or pick her brain. Maybe we can actually do that, I think. Maybe we'll get a bed and a room and some rest.

Dad joins Veronica, inspecting Jimmy and Odessa like cattle at an auction. He even whistles to himself. Jimmy looks at me in alarm, but I don't know what to say to that. Dad takes a closer look at Odessa's leg. "It's been a long time, Odessa." He's bent at his waist, peering close. "Very brave of you to step in front of that bullet."

She smiles, showing a field of new lines upon her face. Not wrinkles, yet, just the beginnings, but I've never seen them there before.

Jimmy flicks his eyes from Dad to me, taking in the resemblance. "Yeah, I see it."

Dad looks bemused and goes on examining their faces from all angles.

"See what?" Odessa asks, tired of being the test case. I don't blame her.

It's Veronica who speaks. She's writing notes now in a little booklet she's carrying. "Odessa, right?" She nods. "You two have the virus. We haven't seen it in humans before. I'm sorry we're poking and prodding you—we should hurry, of course. But it's hard not to collect real data when we can. Sort of hardwired in, you know?"

"But they're growing older by the second," Rob complains.

"You're right," Dad says. It's weird to see him so zoned in on something that isn't me. He holds out a hand to help them up. "Odessa," he ventures, "you going to be okay to walk?"

She nods. "I'm fine, I'm fine. And besides, I got Jimmy here to carry me, right, Jimmy?"

"That's right. Muscleman me."

"All right, then," Dad says. "We've got a ways to go, but not too bad." He keeps his hand on my shoulder, very proprietary, and when Veronica nods approval, we all haul out, with her taking the lead and me and Dad bringing up the rear. We walk uphill, moving fast. *Now* I feel my foot; it aches with every step.

"Where are we going?" I ask. Rob cranes his neck to hear the answer.

"The infirmary. We have a pretty good facility, all things considered."

"What about the virus?" Rob asks, but he keeps his voice low, as if it's a question only he had in mind and doesn't want to share with the others.

"I don't think I want to tell the whole story twice, so I'll just say that we'll take care of it soon."

"How?" Rob persists.

"Well," Dad says, "that man who's doing this, the fake newspaper reporter?"

"You know him," I say, though it's the most obvious thing in the world.

"That's right." He nods. "We all do. He used to work here."

"At Fenton Electronics," Rob says drily. Dad knows Rob well enough to understand his sense of humor, but he looks a little wounded at this comment.

"Yes, Rob. And I promise you both you'll get some answers. But for now, let it be enough to know that since he used to work here, we know what motivates him."

"Did you make the virus?" I ask.

Dad doesn't stop walking—he doesn't even pause. He just shakes his head in disgust and mutters, "You think that ill of your father?" The reaction has me feeling equally guilty and angry, bummed to be letting my dad down and annoyed that he wouldn't think that question had come to mind. I watch him move ahead of me. I let the anger win over the guilt, tired of his deceptions, and sulk after him.

The path is carved out of the rock and entirely mazelike, with a number of twists and turns, and I've lost all understanding of where I am. Not that I ever did know. Every once in a while, we suddenly enter a vast room of stalactites and stalagmites still dripping, still growing, big enough to put Carlsbad Caverns to shame. Spotlights are placed to illuminate the view as well as the path, and I'd like to think that was my father's idea. But then we'll go for stretches of time in near complete darkness, with only a thin walkway of lights guiding us through a narrow tunnel. The air's cold, and we don't talk much. I think we all have this feeling like this walk is *finally* about to get us some answers. The gravity of the mountain weighs on us, pushing us down, keeping us quiet and respectful and determined. There was a time when this walk would have killed me, something this deep and dark. But now the claustrophobia competes with adrenaline, a spike that pulses like my heart, providing a burning fuel to combat my fears. That's how I got over water, by diving in. I've used swimming my whole life for the rush, a safe place to remember my nightmares, until one day I realized I was good, and I found some sort of karmic balance from my success. Now the cave feels oddly the same; I dive into my fears, and am rewarded with an entirely new world. The darkness around me is gentle, as if it's only watching, not trying to harm. That doesn't stop me from imagining some creature leaping from the shadows; I've seen enough scary movies to know that they're lurking nearby, waiting for one of us to fall back. I watch Odessa's slow shuffle-step and feel better. The monsters would eat her first.

Dad finally gets over his hissy fit and checks in with me from time to time. He knows I don't like this wall of darkness, and I wonder in passing whether part of the reason he never told me the truth was that he couldn't bring me here—he was too afraid of my reaction. "Not much longer," he says for the third time. Thanks, Dad. Keep up the lies.

But in this case, he's not really wrong. Suddenly, almost out of nowhere, we hit a different style of tunnel, lined in concrete, man-made or at least man-fiddled-with. The lights that run along the floor are brighter and placed in small circular globes.

"If the lights are on your left," Veronica calls over her shoulder, "they mean you are heading central. On your right, away from center."

Finally, we hit another hallway, then a door, then a series of doors, all locked by punch code.

Our feet start to echo. I realize I have no idea how many people work here, and now that I know that I'm clueless about what goes on in the Cave, every door holds some sort of secret. Where *is* everybody? Surely a place this big can't be entirely empty?

Suddenly, up ahead, Veronica stops. We crowd around her at a door while she enters a code. I can hear Rob muttering the numbers to himself under his breath, and I elbow him in the ribs. The door beeps, then unseals with a release of air, and Veronica pulls it open. Judging by the strain in her arms, it's pretty heavy.

"After you," she says.

Inside there's a room, a dormitory more like it, small, steel and compact. There are only three sets of bunk beds, allowing six to sleep. I see a small door marked LAVATORY, a shower stall and four lockers. There are also a few machines, like the ones you see in a hospital, an IV stand and heart monitor and such, but not much in the way of an infirmary. It's strange, being here, imagining my father working nearby. The place appears safe and sturdy, like a small bomb shelter. Why is it that the people who build the bomb shelters are the crazy ones?

Dad claps his hands together. "Okay, so, here's our infirmary."

"Infirmary?" Odessa repeats, her voice shifting in inflection the way it might back at school, hard to do now that she's aged so much. "This isn't much of a doctor's office."

"At least there's a light switch," Brayden jokes.

"At least there's a protein bar!" says Jimmy from inside a locker he's taken the liberty of rooting around in. "Who wants one?"

I look questioningly at Dad, and he waves us on. Jimmy tosses the bars to everyone, and we rip in, starving. The bar is cold and tastes awful—I got oatmeal raisin—and is hard to chew and won't fill me up but it's something. It feels like the most important thing in the world, and considering that it's healthy, maybe this protein bar really *is* the most important thing in the world at the moment.

Odessa takes a seat on a lower bunk and peers up at Veronica. "Really, I thought you said it was a good facility."

"It is," she says. "We just don't need the standard equipment." They don't need? Did she mean they don't *have*?

Rob's found a power outlet and has his huge clunky OtterBox plugged in already, looking sheepish. And rightfully so—we all took our phones by reflex, but he had the presence of mind to bring his power cord.

"Rob, can I call my mom from that thing?" Odessa asks from her seat.

"You won't get any reception in here," Dad replies with a shrug. "We only use landlines, and those were cut at the same time as the quarantine went into effect."

"So there's no way to call for help?" Jo asks.

Dad and Veronica both seem to flinch, but neither says a thing.

"Come on, Mr. Kish, we already know all about Sutton," Jo says, and she uses a tone I've heard before, a conspiratorial voice she'd pull out in class to get us dismissed early, or into the quad for a lesson in the sun. Rob catches it too, because he has to stifle a smile with his hand. I almost laugh too, and it's a weird thing, because it's like she's messing with our teacher, except in this case the teacher's my father.

Dad appears to mull things over, but he's already given in. In some ways, that makes me feel safer. He wouldn't say a thing if he thought we were in immediate danger. "Our cameras still work just fine. Since Blake knows where they are, he probably left them up on purpose."

"He wants us to watch him," Veronica says, her voice tight.

"Maybe," Dad says, "But the doors we have here are virtually indestructible. He's just trying to scare us, that's all. To force us to make a play."

"So what's the play?" Brayden asks, his arms crossed over his chest, looking, for some reason, unimpressed. "He knows this place, right? You said he used to work here. Don't you think he'd know what he'd need to do to get in?"

"A little much, Brayden," I say, feeling overwhelmed by the bleakness of his tone and defensive of Dad.

"He's not wrong," Veronica replies, and it's clear that she's more worried about Blake Sutton than my dad is. It's as if she's using the moment to bring up an argument that has been going on between her and Dad for a while now. She looks afraid, solemn. Like she knows more than Dad does about Sutton. "Our cameras have picked up his troops, and they're already in position around us. We're just waiting for his move."

"Maybe he's already made it," Brayden says aggressively.

Dad, though, seems unbothered. He pops his heavy eyebrows up and absentmindedly scratches his hairy arm. "He hasn't. We're safe in here. And that's the last I want to hear about it, okay? You didn't risk your necks escaping Westbrook to come to a place that couldn't protect you, right? Now relax, kids, and believe we know what we're doing."

No one says a thing. I try to smile encouragingly at him, but it feels like I'm posing for a picture I'd rather not take. He's clueless, and says, "Okay, now, boys, time to step outside for a moment. The girls need to clean up."

I'd expect Jimmy to grin and make a joke, but he's the first to rise, tossing his head to the boys to get moving. I guess he's really changed from his frat-boyness of Westbrook. Jimmy squats at Odessa's side, his newly adultlike face puppy-dog sad, and he asks if she needs help. She's the one who grins, barely, an expression that eventually turns into a grimace, and then she pushes him away. "Get out of here, Jimmy!"

As Dad leads them out, Brayden glances back at me and mouths, *See ya soon.* I smile warmly, feel the heat spread from my lips and down my body as I imagine seeing him again and soon. Now that we've made it, I find my thoughts slipping into visions of him more often, as if I'm allowed to relax and enjoy the feeling.

"Mia, a hand, will you?" Veronica says.

I snap my mind back into place and move to Odessa, but the ache in my foot swells to a sharp pain, and I almost fall over.

Jo stares at me, confused at first, then with dawning recognition. "Oh, crap, your foot."

I shake my head. "No, it's fine. Let's deal with Odessa."

Veronica's puzzled, but she takes it in stride and points to the bed next to Odessa. I limp over. "Shoe off, now."

I start to untie, but I'm not fast enough for her, so she takes over. I put my hands on the cold bars and stretch my back. Now that I'm sitting, I realize how tired I am. If I were to just lie down, I'd be asleep instantly. I try to focus on Veronica's pinched face.

"So . . . what's your story?" I ask her while she's working, really wanting to know what she and my dad were arguing about.

She glances up. She has the shoe untied now and takes it off slowly. My foot throbs relentlessly. Like I can feel my heart beating in my foot.

"What do you mean?"

"I mean, what do you do here? How come I've never met you? What's the big secret about Fenton Electronics? And why are you so scared about Sutton and Dad isn't?"

"You ask a lot of questions. Does this hurt?" She's got my thick ski sock and is slipping it off.

I shake my head. "Can you answer any of them?"

There's my foot, which shades from normal to splotchy to completely dark purple and black, like a blueberry Greek yogurt before you mix it up.

"Fuck me," Odessa says. "I thought I was the one in trouble." I don't feel the need to remind her that she looks like a thirty-year-old. I try to wiggle my toes, but can't. They look bloated, the skin tight like a hot dog's. There's a huge blister on my big toe, and I don't know how it hasn't burst yet.

"I don't feel much pain," I say.

Veronica digs around the small backpack she's been carrying. She pulls out a vial, one with an eyedropper, near empty, carrying a clear liquid of some sort.

"You don't feel anything because your nerves are shot." She puts the dropper down and lifts my foot to look underneath, at my heel. "Okay, this is totally doable." Satisfied by something, she moves on to Odessa. "Pants off."

"But what about Mia? What's doable?" Jo asks, confused. What *is* doable? I wonder. Does that mean it's doable to fix me up, or doable to cut off my toes?

"She'll be fine. So will Odessa. It's clear the virus is accelerating the healing in her leg, but that's merely her body aging and her cells in rapid reproduction. Soon she'll head over the hump and start moving toward old age, which will, conversely, accelerate any infection. We have to get at the wound now, expose it and take care of it." So Rob was right, the virus is healing before it begins to kill. Sort of like the "tipping point" that Sutton had brought up back at Furbish: the moment before things start getting bad, the body gets stronger. Veronica experimentally tries to pull apart what's left of Odessa's pant leg. "Despite the fact that you're feeling better, this is going to hurt. I just want to prepare you."

Right then, I'm thinking that Veronica's a cold woman, what with her hair pulled back so tight I can almost feel her scalp screaming, but she surprises me by gently putting her palm on Odessa's forehead. Her tight lips curl into a reassuring smile. "You'll be fine. Okay?"

Odessa bites her lip and nods.

Jo and Veronica carefully pull off Odessa's still-wet layers of clothes and strip her as best they can while I watch uselessly from my spot. But when they get to the bandage, every time they pull at the adhesive corner, she gasps painfully. Veronica's eyes go steely, and she heads to a cabinet along the wall. She comes back carrying a scalpel, the blade shining in the overhead surgical lights. I get involved now, clear that they'll need me, and hold Odessa by the shoulders. "This isn't going to hurt at all, Odessa. Don't worry," I tell her.

"I don't believe you," she says. "I believe *her*." Her being Veronica. "Do you have something for me to bite?" she whispers to me.

"What?"

"Like, to handle the pain?"

I glance at Veronica, who stares pointedly at the snow cap I had tossed on the floor when I first got inside. I go pick it up, ball it into a cylinder and place it between Odessa's open jaws. She looks at me gratefully, then slowly closes her eyes. Veronica starts cutting at the gauze wrapped around her stitches with expertise, almost surgeon-like. Odessa doesn't even make a noise. There's the wound, high up on her thigh, an angry red line of stitches, puffy and gross and flaked with silky pus.

And the smell. The wound smells like a garbage bag with a very meaty leftover in it. I purse my lips together so hard they hurt. Jo and I eye each other grimly. The bandage is a rusty red, superwet, and I can't bring myself to keep looking at it.

"I thought you said the virus was speeding up the healing," Jo demands of Veronica.

"It *is*, see?" She points to the stitches. They still look bad to me.

"Odessa must have had a serious infection, and that smell and that pus and that blood are all appropriately indicative of that. The virus helped the muscle regenerate, the wound close. It didn't kill the infection, though. It just sealed it up inside."

"But," I say, trying to understand, "that means she's still infected?"

"That's exactly what that means," Veronica says. "This *will* hurt, Odessa. But it won't take long."

And with a flick of her wrist she slices the wound open, splitting the stitches. Odessa's eyes roll back, and she screams through the cap's fabric. It's like Veronica popped a soft-boiled egg, and the sight of the pus oozing out of the newly reopened wound has me dizzy.

"Okay," Veronica says. "You can take the cap out of your mouth." She moves back to the eyedropper and takes it up and then shoos me to my perch on the bed.

"What's that? Some type of antibiotic? Will it even work in time?" Odessa asks, her voice shaky. She's breathing hard, and soon she coughs, a deep hacking cough, spraying blood on the ground.

Veronica eyes the blood; she appears fascinated, as if she's going to touch it, which I find creepy as hell. Then she turns back to Odessa and says, "This works fast enough, believe me." She uncaps the bottle carefully, like she's defusing a bomb or something, and then squeezes one drop onto the wound. Odessa grits her eyes closed, but then she opens them and looks up in disbelief.

"That's it?"

Veronica nods her head. "Open your mouth. You too, Mia." She glances back at the blood. "Jo, you too."

One drop each. There might only be a dozen drops left. It tastes like nothing, and I can't even tell it's in my mouth. Veronica looks satisfied, though. She stoppers the bottle and puts it away, then gets up and goes to one of the lockers and pulls out some scrubs. "Here," she says, tossing a pair to each of us, and a towel. "Get showered and changed and then we'll grab the boys."

"Wait," Jo says, wrapping the towel behind her neck. "You never answered Mia's questions. What do you do here? Can you tell us more about what's going on?"

Veronica looks around, and it's clear that she doesn't normally speak about this place freely. In the moment, she hesitates; I wonder if my dad gave her specific orders not to speak more to us about the Cave. I wonder if she'll get in trouble.

"I'm a biologist," she says finally. "But we all sort of do some of everything here."

"What does that mean?" Jo asks. "You work with animals and stuff?"

She smiles, her mind now elsewhere. "Yeah," she replies. "Lots of stuff. You girls shower up. I promised your dad I wouldn't say a thing."

The shower might have been the best thing that's ever happened to me. Afterward, I'm so exhausted, I want to just pass out. Odessa already has. I glance at myself in the mirror and see that my body looks like it's lost some weight in the last two harried days. My broad shoulders are still lined with muscle, but I can see my hips and ribs more than I used to. I suck in my gut and pat my belly. Jo joins me and does the same, and for a moment, I can see us back in our dorm, getting ready for school or a night out. Jo's body, of course, looks just as good as ever, despite the bad lighting. But it's the smile on her face that has me feeling good. This is what it's like to feel safe.

"You ready?" Veronica asks us, and then pops the door to the hallway and hollers to the boys like a drill sergeant. "Let's go, let's go, let's go!"

Dad enters first, his face etched in concern. In the light I can see him better. The bags under his eyes are literally purple. He smiles at me, kisses my head and then moves to check on Odessa.

"Nice outfit," says Brayden, his eyes taking me in. It's cold in here, and I self-consciously cover my breasts with my arms, even though scrubs aren't exactly revealing. He swipes his hair out of his eyes and grins.

"How's Odessa?" Jimmy asks, after seeing her asleep. He's almost comical, his enormous, ill-postured body filling the entire door frame.

"She's good, she's going to be fine," Veronica answers for me. Jimmy sits down next to Odessa on the floor and takes her hand. "Time for you all to get some rest."

"What are you, our RA?" Rob asks, taking off his boots and claiming a bed, so I don't think he's really arguing.

"And what about the virus?" Jo adds. "What's going on outside?"

"Hey, now," Dad says. "Nothing outside of these walls will hurt you, not in here."

"But we don't have—"

"It doesn't matter," Dad interrupts. "I know you're worried, that you've been chased by a lunatic. But with the back entrance blocked, there's no way he can get in here. He'd need a nuke to break down our doors." The others watch him like he's their own father. Jimmy closes his eyes and keeps listening, nodding all the while. "It's been a long day, you've just had a really trying experience. Why don't you take a shower and go to sleep, and we'll talk about this first thing tomorrow morning."

Rob's face is covered in grime, and I can see him eyeing the shower.

Just then, Brayden spots my foot and sucks in air. "I forgot about your toes!"

Dad's there in a heartbeat, lifting my leg. I have to balance by putting my hand on his shoulder as he crouches.

"What happened?" he asks, squeezing the skin lightly. It's tight, it still feels thick. I would tell them that Veronica already checked me over, but I'd rather have the attention.

"Mia swam underneath the ice at the lake to get us off campus. It was nuts." It's hard to reconcile the wild and inarticulate motions Jimmy makes with his fully adult body.

"You did?" Dad asks, incredulous. He runs his hands through his thick hair and tugs in disbelief. "*Under* the ice?"

I nod, suddenly shy. He looks over to Veronica, who's fiddling with her ponytail, her mind elsewhere. "She's good," she says reassuringly.

Dad stands up and shakes his head. "I can't tell whether I'm extremely proud of you or angry that you'd risk your life doing something so dangerous." Before I can get annoyed, he grins and rubs my head. "I guess I'll take proud . . . I thought I told you to get out of Westbrook, not do something crazy!"

"If you had just told me why, I might have listened." I'm semiserious and remember what Sutton said about him leaving me there. It makes me sad. "You abandoned me. I told you he was coming, and you left me."

The look of concern and shock on his face is enough to make me forgive him. "I'd never, Mia." He touches my nose with the tip of his thumb. "I thought you'd listen to me and go. I knew you were up for the challenge, and I knew I wouldn't be able to get there in time to help. You did well, honey. You did great." I swallow back a lump, not because I'm so glad he's praising me, but because I'm not sure I believe him anymore.

Dad takes a deep breath, claps his hands together and takes the eyedropper from Veronica. "Okay, you boys, line up and open your mouths." I guess that's the end of father/daughter time.

"Why?" Rob and Brayden ask in unison.

"Because this," Dad says, holding the eyedropper up in the light and swishing the liquid around, "is the antidote."

I frown, thinking of how Veronica dropped some on Odessa's wound. That's weird for an antidote; this isn't Neosporin. Rob's face bends in wonder. "So that's what you do here? You run an experimental pharma lab? That's why Sutton's trying to get in. For the antidote?"

The two adults exchange glances. "That's true," Dad says. "He needs this, and right this moment, boys, so do you."

"But what is it?" Brayden asks, his voice quiet. He's watching my father like a hawk.

Dad shakes his head. "Not right now. After you get some rest, okay?" We're quiet, and Dad looks at me. "Okay, Mia?"

"Okay, Dad," I respond automatically, feeling somehow like I was just chastised and hating it.

They take the drops without further complaint, and Jimmy soon lies on the floor near Odessa's feet. Rob pulls off his shirt, indifferent to the fact that we are here, and walks into the shower. It has a curtain, but none of us are looking. I can't help but notice that Brayden's swollen lip has gone back to normal. He keeps touching it, then looking at his fingers, searching for blood.

"Want me to kick you in the face again?" I say.

He smiles. "No, actually. I'd rather not."

Brayden takes the bed below me, atop an extra blanket we took from one of the lockers. I can hear him tossing and turning, even before Dad kisses me on the head and goes to the door.

"We're going to lock this, but just so you don't get lost, okay?"

"What time is it, Dad?"

He checks his watch by the light of the hallway. "Four thirty P.M. on Saturday."

"I haven't slept in two days," Jo says wearily into the dark.

"Well, get some sleep now, okay?" Dad says.

No one answers. Either they're asleep or they don't believe him that us getting "lost" is the biggest of his concerns.

His shadow remains in the doorway, his eyes sweeping across the room. "I'm glad you're safe," he says to us, and then closes the door. I can hear the muted sound of him punching the code and the lock clicking into place.

Rob's out of the shower and sneaks through the dark onto the top bunk of Jo's bed, whispering "I love you so much" to his mattress.

Brayden holds his hand up and takes mine. I peer over the bed. "Don't keep stuff like your foot secret again, okay? That's dangerous." His voice is soft, and it seems to slip from his mouth.

I nod a few times, but don't say a thing. I don't want anyone to wake up. I want to have this moment for myself. Staring over the side of the bed, at his disheveled hair and his face peeking over the blankets, at his worried smile, I find myself moving before I can think about what I'm doing. The bed creaks as I climb down and Brayden opens his blanket and lays me comfortably on his chest. He covers us both, and we lie there, our chests rising and lowering together, the heat of our little cocoon so acute that I begin to sweat immediately. I have never lain on a boy's chest before. I can feel his rib cage and the softness of his belly. I can feel the muscles in his arms as he holds me, and most of all, I feel safe. Small and safe.

I'm so tired that I can feel myself fading even as I fight, wanting equally to press myself harder against his body and to curl up and sleep.

"I want you to be safe, Mia."

I want to tell him that that's exactly how I feel right now, but I don't. He rubs his hand gently along the ridge of my brow, down my chin. He kisses me; his lips are soft and gentle and don't ever leave mine.

16

MY EARS WAKE ME, REGISTERING THE DOOR'S ECHOING *pop*. Then the now-familiar *buzz* of the overhead lights. For a moment I panic, imagining everyone seeing Brayden and me tucked together on his bed, but I'm back on the top bunk. I don't know how I got here. I don't remember leaving him. It's hard to tell the time when you wake in the same sunless place; I'm not sure I want to ask. My body feels so heavy and poorly rested that I don't know whether I managed to get eight hours or three. After two days of being shot at and chased around, cold, wet and scared, I'm not even sure sixteen hours of sleep would have helped much anyway.

At least everyone else seems to be in rough shape too. Rob's standing over the sink, gargling water, his shoulders slumped and elbows resting against the metal bowl. If I didn't know better, I'd say it looks like he's about to puke. Jimmy's still sleeping, his mouth half open and his left arm tossed over his head. Jo's face is red, and she's trying to clear the grit from her eyes. Brayden sits thoughtfully against the wall, his knees drawn in, a pile of sheets folded next to him. He smiles, though it's a bit thin, not the type of greeting I was expecting after last night. Looks like he's been up for hours, ready to go. Why isn't he as tired as I am? I mean, it's not like I'm out of shape. I'm only a nationally ranked swimmer.

Dad pokes his head in, eyes closed, and calls, "Everybody decent?"

I'm embarrassed as only a daughter can be, but no one else answers either. We just sort of sit there and look at his long, stubbly face. Finally, he opens his eyes and enters the room. He's wearing a one-piece like Veronica had on yesterday, his body shapeless. He seems rested compared to us, what with his combed hair and bouncing feet. "Okay, everyone. Let's get moving. Breakfast is ready, and we've got a lot to do today."

Jimmy's awake now, but I can see his eyelids drooping closed. His cheeks are sallow against his dark eyes and beard, and it seems like he could use the sleep. I'd like nothing more than to roll over myself, but this is my dad here, and ever the dutiful daughter, I lug my feet off the bed and hop down onto the floor, which is so cold that I squeal. Which means I felt something. Which means I'm not hallucinating when I see my perfectly healthy feet.

"Dad!"

He's at my side, looking scared, his eyes roaming my face for signs of injury or hurt. "What is it?"

"My feet!"

"Whoa," Rob says, looking over Dad's shoulder.

Dad takes a foot and prods the skin, which I have the pleasure of feeling and seeing is as normal as it's ever been. A giddy, almost giggly pleasure. "How does it feel?" he asks.

"Fine," I say. "But how can my feet be healed already?"

The look in his eye tells me that it isn't strange at all.

Everyone's standing near me now, checking out my feet. Brayden's

236

smiling, and I notice that something's different. His lips are normal. There is no swelling anymore from where I kicked him in the face. They are pale and perfect and fade into his skin just like they did at Odessa's party.

Suddenly Jimmy seems to remember Odessa, because he hurries over to her side. His energy is infectious, and we all follow him, curious to know how she's doing.

"Is she okay?" he asks, speaking to no one and everyone. Odessa's waking up now, alarmed at the noise. Jimmy shushes her and puts a hand to her head.

"What's going on?" she asks.

"Just checking on the progress," Dad says, inspecting her wound. The skin is almost seamless, the red nearly gone, and the wound doesn't smell at all. "Looking good, looking good."

"How does a drop of an antidote to a virus heal a gunshot wound?" Brayden asks.

"And frostbite?" Rob adds.

Dad ignores them. This is a tactic he's used for years whenever I've wanted to know anything secret, and I almost say that out loud. The two boys share a glance of frustration. Odessa's dazed, but otherwise seems fine. Her newly aged face is angular and proper, and her freckles seem to have faded to the background behind her brilliant blue eyes. Suddenly, the obvious becomes clear.

"The virus is gone," I mutter, but the others hear.

"What do you mean?" Jo asks.

"Yeah," Odessa says from her perch on the cot. "Who made you a doctor?"

Dad watches me with interest.

"We slept for what seemed like hours, and the virus moves much faster than that. Jimmy still looks thirty. So does Odessa. They haven't aged, they haven't died—therefore they must be fine."

"Really?" Odessa asks, taking all the good news in at once. "I'm not going to get all wrinkly and shriveled?"

I glance at Jo, but she truly seems to be focused on the good news and not the memory of her father. She's smiling, and she rubs Odessa's arm. Her fingernails still have specks of the purple nail polish I applied for her days ago.

Rob pulls his glasses from his face and begins to clean them. He speaks grimly. "This is awesome, of course, so, that's great. But, Mr. Kish, you can't think we're dumb enough to believe you just gave us something like penicillin. Not after Mia's foot."

Of course he wouldn't. I'm allergic to penicillin.

Dad's quiet for a moment. He rubs the ridge of his thick nose, thinking about how best to respond. He looks at me, then at Odessa's wound. "I promise this will all be easier if we explain naturally. Just . . . yes, you're right. There's something special about that liquid. That's why we need to hurry, so we can show you firsthand. It's an immunization to the virus."

"And frostbite?" Rob presses.

"Yes, Rob. It cures many things."

And suddenly I get a glimpse of what's so important about the work my dad does in the Cave.

"So we're not sick anymore?" Odessa asks.

Dad shakes his head.

"But we are stuck this age?"

He nods, his brow furrowed apologetically. Rob whistles low.

There's a tense pause, and we all watch Odessa think it through. I can actually tell that she's chewing the inside of her cheek.

"Well, all right, then," she finally says. "At least I can get into bars now."

Jimmy scoops Odessa up in his arms. She laughs and says, "I never thought I'd be glad to be thirty." Jo's happy too, and she jokingly steps on my once-dead toes.

I'm curious and proud and fascinated. Is my dad a chemist, then? Runs a private section of a big pharma corporation? Is he working on a cancer cure or what? It must be top secret, like he's sworn against telling me anything. Maybe he had to sign a confidentiality agreement. This is way better than microchips. And the reason for Sutton's interest in the place is beginning to crystallize as well. If there's a liquid that cures everything from the plague to frostbite, the demand for it would be beyond enormous.

"Leave your things here," Dad says, breaking up the fun. "There should be slippers in the lockers. Put those on and follow me."

I find myself hurrying, eager to know what's next, what more I can learn about my dad. I kind of want the private tour, but this isn't really the place to be whining about father/daughter time.

We're soon back in the hallway, wandering empty halls with many doors, and something occurs to me. "Where is everyone?" I ask.

"Good question," Jimmy mutters. "Feels like *The Twilight Zone.*"

"When the facility was built," Dad answers, not even breaking his stride, "we prepped for growth. It's extraordinarily inconvenient and expensive to expand quickly underground, so we built for the future."

"So how many people work here?" I ask.

For some reason this is too much for Rob. "He never told you?" he asks angrily.

"Well, he did." I pause, speaking carefully. Dad makes a sour face, pulling his stubble tight across his jawline. I feel like I'm betraying him. "But now I don't know if he was telling the truth." I look right at Dad. "Were you?"

"Not really, no." His brown eyes flash at the challenge, his eyebrows bend in annoyance.

"Then how many?" Jo asks. We're all on one another's heels, wanting and needing to know more.

Dad doesn't say anything for a moment, and his sturdy work boots echo through the corridor. He stops at a double door, one without a keypad, and pushes the doors inward. "Come meet the employees of Fenton Electronics."

There are three long tables, which I take to be more room for expansion because there are only two adults sitting at them, including Veronica. The room feels so immense, I can imagine that this place was designed as a hidden bunker for the president or something. We all file in, and there's an awkward moment as the two adults stand and march across the room toward us.

"Three," I say, almost in disbelief.

"No way," Brayden says, fiddling with the spot where his bracelet used to be. "There has to be someone manning the controls, right?

Dad grunts. "I wish that were the case. Only three, at the moment. We were supposed to have six, but the circumstances have changed of late."

"But what if Sutton tries to get in?" Rob asks, adjusting his glasses.

"He's already trying," Dad replies, his voice less carefree than last night. "Our monitors show men attempting to puncture the outer door with high-density drills. We already had to manually disable our alarms, or the sheriff would have showed up."

"Why is that a bad thing?" Jo asks.

"Because," Brayden answers before my dad can, "Sutton would have no choice but to capture the sheriff and then threaten the town too." What, did he pipe up just to impress Dad? Whatever the case, it seems to be working, as Dad nods approvingly. Sir, I'll have your daughter back by eleven, if we ever get out of here.

"I still don't get it," Jo persists, and she tugs at her ponytail in annoyance. "That seems like a good thing. More people coming to help us."

"Not if it means the outbreak spreads beyond Westbrook and his soldiers," Dad says. "There is literally nothing the local police could do quickly enough to help us out. These are just automatic alarms. We can't explain what's going on here, we can't warn them, so if we hit the alarm, we're just sentencing the sheriff and his deputies to death." He checks his watch. "I'd say we have seven to ten hours before Sutton's engineers can burrow into the rock. Maybe double that before he can breach both doors with the fancy gadgets he has." He seems to be talking to himself now. "Hopefully that's long enough."

By now, Veronica and a very tall man have reached us. He seems familiar in a way that Veronica wasn't. He's got a buzz cut; his hair's already gray, though he doesn't look older than Dad. His face is tan and long, and he's wearing what looks like a flight suit.

"I've seen you before," I say, trying to catch the fleeting memory. The man smiles, pleased at my recall, his teeth stained by coffee or cigarettes.

"I'm Chuck. I was your doctor after the well. I set your bones and stitched you up."

I look to my dad, and he nods in confirmation.

"But why haven't we seen you around town?" Odessa asks. I agree with her. This doesn't make any sense.

"I was working here," Chuck says, "and this is where I am most of the time. I have a house, down on Breakers Lane, but I don't really leave it except to buy food. Otherwise, I live in Denver." Odessa shrugs, already bored, and he notices. His face shifts immediately, as if slighted and incredibly annoyed. "What, you think you kids pay attention to who's in the supermarket with you?"

"I guess not," Odessa replies, and I have to stifle a laugh because I can't really see her doing much household shopping.

Suddenly, as if out of nowhere, I'm hit with a waft of the smell of eggs, and it makes me almost dizzy with hunger. We slept until Sunday morning. Is must be my birthday! Weird, this isn't how I expected to spend it. We take the long walk to the tables and have a seat, and soon enough Veronica and Chuck are back from behind a swinging door with heaping trays in their hands. There's juice and water at the table, pitchers and glasses. I'm in heaven.

I try to pace myself. Jimmy has no such qualms; he uses the big spoon to pull a good quarter of the eggs onto his plate. At first I thought they were for Odessa, but she's already managed to fill her plate on her own just fine.

It's almost a sideshow at first. The adults arrange themselves across the table from us, like a panel of professors or something, sipping their steaming coffees and watching us closely. Sitting there, my body shifts to normalcy through egg yolk. It's strange to see the people Dad works with. Chuck's the hardest to read; he keeps checking his watch and swirling his coffee like you would a glass of wine. But it's Veronica I'm drawn to anyway. She's tough, and I like that, but she also smiles when she catches me looking, and I feel a genuine warmth for her. I guess I was wrong yesterday about her being so stiff and cold. I wonder if she's one of Dad's close friends. Dad doesn't really take his eyes off me, as if my life depends on each bite I take. It's getting kind of annoying. Even their silence is. I know they're anxious and ready to go. Though I wish I knew more about what that means. I wonder, fleetingly, if once we're out of here, I'll ever be able to take anything he says at face value again.

My stomach almost hurts from the food.

"Good, good eggs," Jimmy says, from a couple seats down. "You guys bring 'em in, or are they powdered?" Chuck frowns, offended at Jimmy's suggestion, and the others chuckle. I watch them with my chin close to the plate, food dangling from a metal fork.

"Chuck never gets any compliments from us," Dad explains. "But, then again, I'm not sure he deserves them." We all stare at Chuck, who's looking pleased with himself, a doctor and a chef.

"Whatever, Kish. If you guys ever thanked me for meals, you might get as good as this."

"Duly noted."

They're kids, I think. Or maybe they've been trapped in a cave for almost seventy-two hours. Heck, who knows how long they've been here.

"So, guys." Veronica leans forward, studying us all. She seems the most businesslike of them all, even my dad. Her eyebrows are thin and carefully tended, and she's wearing pretty hefty diamond studs, probably her default keep-the-holes-open pair. She's not always here, I think—I can see her in a ballroom; her face is regal enough. Or behind a podium. "You fled Westbrook on Friday, and it's early Sunday now. We have an inkling about what's been going on out there during that time, but why don't you tell us in your own words, okay?"

"But that's not fair," Rob complains. "You know all the answers and haven't told us anything."

Veronica pats Rob's hand, a gesture I think would normally piss him off, but for some reason, he seems mollified. He crosses his arms over his chest and waits.

"The thing is," Chuck says, "we *do* have answers, but we'll have more when we know all the facts. Like detectives." I don't like that he condescends to us. Odessa snorts from behind her mound of eggs. "And with that crazy man trying to get in here, we need more facts fast. So who's going to tell the tale?"

We exchange looks. They expect me to answer, I'm the bridge here. But that doesn't seem fair, and I look to Jo for help. Jo's mouth is set, and I realize that things have changed since Westbrook, when I'd always wait for her to take the lead. Now she's waiting for me. They all are.

I run my tongue back and forth on my teeth, trying to get the taste of the tale out of my mouth. The adults appear shaken; my dad especially so when I talked about Wilkins's death, even though that's old news. He must have felt the same way about Wilkins as I did.

"Jo, sweetie," Veronica finally says. "Can you tell us a little more about your father's death? Are you up for that?" Her voice is firm, but slow, like she's carefully controlling each word, trying to be sensitive. While I was storytelling she pulled her hair out of the bun and ran her fingers through it, like an involuntary habit. Now she's tied it back up, all business.

Jo takes a deep, rattling breath. "Later that first night. One of the kids who tried to escape told us about the dead teachers, and we investigated. That's how we found Dad." Her voice catches, and I rub her back, which hunches in on itself. "He was alive, but died right there. He got really old and died."

Chuck leans forward. "I just want to be clear for the sake of certainty—I'm not trying to rub salt into the wound. Did your father have a long beard, wrinkles and rheumy eyes?"

"Chuck!" Veronica barks. He backs into his seat like a chastened dog. Everyone else gets some of the same feeling, ducking their head down to their plates. I grab Jo's hand under the table. No one speaks, until Veronica looks at Jo and says softly, "I'm sorry—we're scientists. It's in our nature to be thorough."

Jo, though, doesn't look like she's up to speaking anymore. Her lower lip, pale without lipstick, quivers uncontrollably. She's having this crazy seesaw life right now. I realize she's been able to put her grief aside, only now to be brought right back to the moment

"He's right," I say, taking up Jo's slack. "Down to the detail. It was like everyone turned ninety in a few hours."

"For an adult male in his fifties, fourteen hours," corrects Chuck. Jo's hand squeezes mine to the point of pain, but I'm not going to pull away.

"What did you say?" Brayden pipes up in disbelief.

"Yeah, fourteen hours, based on what we can extrapolate from our live-specimen research. That's how long it takes for someone that far into their life span to age to death. Though there are bound to be some anomalies to that estimate."

"A few of you didn't age at all," Dad says, smiling brightly. "Which means you hadn't yet contracted the virus."

"Well, aren't we lucky," I reply, feeling annoyed at both of them for being so insensitive to Jo. We don't need statistics right now. We need a plan.

Dad's face glooms up, and he squints at me, gauging how to respond. When he squints like that, he looks like he's blind, and the wrinkles at the corners of his eyes web all the way to his hairline.

Chuck, though, has taken offense at my snide remark. "You *should* feel lucky, missy. Your friends wouldn't have made it until morning." There's a blankness to his features now that seems in direct contradiction to the food-bearing kindness we saw before, and I get the feeling that this is the real Chuck.

I don't like the real Chuck.

"You shouldn't act like you're superior here," I say quietly, surprised at my own vehemence. "You know details about the virus. You have an antidote!" I look at my father, ignore the sadness that's creeping onto his face. "I was right all along. *You* made it here. *You killed all those people.*"

"No, honey, I promise—"

But I don't care, I'm too angry, and I storm on. "Not just all those people. You killed Jo's DAD! You endangered the school and the town. And now the virus is spreading. It's even killing soldiers in hazmat suits. What does it matter if you have the antidote if you're sitting on your asses in a cave?"

Jo swallows hard at my comment. The others look shocked too, but in a good way. I feel strong, my breath heaving, like I'm on the block about to dive deep into the water, except this time it's clear I've already jumped. The adults eye each other, genuinely surprised. Veronica almost gets up to leave, as if she now has something dreadfully important to take care of.

"Sit down!" I scream. Veronica inches herself back to her chair. "You're not going anywhere. No one is until you explain yourselves!" I see the others watching me with approval. Brayden has a grin on his face, and I think he's proud of me. My heart beats so fast that I'm almost dizzy.

"Dad," I say, my voice more even. He looks chastised. So does Veronica. But not Chuck. Little lab rats. "What did you do? What is this place?"

"What's the Map Room?"

Dad pauses; so do I. Everyone turns to Brayden, who's wearing a curious smile, looking at my father. Chuck and Veronica grow perfectly still, as if maybe the question won't see them and will pass them by.

"Where did you hear that?" Dad asks, his voice dangerous. He leans forward on his chair, his eyes flashing. I can't help but wonder the same thing.

"When I was sneaking through Furbish," Brayden says, "when I was in a secret tunnel in the wall, I heard a soldier say, 'They aren't as important as the Map Room.' I assume he was talking about something you have here. Something they want. What's the Map Room?"

It's so obvious from their reactions that the adults know what he's talking about, enough so that Odessa blurts out, "Yeah, what's the Map Room?" I want to know as well, but I also want other answers, not some new mystery. Including the one where Brayden overheard information at Furbish and why he didn't tell us about it.

The adults eye each other; apparently their tempers are in check. Dad raises his eyebrows and doesn't say anything until Chuck and Veronica give their grudging nods.

"Okay, kids. You're right. We owe you a full explanation. But in order to do so, no more arguments and interruptions. You need to understand what's going on to be of any good help to us and to Fenton, but time is short. Let's go see the Map Room."

We all file out of the cafeteria, Veronica and Chuck taking the rear as if we might run off or something. The hallways all look the same, and I'm soon lost. At first the halls are small, big enough for two people to walk side by side, but suddenly they widen, becoming large enough to drive a car through. I haven't seen a door in a while, but then I see two sets, directly across from each other. We approach the one on the right, which looks more similar to the bank vault of the Cave's rear entrance than the submarine hatch of the aqueduct. Dad uses a key card on this door, the first I've seen, swiping it against a magnetic detector and then entering a number of digits.

"Ten numbers," Rob whispers behind me. I throw him a look.

The crank of gears within the door is loud. It opens with a *hiss* and swings heavily toward us, its innards reminding me of the inside of a gigantic clock; this is a serious door. I think that the keypad, even with ten digits, feels inadequate for a door like this. There should be voice recognition, a thumb pad, and two separate keyholes that must be turned by two separate keys at the same time.

As soon as Dad crosses the threshold of the room, lights switch on with an audible *clunk*, the way they would at a sports stadium, the way they do at Westbrook's football field. We're all gathered tight around the entrance, even the other adults, and for a moment, we just stare. I literally cannot connect this place, this room, with my dad, with Veronica or Chuck, with anything but silly movies about the CIA or buried vault rooms. They should make more movies about the kids of superspies so I can know how I'm supposed to be feeling.

Considering the virus, I expected a room with petri dishes and hazmat suits hanging from the wall. But this is something different. There's almost nothing here. Just a dim, smooth-domed room, like an Imax theater or a planetarium. Ten yards in, directly in front of us, stand two black computer consoles on podiums facing a large flat chunk of rock, which is suspended right in the center of the room by wires hanging from the curved ceiling.

The large chunk is rectangular and bigger than Rob's forty-four-inch Samsung. Small, pleasant lights from the dome illuminate the surface of the rock, which is covered with ancient cave drawings, what must be a map. This is the Map Room, after all.

We've all taken world history at Westbrook. We've all seen images of the cave drawings around the world, art of the early civilizations in the hilly Dordogne region of France or the Anasazi in the dry rocks of the Southwestern United States. Those are bare walls with pigment etched in, rough drawings, and our ancient ancestors' rough-minded, rough-handed, doing the best they can. We were all suitably impressed, but think of them as lesser humans, as the original beta male.

This, though . . . this is something different.

"Well," Chuck says from behind us, not without some reservation. He's still unsure whether we should be here. "Go have a look."

We move forward, and I take Brayden's hand, almost involuntarily. He winks at me. We stand in the dark and look at the paintings together. This isn't about crude sticks. There are no red deer figures and buffalo, no spear drawings and fire pits. This is intricate, advanced. Similar to the sophistication of hieroglyphics, except clearly not the Egyptian style we all know and love, with large painted god-eyeballs and sideways facing bird- or dog-headed men.

There's also a depth here, a sense of a third dimension that's missing until the past five hundred years in art history. Trees are vibrant, fish and water glisten. There are carefully etched pathways and images of tall, imposing, muscular humanlike figures. There's a golden tower and a cascading fountain, and when I move the slightest bit, it all seems to shimmer and glow, like it's a hologram or something.

"It's amazing," Rob says, his voice given to awe. He tugs at his sideburns.

"It's beautiful," Odessa adds. For some reason, I'm surprised. Maybe the virus has left her more sensitive.

"What is this?" I ask.

"The map, Baby," Jimmy replies matter-of-factly.

I let that go. So does my dad. "But where did it come from?"

"About a half mile down, actually, in a hole three times this size," says my dad. Veronica shoots him a look, but he just shrugs.

"What's it a map of?" asks Brayden, who's really taking the map in. His eyes roam all over the place, and the scar on his chin is as white as I've seen. I squeeze his hand, and he returns the squeeze, but doesn't look over at me.

"We're not really sure." Dad pauses. "Run analysis B-two," he commands, speaking into the air, and immediately a small red dot appears in the center of the map. It looks like a laser pointer. The dot expands into a rectangle, perfectly covering the map, creating the lines of a grid that crisscrosses the surface. Three rows down, six images per row, each image in a contained red laser square. The computer seems to run for a moment and then beeps. The grid on the map disappears like nothing has happened, but suddenly the bare walls around the room are splashed with magnified images of the map, close-ups of individual grid pieces and drawings.

"Chuck," my dad says over his shoulder, "want to take this one?"

Chuck seems less confident than he did back in the cafeteria. He's bent, his posture bad, and he appears cold and distant. I remember the coffee stains on his teeth. The offhand tone he took with Jo. I think I can safely say he's not my favorite person here.

"Well," he begins with the air of a professor, "we think this map is a primer. The first note." He points to the wall behind him, which now holds a blown-up version of the map. "Do you see the bottom-right image on the map? The last image? It's pretty complicated. We assigned each image on the map a number, and that one is eighteen. Enhance image eighteen," he calls into the air, and instantly we zoom in on the corner drawing. I get this weird sense of déjà vu, though, because suddenly we're staring at the entire map again. "You see?" Chuck says, his voice triumphant. "The final image on the map is a miniaturized repetition of the *entire map*. And, using our advanced imaging, we can see that somehow whoever painted this made *another* replica on that map, and so on. Enhance image analysis B-two," he says. We zoom again, and now I'm dizzy, but we're still staring at the entire map.

"I'm going to throw up," says Jimmy.

"Please don't," Veronica replies.

"This goes on forever?" Brayden asks. "How is that possible?"

"I don't know." Chuck sounds wistful.

Rob's having a field day. He bends and stares at the real rock so closely that he almost falls over. The replica is big and on the wall, but he wants to see it in real life. He pulls out his clunky OtterBox and snaps a picture, and I see Chuck open his mouth to protest, but my dad stays him with a hand motion.

"Wow," Rob shouts, pointing at the real map. "You can make out three of them right here."

Veronica nods. "That's right. There are seventeen replica-maps that we can find with our electron microscope. Want to know the strangest thing?"

"That each progressively smaller map is a bit different?" Brayden offers.

Veronica looks alarmed. Dad and Chuck murmur to each other like concerned teachers. "How did you know that?"

Brayden points to the map on the wall. "That moon in the middle left, what number is it assigned?"

"Twelve," she replies cautiously.

"Enhance image B-twelve," Brayden says loudly, and we all stare at him as if he's cracked some kind of crazy code. "See, moon twelve, in the original map, is full. Moon B-twelve is waxing. The moon in map C-twelve is probably a gibbous waxing. It's an infinite but changing map."

"Yeah, that's right," Veronica says, clearly impressed, as am I, at his astronomy knowledge. "The moons are different. What we consider our only clue."

"Clue to what?" I ask.

Veronica looks to my father, and it has become increasingly obvious that my dad runs the show here. He's rubbing his thumbs across the tips of his long fingernails. An odd habit of his.

"We're not completely sure. But we do think the fact that the map has an image of itself is an indication of where to start. How to read it."

I think that's a good thing, an internalized Rosetta Stone. Everyone's all hung up on the mini maps, but I keep finding myself drifting to some of the other incredible images there. There's a huge golden gate, its pointed rails swirling with intricate filigree that catches my eye, and right next to it, as if to counterbalance the shining gold, is a simple black hole. Or, rather, not a hole—it's just a big circle of black. Around the edge is a ring of light, like a solar eclipse. I bet it *is* a solar eclipse, considering everything I've been taught about ancient calendars. The Mayans were all about sundials, right? Next to the eclipse is an upside-down man, his skin milky white and his eyes closed in slits. The eclipse is so dark, the circle so perfectly round. It feels almost familiar. How could a human hand do that? Who were these people?

"But," says Jimmy in a tone that might mean he has been confused this whole time, "who made this? Indians?"

Dad shakes his head. "Maybe, but if so they'd predate the earliest known Native Americans by tens of thousands of years. The earliest known cave paintings anywhere, actually. We've carbon-dated the paint: a pretty advanced combination of plant pigmentation and animal-fat rendering. Some of the compounds we can't even trace."

Veronica speaks up here, her voice getting excited, even though I'm sure she's seen this room hundreds or thousands of times. "Which has us conjecturing that perhaps the paint was made of now-extinct animals, like ancestors of the mammoth or giant sloths that used to roam North America."

"But what does it mean?" Jo asks, and there's a hint of desperation in her voice. "What does this have to do with the virus, with that crazy guy and the army he has with him, who want to get in here? Is it a treasure map? Is that all you guys do, hang out here trying to figure out the map?"

My dad is a pirate. He's Blackbeard, hidden here in this incredibly vast network of caves, keeping his treasure map safe from the world. Was my mom some passerby he knocked up on the way?

I don't think I have the mental energy to even open that can of worms. My dad may be a liar, but he's never been anything but a good father. All this has to be for a reason. What better reason for a mysterious cave than a mysterious map?

Veronica says, "Greg, you've let them in the Cave, you've shown them the map—just go ahead and tell them everything."

"You okay with that, Chuck?" The tall man doesn't really reply, not voting against, but certainly not voting for. He doesn't even look at Dad, just bends his neck one way until it pops. "All right, then. Follow me."

We walk to the other side of the domed room, behind the rock, where there are eight stadium-style chairs, each with its own work-station and console. As soon as we all pass the stone, it begins to swivel and follow us. Dad wipes a sheen of sweat off his face and then claps his hands once, which reverberates loudly in the room.

"Pick a chair and take a seat. And yes, we sometimes watch movies in here."

We all shuttle into chairs, and by the time we do, the map locks into place, facing us. In front of me is a console, keyboard and a dozen other buttons and readings. I immediately look at Rob, whose fingers are lying gently on the board in front of him like a piano player's at rest.

"Don't mess with it," I mouth to him, and he pulls his hands back guiltily and sets them in his lap.

"Okay, so, the map is only one part of the puzzle. The virus is another, and though it has been causing a great deal of devastation, it is, in fact, just a small part of what's going on here. There's a reason we built a multimillion-dollar facility here in Fenton, a reason we have the money to do that and a reason Blake Sutton has raised an army to break in."

He turns to the ceiling and calls out again, "Initiate file: history." I wonder fleetingly if he built all this, or at least designed it. The whole setup is superimpressive, and it reminds me of a giant Siri.

Instantly, four images fill the entire wall above our head. One shows a three-dimensional view of a vast tunnel system under the mountain, like a giant ant farm. Wow, they've really put some work into this place. We've barely scratched the surface.

The other three images are old and grainy. In the first image, we're looking at a mountainside. The sun is out, trees are bent and black, as if there had just been a forest fire not a month back, and there's a small hole in the cliff face, barely visible. It looks no different from any other hole you might see while hiking. Something to stay clear of, to imagine a home for a fox or a nest of snakes.

The second image is of my dad's high school class. The very same one that's in the administration building back at Westbrook. The very same one Sutton was looking at that day he interviewed me. The students are standing in front of Dylan, where all class pictures are taken. I get chills, picking my dad out of the crowd. His hair is longer, caught in a breeze; his smile is hesitant. Why are they showing us this?

The final image is a repeat of the hole in the cliff, with the opening much magnified, taking up the majority of the picture. There's nothing small about this cave. It is a maw, a gaping mouth, and the darkness appears endless, deep, forever.

I shiver. It looks familiar.

17

THE STORY, PART I

MR. AVERY'S "EXPLORATION" CLASS HAD A CAP OF TEN students and, as an elective, was only offered every two years. But even that cap was misleading, as he'd only allow in the students he thought worthy, those he had handpicked from his American History I course. Greg Kish's year, there were only six.

Greg had been looking forward to the class for most of his Westbrook life. Avery was the type of teacher most students hated, but mainly because he was demanding and exacting, assigned way more homework than most, only offered two As in his entire Early American History class and tended to ignore the fact that most students came from the upper echelon of the world's elite. In fact, until Greg's year, there were no scholarships offered to anyone of median or lesser means. And, according to his mother, he was the first townie boy ever accepted to Westbrook. Maybe it was politics: the town got tired of this bastion of elitism. Maybe Greg Kish deserved it; he did, after all, spend his summers at the Gifted Future Students Program of the Colorado School of Minds. Whatever the case, Greg was different, noticeable and worked nonstop to make up for his financial inadequacies. He received one of the two As in Avery's EAH class. And then, at the beginning of his senior year, he received a handwritten note inviting him to take part in Exploration 101, Avery's famous hands-on class about the local American histories.

Greg lived at home and commuted to school. Before he was accepted into Westbrook, his life consisted of homework and full-day Atari sessions with his neighbor, Terry Wilkins. Once attending the prestigious prep school, his routine remained remarkably similar. Greg knew a few of his new classmates, but since he was basically useless on the sports field, plus a nerd and a half *and* a townie, none became close. He was a failed experiment in the eyes of the students, a foreigner almost—and Greg couldn't help but agree. He hadn't thought there'd be *that* much difference, but these kids knew languages, knew wealth, knew way more *things* about the world because they'd been traveling since they were toddlers and had been trained by nannies since they were swaddled. On the other hand, to the staff, Greg Kish was exemplary. He was polite; his grades were impeccable; his contributions to the brand-new computer science lab, with its freshly constructed supercomputer, actually paid for his tuition many times over. To put it simply, Greg didn't really have any fun at Westbrook, and he longed for the day he'd be at a normal place. He applied to state schools, read books and waited for his next Avery class.

Every Friday—and yes, a Friday class for a senior was usually considered a drag—Avery would demand his students gather at the crack of dawn, and they'd hop into his rented white van and scour the countryside for hands-on history. He took them panning for gold, and no one but Alex Stedman found a flake, but no one cared. Took them on a weekend hike up Pike's Peak. On a replica raft down the Gunnison River. All in the name of exploration and education about early settler life. They were a rougher group than most at Westbrook, and their class often slipped over into the weekend, into tents and hikes and waterfalls.

It was here that Greg Kish made his first friends. Outside of the school's walls, barriers could be let down and social norms bent. The small group seemed at least willing to interact with a townie. Because out in the wild, with Avery's gruff companionship, things *were* different. Make no mistake: as soon as they hit campus, the boys and girls would separate, shower and head out to Aspen for the remainder of the weekend. But you can't ignore a person's hand when he's helping you up a steep incline, regardless of whose hand it is.

Avery's most famous "lesson" in the Exploration class was the daylong spelunking session. And that day was finally here! It was perhaps the very reason his class became famous, because eight years ago, they had stumbled on some old Anasazi cave drawings and were written up in papers around the world; there was even a photo spread in *National Geographic*. Avery hadn't found any more cave drawings, of course. Once-in-a-lifetime finds happen that way. But the idea, the *potential* of such a find, kept Greg's imagination burning throughout the semester.

Rumor had it, though, that in the past few classes, Avery had become reluctant to delve into any new locations. Maybe he was resting on his laurels. Maybe his famously rotund belly wouldn't fit through tiny nooks and crevices. Apparently, Avery started his spelunking day at the very cave of his famous discovery, now a small local museum. Students would re-create his famous hike; a relatively safe and adventureless affair, with no sight of actual exploration involved. Unless you counted the occasional make-out session. Not that Kish was making out with anyone. Though he certainly wanted to. In fact, the girls' dorm, separated from the main campus, was like a den of desire for Greg. No *particular* girl stole his heart. For someone like Greg, they were all unattainable and therefore alluring in some way: Wendy Chandler or Heather Fain, Tammy Henderson or Alexis Hanes (yes, the underwear). He'd walk past their dorms on the trudge into campus and often see boys sneaking out, smoking cigarettes, their girls tossing out the occasional forgotten rucksack.

The morning of the spelunk, Greg had spotted Veronica Little on his way to class. She wore only a black, lacy bra and was halfway out her window kissing Tripp Berry III. Greg felt that he was intruding, that he shouldn't be seen, so he froze, right by the wall, trying to blend in. Tripp, the kind of guy who wouldn't like to see Greg peeping at his girlfriend, was oblivious, and after grabbing a handful of Veronica's breast he took off, class jacket over his shoulder, hair perfectly gelled into place, whistling the Westbrook fight song. Veronica stared after him contentedly and was beginning to pull herself back into the window when she noticed Greg.

Kish shrank in embarrassment, but Veronica didn't seem to care. The class had been ongoing for a few months, and Veronica had been talking about today's trip for weeks. She was as obsessed as he was.

"Greg, hi! You think we'll actually get to see some good caves today?"

He inched forward, keeping his eyes on her face. "I don't know. Who can tell what type of mood Avery will be in."

Her smile turned into a frown. "But that's half the reason I took his crazy class."

"Maybe we can just ask him to take us somewhere new."

She laughed and actually shook her breasts at him in mock seduction. "I *have* been known to ask nicely!"

Greg didn't know what that meant, but he blushed anyway. He waved off Veronica, telling her he'd see her at the parking lot, and hurried on. He didn't have a thing for her. Not really. She was just the only person who would talk to him outside of class.

He was there first, of course. And when Veronica did arrive (late, and in the midst of Avery's morning pep talk), she was wearing Tripp's plaid flannel shirt.

Veronica nudged him with her elbow. "Hey, no biggie, right? You won't tell anyone about Tripp?" The ritual of sneaking boys into the dorm was well practiced, but that didn't mean you couldn't get in trouble if caught.

He shook his head.

"Great. Now, watch this."

Veronica raised her hand, interrupting Avery's flow. He had been pointing at the surrounding mountains, moving from one to another, tracing their itinerary in the air.

"What can I do for you, Miss Little?"

"Are we going to be exploring any new caves today? I heard we don't do that anymore." The group turned to Avery expectantly. He frowned, his face lined with heavy wrinkles from lots of sun. Avery always had stubble but no beard, as if he shaved every morning and it grew in immediately after. His long white hair whipped about in the wind, and his voice was gruff and pleasant, a grandfather through and through.

"Well, Miss Little, we will be making some incursions into a system just off—"

"But any *new* caves," she interrupted him. "I mean, you actually taught those students something when you found that cool drawing. They *were* explorers. Can't we get that type of experience? I know that's what I signed up for."

The other kids were excited now, and clamored their support. If anything could make Avery bend, it was enthusiasm for his very own work. He seemed to be teetering.

"As tempting as off-the-beaten is, Westbrook no longer allows me to take students for a proper spelunk."

For some reason, this bothered Greg. Wasn't a little adventure the entire point of this class? He looked at Veronica, who stood there scuffing her leather hiking boot against the pavement, and saw the disappointment in her eyes at Avery's answer. He blurted out, "We don't need anything more than our flashlights and water and rope, Mr. Avery." Greg was shocked that he found himself speaking up. The others seemed to be as surprised. Veronica's mouth actually opened, but there was a glint to her green eyes. Greg was Avery's wunderkind. The quiet, perfect one. Elsewhere in the school he was a ghost, drifting from one class to another. But now, with five bodies standing straighter, their toes bouncing in excitement, he felt emboldened to continue. "With you guiding us, we won't fall into any holes or anything. Just give us a chance to go into a place we've never seen before. That no one has ever seen in hundreds of years. Let us feel what it's really like to be those early explorers."

No one made a noise—the speech was too perfect, and they didn't want to blow it. Avery mulled it over like a cow chewing cud. Finally, he let out a breath and said, "There is a place . . . I've only touched the surface of what potential it has. I guess it might be worth checking out."

The group cheered; they would have tossed hats into the air if they wore any. Chuck Vaughan picked Greg up and down in a semihug, and Veronica kissed his cheek.

"All right, all right, you crazy crazies. Get in the van. It's getting dark already." The sun was barely up, but this was what Avery always said. "Miss Little, front seat. You want the adventure, you get to be the navigator."

The van sputtered and smelled of tuna more than usual, but that was okay. Something felt different about this trip. Something felt big.

Greg felt a tap on his shoulder, and he looked behind him at Blake, the closest Greg had ever had to a best friend. He was wearing a blue rain jacket, and for some reason had the nylon hood pulled tight over his head, the cinch digging into his skin. He looked funny, his nose too big for his narrow face, his deep-set eyes glittering with delight. Blake was pointing at Westbrook, at all the freshmen walking through the quad to their early Friday morning classes.

"Chumps," he said. Greg couldn't have agreed more.

An hour later, they stood halfway up a mountain, lost to the world. The sun was hot, even if the air was cool, and they all were reminded to stay hydrated. The cave entrance was small, barely wiggle-room big, and before they went in, the group of kids stood semicircled and staring.

"You sure about this?" Chuck asked Veronica, his voice squeaking with indecision. Chuck was the tallest of the group, no muscle at all, just skin and bones. He'd have to duck more than anyone; whenever he took a step, his Moe bowl cut would bounce like a sea anemone. Avery had already entered and was standing inside, shining his light about, scouting ahead. *"Come on, you rascals!"*

Veronica punched Chuck playfully. She loved doing that, and whipping her braid at his head. She flipped on her flashlight and crawled in, disappearing into the dark. Brenda next, Blake and Greg, Chuck and Alex. The passage only stayed narrow for a spell, and soon they could stand up. Avery had the only high-intensity beam, and he was twenty feet ahead, clearly on a ledge, shining his bright light about the walls.

"Not much to see here," he called back. "Not yet at least. We'll go ahead and take a gander. You can see some guano at your feet, but nothing much fun that is."

The six students immediately scanned the dirt at their feet, and sure enough: dried guano in prodigious amounts. Bats must fly from the hole every evening. Veronica grabbed Greg's arm. The simple touch was a shock to him. He was glad it was too dark for her to notice.

The cave cancelled out any of the heat of the sun, and suddenly everyone was shivering. "Forward," Avery cried, and they did exactly that, single file, squatting and stopping occasionally, unused to the emptiness and fear that darkness brings.

"All right, then, lads and ladies." Avery had stopped and was pointing with his beam to a slit in the wall about fifteen feet high, but narrow, the width of a shoulder. The group was huddled a few yards behind him. They had never experienced this level of dark. Blake kept running his hands through his hair, a nervous tic. Brenda and Alex held hands. Chuck fidgeted, though he was smiling broadly, his crooked teeth reflecting more light than his clothes, and Greg couldn't tell if he was excited or nervous, or both. "You up for the new, for the real adventure? Who's going first?"

"I thought you were going to lead us," Brenda said, her nasally voice not entirely trembling, but close. She always scrunched up her face when talking, her cheeks pushing up to her eyes.

"Sure, sure. But you asked for it. Nothing dangerous here. Just go on to the other side and then turn and shine the light back through the path to guide the others. Any volunteers?"

"I'll go!" Veronica said, stepping forward. Greg felt a twist in the gut—why couldn't he have taken the lead? If there was ever a place to be the person he always imagined himself to be, it was here in the dark.

"I'll go too," he piped up, raising his hand, his red jacket swishing against his skin. Blake started making smooch noises.

"Enough now, pissant," Avery barked at Blake. "Sure. Just go on behind her. Let her do the leading, okay?"

Greg nodded and hurried to catch up to Veronica, who was already well ahead, halfway into the slit. Her body turned sidewise, she stepped carefully, squatting some. It was too narrow for her to even look back. Greg followed, feeling the wall tight against him, the rock slick from centuries of drip, cold and smelling of an inoffensive mold. A familiar smell, like that of a basement or an old washcloth; it was somehow comforting in this enormous place. His blue canteen, attached to his belt, snagged for a moment on the rock.

When he looked up again, Veronica had disappeared. One second he could see her knee-high socks, her dangling braid; the next, she might never have been there at all.

"Veronica?" he called, but no one answered. He couldn't turn his head either, but tried anyway. "Mr. Avery, I can't find Veronica!"

"You're not even through yet, pipsqueak! Keep going."

Greg kept sliding forward, step by step, almost there. "Veronica?" Nothing.

And then he popped out into a larger room, so big he couldn't find its end with his flashlight. But that wasn't what he was looking for. Up ahead, on the dirt, maybe fifteen feet beyond him, was Veronica's flashlight.

He slid frantically down a small slope, scattering dust, hurrying to the fallen flashlight. "Mr. Avery! Come quick! Veronica! VERONICA!"

But she wasn't there. He expected her to be lying prone, unconscious or moaning from a fall, but instead he was all alone with two flashlights in an enormously dark room. There was a small twinkle of light piercing the slit behind him. Someone must be coming through. He picked up her flashlight and used both to illuminate the walls.

There! Her boot, just sitting on its side. Greg was so afraid he could barely move. He took a slow step, then another, swinging his gaze around. No one. He picked up the boot, felt its weight in his hands. He tried not to hyperventilate, he was breathing so hard.

Blake had made it through the passage, and his beam of light was zooming around the cavern. "Down here, hurry!" Greg called up. Suddenly he was pushed from behind and Veronica yelled, "Gotcha!"

Greg screamed and dropped the lights. A real girl scream, high and loud and long. It echoed around the unseeable walls, like a dozen damsels in distress. Veronica was on her ass laughing, rolling in the dirt, and Blake, the one who made it through, was shouting something at them both, but Greg didn't hear or care. He felt so hot all of a sudden that he was dizzy, and he stumbled away before he could think about it, the flashlight left behind rolling on the dirt.

And then he tripped. It must have been over a rock, something just big enough to catch his boot. But the strange thing was, he didn't slam into the ground as he expected. The sound of Veronica laughing disappeared above his head, and Greg felt wind and a whistling in his ear, like he was almost somersaulting in place, moving faster and faster, Veronica's laughter still there but so high overhead in the darkness, and suddenly there was no more light, not the faintest echoes of the flashlights, and he didn't even have time to scream because he was too terrified. The wind kept pressing against his face, and he knew he was still falling.

Greg tried to look down, but didn't know which way *was* down.

He could see a faint, glowing haze out of the corner of his eye and managed to think one thing before he hit.

I'm in a black hole.

The pain burst through, waking him in a jolt of agony. There was a light, so blindingly bright that for a moment Greg actually, *actually* thought he was going to heaven, and then the beam slipped from his face and he could make out the hazy silhouette of Avery hanging in the air about five feet above him, one hand on a rope that was twisting in the darkness.

"Hold still, son. Hold still. I'll be right there."

There were a few flickers above, way, way, way above, and he could only guess that was where he'd fallen from. Too far to tell. He tried to think about the distance, but his head squeezed in protest. He moaned; his leg felt like it had been cut in half and dipped in salt. There was a ringing that began to fade. Avery pulled close, and Greg attempted to sit up, but his body was heavy and weak. And, he belatedly realized, he was wet. He'd landed in a puddle. The water, which he hadn't even felt before, rose about halfway up his body and was warm; maybe he'd pissed himself after all.

Avery rappelled down a few more feet, his rope hissing as it gave way, but then he stopped again, swinging gently back and forth.

"What the . . ." He was not looking at Greg, but rather shining his light all around him. Greg craned his neck over as far as it could go and saw where the beam landed: on a pale white tree, not dead but very much alive, its branches long and willowy, with leaves dripping down to float in the shifting pond of water where Greg was lying.

Avery recovered and splashed down next to him. A drop hit Greg's face and felt almost hot, soothing, like a bath.

"Greg," Avery whispered, his voice urgent. He put his hand to Greg's cheek and gave a half caress, half pat. "It's going to be okay, son. I'll send one of the kids to get help." The teacher's eyes frantically searched his body. "I can't believe you survived that, kid." He laughed in relief. "Holy cow, I thought you were done."

Greg tried again to get up but Avery's face grew alarmed, and he gently pushed Greg back down. "No, no, best you don't move. You might aggravate any injuries you have."

"But I'm feeling better."

And he was. The agony he'd felt upon waking was already subsiding. Though that might not have been a good thing.

Avery scanned Greg's body and gasped. His jeans were cut open, torn by the fall.

Greg leaned back, defeated. "My leg is broken, isn't it?"

Avery didn't say anything, just widened the gap in the jeans and let out a breath of disbelief. Then he looked back at Greg.

"What? Mr. Avery? What's going on?"

He shook his head. "I don't know, son. But something's happening."

Greg forced himself up, feeling lightheaded but otherwise okay. Avery's beam was on the wound, and Greg squinted his eyes near closed, expecting to see a bone or three jutting out. Instead he saw his leg and yes, a cut, but one that was only three or four inches long and not deep at all. There was blood all over his leg, though. Avery squeezed him on the shoulder, not to comfort him but in shock as they watched the wound get smaller, slowly but surely, tightening and whitening and then, finally, disappearing completely. No scar. Nothing.

"Mr. Avery!" Greg breathed, unable to tear his gaze away from his pale but perfect leg. "What's happening?"

His teacher didn't answer. Instead, Avery ran his finger lightly along Greg's leg, his hand leaving a trail in the drying blood. There was no pain. In fact, Avery's hand tickled Greg.

"Hey!" came a voice, faint and faraway. "Is he okay?"

Avery looked straight up, his mouth open and his eyes glazed, dumbstruck. But the voice reminded the teacher of his surroundings; he flashed his light around them. Greg followed this beam of light as Avery twirled it in a circle. There was not just one impossibly lush tree, but many, a whole tight forest of plant life. And not just trees. There were bushes and ferns and flowers and, with some focus, they made out insects buzzing around and even what appeared to be some type of bird rustling in the branches.

"Inconceivable," Avery whispered.

"Guys?!"

Avery called up to them. "We're okay! He's okay!" Avery looked all about, wide-eyed, his hair in a frazzle. "What are you doing, Sebastian?" he muttered to himself, peering close to the water's surface, lifting up a handful, sniffing it and letting it fall. "Are you really going to do this?

"Youngsters," he cried, "you best come down here. All but one, we have to leave one up top. Who's strong enough to help pull us back?"

"No one wants to be alone, Mr. Avery!" the voice came back. Greg was sure it was Veronica. "We all want to come down."

"If we all come down, we won't all get back. I promise whoever misses his turn this time will get it later. Alex, you're a strapping one. You harness the rope, son. Everyone else, remember what I taught you. Lock yourself in and rappel down! You wanted an adventure—Mr. Avery got you one!"

Avery had Greg stay put until curiosity finally got the best of the teacher and he left his patient's side to go examine a tree, giving Greg the opportunity to try to move. He didn't expect to be able to do so, but his body tingled, energized, probably in shock, and he happily heaved himself up from the water. He walked gingerly around the perimeter of the oasis, and each time his foot sank into the water, he felt a warmth surge up through his leg. He was stronger by the step.

Chuck and Blake had already landed, having rappelled down with ease. Brenda next, you could hear her squeaking on the way. Greg had waved Blake off, wanting a moment to get his bearings, and the two boys were with Avery, cataloging everything they saw. When they had given Greg his flashlight back, they had gazed at him in disbelief. Blake looked like he had been crying, his eyes red and puffy. They probably didn't know how to handle his fall. He certainly didn't. He should be dead. That was, like, two hundred feet or more. *Well,* Greg chided himself, *the rope is only one hundred and fifty feet, so not* that *far.* But close.

Brenda held the rope for Veronica, who, when she landed, rushed directly to Greg and was about to give him a big hug when she paused, worried about hurting him any further.

"I'm okay," Greg said, not sure he wanted to reassure her.

"Greg"—she was clearly as upset as Blake—"Greg, I didn't mean to do that. I mean, I did, but to have you fall? I'm sorry. It's a miracle you're okay. I don't . . . wow."

"Greg, son," Avery shouted to him from somewhere in the mass of branches, "you feeling good? Nauseated? Headache? Don't move now, you hear? I want you to just sit still, and we'll get you out of here soon." To Greg, and clearly the others, their teacher's words were hollow and distracted. They should pull Greg out of there, come back another time. But no one objected, least of all Greg. Something was going on here, something special, and they all wanted to be part of it.

"Mr. Avery, I'm great. Totally fine. Lucky one, I guess." He felt weird speaking to dense foliage; you couldn't see anyone clearly through the branches. Veronica was on her knees, peering at something, already distracted by the oasis around them.

"In that case, dig out your notebook and start cataloging what you're feeling. How you fell in, what you first remember when you woke, painwise, and how you're feeling now. I want to know everything you see here. I don't recognize most of the vegetation or the animal life. From where you're sitting, draw what you can. Everyone else, don't touch anything, just record. We may have found a unique bastion of life here. This could be a major find, kids, a major find!"

Greg squatted next to Veronica. She was cupping her hand around a flower, a pale thing, so pale you could see right through it. The leaves were tricornered and small, but the flower itself was a twisting knot of petal. It reminded him of the creatures that lived in the deep of the oceans. The fish that had their own lights dangling over their heads to illuminate their way.

He remembered the haze of light he'd seen during his fall, from below, and got an idea. "Turn off your flashlight."

Veronica stared at him, puzzled. He clicked off his own, and then shielded the flower from any stray beams flickering from the rest of the group. Veronica shrugged and turned hers off too. Sure enough, the flower's outline began to come clear in his palm. It was like a lightbulb warming up, until suddenly it burst on, incredibly bright, catching the air ablaze.

Veronica gasped and clapped her hands in childlike delight. Greg was feeling pretty blown away himself. But as soon as he moved his hand, the smallest hint of a flashlight beam from one of the others came vaguely near the plant, and it shut down.

"It's afraid of the lights," Veronica said.

"Mr. Avery," Greg called, "turn off your flashlight. All of you. Turn them off and stand still."

"What are you talking about?"

"Trust him, guys," Veronica shouted. "It's incredible."

One by one, the flashlight beams disappeared. The last one danced on the far edge of the oasis, holding out for a good twenty seconds until Avery bellowed at Chuck to shut his down. Then they were in total blackness again. Someone made the *ooooooooohhhh-hhh* of a ghost, and there were snickers. This time, Veronica and Greg knew what to look for, and they watched the flower begin to glow, its iridescent brilliance pulsing bright. Greg was about to call everyone over when he heard murmurs of surprise from the group. A few feet away from him, there was another flower, then another, and more. The room had brightened incredibly, lit up all on its own, a mask of beautiful floral lights.

"Holy shit," Avery said. Everyone laughed, so giddy at the find that they couldn't move.

"Do we take one back?" Chuck asked. The group had congregated now in one place, watching the symphony around them.

"We try," Avery responded. "Though I get the feeling they aren't going to last long up top."

Two things became very apparent in the light and silence. One was that the inch-deep water was flowing, gently, toward the center of this amazing oasis. The other was that in this center, there was an outcropping of rock jutting from the ground, something that was easy to realize now that the room was bright. The group, needing no prompting, seemed to move as one toward the center.

Through the folding branches and leaves of an enormous tree, their boots splashing the entire way, the group came upon a hole in the ground, a natural well. Not a big thing, small, maybe big enough for one of them to fall through. And not man-made. It looked like an anthill, like a small mound. Brenda said it looked like a miniature volcano, except instead of lava there was water. In the light around the rest of the oasis, the group could all see the silty bottom of the pond, but here, their boots planted along the edge of the well, they saw darkness straight down.

"How is it flowing *into* this hole? Shouldn't the water be flowing out of it? Isn't that a contradiction?" Greg asked.

No one had an answer, but Avery bent down and tentatively stuck his hand, then his arm, then his shoulder into the hole.

"Not too shallow, I couldn't feel a bottom," he pronounced, coming back up, shaking his arm free of water.

"Guys, what's that?" Blake asked. He was staring at the outcrop of rock, which seemed nothing special from Greg's vantage, just a flat rock face covered with a pulsing mosslike fuzz. Nothing compared to the anthill of a well. Looking closer, though, he realized quickly how wrong he was. In the center of that mossy fuzz was a clearing, where a series of images was visible—it was as if the drawings repelled any plant growth. The most beautiful cave drawings the students could imagine. Not the familiar renderings of early man, like the slides Avery had shown them in class, these were *different* drawings. Big trees, golden cities, flowing fountains, pale men with piercing blue eyes.

Avery started jumping up and down, his feet splashing the water and his belly jiggling. He was not the type of teacher you could see freak out without at least breaking a smile. "Oh, my God, oh, my God. Look at this! We did it! What is this place? Oh, my God." He flicked his light on, maybe to get a better view, but it was like he blew a fuse; every flower dissolved immediately into the blackness. Greg felt suddenly disembodied, floating near the loud breaths of his friends. Brenda squealed. Veronica tried to hold Greg's hand but instead grabbed his shirt. Blake just muttered, "Insane. Freaking insane."

Avery went as close to the drawings as possible, his lips moving, trying to get some idea of their origins. They were pretty crazy, large and detailed, and the students stood off to the side in awe, anxious for the teacher to finish his inspection so they could get closer themselves.

Abruptly, Avery pulled back and turned to the group of students, aiming the flashlight up at his own face as if telling a ghost story. "Boys and girls, this is the real thing. They will talk about this in every classroom for hundreds of years." The kids felt their arms go goose bumpy. Greg's whole body was tingly warm still. "Nice fall, Kish, though you probably shouldn't be moving." He stared for a moment at Greg's leg, shining his light there, and since they were in a cave in the dark, the only place for anyone to look was at the pale and bloody but otherwise unblemished leg. Avery seemed to shake himself awake and went on: "But if there's one thing I know, it's that this all has to be done right. And I feel we are wasting precious seconds standing around here, improperly outfitted. Let's all forget samples—I don't feel comfortable taking from this potentially fragile ecosystem—and return surface-side. There's a chance that just us being here is killing the plant life as we speak. We'll regroup, call it in, and come back tomorrow with better equipment and a few more hands. Sound like a plan?"

The group was sullen, despite understanding Avery's logic. They had just gotten there. And the idea of him sharing their prize, their discovery, was oddly rankling. Avery seemed to notice this and sighed deeply.

"Okay," he said, pointing at the wall. "You want to stay? Can anyone tell me what these drawings mean?"

Greg's eyes felt crazy, and everything began suddenly to swirl with a halo of light. The images on the rock face seemed to fit together, not like the story of a hunt or a dance, but like a sequence. One thing after the other, all leading to something. He followed the images to the end, to the bottom, where somehow, some way, there was a tiny image of the entire wall all over again.

"It's a map," said Greg, knowing that he was right.

The others peered, and Avery *hmm*ed, conceding the possibility.

Greg traced his finger from the first image—clearly the sun—to the last, forcing Avery's eyes to follow.

"Maybe it *is* a map," Avery said, "but that's neither here nor there at the moment; this will exist tomorrow. Kids, let's go." Still there was an inch of mutiny among the students, but Avery pulled his last card. "Here's the deal, the real deal. Greg just fell eight stories and survived. That's a miracle in its own right. Now the wound seems all fine and dandy, but I will go to my deathbed remembering the blood on his leg. I have no idea how he's standing here making assumptions when he should be a goner. The only reason he's standing at all is the adrenaline coursing through his puny frame. He could have internal bleeding. We have to get him checked out. Tomorrow we'll be back, trust me."

Everyone agreed and made their way to the rope, where they gave a tug and began to climb slowly out of the cavern. A few glances went Greg's way, as if this was his fault, and he wanted to shout that they wouldn't even be here if not for him. Veronica hovered, but he hunched his shoulders and turned away, so she volunteered to go up next. He stood off to the side, squatting in the water. Something was missing, he was sure. To him it felt like the tree, the flower, even the map, weren't the big deal here. He prodded his wound, now healed, and tried to puzzle through it all. He was intimately aware of this fact; his body felt entirely different and buoyant and wonderful, and it couldn't just be all the adrenaline and shock like Avery said. He felt his blood shooting through his veins, singing. But it was his feet and his fingers, soaking wet, that glowed with heat.

"Your pants look gruesome," Blake said, coming up to him and taking a swipe at the fabric. "Like you dipped them in blood or something." He held up his fingers and showed the red to Greg. For a moment, Greg thought Blake would make marks on his own face, like Indian war paint, but instead he just pretended to, his fingers tracing the contours of his sallow cheeks. Blake rinsed his fingers off in the water. "Don't fall on the way up, Kish."

Greg didn't hear him. He was staring at the ripple in the water left by Blake's fingers. He bent down and splashed some onto his leg, up his shin and over his knee, and it burned, not painfully but in another way, a very intense feeling of heat and pressure and even, he admitted to himself, pleasure. Greg cupped a handful of water, sniffed it, tentatively tipped it onto his tongue. And his mouth immediately felt warm and happy, soothed and relaxed. Even his teeth buzzed. He glanced at the others; they were getting ready to climb. Greg unstoppered his small canteen. He chugged the water already inside—no use wasting—and in a quick motion, dipped the empty container into the pond.

No need to be sneaky; no one noticed him. They rarely ever did.

18

THE STORY, PART II

THEY DID NOT RETURN THE NEXT DAY.

While the group was spelunking toward their extraordinary find, Blake's mother had made a surprise visit to the campus; she owned a house in Aspen and came out year-round. It wasn't, in itself, a problem that she didn't find Blake. Mary Sutton did not especially like to wait, and Fenton had little to offer her in the way of entertainment, but if her son was out on an exclusive field trip, so be it. She found herself in his room, sitting on his unmade bed, convinced that she should fly Elsa in from Connecticut to clean the place once a week.

Five minutes after he was due to arrive back, Mary's patience ran out. Ten minutes after he was due to arrive back, she sat in the dean's office, an eyebrow raised, lips impeccably twitched into a frown.

Inquiries were made, and Avery and class were not to be found at Baker Canyon National Park, their original destination. The lips twitched again with, some might be kind enough to say, concern.

The sheriff was called. Deputies went far and wide.

Not two hours later, a lead: a gas station attendant on Interstate 70 had seen a Westbrook van turn off into the foothills. Twenty minutes beyond that, the van was found.

By the time Avery—he had demanded to be last—was pulled forth from the hole by his six students, four deputies and two emergency-service technicians were standing at the cave entrance, shining their lights, playing rock, paper, scissor to see who would go in first. A deputy named Colin Banks lost, and, being terrified of the dark but afraid to show it, he pulled his flashlight *and* his gun, and crouched through the hole.

Call it surprise or inexperience, but the sight of a man like Avery, with his long white hair and dirty, jowly face coming at him in the dark could scare most humans, even lawmen, especially one scared half to death already. Colin Banks discharged his firearm, thankfully hurting no one at all—just a hole through Blake's lucky canteen—but this caused his colleagues to draw their own pistols and push their way in, and there was screaming and crying and shouting and much, much flashlight pointing.

No more gunshots that day. But the blame for the entire affair fell square on Avery, who was dismissed before Mary boarded her tiny private airplane to return to Aspen. A gun discharged during his non-approved class outing, which nipped the son of the school's third largest donor—what other conclusion but termination could there be, star teacher or no? Throughout the entire harried ordeal, through some wordless agreement, no one spoke of the map and the strange forest, even after the paramedics saw Greg's bloody pants and spent thirty minutes searching for a wound. The kids assumed Avery would talk, but he didn't either, perhaps worried that someone else would take credit for the discovery. In any case, if it weren't for Colin Banks, it's conceivable that Sebastian Avery would still be teaching at Westbrook. But as it was, Greg viewed the dizzying array of events as nothing less than fate.

A week after the incident, Greg left letters for the other five students. Midnight, near the base of the statue of Socrates, he shivered and whistled to himself, trying to make a coherent noise with his cold lips; sure enough, the group arrived. They didn't realize that he'd never snuck out of his house like this before. That he didn't come here to neck regularly with the opposite sex, like Brenda did.

"What's this all about, Greg?" Chuck asked with a note of real curiosity, his bowl cut wispy in the night air.

"I think we have to go back."

No one said a thing. No one disagreed. They all had been thinking it. Veronica, in a cashmere hoodie, moved close to Greg and hooked her arm around his.

"I think something important is down there," Greg continued. "Something that could change the world."

He reluctantly pulled away from Veronica to demonstrate.

"The map must be important. But . . . guys. The water. Check this out. One of you shine a light on my arm."

Greg pulled out his canteen, handed it to Veronica, and then drew a knife from his pocket. The group stepped back involuntarily.

"What are you doing, Kish?" Blake said, his thin face etched with concern.

Greg held out his hand and rolled up his checkered-wool sleeve. He took a steadying breath and sliced his arm, relatively deep, sending forth a nice burst of steamy blood. Veronica dropped the canteen, Alex gagged, Chuck put his hand to his mouth, but they all stared when Greg picked up the canteen and poured what remained of the water onto his arm. The blood thinned, and the cut stopped steaming. The cut had been about a half inch wide, and they could see his muscle underneath, but slowly the gap grew smaller, the skin resealing, leaving just a swirl of dried blood.

"I should have died when I fell," he said, and he knew it was true. He had already cut himself six times before this meeting. "I landed in *this* water. It saved my life."

The proof was indisputable. No one made any jokes. No one denied the miracle of his survival. Veronica kept running her hands up and down her own arms to keep herself from shivering. Chuck couldn't get enough, and he stuck his long nose right onto Greg's arm, as if sniffing for the solution.

"But how are we supposed to get down there?" Brenda asked. She looked tiny amid the others, bundled in all her winter gear.

"We steal the equipment and go this weekend," said Blake. He touched Greg's skin again, just like in the cave, and examined the bloody digit. His eyes sparkled in the starlight, his eagerness so apparent that it gave even Greg pause.

There was no disagreement. It was as if the entire group was looking for this, a purpose, and they were suddenly a unified team ready for anything. There was something powerful happening, and each felt it deep in themselves and the air they breathed. Blake reached for the empty canteen and managed to pour a few drops into his open mouth as they watched in fascination. He swallowed, looked down at his hands, then at the others, and shrugged.

"We can't tell anyone," Veronica whispered, her face stern and set in lines.

"Why?" Chuck asked.

"They'll think we're crazy. We're just kids."

"What about Avery?" Greg said

"What about him?" Brenda replied.

"What if he gets there first?"

Blake took deep breaths of air, and his eyes began to water in the cold. He clapped his hands together to keep warm. "How is that a bad thing?"

No one spoke. There was a current passing between them. A shared vision of wealth, fame, of immortality. Not telling anyone was a big deal, they were realizing. No parents, who expected them to follow a certain path of education and employment. No teachers, who could help procure equipment and material. No friends but themselves. The group stood there for a while, breathing in the cold air, thinking their newfound thoughts, and then dispersed, changed forever.

Veronica, Blake and Greg strolled back to campus. Veronica was holding Greg's arm and rubbing the place where he had cut himself. Then she glanced at Blake, the curiosity plain on her face. She almost licked her lips.

"What did it taste like?"

His eyes lit up. "Like water," he said without hesitation, "but with a kick."

"Do you feel different?" Greg asked, because he wanted to see if it caused the same effects on Blake. When Greg drank the water, his lungs felt full of fresh air.

Blake stopped walking and began to breathe heavily. Greg got excited. *He* did *feel the same thing!* Blake squeezed his fingers into fists and huffed his shoulders up and down, all the while keeping his eyes closed. The steam of his breath shot into the dark.

Greg and Veronica watched him with bemusement at first, and then alarm. Veronica came close, put a shivering hand on his shoulder. "Blake? Are you okay?"

He didn't respond, but kept breathing harder and harder and then, suddenly, stopped. His head drooped. His arms dangled at his sides.

And then he lunged at Veronica and encircled her waist and screamed while spinning her around and around, her feet in the air and her white sneakers flashing. She freaked out, shouting as loud as anything Greg had ever heard, but then she began to laugh and laugh, her face turning bright red and happy, and she let her arms loose into the sky and Greg watched the two of them go round and round. When Blake let her down, they stared at each other, and Greg had never seen that stare before.

He was not surprised to see them holding hands soon after.

They didn't have to steal a thing to help them on their way. Aside from Greg, each of the students had a trust fund to pull from. By the weekend, they were decked out in serious spelunking gear, with laboratory equipment, cameras and plenty of rope. But upon arriving at the cave, after a few nerve-racking hours of setting up everything and imagining police sirens, the Westbrook students found the well dry, the water gone.

The forest was still there, but already it was aged, thirsty, desperate for sustenance. The group was devastated, certain their previous visit had somehow contaminated the environment. Greg wondered if true sunlight would kill these plants that had evolved in darkness, anyway. There were no more insect noises, no more strange creatures. The place was dying. Everyone felt awful but for Greg. He stared at the map for a few hours, his flashlight puzzling over every clue. The white men, the blazing solar eclipse, the upside-down mountains, the vividly bright colors and the endlessly blue water. He smacked his lips together, lost in thought, until it came to him in a flash of gut instinct.

"The water's coming back."

The map was near impossible to decipher, but Greg was convinced that the water had to return on a cycle. There were so many calendar events noted on the map: a solar eclipse, a moon, the sun. Surely whoever painted the thing had a time in mind. More important, he reasoned to himself, it was a *map*. There was a purpose, and that was to explain where something was. In this case, Greg knew it had to be the water, the magical, wonderful, healing water. Blake wasn't so sure, but Greg kept pointing to the bottom corner of the map, the miniature map within a map, at how it had to mean there was a cycle. He couldn't tell how long—only that the water would return, he was absolutely, positively, somehow sure of it. He dug around until he found some petrified wood, which he claimed was evidence of an earlier oasis. They just needed patience. Everyone else was pretty disappointed, almost angry. They had witnessed a miracle and had, in that dead forest, all the proof of its reality they needed. But they didn't have the miracle itself. There was no water left. They returned to school, trying to forget anything had ever happened.

But Greg wouldn't let them.

By the time they graduated, the deal was made: Greg would stay behind—it was his city, after all. He was happy to sacrifice his college plans for an opportunity like this. He'd check the well three times a week, examine the decaying plant life, and would get financed by his classmates' trust funds. Normally he'd never take a penny from someone else, but Greg had plans for this money, and so he accepted, and the others dispersed to lead their lives. Veronica and Blake moved to New York together, where they both went to Columbia University. They visited Greg the most frequently, on winter breaks or in summer. But even their visits began to slow when, after a few years, not a drop of water had appeared in the well. Soon Greg was alone, a quiet watcher, in the only place he ever knew. The others became doctors, engineers, lawyers, and for a very long time, they really did forget that their classmate once rose from the dead.

Even Greg almost stopped believing.

Seventeen years passed, and he hadn't heard from Blake in six months. That call was only to say that Veronica had left him, the divorce messy but—thankfully—childless. All of his pact-mates had stopped sending checks a while back, and Greg no longer visited the cave three times a week.

When it had all started, so long ago, Greg was enthusiastic and determined. He had cleaned up the place, made a lighted path and a long, well-made ladder to the site. At the age of nineteen, he got a job in construction, to better learn how to rig a path and build from wood. He kept studying, both his computers and everything he could about local Native Americans. He had early translations of the conquistador Cortés's expeditions in his study. But after a time, the Cave became sort of secondary. He became a foreman at his construction company, then manager, then owner—an early adopter of computer technology in the workplace. His firm, Fenton Construction, won the contract to build an ambitious aqueduct straight from the mountain to Fenton, and Greg installed his old friend Terry to run the place. Fifteen years in, Greg had met a woman, a lovely librarian named Amanda, and a year or so later, they were married and she was pregnant.

It was almost on a lark that he went to the cave the day Mia was born. He was driving home to pick up some supplies from the hospital, after having just left his wife and newborn sleeping peacefully in their room. There was the turnoff, and on a whim, he took it. Greg went there to say good-bye. He was going to write letters to the others, tell them he was foolish, let them get on with their lives (which they were long since doing anyway). He remembered whistling as he took the path, tossing his keys in the air and catching them, outfitting himself in his harness and peeking over the ledge to see an incredibly bright light below him. There was no darkness, no petrified trees. Instead, he found a forest, teeming with impossible life.

Amanda didn't know about any of this, and, according to the

rules of their little group, she wouldn't. The others had spread far and wide. Greg went home and made some phone calls, and by the time he returned to the hospital, they had all booked plane tickets, ready to sample the wonder of the well and their long investment. They came ready to work, though there was a palpable tension between Veronica and Blake, who did their best to stay away from each other. Greg skipped out on his newborn as often as he could, feeling only slight guilt—he'd make it up to her, she'd see. Gallons were taken and stored, some refrigerated, some not. Tests began; instead of cutting his own arm to see if the water healed, Greg started to use mice—the water worked. And the reunion was kind-hearted and happy. After a week, even Veronica and Blake seemed to be getting along better. Suddenly everyone was closer than they could have ever been, and the project began in earnest.

Seventeen years. The cycle ran seventeen years. And the water lasted for ten days, at least from the time Greg had discovered it, though he had an unshakeable hunch that it began on the day of his daughter's birth. He found the coincidence of her birthday timed to the water's flow to be too much for his proud-father mind to ignore.

But this time, with the water in storage, the others had all the reason in the world to maintain a constant and regular presence. There was a meeting at Brenda's Aspen mansion that went particularly well. The biggest difference was in Greg, who had changed when the water came forth again. He carried himself with an air of command and confidence. He knew the Cave and its environs intimately. And he was, importantly, not of their social strata; he was a neutral party. They recognized plainly that this man would take them places, would be in charge, would be their guide. There was a vote, and aside from a brief, perfunctory conversation about the potential of a rotating leadership—initiated by Blake Sutton—Greg was chosen unanimously. Before, he was the night watchman. Now he was their leader.

The land around the entrance was purchased from the state of Colorado, an impenetrable door implanted, a road built in, the map dug out and placed in an air-controlled environment. Greg tried to call Avery but discovered that he had been dead for some time now, killed in an accidental fire some sixteen years back. With everyone else together, the Cave became a real and complete entity. The well, quite oddly, was an empty abyss when there was no water. The group considered, perhaps, that this was a tributary of some underground aquifer, perhaps an offshoot of the one that fed the town's aqueduct, but any time they tried to find a source, to follow the tunnels that continued below the well, they failed to make headway. There wasn't any evidence of petrified plant life deeper within the earth, nothing similar to the cavern with the well and the map.

Seventeen years until the next cycle . . .

The group hired Greg's construction company and used the interim to create a vast complex of caves and tunnels and rooms. After these were in place, Greg sold the company to focus entirely on the project and began a front company, Fenton Electronics. He used his skills in computers to install a state-of-the-art lab and security system. He familiarized himself with everything. Named director, he was rewarded for his faith. He oversaw all aspects of the organization, from Chuck's purchases of medical equipment to meetings with Blake's private security contacts about on-site protection.

Greg sent Veronica and Brenda off to receive degrees in biology and chemistry. He refused such a path, himself, and remained full-time in Fenton to manage construction and be near his growing daughter and loving (but oblivious) wife. Chuck was already a medical doctor; so was Blake, but Blake went to work for the CDC to learn about pathogens. Two doctors were imperative: one for practical medicine (Chuck) and the other for clinical and theoretical (Blake). Early testing was quite successful, and new strains of healthy and insect-resistant plants were bred through research in the greenhouses below. A couple of the more common strains—tomatoes and spinach—went to market, bringing in additional revenue for the project. Farms were purchased in the neighboring counties by Fenton Organics, a well-disguised subsidiary, and it was there that these hyperseeds sprouted.

It took eight years to fully build the Cave—they expected great things to come of the place, and took advantage of the lengthy dry spell. Day in and day out, the water samples were beaten into submission, endless data charted for everything from sunless crops to cancer remission in mice and monkeys. They worked especially hard to attempt to re-create the water's effects artificially, reasoning that they would not have enough to sustain its use worldwide over seventeen years when they went public.

They failed, over and again.

Seventeen years was a long time, even for such a find. These denizens of the cultural elite couldn't just drop off the face of the earth for almost two decades. In order to keep everything fair, the entire group of six agreed to spend at least three months a year within three hours, driving distance from Fenton—and to devote most of that time to working in the Cave. As a side effect (perhaps of boredom), most became major sponsors of Westbrook Academy. Chuck built a mansion in Denver and hosted fund-raisers, and Veronica's family name crested the new gymnasium.

And there were, of course, some major pauses in construction and research. Alex's family lost their wealth in the dot.com bust, and he disappeared for a few years. Brenda's husband was elected a senator of Connecticut and she was often away in DC or campaigning. And Greg's daughter, Mia, fell down a twenty-two-foot well. The hole was only eighteen inches wide. National media swarmed. The country watched, held vigils and dug up background stories for anyone involved. The group had to use all of its influence to keep the press from the Cave, no easy feat considering the parties involved and the mysterious nature of the shell corporation. For most of six months, Greg barely went to work.

Ten years later, when Amanda lay bleeding beneath a tree trunk, Greg had a choice. He could stay with her as the blizzard raged, scooping snow away from her mouth and nose. Or he could race to the Cave, break his own rule, and steal some water for his wife, even though it was surely too late. He heard Mia call his name, back on the porch. She couldn't see them. She didn't know her mother lay dying thirty feet away. Greg stayed, held Amanda's hand and missed only three days of work after. He barely left the Cave again.

Despite his renewed vigor for their cause, failures continued and until the well sprang to life once more, they'd have nothing but a limited supply of the most valuable item in the world.

Greg was convinced they'd found the Fountain of Youth. He started tasting the water when no one was looking.

They all did.

Greg aged slowly, never had a cold, never broke a bone, never needed glasses. He could hold his breath underwater for fifteen minutes at a time. He could remember things photographically. Everyone at Westbrook was smart, but this group became more so. Their extra studies took no time. They excelled at all things but solving the mystery of the water.

And now there was but one diluted vial left. On the morning of the next cycle.

Mia's seventeenth birthday.

19

THE LIGHTS GO ON, AND I FEEL LIKE I'VE BEEN IN A planetarium. During the entire story, Dad showed as many pictures as possible. Of the lab, the dead forest, the well. Of the group of students standing in black-and-white, my father is clearly recognizable by his thick shock of hair, his tepid smile. Veronica did, in fact, look like a typical pampered richie. There are two others I don't recognize, the kids from the story who aren't here. Maybe it isn't their "turn." Dad had slides, he says, to help document the entire process for when they "went public."

When he first said Sutton's name, we all looked at each other. Dad had paused, his face grim. He gave me an apologetic look. My face went cold, but I never bothered to interrupt (and neither had anyone else). Now, though, even with so many unanswered questions, there's nothing more pressing than the sixth kid.

"Sutton didn't seem like such a bad guy in your story," I say, remembering the man walking easily through the Westbrook halls. "Why's he doing all this?"

"You said he was with the CDC, so is he, like, working for the government now or something?" Rob adds on. He's up and staring at the map again. I'd like to join him, but looking that close at anything gives me a headache.

Veronica clears her throat, her stern face a bit stricken. I can only assume that knowing what her ex-husband is doing out in the world is killing her.

"He wants the water. He knows it's coming later today. And when he asked nicely to be let back in, your father said no." There's some vitriol to her comment, some real spite. Dad flinches.

"Veronica," he says, spreading his hands out before him, "we all agreed on that course. I had no idea he had stolen samples of the virus. Or samples of the water."

"He's killing innocent people!"

"We'll save them," Dad says, his face determined. "The water is coming, and we'll save everyone as soon as it does—"

"You're too late," Jo interrupts, her voice sad. That shuts them up. And it should have. It's ridiculous to see them like this, even my dad, bickering like little kids.

"What happened to him?" Odessa asks. "Why did you kick him out?"

Dad and Veronica exchange glances, another secret to tell.

"Come," Dad says, "we'll show you."

We follow him out the door, walking woodenly, dazed. How far will the virus get before Dad opens the door to Sutton's men?

We make our way past a few rooms that look like laboratories until we arrive at one that is sealed off with duct tape and plastic sheeting. From a window, we can see that the inside is a dusty white, a ghost room, the beakers still partly full of moldy liquid. The place looks like a video game, or a horror movie set, with an emptiness that hints at happier times gone wrong.

"This used to be his lab," Dad starts, indicating the place with a needless gesture. I am standing next to Brayden and find myself leaning against him. I'd like him to put his arm around me, but I don't think he will in front of Dad. "Blake's time at the Centers for Disease Control was supposed to provide insight on cures and antidotes, research into properties of healing and how that might relate to the water. At first, that is what he studied. He managed to stretch a single drop of the water far enough to eradicate stage-four cancer in a full-grown chimp. But what he really wanted to do was to enable that one drop to create a series of antibodies that could stop cancer in more than one chimp at a time."

I press my nose to the glass and look again, and sure enough, there are large cages stacked against the far walls, empty now.

"Blake tried to isolate the blood of the healed chimp and use the antibodies found there to create a vaccine for other chimps, thus negating the need for an endless supply of water."

"It was brilliant, actually," Chuck says from behind us. Veronica scowls, but he just shrugs. "What? Treating cancer as a virus *worked*. These blood cells were primed by the water to defeat all forms of illness, and if they could be replicated, they could act against cancers, filoviruses, bacteria, any type of pathogen. If we don't have an endless supply of the actual water and can't replicate it, the next best thing is the research Blake was working on."

"What I figured out from his progress," Dad says, his arms crossed in front of his chest, "was that if a sovereign nation controlled the water that granted immediate healing and growth, it could create global conflict. Think about it," Dad goes on, pointing into the lab, "if a nation had access to the water they'd have the means to grow endless crops and no illness."

"Isn't that a good thing?" I ask. It seems too conspiracy-theory. So vast. But I'm standing in front of a lab underneath thousands of tons of earth, so it's all real. Chuck smiles a pasty smile at me. "In theory, yes. But that's only if *everyone* is granted the same access. I'm not too confident that would happen. Blake believed that if he could replicate the effects of the water, we could distribute the healing properties of the water without being chained to the time line and limited quantity or the *geographic location* of the actual source. In other words, America wouldn't have the monopoly, and therefore wouldn't have any reason to keep the water's healing properties from the rest of the world. Blake's research wouldn't fulfill all the potential the water had, but it would be a major part."

"So what happened?" Jimmy asks.

"Exactly what you think," Veronica replies. "At first it seemed like his serum worked. The cancers in the monkeys went into remission, but then they died, aging quickly, abnormally."

"We told him to stop," my dad adds. "And he did for a while. He went to work on hybrid vegetation. Plenty of exciting and important things you can do with the water in that area of research."

"Like the coconut bananas and those blue eyeball berries from the greenhouses," Rob offers, looking expectantly at Odessa. I'm sure she'd rather hear their proper names, but she seems interested enough.

"Exactly like those," Dad says. "In a way, they are a perfect metaphor for what he was doing. The coconut ones, they're new and healthy and wonderful, and the things you called eyeball berries, they turned out to be more poisonous than the worst mushroom. This went on for some time, but then his mother got ill. Turns out she had cancer all along and that was part of what was driving him. He started to work again in secret."

"Why didn't you just give her some water?" Rob asks. Brayden nods his head in agreement.

"We had a rule," Veronica replies, her eyes far away. "No water was to leave the facility without a unanimous vote of approval. We didn't want anyone sharing its secrets with the world yet."

"Not very trusting are we?" Jo asks.

Veronica eyes our group with amusement. "Would you be?"

I think about us. About how I'd trust the world to Jo and Rob. But Jimmy and Odessa? I feel the heat of Brayden against me, his shoulder against mine. I see the shadow of stubble on his chin, and watch him flick his hair back to look at me. Would I trust him with *this*? Haven't I already?

"Where are the other two members?" Rob pipes up. "Brenda and Alex?"

"They aren't here. They were due to arrive today, but we haven't heard a thing from them, and we can't open the doors." Dad looks worried and chews on the inside of his cheek. "Blake might have them."

"So he stole the water?" I ask.

Veronica shrugs. "Blake adored his mother, but he wouldn't take the water out of the Cave. So he did what he knew how to do—he secretly went back to his work." She touches the glass door of the lab, almost tenderly, as if she were remembering watching him here those nights, the lights dim, his doctor's coat splattered in monkey blood. "All night long, without us knowing, he'd be in here killing animals . . . He used to say that by understanding death, he could better understand life. He purposefully manipulated the water's properties into a virus." I can barely control my shivers thinking of him in there.

"He always was the best of us in the labs," Chuck adds, his voice a mixture of jealousy and disgust.

"I remember the night I found out; at first I couldn't believe it," Veronica continues. "I just sat there watching him kill mouse after mouse. He was using the same antibodies he'd developed before, forcing cancer out of their bodies and then watching the animals die, cutting open their brains and organs to learn more. I could see the monkeys in their cages, dangling against the bars, their arms limp and tired." She shakes her head, and Dad pats her shoulder, his lips tight. "He found a way to turn the water upon itself, to kill rather than to heal. We are a secure facility," she says, pointing at a sign above the door that reads BIOHAZARD LEVEL 4. "And even after he created the virus, he didn't bother to wear a hazmat suit. He just started taking a drop of the water after every test session to protect himself—he told me this later. I think about how I was standing right here outside the lab, so close to that killer virus, completely unaware."

I look down at the bottom of the door to the lab, relieved to see it sealed shut. The dust in the lab seems deadlier now, sinister and teeming with the virus.

"After a while," Chuck cuts in, "he could accurately predict just how long it took a mouse to die. He showed me once. He'd say 'seven seconds' and then, sure enough, the mouse would die. He could literally time death with that virus. It was the worst thing

I could imagine, and he refused to see that instead of the perfect cure, he was creating the perfect instrument of death."

"We held a secret meeting," my dad says, "and decided to give him one dropperful of water to go save his mother. We thought maybe that would help. But we were too late. She had died a week earlier, and he hadn't told us. He was just obsessed."

"So you kicked him out?" I ask.

"We kicked him out," he confirms. There's a sadness to his voice. The weight of that decision still haunts him, especially with the current outbreak. The bags under his eyes, the sheen of sweat on his skin, his broken posture, must all have to do with letting Sutton go.

"He doesn't need a hazmat suit. He's never sick. He must have some water with him," Brayden says, bringing us into the present, and suddenly it feels very cramped in that corridor.

"I wouldn't put it past him, if he stole the virus," Veronica says, her face severe. "Blake's old money and brilliant to boot—even without the water. It wouldn't have been hard to hire those soldiers. Now that a few of them are sick, they are probably even more hell-bent on getting in here."

"Maybe," Dad says, "but we can't let him in. We have no leverage and no water. We can't save anyone without it."

"Sometimes I wonder whether this really is the Fountain of Youth," Chuck speculates, staring at the empty monkey cage.

"The Fountain of Youth?" Jo repeats.

"Well," he replies, his lips curling defensively, "they didn't find it in Florida, did they?"

"More like the Fountain of Life and Death," I say, the thought rolling off my mind. It's true—who ever thought that you could find life-healing water and then manipulate it to create an unstoppable virus, a pathogen designed to rush your body to death? Only humans could come up with such an awful way to turn a gift to a curse. I'm having a hard time not being disgusted, even resentful of this whole group of alums. With my dad *leading* them, they let the worst scenario come true.

"Whatever you want to call it," says Veronica, "we have water pumps this time, ready to extract as much as possible, and we can't miss the ten-day span. Even if Blake's just going to try to take the water. We've worked too hard to just open the doors because he's back in town."

Brayden snorts. Something Veronica said really bothers him. His skin's pulled so tight, his scar looks like white paint on his chin. "Right, forget about the virus. And after the ten days of pumping, are you going to keep yourself locked up here for another seventeen years, hoarding the stuff?" The adults stare at him. "What?" he replies, defiant. "You're trying to tell me it's okay that you sat on this for seventeen years? You couldn't have spared a dropperful? If you had just gone public, you might have been able to stop Sutton *and* share the secret of the water."

"Brayden . . ." I admonish, feeling embarrassed despite what feels like truth in his words.

"Go ahead, Mia. Ask him why they kept the secret. I want to know."

My dad speaks softly, his lips barely moving, so that we all have to quiet down to hear him. "We had two hundred gallons of water the first time around. Can you imagine the repercussions of going public with our discovery on two hundred gallons of water alone? If I knew where the map led, if it took us to the source, maybe I'd be willing to open this up. But we haven't figured that out yet, and without it, this place is just a stepping stone. I mean—" He pauses, flicking his hand toward the lab. "Not everything is answered yet. We can't let someone as misdirected as Blake have access to this place."

"A bit too late for that," Brayden mutters, unwilling to cede. "Or did the virus *not* come from Sutton's time working here?"

"I thought Sutton wanted to stop the virus," Odessa says, her eyes going involuntarily to her leg.

"Of course," Dad says, his gaze pensive. "But he *released* the virus. He's forcing his way in here. He couldn't have caused all this death solely to use the water to heal the people who are still alive."

"He wants the Cave," Veronica says grimly. "He wants us, he wants this place, and he wants to control the water."

"For what?" asks Rob. "Money? Fame? Is his pride hurt enough to do something like this?"

"I wish I knew," replies Veronica. I can't help thinking that, of all of us, she'd have the best chance of knowing Sutton's motivations.

"Well," Dad says, "if we don't get the water, we don't help anyone. We can't. There's only one vial left."

"Where is it?" I ask.

"The vial?" Dad asks.

"No, the well," I reply. He frowns at me. "We want to see the well."

"I'm sorry, Mia." He shakes his head. "Can't let that happen. We actually are going to need to end this tour now and put you guys in our break room. We have lots to do before the well refills."

"No," Jo blurts out, surprising everyone. She's standing very tall, her blond hair dark with sweat and stuck to her forehead and neck. But she looks fierce, her blue eyes blazing and her lips open just enough to see her teeth. "You are going to show us the well. You are going to take me to the place where this all began. My father is dead because of it. Because of *him*. You owe us everything."

Dad stares at her, his lips tight. He glances at Chuck, who shakes his head, and then at Veronica, who crosses her arms and nods.

Dad puts a hand on Jo's shoulder and her jaw clenches. Dad's face quivers, his forehead so notched with wrinkles and worry that I feel sorry for him. The last time I saw that face was when Mom died. "Jo, I'm sorry about your father. I'm so sorry. He was a good friend; I can't imagine how you're feeling right now. If you want to see the well, I'll take you. But please understand we have to be quick."

She nods, her eyes tearing up, and Dad, not really used to this type of emotion—he certainly doesn't get it from me—turns abruptly to start down the hall. His shoulders sag, and I guess I didn't realize how much he lost in all of this. His friend died too. Kids are dying, and he clearly feels responsible. I put an arm around Jo's shoulders, and she leans against me. Then she sniffs once and steps away, wiping tears from her cheeks. *I'm fine*, she mouths. And smiles, her eyes glistening.

"You shouldn't, Greg," Chuck warns. "These kids aren't here to replace the others." I assume he's talking about Brenda and Alex.

"They're here, Chuck," he replies through gritted teeth, "because that psycho we used to be friends with built a personal army and loosed the plague upon our town. Their school, Chuck. Their *families.* They have every right to this place. As much right as you and I."

Chuck grimaces, his thin face etched with annoyance, but stays quiet, and we follow Dad into the tunnels. Brayden's ahead of me and I watch him as we walk. I haven't really been able to get a moment alone with him since last night. He's mad, in a way I have never seen before. I realize just how little I know about him.

As we walk, I rub Jo's back, and she looks at me, her chin still quivering. She speaks with a voice thick with tears. "Happy birthday, Mia."

"You always give me the best presents," I say, smiling.

We laugh, and she puts her head on my shoulder. For a moment, everything feels like it's going to be okay.

I'm surprised at how we get to the well. It seems that the part of the Cave we've seen so far was built into the upper level of the mountain, probably near the entrance the alumni found with Avery all that time ago. And, maybe to keep it safer, they never dug deeper into the cavern that my dad fell into. We're taken to a dead end, another door, though this one is large and commanding, filling the entire wall in front of us. Dad uses his key card again and enters the code, and the door hisses and swings open, revealing an entrance to a large elevator.

"That's big enough to hold a truck," Rob muses.

"We have to be able to move efficiently," my dad explains.

"How much did this cost?"

"I'm not going to share our tax forms, son."

Rob's not chastened at all and pushes his glasses back on his face eagerly. "But, wow. This place is incredible. How did you even get workers in here to build?"

Dad tosses a meaningful glance at Veronica. "Took a lot of work and a lot of time to get this place ready. We needed a self-contained environment, storage capacities, and defense. All underground, all in secret. My construction company outfitted crews from across the country, in shifts, so that they wouldn't know what they were working on. Come on, guys, step inside."

The space in the elevator is so huge that there's no need to squish together, but we do anyway. Even my dad and Veronica and Chuck. Like we're so trained by elevators for narrow spaces that we can't help but pack in near the door.

"Only one stop?" Jo asks, pointing at the two buttons on the wall. No one answers.

The elevator hums, and I guess it's moving, but you can't tell. Before we realize it, the doors are opening. Heck, we could have gone up, for all I know.

Despite the construction the Westbrook alums inflicted on the Cave, they clearly tried to maintain the integrity of the well's cavern. Aside from the massive water tanks hulking on the edge of the clearing and the multitude of well-positioned spotlights, the cavern that spreads before us is enormous and apparently untouched. Stalactites hang from the ceiling and stalagmites jut forth from the ground in crazy shapes. Already my mind is trying to find images and animals among them.

But that's nothing compared to the broken wood and petrified forest that stands before us rimming a basin. It's as if everything froze in time, with the stumps of dead trees scattered. The remains remind me of a cemetery—we're only missing the fog.

Apparently Jo has the same thoughts, because she whispers, "Ghost town."

We follow Veronica down a well-lit walkway of grated metal and railings, our shoes clanking loudly, and into the dead woods and toward the well. The walkway is a few feet off the ground, and looking down, I can see how the water would have formed a small pond. In the center of the dead forest, jutting from the earth, is a hunk of rock, and I can see a man-made incision in its face that has left a white, empty space. This must be where the map was taken from. But I barely give this more than a glance; something else has my attention.

Next to the rock face, on the ground, is the well. It's smaller than I thought it would be. About three feet in diameter, with sloping sides, a mini volcano. I grip the handrails tight, my knuckles going white. I'm surprised at the nostalgia I'm feeling. I glance at the others spread out along the walkway, peering in, and I'm not sure I want them to feel what I'm feeling. This is *my* memory; it's a place I've been before, owned before, although I was stuck at the time. And here I can't help but find myself leaning toward the well, curious, wondering if the memory of my childhood fall is accurate. I close my eyes and can see the same nothing I saw when I was stuck in the well. I wonder if my shoulders would be a tight fit. I wonder if they'd bring me sandwiches in a lunch pail.

"Come on, Mia," Brayden whispers, pushing me ahead gently.

I break out of my trance. The others are all walking back up the ramp. How long have we been standing here? I glance back at the well and feel a burn along my stomach, which at first confuses me, but then I realize it's where the metal railing was pressing against my skin, holding me.

No one is looking, and Brayden uses the moment to kiss my neck, an act that shocks blood through my body again, as if my heart had slowed and I wasn't breathing. I pull my gaze from the well and smile, brushing his hair out of his eyes and letting my fingers linger on his earlobe. We head toward the elevator, and up ahead I see my dad, who's staring, frowning, looking from me to Brayden.

The return walk is unpleasant. Dad moves us at a quick clip, and everyone feels the urgency building. Stuck in the Cave for a while, we began to let our guard relax, but Sutton's still out there, as is the virus. We don't have much time. I keep my head down, trudging along, trying to quench the equal dose of embarrassment and indignation that's coursing through me. *Why* that *look, Dad?* I want to scream. I know he's just being protective, but why in the midst of all that's going on does he have to care about who's kissing my neck? I clomp after Brayden, my eyes on his shoulders rising and falling, and yes, maybe I take in his form and his body and maybe his ass, but it's only to keep me distracted.

They drop us off at the rec room, complete with a couple comfy couches and chairs, a big flat-screen TV, a wall of books, a few tables and, of course, foosball. That would be Dad; he loves foosball.

"But what about the lights?" Rob asks.

"What do you mean?" replies Veronica with a tilt of her head.

"The lights you have in there. How can you see the glowing stuff you mentioned in the story?"

"Oh, that," she says. "We've been studying the nocturnal luminances for years. We're actually making pretty good progress on that front, replication-wise. They are bright, but won't occur until the vegetation has returned, and we're not sure how long that'll take. We have to be able to see what we're doing there, so we have the lights."

"Will that hurt the plant life?" Odessa asks.

Dad shakes his head. "The water is Miracle-Gro, inside and outside. We can grow a seed on a drop of it in the desert."

"Cool," she replies, taking it all in, imagining the possibilities. I wonder if she'll ever be able to go back to high school botany. She looks the part of a PhD student now, what with her jumpsuit and eager thirty-year-old face. I bet if we survive all this, she'll ask for a job.

It's clear that the adults are ready to get to work, whatever that really means. They stand sort of inside and outside the door. Chuck's completely lost all signs of patience with us, and his initial pleasant veneer has long since faded. He turns abruptly and disappears down the hall, more important things to do.

"I've got a question," Brayden pipes in. "Where's the vial?"

"They aren't going to tell us that." Jo sniffs, dismissive. She's back in form, playing with her necklace, all traces of her earlier crying gone.

Veronica surprises us, though, with a semi-answer. "In a vault, next door to the Map Room. Safest place in the Cave."

Dad opens his mouth to add something, but before he does, I

blurt out the question that's been harrowing me since a drop hit Odessa's lips.

"Does it make you immortal?"

I can *feel* everyone lean forward. I can *feel* their pulses quicken. Dad and Veronica share uncomfortable eyes.

"We don't know . . . we haven't experimented that far. Not on humans, that is."

"So you've tested it on animals?" I ask.

"Immortality?"

I nod. And find myself holding my breath.

"On mice, rabbits, and one dog, yes. And also yes, they died, some of old age."

"You killed a dog?" Jo gasps.

Dad looks sheepish. "Well, we had to test everything. That's the point of all this, isn't it? The thing is, the life-preserving effects fade in direct proportion to the water dilution. Odessa will heal, Mia's foot healed, Jimmy won't have the virus anymore, but you need a lot more water to effect any permanent change. If a person had it pure, and drank it in larger quantities, her eyesight would get better, any blemishes would clear up, memory would improve, and for a limited time, she'd be immune to further exposure of pathogens and quick to heal from any superficial wounds."

"So you've drunk the water . . . you must have felt all this, right? You're sort of like Wolverine?" Rob asks. I roll my eyes. We all do. But only I remember that Dad dressed like the superhero for Halloween three years ago.

"Not anymore," Dad sighs. Veronica has the same look of longing, and I notice more than ever the sparks of gray in her hair.

"When we had more water, we all partook. Used to be I'd prick my finger to see how fast it would heal. Not anymore. We don't have that much left, so we started to drink some diluted, using ourselves as the guinea pigs. I even got my first flu in thirty-three years a few months back." Dad's face sags, and he shakes his head. "It's hard to say how long the pure water lasts. We just didn't have enough of it."

"Blake used to say that if we fed a mouse water and *then* cut a leg," Veronica adds, "it would heal. But if we cut the leg off, it wouldn't grow back. Maybe that was when he started thinking negatively."

"Wait," Jimmy speaks up. It has been a while since he's said anything, but he's paying attention now. "You're saying that I'm not immortal?" Jimmy asks, looking crestfallen, but he's clearly joking. Odessa punches him in the arm and he squeezes her into a headlock. The two of them are distractible, somehow not connected to the reality of the situation. It's bizarre watching them push and shove against each other, their adult bodies a poor fit for their personalities. We all watch for the briefest of moments, lost in the strangeness.

"So they're going to be like this forever, right?" Rob asks quietly.

"I believe so," Dad admits.

"Lucky for them that's all they lost," I say with a note of urgency. There's still our school out there, and the infection surely has spread. Todd Silver could be fifty, Rory could be dead. I might think he's a douche, but I don't want him dead.

"All right, all right," Dad says, bringing us back. "We have to go. We have to keep prepping for the water. I hope you're comfortable here. We'll be by with food soon enough—but for now, there are loads of DVDs in the box over there, and feel free to play whatever game you find."

"What about our parents?" Rob asks. He's taken his glasses off and is cleaning them on his shirt, which I think is an excuse not to look anyone in the eye and show his concern. But we're all concerned. Jimmy and Odessa stop roughhousing and pay attention.

"Rob, see—" my dad begins, but Veronica interrupts him.

"We don't have any more time, Rob. We have to prep for the water. We can't help anyone if we leave the Cave now. As soon as we harvest a good supply of the water, we'll try to figure our way out of this and inoculate everyone."

"But you have the vial," he persists, his voice going a bit shrill.

Dad takes Rob's pleading gaze head-on and speaks with a quiet authority. "Rob, I understand what you're saying. But what if that water ends up in Blake's hands? He'd use it on his troops. We're surrounded down here, and we'd never make it to Westbrook or Fenton with the vial. We have to wait for an ample and sustainable supply. We can't risk losing it, not yet. Your parents are in town, and town is probably okay."

"Probably." Jimmy snorts.

"Yes, probably."

"This is wrong. You can help them—you *have* to help them." Rob's cheeks are red now. Everyone's quiet, watching him try not to cry. I've never seen Rob cry, and my heart aches for him.

"Rob," Dad says, "I swear to you we'll leave as soon as we can. It's supposed to happen in a few hours. When the pumps are running and we have a few gallons in hand, I promise you we'll leave then, Blake or no. Okay?"

He takes in a shaky breath and heads toward one of the couches. The others follow him into the room. No one's too happy right now.

Dad pulls me off to the side. His shock of hair is scattered all across his forehead, making him look like a mad scientist. Maybe he is one. "You okay?"

I shrug and pick at my fingernail.

"Need anything?" His eyes split to Brayden and back.

I shake my head, annoyed he has time to focus on Brayden and me. He's going to lecture me, isn't he? A rage builds, and I just wait for him to bring it up so I can yell.

"How's Jo holding up?"

That dumps water on the fire. I didn't expect that. The others are worried about their parents, while she already lost one. But she's already more focused, less full of grief. All things considered, she's totally surviving. I don't know if I could do as much. When Mom died, I cut school for a week and didn't speak to anyone for a month.

"I think she's okay," I respond tentatively. "She has a right to be upset, you know?"

"I know," he replies. And I believe him. He's more tired than I have ever seen, and his breathing is harried. In the bright light of the room, he looks almost sick. "Trust me," he goes on, "I know. Kids are dying right now, the virus might be creeping onto the highways and spreading across the state. But you realize, Mia, you *know* that's why I'm waiting for the water. Without it, we are all dead anyway. With it, we're in the position to just give Blake a little water to go away and then we *help everyone*." He swallows hard, his eyes rimmed in red. He's boxed in, decades of waiting for this moment, and it's surrounded by tragedy. He leans in, kisses my forehead. Then brings his eyes to mine and tries to smile. "Listen, hon. I know this isn't how you envisioned it, but happy birthday, and I'm sorry I don't have anything planned. But I promise I'll make it up to you when we're out."

He sounds so earnest it's bizarre. Like he actually thinks my birthday is on my mind at this moment. "Dad, I don't care about that."

"Maybe you should," he replies, smiling. "I think that somehow all of this has everything to do with you. Remember, you were born on the day the water came last time, and if it comes today . . ." He takes a breath and then his face gets serious, worry etched into the skin. "I might not see you for a while, hon. If the water returns, I'm going to have my hands full. You understand that, right? If you need something, use the intercom near the door, but don't leave. I want you safe."

I nod grudgingly, trying to fight back silly irrational tears. This isn't the end of some movie. I don't need to say good-bye to my dad like I'll never see him again.

He pats my head, and then follows Veronica out of the room.

20

ALONE IN THE REC ROOM, WITH NOTHING TO DO beyond the mundane, I'm suddenly antsy. So are the others. Jimmy and Odessa gravitate to the foosball table. The rest of us do too, and end up watching the game, Jimmy's tongue poking out of his cheek, Odessa blowing her hair from her eyes.

"It looked like a diorama in the Museum of Natural History," says Rob out of nowhere, talking about the cavern with the well.

"That's in New York, right? I've never been to New York," Jimmy says, looking thoughtful. "My aunt lives in Queens. Maybe when this is done—"

Odessa scores during his lapse in concentration. She lifts her chin cockily at Jimmy, which prompts him back to the game. Brayden idly flicks the wooden wheel indicating a point for Odessa.

"The weird thing is," Odessa says, not looking up, her curly hair bouncing from side to side as she plays, "I feel the same. This body, it feels natural, like it was always mine. I can't even tell my leg was shot." She snaps her wrist and sends the ball into Jimmy's goal, then looks up at me, her eyes as blue as ever, maybe the one unchanged thing about her appearance. "But I'm never going to be myself again, you know? What, when this is all done, I'm going to return to Fenton and live in a dorm room?"

"Why not?" Jimmy says, rooting around for the ball. "Why not try to be normal?"

"Jimmy, we've lost the very *best* years of our lives. And now I'm stuck in a cave playing foosball." I've never heard her like this, ever. Jimmy holds up the white ball and rolls it between his fingers, looking at the woman he's playing against.

"We could steal our parents' money and elope."

I think we all gasp at the comment, and I *know* that Odessa likes what he said. Her newfound crow's-feet dance around her eyes. But then the light seems to go out. She ducks her head back to the table. "They gotta be alive for us to steal it from them," she says, and waves at him to play. Jimmy looks at me, and his round cheeks bounce in an odd, almost apologetic smile. I don't know why he's apologizing for anything, much less to me. He pops the ball into play, and Brayden and I share a glance.

Jo has wandered away and is sitting Indian style on the floor, sifting through the DVDs. Her shoulders slump, and her legs jitter.

"Mind if I join?" I ask, taking a seat next to her once she selects a movie. I feel like we're back in our dorm room, about to watch *Dexter*, talking about Todd. Even the way she nudges me with her knee is natural.

"Why would he release the virus this long before the water returned?" she asks.

It's a good question. I've thought about it myself. "I think because he wasn't expecting this whole situation to keep going. He thought he could use the virus and me to get my dad to open this place up. If the water had already arrived, Dad would have just used it to heal everyone. Sutton screwed up because he never thought we'd escape."

"But Westbrook . . ."

It's hard to imagine the school right now. Most of the students would look like they were in their sixties or seventies. Maybe they're dead. I pull gently at her tangled blond hair, unable to articulate anything else.

"I bet Todd's hot as an adult," she ventures, a weird smile on her face.

I can't help but crack, "Slick hair, six-pack, chiseled jaw."

"He had that already," she reminds me.

"Fine," I say. "Chubby gut, receding hairline, back hair."

Jo leans close to me and whispers, "He has the back hair already!"

We both laugh, such a foreign sound that the others stop what they're doing and watch us. But they grow bored as we keep going, laughing and hugging and happy to feel even a little normal again. The movie she's chosen is an old one, *Toy Soldiers*. With that guy from *Goonies* and *Lord of the Rings* and *Rudy* . . .

"Who's that actor? The one that played Frodo's best friend/ lover?"

"Sean Astin," Rob says. He flops over the couch and lands on Jo's other side, and now we're really back in our room. He pulls out his phone and tries to take a picture of us.

"Rob, what the hell?" I say, pushing his hand away.

"What?" he says, looking hurt, his tiny nose crinkling. "I just thought, you know, that we could use *some* documentation of this place."

"You get any reception yet?" I ask.

"No, nothing." He waves the phone around the room, his calculator watch dangling.

Jo puts her head on my shoulder, and I have to push the strands of her hair out of my face. "I wish we could watch the news," she says. "See if they are reporting on Fenton."

Something about the phone and the news clicks in my head. I look over at Rob. "What happened with the walkie-talkie?"

His mouth twitches, and he stares at the floor, not making eye contact. "I should have held on to it."

"When?"

"In the water. I lost it when the aqueduct exploded."

Jimmy must have scored, because he screeches in delight. I look over at the sound and see the two of them in their scrubs, faces intense, playing their game. Behind them, Brayden's standing at the door, his hand on the latch. I'm confused. What's he doing?

"I'll be back," I say, and lift Jo off my shoulder. Rob raises an eyebrow at me. "Take my spot."

"Do you need help?" Rob asks. And I wonder what the answer is. I hesitate, then whisper, "No."

Brayden waves me through the door. I turn and look at Rob, who's watching me, and mouth, *One minute.*

We step out into the hall, Brayden closing the door softly behind us.

"What are you doing?" I ask, reaching for his hand. He gives it to me.

"I'm sorry. The three of you seemed so comfortable. I didn't want to bother you."

"Bother me with what?"

He peers down the hallway. We can't hear a thing. His face is pensive, his eyes quick and suspicious. There are sweat stains blooming in his armpits. He's making me nervous. "I think there's something more going on."

"More than miracle water and a killer virus?"

He flashes a set of crooked, bleached teeth, his expression rueful. "This place is too complex not to have access to the outside world."

"Dad mentioned cameras, but so what? They're not going to let us see them."

"That doesn't bother me," he replies, and starts walking down the hallway. I hesitate, looking at the door. He glances at me, his face soft and forgiving. "You don't have to come. That's okay. I'll be back soon."

He disappears around a corner. I reach for the door but stop myself. I can hear the light sound of his footsteps on the floor. I'm hurt a little that he didn't pull me along with him, but my curiosity is too great. I don't like the idea of him knowing more about the place where my dad works than I do. In some weird way, I feel like this is *my* cave, and it's not for Brayden to see without me. I've known about it all my life, Dad discovered it, runs it, and the key to saving Westbrook is here. I will not just let the chance go or let someone else experience the Cave without me.

I jog, hurrying to catch up. And when I do, he takes my hand, his skin dry but warm. My heart rate is up, and I control my breathing instinctually. This narrow hallway feels like a swim lane. But I've never had anyone partner with me before. Brayden looks at me, his raven hair flying past his ears, and for the tiniest of moments, I swear he seems dismayed. His thin lips turn down, and his eyes narrow, but then it's gone. Now he's smiling, and his dimple flashes, and all's well again. I fight the urge to touch his face to make sure he's okay, but then he pulls on my arm, and we turn into another hallway.

"Are we gonna bump into someone?"

His face is grim. "The odds are small. We should be fine." This place is so huge, I don't remember where we are and where we've been, but Brayden seems to walk unerringly.

Suddenly he stops, his arm going rigid in front of me, like my dad does in the car when he hits a red light. We're in a hallway that looks exactly the same as the previous one. I feel a sense of déjà vu. We're breathing at the same pace, and he keeps his arm in front of me.

"What?" I whisper, but he shushes me. I try to listen and then—there! A sound. A *thud*. A *boom*.

"What is it?"

"Not sure, but I want to find out. This way." We're moving slower now. If I were in charge, I'd be going *away* from the sound, not toward it. This excursion was his idea. And I can't say I don't admire his bravery. We reach a Y-junction and head down the left corridor, the wrong one, because the sounds recede quickly, so we double back. The *thud* gets louder now, methodical.

There's a door with a keypad. I put the phone number in, and it beeps open. Brayden grins. "You have to make your dad change that."

I laugh, I can't help it. Maybe it's the nerves. "I'll tell him *after* we break into everything."

The door opens into an indoor parking lot, like the garage at a mall, not at all what I was expecting. The sound is violent here, shaking the walls, and bits of rock and dust are falling from the ceiling. There are only three cars and a van. I'm surprised at the sudden pang I feel at seeing our Camry.

"They're trying to get in," Brayden says, his voice sure of it.

Beyond the cars is a giant set of doors. Enormous and familiar. These must be the inner doors. I've pounded on a pair just like them, not a hundred yards away at the entrance to the Cave. *Thud, thud, thud.*

"Sounds like a battering ram," I say.

"More like a tank shell," he replies, his eyes on the shaking ceiling.

"We should tell my dad."

"How can he not already know?" he asks.

"Come on," I say, tugging his arm. "We have to find him."

"They're almost here," Brayden says, his voice strange. "Your dad said they'd breach the outer door. That can't be long now."

I finally get him turned, each of his steps slow and clumsy. "What's wrong with you?" I shout. The *thuds* slam in a steady beat, like a harrowing clock. Sutton knocking at the door.

We hurry down the corridors again, aimless as can be, but we have better luck this time. A few hundred yards in, we hear Chuck's voice coming from around a corner. We plaster ourselves to a wall, and my heart is beating so fast I'm sure he can hear it.

". . . be sure," he says.

"I'm not," a voice replies. Female. Veronica. "But Kish is right. If we have the water, we have the leverage."

"I'm more worried about my life."

"Chuck, Blake wouldn't do that."

"Fine—I'm going to the pump room. Buzz me if that crazy fuck gets in."

Chuck pauses in the hallway, and I can imagine him craning his neck in our direction, wondering if this way is faster than that. Brayden puts a finger to his lips, his eyes flash with warning. Chuck begins to walk, his footsteps echoing loud, and I turn to run, but Brayden snatches my wrist hard enough that I have to bite my tongue to keep from shouting. Sure enough, the echoes fade and he's gone, deeper into the mountain. Brayden unlatches his hand from my wrist. I try to keep hold by grabbing his sleeve.

"Let's go," he whispers, moving toward the very room Veronica is in.

"But you were right. She knows about Sutton trying to get in. Won't she just be pissed that we're out of the rec room? Let's go back."

"She's where I want to go," he says, his eyes distracted. "I'm not worried about her."

I wonder why, but I don't say anything. And I follow him down the hall and into a control room, full of panels, switches and security videos for the Cave. A display three times as large and a hundred times more sophisticated than what we saw at the aqueduct. It looks like a semicircular mission control for NASA. Rob's mouth would water just seeing this. How did Brayden know this was here? On the screens I see the greenhouses and the door near the exit. There's the Map Room. The rec room, where Jimmy and Odessa are still playing in their old-people suits. I don't see Jo and Rob, but

I can't see the couch either. And there's the front entrance and, yes, the tank.

"Took you long enough," Veronica says from her chair near the screens, not spinning around. Her hand is on a lever and is pulling it slowly back. I have no idea what it's for. I realize that she must have been watching us the whole time. Sure enough, there's a screen that shows the parking lot.

"What's going on?" I ask, hoping the fear doesn't come through my voice.

She still doesn't turn around. "He's an idiot, you know?"

"Why?" Brayden asks.

Her hair's in a bun, and it bounces as she nods toward the video showing the front door and the tank barrage. "Blake helped build the place. He knows the blast doors can withstand artillery."

"Forever?" he asks.

Veronica shrugs. "Definitely not. Greg's estimate might be off, but they'll hold long enough."

"Where is he?" I ask, moving forward to get a closer look. She shoos me away, and I pull back. I can see soldiers, still in their hazmats. They are grainy and gray. The screen shivers and goes black, then returns slowly to normal, a layer of dust settling outside in front of the camera. A boom echoes through the Cave, a split second behind the feed. The tank rocks and reloads.

"Where's Dad?"

"Should be down at the well," she replies, turning around. "But don't go there, please. He'd kill me if he knew I was letting you run around. When it comes to the well and to the Map Room, he tolerates nothing but discipline."

I open my mouth, about to make an indignant remark, but Veronica stands up and brushes past us. She stops in the doorway and looks over her shoulder, her bright eyes indifferent and bored. "You coming?" I look at Brayden, and he nods. I wish I understood how he can be so confident right now, how this is what we went looking for.

We follow her into the hallway, and she locks the door to the control room. "Listen, I just changed the code, so don't try to go in there. Don't go anywhere. Go back to the rec room." She starts to give us directions, but Brayden interrupts.

"I remember the way," he says. I'm impressed, because I'm definitely lost.

Veronica doesn't seem to buy it either, so he points back the way we came. "First right, then another right, then a left and up a corridor, second door on the left."

She thinks about it, maps that in her head and finally nods grudgingly. "Okay, good. This is going to be fine, you know?" *Thud.*

As soon as she's out of sight, Brayden grabs hold of my arms. "I need you to go back to the rec room." His eyes are intense, fierce and desperate. He's up to something I don't understand, but I know he's trying to protect me. It's like we're back in the locker room at Westbrook, right after he knocked out the soldier.

"What? Why? Where are you going?" I try to keep my voice from sounding anxious. Not sure I succeed.

"Please, Mia. I don't have much time." He's breathing hard, clearly troubled, and he flinches when another *thud* lands. This time, there's actually a small crackling of rock somewhere overhead, not the sound I want to be hearing.

"I don't get it. What's going on with you?" I say, shaking my head. I don't like this, or the anguish in his face. I touch his hand, and it's burning. "No. I'm not going to leave you."

I can see the warring emotions in his eyes, in the strain upon his face. He moves closer to me, and I can smell his sweat and his fear and heat. I tense up, pulling him to me.

"Do you trust me?" he whispers, his lips near mine.

"Brayden, what's going on?"

"Do. You. Trust. Me?" He clenches my arms, and a part of me is scared, but another part, a stronger part, is incredibly excited. In the moment, I think about the locker room and the snowy fields outside Furbish, about the tunnel before Dad found us, but most of all, I think about the aqueduct, and how he came back for me. His fingers feel like fire, and my mouth's so dry it's hard to swallow.

"Absolutely," I say. I hope he sees it in my eyes.

"Good." He peers around as if someone were watching. "Follow me, then. But you have to do what I say."

I pull away from him, concerned. "What's going on?" The hallway is incredibly bright and endless, and I have to whisper to feel safe.

Brayden stares at me for a moment, considering. I try to keep his gaze. His jaw clenches like a stopwatch. "I'm going to save my parents."

"What?" I say, shaking my head. I remember him in the parking lot, staring at the door. He's been trying to get out of here. "How can you?"

"There's not much time," he says. "They're stuck at Furbish, they contracted the virus, they *need* the vial."

"But—"

"No, Mia!" he says fiercely, his teeth flashing. His brows furrow and his voice is angry, but I'm not scared of him. I'm scared *for* him. "I have to do this. There's not enough time to wait for the well. It might be too late already. Your father will save everyone else. But I have to save my parents."

I'm quiet, and his fury breaks, his forehead eases, and his eyes soften. His conviction turns into a plea. He needs me. He needs me to help him steal the vial from my dad. That's why he didn't want me with him: he didn't want me to hurt my father. I put my hand on his pale cheek, sheened in sweat. Brayden's not going to sit in the rec room waiting, like my father, for the water that might not be coming. Especially when his parents are in danger. I wouldn't wait either, in his shoes.

"I'm coming with you."

He takes my hand to his mouth and kisses it. His lips are chapped but tender. They make it hard for me to breathe. "I'm sorry," he says.

"Don't be," I say gently. "Lead the way."

He stares at me for a moment more. He seems sad, with puppy-dog-brown eyes, as if putting me in danger is the last thing he intended. Like he's about to argue.

"Brayden," I say, "it's now or never."

He takes a breath, and his face lights up, his dimple coming back in his smile. And I know the pleasant feeling spreading inside me means I'm doing the right thing.

Down the halls, our feet silent in our slippers. I follow blindly but he moves with a mission, and with no lack of confidence. We hit the infirmary, where our skiwear is stored. I don't even bother to take off my scrubs, I just add layer after layer. Because I left my jacket at the aqueduct, I grab Odessa's. It's heavy and warm and feels like armor. I put my hands in her pockets and am lucky I don't cut myself, because inside is a serrated steak knife from the kitchen at Furbish Manor. I actually let it cut through the fabric so that it holds in place. I also find the little squishy blue-and-white berries from the greenhouse, which she must have stashed away. Can't blame a botanist for hoarding. Satisfied, I move on: my boots are thick and impenetrable, and I can wiggle my toes this time. We don't say a thing. We don't have to.

Then we're out again, my mind a mess of turns and junctions and the *hum* of the lighting. I fight down my panic at the endless tunnels and the sweat already gathering in my pits and trust Brayden. And sure enough, we find a familiar-looking set of doors. I enter the code, and it beeps green. I guess Veronica's lock change applied only to the control room. Brayden was right; Dad really should have changed the codes.

But we hit the wrong room. The door opens on its massive hinges to reveal the Map Room. The map itself appears to float in the darkness, a single light illuminating the block of stone like a carefully curated museum exhibit. It's hypnotic and beautiful; the painted images seem to glimmer. I swear they're brighter than when we first saw the map. There's something different going on here.

"Mia, this way," Brayden hisses.

He's already down a couple doors, trying the code. Another *beep*, another huge vault door opening.

I wave him on. "Go ahead. I need to see something." He makes as if to protest but then changes his mind and disappears into the room where the vial of water is stored. I wonder, idly, what that room looks like. If there are rows of empty vials, storage containers for the water. Or if it sits there in a slot, illuminated just like this map.

I step into the room, and the air chills around me.

The map reads like a puzzle of an alien sky. I wish I could figure out what drew me here, what about the map has changed. I can feel it on the tip of my tongue, in the corner of my vision. In the darkness of the planetarium-style space, the images on the map might as well be a set of constellations that I have never seen before. Dad spoke before of grids, a certain number of images on each row and column, but now they seem to writhe in place, desperate to move. Without any context, though, there's no way of knowing what any one of them means, what the shrieking red bird there or the giant ram's horn here symbolizes. I find myself reaching out to touch its surface, but then imagine alarms blaring, so I stop.

Brayden is probably pulling the vial from the shelf now. He has to be quick, so I have to be quicker. The first time we looked at this, the focus was on that never-ending map in the bottom-right corner, the replica in miniature. But we didn't pay much attention to the rest of it. The golden gates that seem to sparkle. Or the bloodshot eye of a wolf. The deep blue of the water, painted with a pigment that seems to have come from the sky.

And then I see it. *Holy shit, I see it!*

The map is a grid full of paintings, and the paintings have changed. Aside from the replica map in the corner, the most eye-catching image is a spray of water, a fountain jetting into the air. At the top of its spray, the water curls over to fall back down to the earth. It's a simple thing, but it's somehow bright and brilliant and appears to shudder. After all the talk of healing water and the Fountain of Youth, of course that's what stands out.

But higher up on the grid, something is entirely different. Last time, my eye kept drifting to the black hole, a single dark circle that seemed to somehow shine around its edges, like an eclipse. Dad and the others actually thought it was an eclipse, a solar event that marked a major religious ceremony like the drawings of the Aztecs or the Incas. But now I'm not so sure. The thing is, I've seen this image before, and suddenly I am certain. This is not a solar eclipse. It's a unique perspective, one I stared at for days deep down inside my childhood well, looking up, where all I could see were the flashes of light bursting around the edges. That hole is not an eclipse, because it is the well, the spring where the water comes from. I know this now because it's blue, shimmering and filled with water. Dad was right, the water will come today.

I look closer. I can't believe it. My arms tingle, goose bumps raised so high they hurt. The painting has *changed*. What is this? Magic? Has Dad seen this? Am I the only one who knows? The well is full. The water is here.

My legs literally weaken from excitement. I shift my gaze around the map, seeing if I can find any other differences in my memory of the images. There's a pair of high gates, closed if I recall, but they're now open, and there's a road in between them. Farther down the map, there's an intricately depicted city, pulsingly gold. There's a thin figure, nondescript, so blank that it might not indicate male or female, but its skin is white as milk. It appears a few times on the map, the same figure. But this time, there's one figure that looks different. I'm not sure I'd normally notice this, so it might not really have been different, but now that I'm looking for differences, I can't help noticing that in all the other images of figures, the eyes are slits. Slits, that is, that made me think nothing special before. But now this one figure, I remember him from last time I was here— he's upside down, his hands pointing below, and he's painted right in front of the blue of the well.

His eyes are open. His eyes *are open*!

The others, they don't have open eyes, and now I think those slits mean they aren't awake. Suddenly I remember Dad's story, about how their eyes were blue! I hadn't thought on it before, but he's right. If the blue in the well means the water has returned, what do the open eyes mean?

"Do you see anything you like?"

I am so scared I can't help but scream, my hand flying to my mouth. Chuck is there, standing with his legs apart, his face stern and disappointed and bemused at once. In Chuck's hands is a long length of black tubing. He must have seen the open doorways as he went for a replacement part. Hopefully, his finding me is just very bad luck.

He doesn't wait for me to answer. "Your father's like that too. He'll just come here and stare, for hours. You'd think that after thirty-four years, he'd have learned something by now. But then again he's always been a bit of a zealot, always looking at that thing even after he figured out that the water flowed on a cycle."

I try to calm myself. Chuck seems relaxed, more like he caught me out of bed than anything else. My voice is dry when I speak. "You don't buy all this?" I ask, saying the first thing that comes to mind. "You don't think the water is coming, do you?"

"Buy?" he repeats, smiling, his long face peering down at me. "I buy it all. I will buy a lot more after all this is done. No, your dad thinks this all *means* something. I think it's just a magical collusion of natural forces, creating a universal healing property. A very lucrative one." He laughs once to himself, lifting the tubing to his chest, thinking of something far away. "I can't believe I've spent so much time here. But it'll all be worth it. I'll be known as the doctor who cured illness, *every* illness." He looks around the room, almost with nostalgia. He even pats the door gently. "But, man, I can't wait for this all to end."

"But what about the people dying? The infected?"

He nods thoughtfully. "Yes, that's tragic. I truly think so. But when you've been around the water as long as I have, you learn what it can do. No one will be sick for long. Now, let's get moving and check in on the others. We'll see if anyone else decided to wander away."

He holds out a hand, not at all threateningly, and at that moment, an arm comes down hard on the back of his head. His eyes roll and his mouth slackens, and he falls, knees first, hitting the ground; at the same time I hear another reverberating *thud*.

"Whoa, you didn't have to do that," I say. "He wasn't trying to hurt me." How did he learn to hit that way?

Brayden just shrugs and flashes the vial of water at me. Is it even water? Can it be called that? It's clear and pure and healing, but is it water? Brayden checks Chuck's pulse, then his pockets. He pulls a key card and waves it triumphantly in the air, then tosses it to me. "This could be helpful." He's smiling now, flipping his hair back as he takes my hand. "You okay?"

I nod dumbly, still trying to get over the slumped body on the floor and that this is the second time Brayden has knocked someone out for me. I open my mouth to tell him about the map, just as Brayden hisses sharply, "Someone's coming!"

I can hear the footsteps now. Nondescript, beating loudly, they could be anyone's, even my dad's. And for a second, I want to stay here and wait for it to be my father, and for him to come into the light and for me to show him what I just learned. But I guess that's impossible and now I feel like I'm betraying my father. I'm leaving here, I'm stealing the vial and I'm choosing Brayden. Not him, not my father, but this boy.

For a heartbeat, I pause. I almost just give it up. This is crazy and stupid. But Brayden needs my help. And I trust him.

We take off down the hall, away from those nameless footsteps. I don't look to see if anyone's following. Brayden and I race through the Cave, deeper and deeper, until the concrete walls go rough and turn to stone, and I can feel the air around me get hotter and muggier. Sweat stings my eyes, and my hiking boots feel heavy as I run. The ceiling seems to get lower, and I find myself ducking down, scared I'll smack my head into the wall. I look behind me, but the light globes on the ground begin to fade out.

Suddenly, the Cave expands, and we find ourselves in a familiar setting. I put my hands on my head to control my ragged breathing; my coach would be proud. There before us are the greenhouses, now filled with a new meaning. Each house a birthplace of a unique life form, all created through experimentation with the water and genetics. I bet Dad's pulling the stuff from the well right now. As we walk between the opaque windowed units, I can't help but think that just one leaf from one of the plants inside would be enough to set Odessa's professional career for life.

Seeing the rear exit of the cave gives me another hit of energy, enough that I have to shake my arms to release the jitters. I reach unconsciously for goggles to pull down onto my face.

I realize, as Brayden must surely, that we might have a difficult time descending from the wrecked remains of the aqueduct station, but that isn't what matters now. If Odessa is any proof, then even one drop of this vial could save either of our lives from whatever Sutton and his men might throw at us. As if reading my mind, Brayden says, "Holding this makes me feel invincible."

"But you haven't had any of the pure water."

"Still," Brayden replies. "Now take it." He hands over the vial to me for some reason, like it's my right. I don't argue, but secure it in my pocket, snug, where I can feel it digging against my hip.

The heavy metal door seems insignificant now, compared to the vastness of the Cave, but it's a porthole to something much bigger. When we open those doors, it'll be like we're moving backward, from the Cave to the aqueduct to Furbish Manor, then through the woods to Westbrook.

Brayden's not even looking at the door. In fact, he's staring at me. The corners of his lips turn downward, making him seem sad and broken. His brow is in a knot, and his eyes . . . they catch my gaze but are glassy and seem to be lost somewhere else. He blinks and suddenly is here, his eyes clear and bright, dimple and all, but his face remains miserable. He closes the distance between us and puts his hand to my neck, his thumb resting against my cheek, where it presses lightly. For some reason—reflex maybe—I grow incredibly embarrassed and instinctively try to duck away, but his gentle hand turns solid, and he keeps me there; in fact, he pulls me closer.

"Mia . . . I'm sorry."

I'm about to say, *for what?* But then he kisses me, as if he doesn't want to hear me speak. The kiss takes all my thoughts away. Our breaths go desperate, and the taste of his tongue lingers. I feel the thrill of his body against mine, and I tug at his jacket and nip at the tight skin of his scar, somehow desperate for his touch. We're about to leave the safety of the Cave, and who knows when I'll be able to kiss him like this again?

"Mia," he whispers as we kiss, and I pause for air but not to answer. "Mia, stop it . . . We have to stop . . ."

His tone is weird and splashes like cold water against me. I pull back, confused.

"Mia," he says, his voice serious, "I'm sorry."

Brayden steps away from me, but his eyes don't meet mine, and the smile that was thick on my face has vanished. He turns and walks to the door. I wonder—if I had more than a second, would I have figured out what was going on? But I didn't. I watch Brayden swipe Chuck's ID and hear it *ping* with an echoing, metallic *clank*. He moves back from the door and, almost absentmindedly, he hands me the ID. Brayden stares at the door, and I flip the plastic card in my hand end over end. The door lurches. I remember how, on the way in, it took the three boys all their combined strength to move that door, but now, as if by magic, it swings inward, and we stare at the shape of a man, his smile dripping, his eyes bright.

"Brayden, my boy, I knew I could count on you."

21

SUTTON'S NOT ALONE. HE'S STANDING WITH A HALF dozen of his soldiers, each unmasked, each armed with serious-looking firepower, big heavy machine guns that I'm sure have impressive-sounding names. As if they expected us to come packing heat. Or, more realistically, as if they were expecting to have to storm the place.

Brayden stares at the floor. Sutton ruffles his hair with affection.

I don't have to ask Brayden to figure out what's going on. All I want to do is scream, but first I need to hold back from vomiting. Really—my stomach is queasy, and I'm so hot all of a sudden I think I'm going to pass out.

"What the fuck?"

"Now, Mia," Sutton drawls. "That's no way to greet a friend." He's still in his jeans and fleece, like he's never once changed since I first met him, which seems like so long ago. But something seems off about him, different. He appears aged by the ordeal—his skin has an unhealthy pallor, and his eyes are bloodshot. But his apparent exhaustion does nothing to dampen the enthusiasm in his voice.

"You're not my friend," I reply woodenly. Sutton's troops fan out and take positions against the nearest greenhouse walls, then move to secure the room. One stays behind at the door, most likely to guard their entrance. Do they even realize how easy it's going to be to take the place over?

"Little Kish, your father's daughter. Where is he? Where is everyone?" He runs his hand through his hair like he did last time I saw him, his nerves shot.

I don't answer. Why would I?

"Son?" he says, squeezing Brayden's neck. He's not his real father, so the term sounds creepy.

"I don't know where he is . . ." Brayden speaks through clenched teeth. "Mia," he goes on, his voice desperate, "I didn't want to do this!" His cheeks flush, and his eyes plead.

I'm almost blind with anger. Brayden meant to betray me all along. That's why he kept apologizing. That's why he didn't want me to come.

"Brayden."

It takes me a moment to realize his name slipped from my lips. A whisper, almost inaudible. I can feel my own pathetic pain as I desperately piece the clues together. He was separated at the Manor, of course, working with Sutton. And that whole time, he was probably getting some medical help for the injury I caused when I kicked in his face. He probably was eating good food and Sutton was with him, whispering in his ear, detailing the Cave's floor plan and his strategy. I feel manipulated and used, and I slap him. Hard. So hard that a mark is already welling on his cheek from my fingernails. My hand stings, but the pain feels good. He doesn't say anything, just puts his hand to his face and takes a step back.

Sutton looks disgusted by the two of us, as if being in the middle of our squabble is beneath him. "Boy, did you find the vial?" he asks.

Brayden shakes his head.

"Shame," Sutton replies. I feel the knife in my hand and wonder if I could pull it out and throw it at him. "I would have sent a soldier with you to help your parents."

Why did Brayden lie? I wonder. Why did he give me the vial and the key card? What even is the point, if Sutton's here to steal the water? Brayden's staring at me, his expression blank, my hand outlined in red on his face.

Sutton glances at his man guarding the door and motions him forward.

"Keep him here until we're back."

"Yes sir," shouts the guard. I realize, suddenly, that they aren't wearing hazmat suits, as if they've given up pretending the suits worked. The guard's a fierce-looking man, his uniform dark and imposing, and his helmet tight against his forehead and his body weighted with equipment. He takes Brayden by the arm and leads him to the exit. The other five soldiers return now, shouting all clear, and they take positions, creating a path and direction for Sutton to take.

"And you." He points to another soldier. This one is short and dumpy, and I can see sweat through his uniform. But his eyes are intense and his expression serious, and I'm somehow more afraid of him than the others. "Bring her with us." The soldier grabs my arm roughly, and I try to pull away, but it's a steel grip, cutting off my circulation.

"Move on, men. We have to hurry." Sutton starts forward, but he's stepping with a hobble. And then it hits me. He *has* aged since I saw him last. I reinspect his face and can see the ashen sag of skin, the longer graying hair. He's infected. And since he's older than us, things are moving quickly. Suddenly, I realize why the vial in my pocket is worth so much. Every second for Sutton is an exponential moment of his life lost.

"Sutton," I call out, my voice singsongy, "what about Veronica?"

He stops and stares at me.

"Yeah, what are you going to do to her in your master plan? After you kill my dad? Are you going to kill her too?"

"You don't know what you're talking about."

"She said they shouldn't have let you go," I say, repeating her words, bending her intent. Sutton's face shows a stormy mixture of emotions. His hands begin to shake and his body looks smaller, hunched in on itself. They must have really loved each other once. He swallows, and his eyes slant. He's going to hurt someone. It might be me. He takes a step my way.

I fight the panic off my chest and pull out the vial. "You looking for something?" I raise the glass above my head, as far away from the soldier's reach as possible, and tell him to let me go. The guy looks about to break my neck, but Sutton shouts at him to release me. As soon as he does, the blood pours into my arm, making me woozy.

"Give it to me, Kish." His voice is menacing. I have never heard it with such an edge. He pulls a gun from his holster and trains it between my eyes. "Give it to me now!"

336

"You listen to me," I spit out, letting all the rage I feel at Brayden flow through my veins. "This is the last known sample of water from the well, water that can save your life, and you don't know for sure if it's coming back today or not. No one does." I can only hope the bluff holds long enough to make this work . . . "So put your gun down and back off."

Sutton's men shift uneasily. He's about to say something when he begins to cough, hacking hard enough to double over. He spits some blood onto the ground and groans. I never thought I'd be happy to see someone sick.

Sutton shakes his head, clearly restraining himself. His tendons bulge from his neck.

For a moment, I think he's going to do it, have his men put their guns down. Maybe I could get them to back out the door. Without them here, we'd have a chance. I could get away and warn my dad. I could pull the knife that's in my jacket and try to hurt him. But Sutton's less of an idiot than I want him to be. He raises his gun again.

"No, little Kish. I don't buy it. Give me the vial now, or I'll shoot you and take it."

He might or might not be bluffing. But there's no way for Sutton to know, at least at this time and place, if I'm telling the truth about the water.

Brayden's looking small. His face is still red, his scar standing out brightly against his skin, and he's watching me from the exit. I look at him and can't feel a thing.

"Screw it." My words come out no louder than a breath. I bend my knees and launch the vial straight up in the air.

I take a split second to watch it twist, glinting off a light fixture, and try not to think about how Sutton should just shoot me before he tries to catch it.

And then I'm running.

I have maybe fifteen yards before I get to cover (what little there is behind a building made of glass). I run, literally feeling my feet push off the earth. There's a loud *crack* and I feel something brush past my head. I duck and keep going, getting closer to the glass, and then, miraculously, I'm there. I can't stop to look, that would be stupid, so I'm weaving through the greenhouses and finally, almost reassuringly, I can hear more gunshots and glass cracking all around me. They don't know where I am, so they're just shooting, and I run low, as fast as I can manage, pushing toward the tunnel.

I'm hoping that they actually caught the vial. That would slow them down, as Sutton would want to open it right there and drink it down. Or maybe it would be even better if no one caught it and it broke on the rocks and Sutton is even now licking muddy dirt from the floor. But there's no way I'll know. All I can know is that I have to run fast. I take a breath, turn my head and let it out. My legs begin to burn, but I just turn my head and breathe. My ski clothes are my drag suit, and my sweat the pool.

I hit the tunnel at full speed and am probably a hundred yards in when a pair of hands grabs me. I scream and flail out, but then I see that it's Rob, hushing me, pulling me into a corner.

Jo's with him, eyes panicky.

"What are you doing here?" I shout, almost unable to speak. "We have to go!"

Rob looks apologetic. "You never came back, so we went look-ing for you."

"Where are Odessa and Jimmy?"

"We told them to split up and that we'd meet them back at the rec room. I have no idea where they are."

"We don't have time to find them. Sutton's here, through the back door. We have to warn my dad," I say, my voice frantic, my eyes shifting behind me.

"Where's Brayden?"

"Not now!" I say, my voice acid.

Jo controls herself and doesn't ask anything more. "Okay, Mia," she says. "Let's go."

We move, sprinting from tunnel to tunnel, and I don't hear any more gunshots or any boots behind us. But that doesn't mean a thing. Brayden knows these tunnels better than I do, and they'll be coming.

"Where's your dad?" Rob calls as we go.

"At the well!" I reply, sure of it.

"Do you think they have guns?" Jo asks. "Can they protect themselves?"

I don't answer. Nothing to do now but keep going. I'm worried about my dad, about Jimmy and Odessa and even Veronica—and Chuck, who might still be unconscious. But everything we ask now we'll know the answer to soon enough. If, that is, we can beat seven grown men in a footrace.

And then we hear them. Calling behind us. Sutton and his men, all shouting my name. I have heard this before. It's a memory I didn't know I had. "Miaaaaaaaaaa! Miaaaaaaaaaaaaaaa!" Dad shouted it down the well when I first fell in. For some reason it sounds the same here, the voices echoing off the walls. Coming closer and closer. And now we can hear the boot steps, the running. What if Odessa and Jimmy are caught? What if Dad isn't at the well?

So I scream, I scream to warn him and to make me move faster and to scare them behind us as much as they are scaring me. Rob and Jo prove their love for me and maybe also their own fear by screaming too. We fly like banshees down the mountain, waking up the sleeping rock itself. And that's when we come to the fork in the path.

"Which way?" I pant.

"Left!" Rob shouts, and we have no time, so we go. I only hope they didn't hear him shout our direction.

My lungs are about to burst, but suddenly we are there. A dead end.

"The elevator!" Rob points, and we hurry to the door, where I fumble with Chuck's key card and then enter the code. I hope Veronica hasn't come this way and changed it. I jump up and down on my feet. *Come on come on come on.* And a light beeps green, and the doors open. We hurry inside and press the button, sealing us in. There's a *slam* as something rams into the door. Jo screams, and I almost barf my heart up. But the door holds, and the elevator descends. It moves slowly, again with no perceptible direction. When it *dings* and prepares to open, I have a horrifying vision of us having never moved, and the door opening to Sutton and his gun pointed at my head. Thankfully, we're in the right place. My heart slinks back down into my chest, and we go running down the ramp.

"Jam the door," I yell at Rob as I lunge ahead. He stays there, leaving his foot in the door, not allowing it to close.

The Cave. The lights are bright, and the well is full of water, the brightest blue water I've ever seen, as if there's a lamp in the well, like in a swimming pool. Nothing is there but dead trees and huge water pumps, all shut off, and a strange buzzing to the air. No Dad. No Veronica. Jo and I hurry down toward the water, and I see that the buzz is actually from insects, many of them, flipping around the water, the liquid already providing life to some creatures. Where are Dad and Veronica? Maybe they heard the gunshots and locked themselves in a bunker for safety. Or they are in one of the dozens of rooms I haven't seen, slipping on bulletproof vests and loading their firearms. But the fact that Dad's not here, after all this time . . . it can't be right. Something's wrong. Something beyond the fact that Brayden is the devil.

"What do we do now?" Jo asks frantically. We're at a dead end, standing at the edge of the pool. I try to think, but keep on taking in the water. There's nowhere to go. No way to make sure we warn the others. Just a darn hole. A well in the ground.

"Mia!" Rob calls from the elevator. "They're banging on the ceiling. I think they're trying to get through! What if they drop a grenade or something!"

"I don't know! Take off your shoe and leave it in the door and get away from there."

I don't watch to see if he's following my order. My eyes are desperate, looking for a way out. Maybe a tunnel that leads farther into the mountain. Anything! Rob huffs up and immediately begins cupping a handful of water and splashing it at Jo. "Hurry—you too, Mia," he calls. "It could help us, maybe, if we get shot."

Not sure that's how it works, or if that was a sentence I wanted to hear, but I'm not going to argue, so we all suck it down, the water as cold and refreshing as anything I've ever imagined. It's like suddenly the panic in my body just disappears, and the ache in my legs and my feet and my lungs fades, and my breathing slows, and I can think, clearer than ever. My vision, even, I can feel my eyes sharpening, the room growing clearer, my hearing more sensitive, and I know they are arguing about what to do with the elevator. Even my sense of smell is sharper, and I feel the crook of my broken nose to find it straightened, the bump no longer there. I impulsively long for a mirror. Rob and Jo are going through the same thing, Jo rolling her right arm around in its socket, testing her chest, breathing deeply, a look of surprise and satisfaction on her face. Rob keeps squinting, and I lean over and pull his glasses from his face. He stares around with a look of awe. The water healed his eyes; he can see perfectly, and while I don't have any superpowers—I don't think—it's clear that I'm firing on all cylinders. My body is in the best physical condition it could ever be. Despite what might be my impending death, I feel incredible.

And I laugh to show it. We all do. Just once—we aren't crazy—but there's a need to let this feeling burst forth, and we all revel in it, one huge guffaw before our time runs out.

"Not much longer," Rob says, and we stand, looking at each other, ready for anything.

Rob is the one with the brains. He should be figuring this out, not me. I think about the map, and how the stick figure was activated. The eyes open. Staring at the moving water. The well. Jo the diver. Rob the brains. *Baby Mia, who fell down the well.*

The map. The shining gates. The brilliant city. The flowing water. The map.

"It's not of the tunnels," I whisper, realization dawning on me, spreading through me like the water did.

"What isn't?" Jo asks, her eyes on the elevator. Just then, we hear a loud *pop*, and smoke comes gushing out from behind the door. Not a big bomb, they wouldn't want to damage anything. Something small and careful and precise. They'll rappel down the elevator shaft any second now. Things are slowing before my eyes.

"The map. It's not a map of the tunnel. It's a map of something else. Somewhere else."

"Who cares, we have to find a way out!" she replies.

I remember the figures on the map. They were scattered throughout, eyes closed. Except for the one in front of the well, upside down, its eyes wide open. I hadn't thought it truly connected, but it does. Jo's face is a mask of confusion. In that moment, I imagine that she's not thinking of her dad, dead, or her mom, alone in Fenton. She's here with me, and unknowingly is providing me with the key.

Diving.

"Guys. I know this is crazy. But you have to trust me."

"What are you talking about?"

"The well, the water, think about it. It has to come from somewhere, right?"

"I guess." Rob nods, admitting the obvious.

"The water's running now, so wherever that someplace is, *now* it is open, the way is clear."

"I don't get it," he says, looking back over his shoulder at the elevator. "We have to hide!"

I shake my head. "No hiding. You have to trust me."

"Mia, what are you talking about?"

"I'll see you on the other side."

And with that, I take all the fear that's ever been part of me and push it into my feet so that they might be ready, and they are, because they push, hard, and then I'm diving, a dive to make Jo proud: I make almost no splash at all.

EPILOGUE

I FEEL THE ROUGH SURFACE OF THE WALL ON EACH side of me and have to fight the claustrophobia. The tunnel is too narrow—there's no way I can turn around. Forward or nowhere. I keep swimming, down and down and down, my ears popping. My lungs pressing deep into my chest. I'm an idiot for diving in Odessa's ski jacket, but I wasn't thinking, and now it billows like a parachute, slowing me down. Behind me I hear two *thumps*. My friends risking death to trust me. I only hope the water stills before Sutton arrives. That he'll think we disappeared down some sort of side cave, some small hole in the wall hidden in the darkness of the cavern.

It's black in here. There's no shimmering light. No moon through opaque ice above. I'm in a well, another well. Except this time, the water isn't cold; it's exactly right. Like I'm swimming a race, though even that's wrong. I feel as if the water buzzes against my skin and strengthens my arms, and I'm not tired at all. My eyes are open, and they don't sting. My heart beats steady, the only sound I hear.

What's the first thing you remember, your first memory?

I pause, floating in place. In nothingness. Because suddenly I remember. I *remember* the well. No more flashes or broken memories. I remember it all.

I didn't fall in. I found the hole in the ground, I stared down its depth. My father stood in the driveway, and I heard him say to my mother, "I'm sorry. I have to be there. There's nothing I can do." She looked so sad, so broken. I have never remembered her as clearly as I do now. As if I were watching it all happen before my eyes. I can smell the pine. I can feel the chill in the air. I can see my mother in her blue dress, her hair up, her glasses hanging from a band around her neck. I want him to stay. It's their anniversary, and he's going to the Cave. He's always at the Cave. My mother is sad, and so am I.

"Dad!" I cried.

I remember him looking over his shoulder at me. And then I jumped.

I almost choke at the memory, and am jolted back into place, confused—for the briefest of moments, I'm sure I'm back there, lost in the well. But no, I'm not lost anymore.

I swim on, my muscles so strong they tingle; I'm a dolphin bursting downward, and suddenly the darkness fades, a light appears at the edge of my vision, mimicking that of the black hole on the map, and moves closer and closer, until suddenly, inexplicably, I burst through.

I'm breathing air.

I tread water and stare in confusion, and I realize I'm on the surface, in a full lake of the well water, somewhere, down deep below the earth.

I'm dizzy and breathing so hard I almost suck the water into my lungs. A couple seconds later, Rob pops up, then Jo, their mouths agape in desperation and surprise. I grab their hands, try to calm them down, but they struggle, not used to the well, to the fear I have lived with all my life.

We three tread water and cast our eyes around the massive cavern we're in. There are giant gates, beautiful, enormous, impossible. The first thing beyond the well, within the map. It's my birthday. The room is lit, glowing bright enough that it might as well be daylight. I know why we're here.

We're here to find the source.

Turn the page for a preview
of the thrilling sequel,

The Dark Water!

1

THE WATER FEELS THICK, SILKY ALONG MY SKIN. I TREAD easily, the way a bird might fly, lazily pushing down against the current. Even with Odessa's ski jacket on, the water's welcoming. It's buoyant and warm and massages me softly.

Rob and Jo float nearby, and every few moments one of their hands brushes against mine as we tread, like we need to remind one another that we're really here. I open my mouth to let some water in and swallow, tasting copper, like the earth, like our blood. My body shivers, craving more.

We've been in the water for a while now. Ten minutes maybe. We haven't said a thing. It's so quiet, like we're drifting in a vacuum. The shore isn't so far away, but I'm reluctant to move. I think I could stay here for days.

The basin we swim in is large, about the size of the lake that borders my prep school. I can't believe that only two days ago I swam across that lake—under three inches of ice—and nearly froze to death. That feels like a lifetime ago now, though not a good lifetime. This place is something new and impossible, and it makes everything I've ever seen or believed seem smaller. On the shore, some hundred yards away, there's a haze of light, as if the ground itself is glowing. There are trees, plants, a full vibrant green forest leaning as far over the water as possible, as if the water itself were the sun. I peek above me, and can only see black. The darkness is complete and presses down on us. There's no ceiling, no stalactites dripping over our heads. No stars twinkling through the haze.

Then there are the gates. Giant, beautiful, unreal. They jut from the foliage like Roman ruins. They must be two hundred feet high, suspended between massive gold pillars, the opening in a wall that I can now see stretches off in either direction and curves away from us, seemingly endless. The gates are open, beckoning, and between them are hulking shapes I can't make out, the light is so weak here. A city, maybe? What else could it be? My mind is having a hard time processing the shapes, the gates, the endless room. It's just too unreal, this whole thing. But what my mind believes doesn't really matter because right now the light from the gates *is* real, and it shines brighter than the brightest building in my hometown of Fenton, Colorado, or the world.

"What is this place?" Rob says, finally breaking the quiet. A small part of me was enjoying that silence, that pause we were having. His voice floats along the water and disappears. It awakes the memory of why we're here, of the lunatic we're running from.

"I'm not sure," I say, looking at my two best friends. They're watching me, trusting. And why not? I guess I'm the one who brought them here. They actually dove into the well, following me, risking their lives on a hunch of mine that we should swim down and down and down through the water; now we've ended up floating in this underground cavern. I sort of can't believe how amazing they are, how lucky I am to have them.

"How did you know what to do?" Jo asks. "You knew we'd show up here?"

I shake my head and picture the map, the wall of stone covered in paintings that my dad found all those years ago, with its vibrant colors and images and hints. The diving figure, the flowing well, the gates. "Not here specifically. Somewhere, yes. There were a few clues on the map."

"What, clues to get *here*?" Jo replies.

"Remember that pale-skinned figure on the map? The one that was upside down and near the well?"

Jo laughs incredulously. "You jumped into the well because of *that*?"

I make a face. "We're here, aren't we?"

"You realize that we swam down, right?" Rob points at the blackness above. "When you swim deeper into water, you shouldn't break the surface. This isn't natural."

I look once more at the endless space above us, like a vacuum of light.

"Yeah, this shouldn't be possible," I reply. We were being chased by Sutton and his men, running through the Cave, and now I don't know if we're better off at all, or if we can even get back. "Come on," I say, and begin swimming toward the shore. The winter gear I wear is bulkier than the drag suit I have to use in practice, but I'm soon far ahead of the others. I can't help but swim fast; years of training refuse to go to waste. So it's me who steps on the shore first, lifesaving water gushing from my pockets and squishing out of my boots. There's no sand, only a very fine moss that carpets the earth. I kneel and rub my hand gently on the surface, and it's so soft I almost want to take off my boots and go barefoot.

"I wish Odessa were here," Rob says, splashing up from the water and grabbing at an overhanging leaf. It's wide and thick, like a giant piece of iceberg lettuce. Almost as pale too. "She'd know what all this plant life was." I try not to think of how Odessa and Jimmy might be captured already. Prep school townies, they escaped Westbrook with us, and now they're stuck back in the Cave with soldiers-for-hire. Maybe they stand a chance; they're fully grown adults now that they've contracted the virus and it's aged them some. Weird how just one drop of water was enough to kill the virus in them. One drop was enough to halt their premature aging, saving them from dementia and a wrinkled death, like what happened to our teachers. To Jo's dad. Weird to think that there's probably enough water in this lake to eradicate all illness in the world.

"I doubt anyone would know the plant life down here," Jo says, taking off her jacket to wring it out. The nylon doesn't make it easy, but she has the right idea. My jacket weighs a waterlogged ton.

I remember the story Dad told us about finding the well as a student some thirty-four years ago, spelunking on a class excursion. He tripped into the water, the same water that we just dove through, and he found out that it heals everything it touches.

"Do we get to name everything we see?" Rob asks, wiping his face. His jet-black hair is plastered to his forehead, as if he gelled it to look that way. He blinks water away from his eyelashes, then pulls out his Warbys from an inner pocket and tries to put them on. Of course, with the water coursing through his body, his vision is perfect now and he doesn't need them. He gives a goofish smile and puts them away.

We all stop and look into the underbrush. There's a hum to the air, and the branches sway; something, maybe a bird, flits. I'm suddenly aware of the sound of nature, as if I hadn't been hearing it before. Rustling underbrush, quiet chirps. A bug flies slowly by, its butterfly wings familiar but its cicada-like body an odd fit. There's an entire ecosystem deep in the earth, one that's never been seen before. It's thick and impenetrable, like a rain forest, dense enough that standing here below the trees makes it difficult to see the wall and the gates.

"Check this out," Jo calls, squatting near the base of a tree. She's tied up her hair already, looking at ease even in her scrubs. It's like she's back in our dorm, pointing out some calculus mistake on my homework. If my dad had died two days ago, I'd be a mess. She's not even fidgeting her fingers the way she does when she's nervous or distracted. I know she has to be feeling it, that she's purposefully pushing it away, but I don't see it at all. Man, she's impressive.

She's hovering by a patch of tall flowers with long, shivering petals, their stems no thicker than a millimeter each. Almost like spaghetti, like tiny medusaheads. The petals are white, incredibly white, enough so that they actually shine. Looking around, farther into the trees, I can make out another dozen clumps, some flowers even dangling like vines from the branches, illuminating the woods. They make their own sun down here.

Jo reaches out and gently plucks one from the ground, and immediately the remaining flowers in the patch go dark, shockingly fast, as if hurt. But the one Jo holds keeps its light. On a hunch, I

5

squeeze my wet hair and put my moist fingertip to the broken stem she's holding, and as the flower shines brighter, I can't help but smile. I'm suddenly ridiculously grateful for these flowers and the light they bring. How awful it would have been to arrive here completely blind.

"What now?" Jo says, waving her flower around her head in fascination. She's gone a few days without makeup, and she looks like a softer version of herself. Her lips are a pale pink and fade into her skin, her eyes still intensely blue, but without mascara, they seem more dominant.

They both look at me like I've got the answer. Sure, the map gave me clues, but I wouldn't have had the guts to jump into the well if not for Sutton and his men chasing me. They're probably up there right now, searching for us. My stomach churns, thinking of Brayden, how he might be there with them. What if he had found me, if he'd looked me right in the eyes and then shouted for Sutton? I don't like the feeling, the churning, because it betrays me as much as he betrayed us. Brayden, new to Westbrook, the boy who escaped with us, who helped us. Brayden, with his scarred chin and his sly smile. I blink away the thought. He's back in the Cave, helping Sutton get his supply of the lifesaving water. I wonder if they'll leave Dad alone when they catch him. Does Sutton hate my father that much, to hurt him even now? Will he care enough to try to contain the outbreak at Westbrook, to distribute water to all of my classmates and heal them if it isn't already too late? Does that fall into his game plan at all? He doesn't know them. He doesn't care about them. I think of the party where I met Brayden, how everyone there's probably dead. I remember the infirmary, where the first infected went. Where our teachers died, their bodies piled on top of one another, their hair turned gray, their faces so wrinkled they were hard to recognize.

I bite my lip and pull my jacket closer, and I realize I'm not cold. The water keeps me warm as my blood paces through my body. I pull my own flower, and it shines enough so that I can see through the webbing of my fingers.

I take a breath. They're waiting for me. Even if I don't have the answer, it still falls on me. "I saw the well in the map, and I've seen the gates there too—"

"Look," Rob shouts, interrupting me to point down the shore. My instinct is to jump back into the water, where I'm safe and confident I can outswim anything, but I force myself to get a grip and follow his finger. There's a lump of something out of place on the beach, something blue and familiar.

My stomach sinks, knowing what I'm seeing before my mind does. I hurry over, maybe twenty, thirty yards, and realize halfway there that those are scrubs, like the ones we're wearing. The only person I can think of who would have had those on and made it here is my dad. I pick them up, as if I might find him underneath, maybe a smaller version of himself—maybe the water shrunk him, maybe I'm going crazy. The shirt is wet from the lake, but it's also stained red, a smear of blood.

"Whoa," Rob says. I flare up inside. *Whoa* doesn't really cut it. Apparently, my dad came before us, and now he's gone. Hurt too. I can't see any blood on the beach, though. What exactly happened here? Did he know about this place all along? Why didn't he tell us? Why didn't he tell me?

I look toward the gates, wondering whether I can see him, whether he's only a few hundred yards ahead of us, limping in pain. But he's not there. The forest has broken, and there's a clear path from the lake to the gates, which are gaping and bright, but no naked Dad. Tall shadows loom beyond the gates, like burnt-out skyscrapers. I don't know what Dad's doing here, but I know where he's gone. If we hurry, maybe we can catch him.

"We should go back," Jo says.

"What?" I have to stop myself from shouting. "You're kidding, right?"

She's taken a few steps toward the lake, and stares out over its black surface. "We should wait a half-hour for Sutton and his men to clear the room, and then dive back down and swim wherever the hell we need to go to get back out." She turns and looks at us. "We have to save Fenton, and Odessa and Jimmy and Todd and my mother and Rob's family and everyone, if we can." I fight down a sense of panic. I never expected this from Jo.

"What about the map?" Rob says, digging into his pocket. "It's a gigantic golden gate, Jo. We can't *not* go check it out."

"Forget the gates, what about my dad?" I say, still incredulous, holding up the bloodstained shirt for them to see.

"There's no blood on the ground, Mia," Jo says, trying to sound soothing. "That's an old stain."

I rub my fingers against the fabric, unsure.

Rob, meanwhile, pulls out his OtterBoxed phone and starts messing with it.

"You won't get a signal here," I say, clenching my teeth.

"Duh," he replies in a way that I know doesn't mean any harm.

To Rob, everyone's a step behind. He flicks his screen a few times and then holds it up for us to see, his face smug. I remember now, in the Map Room, when he was taking pictures. His obsessiveness pays dividends, because he's holding up an image of the map. Even from here, on the tiny screen, I can see the painted gates. He points to them. "The gates are here, so all these other things must come after." He waves at the remaining images: a city, a waterfall, a cup, a prone figure in white, a spear-like thing sticking right through another pale figure, the strange objects we'd have to decipher if we don't turn back. I can't help but notice that he's at 23 percent power.

"The well. This lake. Dad clearly figured out the map like I did, so he's probably just following the clues. The same ones that led us here."

"To what?" Rob asks. "I mean, I understand that this place is crazy. It's a miracle. Yay. But there's a virus outbreak and you were in the Cave. Why would he come here right now, especially if he knew Sutton was about to break in?"

"I don't know," I say uncertainly. "But he wouldn't come here for no reason."

"That's not good enough, Mia," Jo says, insistent. "We *have* to go back."

I can't believe this. I know she's mourning her father, but that doesn't mean we should abandon mine. "You know I can't do that. He's my dad." I hold up his scrubs and wave them at her. "Why'd he strip? What if he's really hurt?"

She turns to me, her face anguished. "Don't you think I know that, Mia? Of course I do. I want to find your dad too, but you aren't looking at the big picture." She pauses, gathers herself. I can see how hard this is for her, and an ounce of my disbelief fades. "The virus broke out two days ago. It's already infected our friends. We know that the quarantine didn't work. That the virus managed to infect soldiers in *hazmat suits*. It's spreading, Mia. And the only thing that can stop it is this water." She rubs her thumb and forefinger together, still slick from our swim. "Even if this place is like Narnia, even if there's a magical talking bird that spits water from its mouth and teaches you the secrets of the universe, we don't have time. We have to get back and figure out a way to get past Sutton and bring the water to Westbrook and Fenton. If we don't, the whole town dies. Maybe more."

"Jimmy and Odessa can handle him." Even as I say the words, I know I don't believe them at all.

"Are you serious? Jimmy and Odessa? They'll stop Sutton all by themselves?" she asks, eyebrows raised. "Mia, do the math. Every second we're here, the greater the odds that we won't have a home to go back to. Not only that, you said yourself Mr. Kish came here on purpose. He came here for a reason, *without you*. He knows what he's doing and he knows how to get back. The town doesn't have the luxury of seventeen years of planning."

We're quiet, all of us. Breathing deeply. My skin tingles I'm so angry. I'm angry because she's right. Dad came on purpose. He's fine, with or without clothes.

Rob seems to agree; after a moment, he looks at me apologetically and I've lost. "She's right, Mia."

His parents live in Fenton, too, and he must be just as concerned for their safety, but it doesn't make his siding with Jo sting any less.

I take a shuddering breath. "I mean, what's down here? What's he walking into?" I say out loud, but Rob and Jo have the sense not to answer. *He'll come back, of course he will.* I stare at the giant wall spreading out before me, and feel sorry for myself. Until I see something move.

ACKNOWLEDGMENTS

THANK YOU THE VERY MOST TO—

Kirby Kim, my agent and friend, without whom I'd never have applied to Westbrook.

Stacey Barney, my editor, strategist, and advocate, for making this book her own.

My sister, Maya, for that whole thing we did; my brother, Daniel, for never saying uncle.

My nephews, Jonas and Lucas, to find in every bookstore.

My parents, for reading my writing since I was in the ninth grade.

John and Jean Thomas, for the loft (and your daughter).

Matt Block, the human dolphin, for your swimming lessons.

Téa Obreht and Kate Beaton, for their extracurricular awesome.

Ian Dalrymple and Julie Chang, the gatekeepers; Laura Bonner, the world; and Ashley Fox, the Wild West, for all you've done on my behalf.

My extraordinary copyeditors, Cindy Howle, Robert Farren, Chandra Wohleber, and designer Annie Ericsson, who gave me a shave and warned off orphans and stacks, I am entirely grateful.

Vanessa Han and Linda McCarthy, my brilliant cover designers, who hit the nail on the head with the book's incredible face.

And Jennifer Besser, Jay Katsir, Katie Schorr, Eric Gross, Maria Braeckel, Dave Yankelewitz, UEA friends and faculty, Ed White, Liam Brockey, my companions and colleagues at the Gernert Company, my many incredibly talented clients for their teachings, and all who have helped from the day after I couldn't add anyone else to this list until forever.